AWAKENING

Z.R. MCCORMICK

*For Erica—
My endless encourager
my forever love.
You're worth more than
all the words I could ever write.*

I love you

CONTENTS

AWAKENING

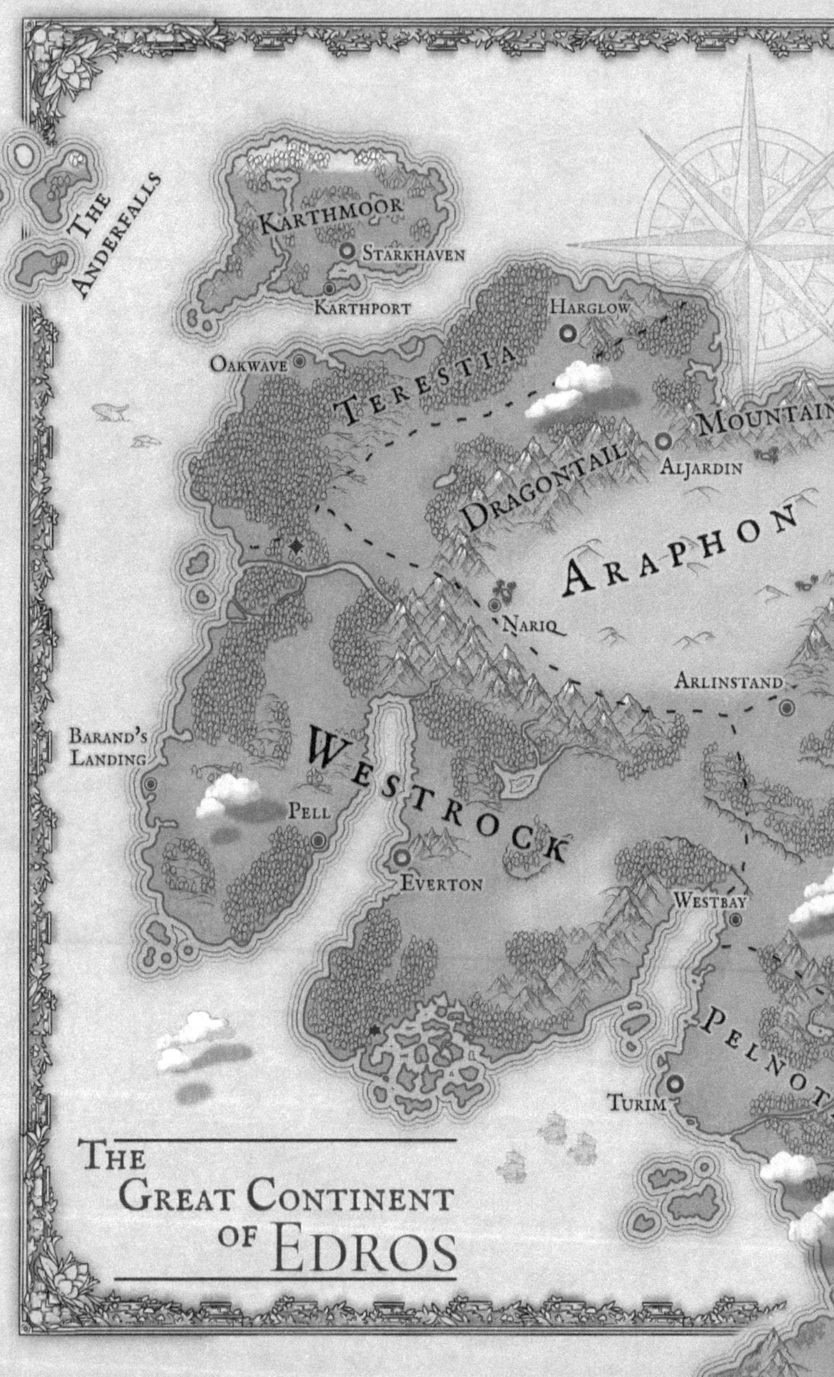

THE ANDERFALLS
KARTHMOOR
STARKHAVEN
KARTHPORT
OAKWAVE
TERESTIA
HARGLOW
MOUNTAIN
DRAGONTAIL
ALJARDIN
ARAPHON
NARIQ
ARLINSTAND
BARAND'S LANDING
WESTROCK
PELL
EVERTON
WESTBAY
PELNOTI
TURIM
THE GREAT CONTINENT OF EDROS

FARGOST
CERN
FELLINOR
BIRNPASS KEEP
ALSALAAM
GLASINIR
ISTWYNEIR
MALGAVORN
THE LOST HAVENS
RAVEN'S WATCH
H A M I D I A
AGONAR
MINDEN
VRALN
DORET
ILAGRON
L Y N R E S T
SHEARPOINT MOUNTAINS
O R D A
N E B O A
CAROCA

TO THE
ANDERFALLS
ANDER SEA
FROSTHARBOR
THE FROZE
BOWMAN'S
CROSSING
GREENWATCH
ARINGOTH
THE GREENWOOD
FAIRHOLLOW
FARSHORE
FALLOW

THE ISLAND OF
KARTHMOOR
ASTES
HAZELCOURT
TAR'AUTH
ELD
DORN
REFUGEE CAMP
HILLMARCH
BINTHIR
FOREST
HARROWMONT
STONECROFT
EBENAITH
STARKHAVEN
KARTHPORT
STRAIT
TO EDROS

Author's Note

Suggested Reading Order for The Oathsworn Chronicles

The Cataclysm - a prequel novella
The Chase - a prequel short story
Awakening - Book One
Arrival - a companion short story
Heir - a companion short story
A Legacy of Ashes - a companion novella
The Mages' Merchant - a companion short story coming late 2026
Well of Souls - Book Two coming late 2026

AWAKENING

PROLOGUE

THE MAN GRIPPED HIS wrist behind him tighter, pacing across the tiled floor. He dared not look out the window again, too afraid of the pale, blue haze swallowing the walls of the city in the distance.

"Blast that mercenary," he muttered, "and blast those bells!"

The man paused, wiping the beading sweat below his graying hair with a handkerchief. The gatehouse bell pealed endlessly over the clamor and cries in the streets below. He let out an exasperated sigh, his wrinkled face turning to the mound of bags piled beside the door.

"Confound him! Where is he?"

He shuffled to the desk in the corner, scooping a handful of papers into a leather satchel in the chair. Suddenly, the door creaked open, letting in a stream of faint sunlight and, with it, screams echoing above the domed rooftops.

The man jerked back towards the opening as a dark figure slipped inside and shut the engraved timbers. He scowled, crossing his arms.

"Took you bloody long enough. The city's falling to pieces. Where in Aldaria have you been? I need to get out of here!"

The newcomer adjusted the black leather pauldron on his shoulder, his dark eyes slowly scanning the shadowy manor. He said nothing. The man clenched his fist, maintaining his scowl as impatience simmered. Finally, he gave a frustrated huff and returned to closing up his satchel.

"We need to leave, mage. Now," he growled.

The mage turned his gaze to the older man. "I'm looking for a vault."

The man snorted, clutching the strap of the satchel as he stomped towards the mound of bags. "You and everyone else. There's no getting into the north now, though. Not with the Mist." He glanced nervously towards the window beside the mage.

The mage shook his head once, bits of his shadowed scale armor glinting in the failing beams. "Not those, advisor. Your other research. The artifact." The man froze, his gaze darting back to the mage. "Did you locate its resting place?"

"That is none of your concern, Garrin," the man hissed, thrusting the satchel onto the floor. "You are a hired mercenary. Right now, your only job is getting me safely back to Hamidia. Then you are to complete your original task. Do you understand?" With a final venomous look, the advisor marched back towards his desk.

Garrin smiled, a gleam creeping into his eyes. He glanced out the window, watching the sickly blue fog pierced by columns of smoke. He stepped closer to the door.

"Locating the marked is quite simple. Did you know?" The advisor paused, turning to face the mage as he spoke. "Once you understand where to look. Why, it's how I found you."

Garrin continued smiling as a look of pure horror crept across the man's weathered face. The advisor shuddered, his hands trembling as he licked his dry lips. His eyes flicked towards the window, covered in the swirling haze. The city was nowhere to be seen. A deep rumble echoed through the pane, followed by more screams. Closer.

Garrin stepped beside the door and, with a single swift motion, thrust it open. Screams washed through the opening, carried atop the tumbling swirl of thick, hideous fog.

The advisor gasped, staggering backwards. "Are you insane?!" He pressed himself against the cold stone of the wall, his quaking finger pointed at the open door. "Shut it! Shut it now!"

The mage merely watched with a cold, almost eager, grin as the man struggled to force his considerable girth farther into the wall.

"Do you know who I am?" the advisor shrieked. "The Archon will hear about this!"

A soft crack resounded through the room as a curve of stone shot out of the floor, latching the advisor's neck to the wall. He gasped, clawing vainly at the immutable rock. His eyes widened, frantically bouncing between the mage and the Mist.

Garrin ran his bare hand through the bank of Mist tumbling lazily through the doorway. It was so thick that for a moment, his flesh disappeared entirely in its depths.

"So much confusion. So much chaos, for such a simple thing," he murmured, gazing at the fog. "And such a small thing for one to simply vanish. A pity."

The advisor wheezed as the stone collar grated farther up the wall, pulling him onto his toes. His pale skin reddened as he gasped for breath. His bulging eyes strained towards the tiles where the Mist lapped closer towards his boots.

"Okay," the advisor sputtered. "I, I'll tell." The collar lowered slightly.

"The artifact. Where?"

The man's chest heaved as he fought for air. He raised a quivering arm towards the desk.

"The letter. On my desk."

Garrin walked over to it, scattering a pile of books onto the floor.

The stone collar retracted into the wall with a crack, and the advisor collapsed onto the floor, panting as he clutched at his throat. He took one look at the Mist consuming the room and scampered into the far corner.

"Now, please, get me out of here!"

"It's already too late," said the mage, his eyes never leaving the desk. He gently rolled up the letter and stowed it at his side. "Don't worry, you are one of the lucky ones. It will be quick."

The advisor jerked his head towards the wall of Mist, blotting out the doorway now, towering over him. His desperate gaze darted back to Garrin, striding into the fog. He jumped to his feet, reaching for the fading figure.

"Don't leave me!"

The sickly blue haze lurched forward, blanketing the man as he gasped and clutched again at his throat. He crashed to the floor, the echoes of his thrashing drifting through the doorway as the mage stepped outside and gently shut the door.

The world was silent now. Nothing but a faint warm breeze teasing apart the consuming strands of Mist.

"Well?"

Garrin turned to the woman leaning against the manor wall and shrugged.

"A possible lead. It will not be easy to reach."

"I wouldn't expect it to be." She glanced towards the unseen city, shrouded by the fog. "The others already left. Took care of the west half on their way out."

He nodded. "We'll finish the rest and catch up. They will not find passage to Karthmoor that quickly."

"And the artifact?"

"After. We have to keep him happy, for now."

The woman grinned, the green eyes below her fiery hair flashing. Together, they strode silently into the gathering gloom beneath the Mist.

CHAPTER 1
FAIRHOLLOW

650 GR, 500 Years After the Cataclysm

A ROOSTER'S CROW PIERCED the world, and Micah sat up, startled. The vision of a small boy giggling on a swing, and a woman calling out, fading as he blinked. A dream? No, a memory. Long passed, yet felt again vividly. A lingering sweetness tasted only briefly before awakening to a new dawn. The serene peace of his dreamworld dissolved as he roused himself out of bed, searching for his shirt.

Pulling it on, he opened the weathered door of the small bedroom and stumbled into the hall, sleep still heavy in his eyes. He splashed cold water from the cracked bathroom sink on his face, shocking himself awake, and attempted to tame his dark, unkempt hair and straighten his clothes. He studied himself in the grimy mirror. It was hard to believe the face staring back belonged to a man of only thirty-two years. _My scraggly beard_ *will have to wait until I find a new blade*, he thought. He still wasn't ready to return to the old cabin from just a fortnight before. He shuddered, pushing away the haunting thoughts of that night and its battle. *Perhaps if luck holds, there'll be time to look around today.*

Micah returned to the shadowy bedroom and pulled on his heavy leather boots, clasping his scabbard to one side and a holster to the other. He was running low on ammunition for his worn-out pistol and made a mental note to check the supplies for additional shot and powder.

At least my sword is in excellent shape. He gripped the leather-wrapped hilt and revealed a sliver of its polished edge. If there was one habit he never abandoned after leaving the Guard, it was maintaining his prized blade. Outside, the buzz of stirring villagers drifted through the window. A rickety wooden door slammed against its frame, likely Francis, the leading elder of Fairhollow, moving to his porch as the sun began its rise.

Micah made his way out of the dilapidated house, heading along the grassy path towards the tavern and the center of the town. What had once been a bustling farming settlement of a few dozen log-framed and wood-shingled homes, was now reduced to only a handful of inhabited dwellings. Many of the scattered houses sat empty, their broken windows and ominous shadows a menacing stain on this once peaceful village.

"Another day," a raspy voice observed to his right.

"Morning, Francis. Another day to give thanks for," Micah tried to muster sincerely as he passed.

"Perhaps."

"Well, that's a fine start," he muttered. While known for his blunt, cynical manner, Francis' simple statement also revealed a bitterly realistic view of the world they now inhabited.

Micah continued his walk, passing more houses with signs of life. Those closer to the middle of the village remained in decent shape, still sheltering those who remained. As mothers and fathers made their way to front porches, the eerie silence was unsettling. Though there were children around, they made little noise. Even sleepy voices complaining of waking would have been a welcomed sound. Yet, even the littlest ones knew the danger of drawing too much attention. While the village was currently deemed safe, their harsh new world's effects were palpable.

By then, the tavern was a bustling sight. Smoke rose from its chimney, beckoning any citizens without the means to prepare their own meals to its tables, Micah included. Many villagers were making their way there, if not for a meal, then for company and whatever gossip captivated their small assembly that week. Delvin and his wife, Maven, ran the tavern, which had become the center of life for the town. While they were more than happy to take your coin for their middling ale, Delvin and Maven selflessly provided meals to those less fortunate in the area, only asking that recipients assist the village wherever they could.

Every hand was needed now, especially as each passing day only added to the difficulty. Every week seemed only to lead to more people disappearing, either fleeing into the unknown or vanishing in the chaos of an attack. While Micah would take anyone to bolster their defenses, there were precious few who were naturally immune to the deadly Mist that signaled an encroaching raid.

The Mist.

Micah shivered as his mind sank into despairing thoughts. Where it came from, no one knew. Not the brightest sages, nor the most powerful wizards could unravel the terrible mystery that was the Mist. Ultimately, to those who endured its relentless onslaughts, survival was all that mattered. Attempts to understand the Mist quickly faded into obscurity. If the wisest minds of Karthmoor and those from among the larger and more powerful nations could not decipher the deadly enigma, how could simple farmers claim such knowledge?

Micah pushed his nervous thoughts aside. There was enough to worry about, and pondering the existence of the Mist wouldn't solve any of them now. He headed into the tavern, looking to cleanse the thoughts from his head and prepare for the breaking day.

Chapter 2
The Tavern

"Good morning, Micah!" exclaimed Delvin as he opened the weather-beaten door. How Delvin, this large, aging man, always maintained his optimistic appearance was another mystery Micah had dismissed. Still, his positive mood had repeatedly proven to be a powerful force in encouraging dispirited souls, and the boisterous laugh that shook his tangled beard could bring a smile to anyone's face.

"We've got a warm porridge heating on the fire and fresh water and coffee over at the bar," he added.

"Thanks, Delvin. Doing well today?"

"As well as any day. The sky is clear, and the sun is warm. A good sign, by my reckoning!"

The tavern itself was old. Passed down by generations of tavern keepers, each leaving their own mark on the place. Its smoky windows scattered faint beams of light spilling in from the morning sun. Countless chairs and shoes had smoothed its creaky floors, the planks hewn from the pines of nearby Binthir Forest. The low ceiling beams could be a danger to anyone of unusual height. Yet, even in the dim light of the fireplace and sparse candles, the building had a comforting atmosphere. Whether it was from the woody smell mixed with Maven's spices or the savory meals and brews of Delvin's design is hard to say.

As Micah made his way to the counter, the powerful aroma of coffee drifted towards him, cutting through the ale-soaked scent of the bar. Since no sustained trade and, as a result, no imported goods had reached the area in years, the magical brew had become a precious commodity. The mere fact Maven allowed Delvin to offer it freely meant everyone must have been in high spirits. He poured a large cup and slowly enjoyed its rich, potent taste. Immediately, Micah could feel his energy rising. With his list of projects growing, he needed every bit of strength he could muster.

Coffee in hand, Micah made his way over to the fire and helped himself to the breakfast. In the bleak lighting, he noticed a couple of villagers at a table in the corner. They too had helped themselves to the gift of the rejuvenating drink, undoubtedly preparing for work in the fields. More farmers slowly filed in, sure to take advantage of their hosts' hospitality. Any break in the weather meant every able-bodied man and woman rose early to head to the fields, sowing, weeding, and feeding their meager crops.

As another man opened the tavern door—Halvid, by the look of his wild hair—Micah spotted a pair of men at a table under the nearby window and caught a moment of their intense conversation.

"It's true, I tell you!"

Peering closer, he recognized Beirand, a man who would have been an esteemed elder of Fairhollow were it not for his extreme fondness for Delvin's ale.

"Posh!" replied the other, waving his hand dismissively. Micah realized it was Gerar, a captain in the Karthmoor Guard before the Mist and now his most reliable leader among the defenders.

Gerar frowned, pulling a faint crease across his weathered forehead as his dark beard nearly touched his rough shirt. "If they had been there, I would've seen them. I manned that section of the wall for over half the day!"

With coffee and porridge in hand, Micah shuffled over to their table. He set the dishes down and pulled out the extra chair as the two looked up.

"Morning, Micah," Gerar said tiredly.

"Gerar. Beirand. What's the word?"

Beirand started to speak, but Gerar cut him off. "This old sack of bones has the audacity to claim my eyes are going dark!"

"I may be old, but my sight is still sharper than yours, Gerar," retorted Beirand, folding his wrinkled arms across his chest.

Micah let out a sigh and slumped backwards. Turning his head towards the old man, he began, "Alright, you two. Beirand, what did you see?"

"His mind is addled! Old Beirand here claims—"

"Enough!" He shot Gerar a stern look. "Let the man speak."

Beirand slowly cleared his throat. "'Twas nearly sundown last evening," he began. "I'd been makin' my way towards the lookout hill after I was, er, persuaded to leave Frederic's shop. Young Frederic was quite upset with my nearness to his forge, though I fail to see what a little ale would harm. Why he has to get himself all worked up just because..."

"Ahem," Micah said, leaning forward. "So, as you were on this walk?"

"Whatsit? Oh, yes," he continued. "So, I was on my way to the hill, a fresh bottle of ale in hand, an' not a worry in me soul. Figured I'd take in the last of the day against the ol' tree. Once I got there, I settled down all nice and comfortable-like you see." Beirand's voice dropped. "And that's when I saw 'em. A whole group, plain as I see you now." He paused, quivering with excitement. "Elk! Strong, healthy. Better looking than any of those other pitiful critters we see 'round here."

"Elk?" Micah asked skeptically. "You're sure?"

"Absolutely," Beirand replied.

"Not a pack of wolves? Or even deer?"

"I know what I saw," Beirand said defensively, crossing his arms. "I've lived in these parts longer than you fresh-faced lads. I remember when the noble beasts were plentiful. Back before the dark days we now find ourselves in."

"He's mad," Gerar muttered. "No elk could've survived this long."

Micah sat back, thoughts swirling. Gerar had a point. No one had spotted a creature near the size of an elk for years. While hunters happened upon deer, it was always a rare occurrence and almost always involved a sick or injured one. Yet, they taught every youth learning to hunt on their island nation to distinguish a simple deer from its grand cousin. Even though Beirand had never been known as reliable, he understood the importance of something like this to the village. A single elk could provide months of meals for a whole family with the right rationing.

Micah sighed. "Alright, Beirand. Where exactly did you see them?"

His face brightened immediately. "From the hill, the herd was to the east," he explained, "grazing on the edge of the forest between the great fallen pine and the rocky mound to the north."

"And where did they go from there?"

"I couldn't tell if somethin' from the village spooked 'em or somethin' farther north, but they suddenly looked up, and the whole lot dashed off into the woods. From the looks of it, they headed east southeast, though I never saw anythin' cross the road to the south," he recalled. "If you ask me, the likeliest spot for a herd of any size is the ol' pond deep in Binthir Forest. Just north of the fork in the road, where it turns south."

"Thank you, Beirand," he replied. "This could be the biggest news we've had in weeks."

Turning to Gerar, Micah formed a plan. "Gerar, once you've finished, head over to Hamill's. See if he's up for tracking some elk. Take Tala with you too. She knows the woods better than anyone nowadays, given her proclivity for adventuring."

"I still think the old man's a nutter," Gerar grumbled, "but you're right. If it's true... Well, the village needs this." He drained the rest of his coffee and pushed his chair out, the feet scraping against the floor.

"And Gerar," said Micah, catching him by the arm, "keep it quiet. Bows only. Use your Guard training. We can't afford any attention—to yourselves or the village. We're still recovering from the last wave and can't afford to lose any of you."

"Aye," he replied. "No arguments here. Plus, what would you ever do without my pretty face?" With a smirk, he nodded towards Delvin and walked out the door.

With Gerar gone, Micah's gaze settled on the worn table. He'd sent other villagers out after supplies or game before. Good people. All of them experienced. Yet, their island was no longer the home they once knew. Brave hunters, well-versed, mysteriously vanished. Many poor souls disappeared forever, their whereabouts greedily hidden in the nebulous Mist. Yet, search parties eventually found a few others. Some of the deceased had no marks, no signs of a struggle. It was as if they'd gone to sleep and never woken up. They were the recipients of the most merciful death the Mist offered. The others... Well, no one dwelt long on their horrific ends. Not a person in Fairhollow wanted to imagine a mauling as vicious as that.

"So?" An inquisitive voice broke the silence.

Micah lifted his head to Beirand, who shifted in his seat and peered at him anxiously.

"So?"

"I did good, right? Maybe good enough to inform Francis of my... assistance?"

"Perhaps," he replied, studying the old man. "It's up to Gerar and the others to confirm it. And don't forget the incident with Merrick's mule. If this hunt turns out for the better, you can consider yourself back on neutral ground."

"Hmph," said Beirand. "An' here I was hoping we'd left that little event behind us." He paused for a moment. "Still... I suppose it'll do. It's a start, at least."

"Aye, a start." Micah drained the last of his coffee, pushed out his chair, and stood to leave. "Thanks again, Beirand. I'll let you know what we find."

Making his way to the counter with mug in hand, Micah realized the room was filling quickly. He hurried to the front, dodging chairs and sleepy villagers, hoping to claim whatever smattering of coffee remained. As he reached for the pitcher, a hand slammed on to the bar beside him, and he jumped.

"Micah Stormcrown!" Maven hissed. "Don't you dare go for seconds!" Several heads turned to see Maven's outburst.

He'd never seen her coming. Maven was famous for scolding more men at her tavern than all the mothers of mischievous children in Fairhollow combined.

"Lord above knows we work hard to provide everyone with a little encouragement each day. We don't put out something as precious as that drink for the greedy!" she furiously continued. "I don't care if you are a former warden or even the leader of our brave defenders. Everyone, including you, will get a single mug. So, you just leave yours right there and head on out to your day."

"Morning, Maven," he answered sheepishly. "Thank you for your hospitality. Give my regards to Delvin for the excellent porridge."

Micah grabbed a chunk of fresh bread from the platter near the porridge and quickly turned to leave. Halvid, finally roused from his sleep, shot him a humorous look as he passed.

"Come on, Micah!" he teased. "Everyone knows not to cross the real keeper of Fairhollow!"

"Aye, a mistake even sleepy wardens won't make twice," he responded, grinning.

Micah reached the door and flung it open, sunlight spilling into the room. With a breath, he readied himself, rolling over the list inside his head.

Another day, he told himself. *Another blessing to those of us lucky enough to be here.*

Chapter 3

Rounding Up the Hunt

The sun was rising over the horizon as villagers headed to their daily routines. The sky held only a few fleeting clouds, an excellent sign the constant rain had passed. Micah paused outside the tavern, mulling over where to head first. He needed to check on repairs to the northern wall, though Merrick was overseeing that project. Then he remembered Rila mentioning Marian was running low on herbs. While he would normally leave collecting them to Rila herself—she was Marian's apprentice, after all—several of the most important were only available near the river outside of town.

If there's time, perhaps I can find Rila before Gerar collects the rest of the hunting group and heads out, he thought. Taking a moment out of their trip to ensure Marian received what she needed for her stock of medicines seemed a worthwhile sacrifice. With his destination in mind, Micah headed south along the dirt road towards the fields, the warmth of the sun growing over the houses.

Rila and Tala, identical twin sisters just barely of adult age, lived together in their family home near the edge of the village. Their parents had been victims of the Mist in an attack almost a year earlier. With no one to support them, and no offers of courtship, each of the girls had found the strength to forge their own paths, something he'd always been proud of them for.

Shuffling his way along with the crowd of farmers heading to the fields, Micah arrived at their home. Its simple wooden frame was sturdy and well built, though its logs were marred and worn. Long gashes in the timbers from unspeakable monsters and thick boards over the shattered windows were all that remained of that dreadful night. A constant reminder that even on a pleasant day like that, they lived in continuous fear.

Micah walked up the slope, spotting the dark shadow of someone moving about the room through the open door. He knocked lightly on the frame.

"Goodness!" she exclaimed, spinning around. "I didn't even realize my sister had left the door open."

"Good morning, Rila. Sorry for the startle."

"Even after two years here, you still can't tell us apart, can you, Micah?" she lightly chided him, folding her arms.

"Apparently not," he admitted with a laugh. "My apologies, Tala."

She shook her head, her playful expression turning somber. "Hard to believe it's been two years now."

Micah nodded, his gaze drifting. He himself couldn't believe it had only been that long since despair had carried him to Fairhollow's gates. Since the Mist had appeared and taken everything from him.

He looked at back her. His wasn't the only life it had ravaged. "It is."

Tala smiled again, wrapping her long, blonde hair with a small band of leather. "Still, it's a rare day that Rila beats me out of the house. Usually, I'm the one champing at the bit to get out there."

Tala had always been an adventurous child. She was infamous for finding every possible way onto the top of the town hall, much to Francis' ire. As she grew older, her curiosity drove her to explore the depths of nearby Binthir Forest. Before the Mist came to Karthmoor, no greater guide could be found. And even after the Mist infested the woods, making any paths through them nigh impossible, Tala remained the only villager still capable of navigating the wild maze. The very thing that spared her from her parents' fate—her natural immunity to the deadly Mist—ensured her place as one of the most valuable hunters in Fairhollow.

"Do you know where Rila headed to?" Micah asked.

"She left her ingredient satchel at Marian's last night and went early to retrieve it. Then she's probably heading to the herb gardens. I think she was trying to save going to the river for last. I offered to go with her first thing, but she didn't seem interested," Tala answered, clearing dishes from the table.

"Thanks. Has Gerar stopped by?"

She shrugged. "Haven't seen him. Why?"

"Someone reported seeing elk in the area. I asked Gerar to recruit you and Hamill for a brief hunting trip."

Tala spun around, quick as lightning. "Elk? Here? Unbelievable! I haven't seen any since I was a little girl."

"It is pretty far-fetched," Micah admitted. "But if it's true, it would be a lifesaver for Fairhollow."

"Absolutely!" She finished clearing the table swiftly. In a flash, she had her pack and a dagger strapped to her waist. "How exciting! Where's Gerar now?"

"He probably headed to Hamill's first, but he's likely on his way here if—"

"Oh, I'll find him!" Tala quickly chirped, heading out the door. "We'll be on our way before you know it."

"Yes, but I actually need you to—" And she was gone, dashing up the road towards the center of town. "—find Rila. But no problem, I can do that," Micah finished, talking to himself at that point.

If I'm going to beat that much energy, I better get moving. Fast.

Stepping outside, he closed the door and headed back in the direction he came from, hoping to find Rila still at Marian's. Marian lived near the old town hall in the center of Fairhollow. As an elder and Fairhollow's resident healer and historian, the village widely regarded Marian as one of its leaders. Her gentle and trustworthy personality made her a natural confidant for advice and guidance.

Maneuvering his way up the road, dodging straggling farmers on their way down to the fields, Micah heard a man shout.

"Careful, careful!"

The clang of metal against rock reverberated off the houses. Glancing towards one of the side paths, he spotted Cole and his son, Mark, along with a freshly dumped pile of manure.

"Keep the front wheel balanced, son. Take it slow instead of trying to rush ahead," Cole explained with a tinge of annoyance. "For your next lesson, take this shovel. Get it all back in the wheelbarrow."

Mark, clearly embarrassed, gingerly took the shovel from his father's hand and began scooping up the pungent mess.

"Morning, Cole," Micah called with a wave. "I see you've got a helping hand today."

"He's as green as a new spring bud, but we'll have him sorted out soon enough!" Cole hollered back.

Micah continued up the main path with a little extra stride to escape the overwhelming stench, reaching the top and turning left past the tavern. A few house-lengths down sat Marian's place, a quaint, compact hut compared to the handful of others around her. A simple stick fence with a swinging gate surrounded her yard, the space teeming with various plants, flowers, and herbs. Some were for her medicinal craft, others purely for beauty. Micah silently thanked Elowë he wasn't a healer—how Marian ever kept the hundreds of plants straight was beyond comprehension.

He opened the creaking gate and walked up the small stone path to her ancient-looking door. As Micah reached to knock, it quickly opened to reveal Marian on her way out. Her round, wrinkled face and bright, gray eyes shot upwards from her small stature to meet his.

"Micah!" Marian said warmly. "How nice to see you. I was just on my way to Lia's to deliver another remedy and a quick prayer. She's still fighting that nasty cold. Did you need something?"

As a retired Keeper for the Temple on Karthmoor, Marian was probably one of the few surviving officials as most Confessors, Temple Elders, and Keepers inhabited the cities where the Mist invaded more aggressively.

"Just a question," he quickly replied. "Is Rila here?"

"She left but a moment ago, off towards the herb gardens near the pond." Marian pointed with a frail hand.

"Thank you, Marian. Give Lia my regards. I hope she feels better soon." Micah nodded, turning around.

Tala has probably found Gerar at this point. Micah hastened his walk to an easy jog and headed north past the old town hall. The decrepit remains of the once lofty building loomed darkly over the empty road. In the early days of the Mist, before constructing the palisade walls around Fairhollow, the villagers fortified the town hall and used it as a shelter during attacks. Until one man, in the chaos of the Mist, dropped a torch near a stack of hay piled against one side to prevent the killing fog from seeping in. Thankfully, the townspeople escaped through the front doors and over to the tavern while the wide roads around the hall prevented the fire from spreading to neighboring build-ings. Still, it was a devastating loss that forced most families to huddle in their own homes or in other buildings closer to the center of town instead.

His trot took him past the town hall and a couple of houses before opening his view to the grassy area between town and the wall. A large herb garden occupied a portion of the field, main-tained by Marian and Rila along with several younger children old enough to help but not of the age where they could handle more strenuous chores. A small pond bordered the garden to the north before reaching the village walls. The modest pool fed a multitude of water plants Marian used in her concoctions. An aging willow tree sat at the center of the garden, its swaying branches enveloping weary villagers in a peaceful respite from the hectic world beyond.

Reaching the edge of the garden, Micah spotted Rila, bent over and delicately clipping fragile new buds into a small cloth pouch. Not far away, a trio of small children were being in-structed by their mother in the art of watering plants, though they appeared more interested in watering each other. He headed towards Rila, cautiously weaving through thorny bushes and twisting vines. She looked up from her work as Micah approached.

"Good morning, Micah," she said in her gentle voice. "Here to help with the garden, or are you heading to the wall?"

"Actually, I was looking for you. You'd mentioned yesterday needing to visit the river for some of Marian's ingredients."

"Yes, you're right." Rila nodded, pushing that same blonde hair as Tala's out of her face as she stood. With a nervous tone, she continued, "To be honest, I've been putting it off. Heading down there is always terrifying, though Tala sometimes offers to go with me. I was hoping to wait until the day was older, and I had plenty of sun in the sky before leaving the village."

"I understand," he said sympathetically, knowing most in Fairhollow wouldn't even set foot outside its walls.

"I'm sure I sound foolish," she chided herself. "Becoming Marian's apprentice, I knew gathering the supplies her craft requires would mean foraging beyond the village. I guess I thought if Tala was so comfortable in Binthir Forest, surely I could handle a simple walk to the river."

"It's nothing to be ashamed of. With everything you've suffered, it's only reasonable to be cautious."

"Perhaps," Rila murmured, glancing away.

"Maybe this will help. Your sister is about to head into the forest with Gerar and Hamill, but I figured they could escort you down to the river on their way. Safety in numbers, right?" Micah gave her an encouraging smile. Her eyes snapped back to him as she beamed with relief.

"That would be fantastic," she breathed.

"Excellent. Gerar should have rounded up the two of them by now," he hurriedly replied. "Are you ready to head out?"

"Of course. Just let me put these pouches in my bag, and I'll head to the gate." She quickly scooped up a pile of small cloth bags holding newly collected herbs, dumping them into the open satchel.

"I'll walk with you, if you like," Micah offered. "I need to check on Matthias, anyway. He's watching the road this morning."

"Thank you." She smiled again as she stood, dusting off her dress. Turning towards the mother and children, Rila called, "I'll be back later to trim the tiger blossoms. Could you tend the mushrooms before you leave?"

"Aye," the mother responded irritably, "assuming these waterspouts leave something to use!" Her children looked at her, then sheepishly at them, before focusing their watering cans back on the surrounding shrubs.

Once out of the garden, Micah and Rila headed off along the grassy path that followed the edge of town. He set a brisk pace, hoping to reach the gate before Gerar's group. Rila easily matched it with her long legs, her satchel securely strapped across her chest.

"How are things at the house?" Micah asked, making small talk.

"Well enough. Halvid brought some fresh pitch and sealed that hole in the roof. And Frederic gave Tala a beautiful new cooking pot a few days ago. If you ask me, I think our young blacksmith fancies her." A playful grin crossed her face.

"Really now?" he replied, amused. "I'll have to give him a hard time when I ask him again to repair a pick head and he says he's backed up."

A moment of silence passed. "I don't suppose any love-struck soul has been lavishing trinkets upon you as well?" he teased.

Rila gave a small laugh. "No, I spend too much time hiding in thickets and covering myself with leaves to be noticed. If Marian can enjoy a solitary life, I can too."

While her words were confident, her voice betrayed a quiet longing.

Whether by fatherly instinct or a simple desire to encourage, he looked over and caught her gaze. "Just because Marian has lived her life alone doesn't mean you have to in order to be her apprentice. You're a beautiful woman, Rila, with a loving heart and spirit. Any young man would be blessed beyond measure to have you."

Micah's words drew a smile out of her subdued face, brightening her downcast eyes. "Thank you," she murmured. "It means a lot to hear you say that."

"Anytime." Micah smiled back, briefly throwing his arm around her shoulders. Although he was only fourteen years their senior, Micah was grateful for the role he'd been able to play in helping the girls gain their footing in the village, and whether Rila knew it, the two of them had provided a comforting solace during the times he silently mourned his own losses.

Yet, Micah worried about Rila's future. With few young men left in Fairhollow and no contact with the other settlements on Karthmoor, the Mist had robbed her of something nearly every young woman looked forward to. Another reminder of the dark times they lived in, and unfortunately, a problem he felt helpless to solve.

Before them, the dirt road widened as it joined with the open area in front of the gate.

"Rila!" a voice cried out from behind. They turned to see Tala running towards them, Gerar and Hamill in tow.

Rila sighed with relief. "We made it in time."

At least we're off to a good start, Micah thought.

"Looks like Micah found you. Did he tell you where we're heading? I'm dying to get out there, but Hamill here was taking his sweet time pulling his stuff together." Tala rolled her eyes and shook her head in feigned annoyance.

"Right. You'll thank me if we get out there and bag a five-hundred-pound behemoth," Hamill shot back good-naturedly. Hamill was one of the younger men in Fairhollow, though the hard work he tirelessly performed as the village tanner had left his hands and skin with a rough appearance. A descendant of foreigners from the south, his dark, curly hair and beard complemented by unusually brown skin, made him a constant focus of attention for many of the girls in town, for reasons incomprehensible to Micah.

With a bow and quiver strapped to his back and holding a pack stuffed with an assortment of sacks for hauling game, Hamill continued, "So then, are we ready to head out? Gerar already filled us in on the details. We'll need to move quickly if we're going to catch the herd."

"Actually, I have a small request. Rila," Micah said, gesturing towards her, "must gather some vital ingredients for Marian. Would you accompany her to the river before you head into the forest? It's not far."

"I suppose we can," Gerar slowly answered as he walked up, "but what about the elk? Won't that give them a bigger lead?"

"It is a risk," Tala chimed in. "What if I go with you when we're back, Rila?"

Rila shot Micah a helpless glance as he started to speak.

"It's also an enormous risk if Marian doesn't receive the supplies she needs to help the sick."

He turned, surprised to hear Hamill speaking up.

"What if I go with Rila and help her gather the plants she's looking for?" Hamill offered. "You two can go on ahead, and I'll catch up. There'll be plenty of daylight left for me to find you, and I don't have to worry about the Mist any more than you do."

Gerar stroked his beard and frowned. "Normally, I would say no, but you have a good point, Hamill. As much as I dislike splitting up, it's going to take time tracking the herd in all the pine droppings. We probably won't get far before Rila finishes, and Marian's work *is* an immediate need."

"It's settled then," Micah declared. "Gerar, Hamill—set a place to meet once Rila finishes her work. I'll make sure Matthias keeps an eye on the path down to the river so Rila can make her own way back."

They all nodded in agreement; a small sigh of relief passed from Rila. Gerar waved up to Matthias on the wall, and he made his way down to help Gerar open the gate to the world outside.

"Hamill," Micah said, catching the tanner as he started towards the gate, "thank you."

He nodded. "It's my pleasure." Turning towards Rila, he added, "Don't worry, Rila. On my life, I swear I won't let anything happen to you."

"Thank you, Hamill," she replied, blushing.

Gerar and Matthias opened the gate just wide enough for the four of them to pass through. Once they were out, Micah took Gerar's place in closing the heavy timbers before he and Matthias climbed on to the wall. After a brief discussion, the group split up—Gerar and Tala quickly moving away due east, Rila and Hamill on the slight path north towards the river.

From his perch on the wall, Micah watched Rila and Hamill making their way down the hill, side by side. The tall grass reached nearly to Hamill's waist. As they walked, he said something to her, and she threw her head back in laughter, lightly shoving him.

Maybe I don't have to worry about her future as much as I thought.

Chapter 4
Repairs

"Road's quiet today, no surprise."

Matthias swept the horizon with his hawk-like gaze. "No signs of the Mist. Though I might have seen a fox moving through the field south of town earlier."

"As good a report as any," Micah gruffly responded.

Waves of the Mist had come from all sides of the village, but the majority seemed to originate from the depths of Binthir Forest to the east. While no one had determined why, the prevailing theory was it preferred the gloomy shadows of the pines and found the wild creatures who called the forest home easy prey.

"Any news from Kells' watch during the night?"

"Quiet as a tomb," Matthias answered, shaking his graying hair. "It's odd. When was the last time the Mist stayed away this long? Mark my words, something is happening. It won't leave us alone forever."

"Then we use this time to prepare. Get as strong as we can. With luck, maybe Frederic will get a new batch of weapons ready for the group," Micah said confidently.

"The boy's been working himself to death lately. The constant rain was hard on the tools forgetful farmers left in the field. And several of the houses need fittings replaced, not to mention all the swords and axes the new defenders ruined in the last attack. He shouldn't have to bear it all."

"Aye."

There was nothing to be done, though. Frederic was technically a blacksmith's apprentice, pledged to Alvin, Fairhollow's resident smith, before Alvin disappeared in a bout of Mist several months back. Whether it was the Mist or he fled of his own accord, the smith's vanishing remained a mystery. Ultimately, the responsibility of the busy forge fell to Frederic. Yet, even with his meager training, Frederic remained passionate about his craft. Whereas the responsibility set before him might have crushed a lesser man, Frederic thrived. He took the smattering of lessons he received from Alvin and improvised on them, learning on his own the proper way to forge an array of invaluable tools, from simple shovels to tempered blades for Fairhollow's defenders. Even with his young age, his tenacity quickly earned him the respect of the village.

Casting his gaze away from the towering pines of Binthir Forest and towards the south, Micah surveyed the dirt road winding its way up to the village from the southeast. Its wide, dusty trail once bore countless hoof prints and wheel tracks from traders and travelers passing through. Nowadays, it remained barren. The only sign of life outside Fairhollow, besides the birds, reduced to occasional sets of soft prints across the weedy soil. Still farther south, he passed over gently rolling fields. Once, farmers tilled many of them low, with rows of beans, potatoes, and wheat sprouting as far as the eye could see.

Yet, the risk of maintaining such a vast area soon became untenable. The encroaching dangers forced farmers back towards Fairhollow, acre by acre, until all that remained were the modest fields Francis' family had passed down. His land was lucky enough to be included in the walls that were built around the village, ensuring those who sought refuge within them could, with forethought, provide for themselves. The fields and houses beyond the vast wooden walls of Fairhollow were abandoned, slowly claimed by the elements and wild creatures who took them as shelter.

"Any guess how long they'll be gone?" Matthias asked.

"Beirand's guess seems reasonable enough. If the herd headed towards Poorman's Pond, Gerar should find them quickly. Hopefully, before sundown tomorrow."

Matthias nodded.

"Assuming they score a kill, I reckon they'll be back the day after tomorrow. Of course," Micah continued with a chuckle, "if the herd gets away and Tala gives chase, I'd add another day at the least. She isn't one for giving up."

Matthias gave a small smirk. "Aye. Sounds like our Tala."

"So, heard anything from Merrick today?" Micah asked him, changing subjects.

"He passed by early on his way to the northern wall. Didn't say much, though it sounded like the work was going slow. We're running low on timber."

He made another mental note. "I'll organize a group to collect some from the forest. Once Torvin and Frederic get that wagon fixed, Torvin can lead a party. Shouldn't take more than half a day to get enough for the repairs."

"For the wall, sure," Matthias responded. "But you know as well as I do there're plenty of other needs in Fairhollow. Those monsters were rough on the buildings in the last round. Before he checked in on the wall repair yesterday, Merrick surveyed the houses to determine which ones were still acceptable for shelter."

"Did he mark the safe houses?"

"Aye, told everyone to look for the red painted circle near the doors," he answered.

"Perfect." Micah gave a silent thanks Fairhollow had defenders with minds for planning.

A moment passed, both of them gazing over the walls into the land beyond. Where once they would have been content to let even their children play freely in the fields billowing softly in the breeze, an aura of danger and violence now hung over the land. Even at a time as peaceful as that, it was obvious from Matthias' demeanor the hidden horrors around Fairhollow had forever changed them.

Suddenly, Matthias' gaze shot northwards. A crow rose from the tall grass near the bank of the river that peeked out from the slope of the hill before them. He gripped his long-barreled musket tighter. His eyes, honed after agonizing months of searching the untamed grasslands for answers they could never give, remained fixed on the spot near the river.

"Trouble?" Micah asked, grasping the end of his pistol.

He was quiet for a moment. A moment longer than Micah liked.

"No," he finally muttered. "Probably a fox or coyote. Too low in the weeds to track."

He watched the northern end of the river a while longer. Micah's eyes traced the river's path as it exited the forest to the north, beyond the rocky mound, before winding its way south. Eventually, the slope in front of the gate hid its course from view, only for it to appear once again as it made its way east, back into the trees near the road. Looking back to the north, he surveyed the wide fields of grass blowing in the faint breeze of the day. Solitary trees dotted the landscape leading to the horizon. In the distance, the top of Tar'auth Eld was faintly visible, with clouds swirling around its peak.

Matthias muttered under his breath and swung his head back to the south, examining the fields and road again.

"I should check on Merrick, see how things are coming," said Micah.

Matthias nodded. "Tell him to be timely in coming to replace me later. I promised the wife I'd help her clean the squash she collected."

"Will do." Micah clapped him on the back. "Thanks, Matthias. I appreciate it."

He nodded again, his eyes never leaving the horizon.

Since the wall didn't have a walkway all the way around, Micah climbed back down the ladder and began trekking north through the grassy ring encompassed by the wall.

Not long after leaving Matthias, he spotted the gap ahead. A group of men were busy moving great beams of wood, shouting to each other. Even at that distance, he could faintly hear the hammers sealing the massive pieces together. Micah ran a hand along the rough surface of the wall, feeling the trunks' grainy bark.

The trees of Binthir Forest were tough, unyielding. Perfect for defenses. In decades past, Fairhollow once housed a booming lumber economy. Lumberjacks had harvested and shipped the timbers of the forest all over the island of Karthmoor, supplying the materials for towering buildings in its larger coastal cities and the ships in their harbors. As stone became more popular and business slowed, logging companies moved to smaller forests farther from the center of the island and nearer to the coasts. Yet, even in recent times, some wealthier citizens paid a pretty price for lumber felled from the great woods of Binthir. A smattering of remaining lumberjacks like Torvin were happy to meet that request. In their present day, however, Torvin and others were forced to shift their focus to fortifying places like Fairhollow. Still, the might of the towering pines had proven invaluable to the small village. Without walls, Fairhollow's demise would have been all but guaranteed.

As Micah approached the breach, he spotted Merrick standing on a boulder, directing a group of men attempting to shuffle the solid trunk of a tree into position. Although he was only of middling age, his thick, gray hair was unmistakable. He still carried an air of seriousness from years of training recruits in the Guard and wouldn't abide anything less than the best from those he oversaw. That drive had often spurred the men of Fairhollow to accomplish what seemed impossible, which was precisely why Micah thanked Elowë that Merrick was here now.

"Steady, steady!" he shouted. "Bolli, push from your side. Torvin, be ready for it!"

The men grunted in exertion. Inch by inch, they shifted the massive pillar of wood to where a deep trench had been dug for the logs to rest upright in. As they reached the edge, the dirt began to crumble.

"It's got it!" one of them shouted. In a flash, the log plummeted into the hole, shaking the ground with a loud boom. They steadied its quaking to keep it from falling and blocking the trench.

"Okay, take a break. Bolli, you've got it first while the others catch their breath. Someone switch him when you're ready," Merrick directed.

Soon, they'd start another round of shifting and shuffling, getting the fresh log as tight as they could to the surrounding wall before binding the two pieces together and filling in the collapsed dirt. It was a tough task, but vital to the security of the village.

As the men sat down for a moment's rest, Merrick spotted him making his way towards them.

"Ho, there, Micah!" he shouted. "Coming to inspect the progress?"

"Aye! Looks like good headway. You all are unstoppable!" It was obvious from their sweat-drenched faces the men needed every ounce of support they could get.

"We've got our work cut out for sure," he hollered back. "But we've got a strong crew. We'll have it done before you know it."

Micah motion him over, out of earshot of the men. He stepped carefully through splinters of busted trunks and trimmings shaved from fresh ones. Merrick's pace was even, but Micah noticed his shoulders sagging. The long days and even longer nights of protecting Fairhollow's citizens were taking their toll. Even their most seasoned soldiers were showing signs of exhaustion. Merrick's gait and sleepless eyes revealed mortality has its limits.

"How goes it?" he asked as Merrick stretched out his hand in welcoming.

"Well enough," his deep voice rumbled, "though we're moving slower as the time passes. And..."

"And?" Micah pressed, raising an eyebrow.

Merrick let out an exasperated sigh. "Honestly? I'm not sure how much longer they can keep this up. The men aren't used to this kind of work. They're farmers, not tree cutters. The lot of them are untrained, and mistakes mean lost resources and injuries we can't afford. Sure, Torvin is vital. He tries to show them how to work it as he can, but he's the only logger left. One logger to train a dozen or more green-thumbs on the job and with little time for rest or organized training."

"Are you concerned we won't finish the repairs?"

"No," said Merrick immediately, "but it's costing us. The men will learn from this one, absolutely. But if another attack happens too soon, we won't be prepared."

"I understand," he grimly replied, thoughts swirling. No brilliant solutions seemed within reach, other than praying the Mist was held at bay. "What about our supply?"

He let out a sharp whistle. "The damage here was some of the worst we've had in a long time. Took a lot of lumber we dearly needed. We might finish quicker with a patch job, but I'd prefer some new stock to seal it up properly. You have an idea for that?"

"I do. Assuming you can spare Torvin for the better part of the day."

"Only him?" asked Merrick with a hard look.

"Yes. We can't afford to take more men from this project."

"Well, I always hate to lose him, but he's got the crew at a good place for now. They've learned the routine. I guess we'll see how much they remember," Merrick conceded.

"Hopefully, it will be a quick run," Micah offered. "There should be some workers in the field we can get to help."

"I appreciate it," he said gratefully. "I need all the men I can get to keep this on pace."

Micah nodded. "We may have calm now, but we know it won't last."

"I understand that," Merrick somberly remarked. He turned away, facing the men as they prepared the settled log. "Lord knows I understand that. There's nothing more important to me now than keeping every last person here safe. I'll see this done, even if I have to give my life to seal this breach," he finished with steely determination.

Then it dawned on Micah that Merrick's exhaustion had additional causes.

How could I have been so blind?

"Merrick," he started, "you volunteered for this when no one else would. You've poured every ounce of your might and passion into keeping us safe since the wall was breached, spending more hours awake than the sun itself, directing everyone."

Micah placed a gentle hand on his shoulder. "But working yourself to death won't bring Niala back. Fairhollow knows how much you care, and so did she. We need you rested and ready for anything. Your men depend on it."

A long moment passed, quietly. Only the echo of the crew working invaded the space. Merrick turned towards him slightly and let out a deep sigh. Pain wracked his face.

"Why her?" he choked. "Why not me? How is it I can breathe the very air that took her from me?"

Micah paused, unsure of what to say.

"I don't know," he quietly admitted. "Elowë only knows why some of us aren't affected."

"Elowë." Merrick let out an exasperated breath. "I want to believe Marian when she says the Creator has a greater plan at work in all of this. But right now, it's hard to see it."

"It wouldn't be faith if you knew all the answers," said Micah. "Plus, if you knew everything, we'd all be worshiping you instead now, wouldn't we?"

A small laugh escaped him. "Wouldn't that be a pitiful sight? Still..." Merrick said, returning to his melancholic voice. "There has to be a reason. A reason the cursed fog kills some, but not everyone. Also, a reason some disappear. That part doesn't make sense either."

"Likely, folks who run are scared out of their wits. Just because we never found their bodies doesn't mean they up and vanished. There's always a chance people escape in the chaos and make it somewhere else. Maybe somewhere safer."

"Perhaps," said Merrick with a shrug.

"Regardless, I meant what I said about being ready for anything. After this shift ends, I want you back at your house for some shuteye."

Merrick raised an eyebrow. "No polite request on this one, eh?" He chuckled. "That's unlike you. Your military days are showing."

Micah waved his hand. "Hmph. Part of me will always be a fighter, I suppose."

"We certainly need that now." Merrick paused before he asked, "So then, what about poor Matthias? We can't leave him to do a double shift. Or triple shift... Whatever it is he actually does. I swear the man is part hawk."

Micah laughed. Matthias' time as a Guard sharpshooter only strengthened Merrick's theory. "I'll get Halvid to cover watch this evening," he said. "He's been asking for some work outside of farm chores, and he's reliable enough. So long as we don't give him a morning shift."

"Very well then." Merrick saluted. "I'll report to my bunk, sir. Just make sure Torvin and his lot bring us enough wood to finish this little project sooner rather than later."

"I'll see to it personally."

Merrick clapped Micah on the back and returned to his men as they busily strapped the new log to the existing wall.

He shouted to Torvin, who was standing on a patch of scaffolding, "Torvin! You've got new orders. Report to Micah over there. Sounds like a little expedition is forming."

Torvin's massive frame passed a handful of tools to the man next to him before climbing down the ladder. A man built for and shaped by years of logging, Torvin was an imposing figure. Easily one of the tallest men in Fairhollow, his grizzled face and powerful body made for an intimidating presence.

Torvin spoke briefly with Merrick before directing his gaze towards Micah. They shook hands as Torvin left the crew.

"Morning, Torvin." Micah welcomed the logger as the man climbed over a twisted branch. "Looks like you've made good progress."

"Some," Torvin said with a nod, his massive, tangled beard pressing against his chest. "Though there isn't much of a morning left. I'd like to make a bit more."

"My aim is to keep it moving. I hear we're running low on timber."

His rough face furrowed with obvious frustration as he folded his arms. "The last bout did a number on the wall. Most of the damage wasn't salvageable, other than breaking it down for use elsewhere. We've only got a few solid pieces left, and it'll take more from Binthir to close it up properly," he responded gruffly.

"I figure you'd be up for gathering some more," said Micah. "How about rounding up a group from the fields to head in? Repairs obviously must be the priority."

"Aye," Torvin agreed. "There's bound to be a sorry lot I can rope into some pine felling. I also need to check on the wagon. Last I knew, Frederic was close to having the axle repaired."

"Let me handle that while you find some men," Micah offered.

"I'll head to the fields and see who I can scrounge up then," said Torvin. "Meet you back at Frederic's?"

Micah nodded.

They split up, Torvin heading towards the main road and fields beyond, while Micah followed briefly before jogging towards the entrance to town.

CHAPTER 5
BINTHIR FOREST

THE BLACKSMITH'S SHOP SAT to the east of Delvin's tavern, between it and the gate. As Micah rounded the back of the shop, the peal of Frederic's hammer against metal rang across the square. At the front, he found Frederic bent over the anvil, pounding on what looked to be the iron ring of a barrel. His open-air forge resided in a covered space, looking towards the gate and providing a fresh breeze to the young smith hard at work. Its workshop provided a convenient place for keeping the town's only remaining wagon, which was occasionally used to haul wood or rocks up from the forest below. The only surviving horses, Francis' beloved Clyde and Noric, provided the strength to move such weighty loads. As the smith's blows slowed, Micah cleared his throat.

"Hello there, Frederic. Busy as usual, I see."

Frederic looked up, startled. "Micah! Fair morning to you. I was so focused, I didn't see you arrive."

Micah shrugged. "Don't worry about it."

Frederic was several years younger than him, a short beard coming in, matching his chestnut hair. His days working the forge had toughened his muscles and roughened his arms, but his attitude and personality remained light and energetic as always.

"What can I do for you? More arms for the watchmen needing work?" he asked, leaving his current project to cool.

"No, no. I think you already have everything we need repaired. I'm actually here to check on that axle for Torvin's wagon. Is it ready to go?"

"Just about," Frederic replied earnestly. "At the rate I end up working on that wagon, I'll be able to do it in my sleep!"

Micah laughed. "Let's hope to avoid testing that."

"I haven't had time to finish connecting it, though. Would you give me a hand?"

"Of course."

Leaving the forge, they walked over to his workshop just north of the building. Originally an old stable, much of it was gutted when the former owner passed away and Alvin purchased the property. The lofty structure now housed a vast assortment of tools, projects, and scrap. In the center of it all was a wide path to Torvin's wagon, propped up with a heap of metal braces, its rear axle half-attached.

"If you would, hold this up while I connect these," Frederic directed. As Frederic hammered the pieces together, Micah looked around. Alvin's workshop had always been a mess, but Frederic seemed to have taken it to new heights. Clearly, his enthusiasm to learn the craft required many hours of trial and error.

"How are you settling in?" Micah casually asked.

"Well enough," he answered between blows. "It's been tough with Alvin gone, as you know, but I've really been hitting a stride recently. Not to, er, puff myself up."

"Not at all." Micah smiled.

"It's just, once I really had the basics nailed down, branching out into the different methods and processes got a lot easier," he continued. "Sure, I may not be making master-quality weapons or a plow blade that slices a field like fresh butter, but my knowledge has grown. Each lesson I've learned in fixing, and sometimes breaking, simpler tools means I make better complex ones. Hopefully, that will mean stronger weapons and defenses for you all."

"A wise attitude." *While I may be older,* thought Micah, *Frederic's wisdom likely far exceeds my own.*

As the smith finished connecting the axle and wheels together, he turned to Micah.

"What about you, though?" Frederic asked. "You're just as much a newcomer here as I am, and everyone looks to you for leadership."

Micah hesitated. Whether from his training or natural inclination, he wasn't used to revealing matters of the heart.

"Well, I have plenty of experience commanding men. The situation has changed, but the principles are the same," he said evasively.

"Same principles, perhaps, but I'm not sure, in my humble opinion, anything in the Guard could prepare someone for what we find ourselves in now," he observed. "It can't be easy."

"No," Micah admitted, "it isn't. I'm used to fighting enemies I can face and keeping the peace. Neither of those are of much use now. There was always someone higher leading us, too. Now, I'm all that's left. We're hard-pressed to keep everyone safe. Hard enough that we still lose people. Good people. It's hard not to feel that guilt."

They were both quiet for a moment. Lingering on bitter pains multiplied countless times over as the names and faces of loved ones passed by in a mournful reverie.

"Yet, we keep on. Forward, no?" Frederic offered.

"Forward." Another moment of silence, though briefer than before, as their resolve built.

"The wagon is ready whenever Torvin is," Frederic finally replied.

"Thanks, Frederic," he said, shaking Frederic's hand. "Now I'm off to find Francis."

"Last I saw, he was heading home from the tavern. Said something about an argument between Lisra and Coraline," Frederic cautioned.

"Thanks for the heads up."

As Micah left the blacksmith, he glanced over as Matthias and another villager opened the gate for Rila, returning from her task. *At least she's safe.*

Rila waved, and Micah returned the gesture, then began his walk towards the center of town.

In front of Delvin's, he made the turn south, retracing his steps from the morning. He wove between houses until he was heading away from the center of the village and towards Francis' house. As the jumble of buildings spread out, it drifted into view. A small enclosure sat behind the structure where his two horses grazed on fresh grass, the last of the dew burned off long ago in the warm sun. Francis owned a larger home, built generations ago by his ancestors. A wide porch surrounded the brick and timber front, a welcoming sign contrasting the worn, fading splendor of the rest of the home.

Leaving the grassy path and coming to the steps, Micah heard a shout from inside.

"It was mine!" a woman's voice cried. As he reached the door, the woman spoke again, but Francis' gnarled voice cut her off.

"Enough!" he rasped. "The both of you ought to be ashamed! Fighting over half-feathered hens as if you were pouting schoolgirls." The room immediately silenced as he continued. "Now, Coraline, you said your coop has five healthy birds, yes?"

"Yes, sir," Coraline curtly replied.

"And Lisra, yours has eight, correct?"

"That is the truth," Lisra's quaking voice answered, "but there was an egg just a couple days from hatching and—"

"So was mine!" Coraline retorted.

"Ladies!" Francis barked again. "Now, there are few enough fowl around that I know both your flocks quite well, and they are veritably different. So here is your task: Coraline, bring me the shell from the chick who hatched as well as the chick itself and a fresh egg from your flock. Lisra, retrieve an egg from yours. Both of you return here within the hour with what I've requested, and we will determine the owner."

"But what about the hole in my fence?" Lisra shot back. "I just know she loosened that board when—"

"Enough!" Francis shouted. "You have my command. Go on!"

Shoes clattered harshly against the wooden floor as someone turned to leave. Micah backed up quickly. The door slammed open as Lisra stormed out, nearly knocking him over. She jumped in surprise, her normally calm, motherly face swept up in anger.

"Micah!" she cried before composing herself. "Apologies." Lisra stalked off the porch, her raven hair twisting in the breeze.

Then Coraline made her way out as well. While she was younger than Lisra, it was obvious Coraline wasn't giving any ground to the older woman. Her green eyes flashed as she passed, nodding briefly before offering a passing, "Micah."

Looking into the house, Micah spotted Francis standing in the middle of the sitting room, a hand rustling his sparse hair. Letting out a great sigh, he dropped into a large leather chair before noticing Micah at his door.

"Micah, come in." He motioned.

Micah closed the door and walked across the entry into the room. His dirty boots creaked loudly on the old boards.

As Micah took a seat in the wooden armchair across from him, Francis began, "No doubt you heard the... lively discussion by our very own gentle ladies of Fairhollow. Unfortunate."

"Will it be okay?" he asked, concerned.

"They may be spirited and prideful, but even in my brittle state, they'll listen to reason. These tired old bones still command a little respect around here." A worn smirk crossed his wrinkled face. "I wouldn't be Fairhollow's elder guide if I couldn't corral a couple fledglings with their feathers ruffled."

"With your experience, there's little reason to doubt," said Micah, grinning. "But... Eggs?"

Francis chuckled. "A shrewd double play, if I may say so myself. It takes time to collect everything, which forces them to blow off a little steam. The eggs' colors will also tell me which hens laid them. We'll have our answer before the sun is down."

Micah smiled at his witty move.

"It's a good thing you're the arbitrator here and not me. I'd rather avoid a duel with Lisra."

"Indeed," Francis answered. "And how fares our weathered village? Is the wall made safe again?"

"Merrick has men working around the clock on it, though Torvin needs supplies."

"Ah," Francis exclaimed. "So that's the reason. You'll be wanting my Clyde and Noric, then."

"If you would," he respectfully said. "Torvin is getting the men together now to head out."

Francis waved his hand dismissively.

"They may be my only family left, but they're poor company. Take them."

Micah nodded. "Thank you. We'll be careful."

"As you should be," Francis warned. "Binthir Forest is not a place to tread lightly. It would be a grievous blow to Fairhollow to lose you all. We'd probably lose the village along with it."

"Thanks for the encouragement," Micah dryly replied.

"It's a truth more real than crumbled eggshells," he retorted. "Fairhollow is in a delicate way. A razor's edge, if you will. Most are scared senseless. They'll panic when it comes down to it. Mark my words. Without their key leaders—you yourself included here, young Micah—they are but wandering sheep. Easy prey for... Wolves."

Micah was still for a moment, letting the truth of the words ring clear in his head. Fairhollow had survived well enough before he came, but they were failing when he did.

"I may have played a role in building up our defenses and training the men, but there are plenty of capable leaders now," Micah responded modestly. "Nowadays, I'm little more than a glorified secretary."

"In a sense, yes. But folks need someone to look up to. Warden or not, you've played that part for years. Maybe you didn't lead simple field hands, but certainly to the soldiers you led under Karthmoor's banner, you were a figurehead," Francis observed. "In the dark times in which we find ourselves, even us simple folk need heroes, Micah."

"I hope to prove myself worthy of that trust."

A small, almost gentle, look crossed Francis' face.

"No doubt," he murmured. "Still." He frowned as his gruff manner returned. "I'm sure if you die horribly, we'll find someone to take your place."

"Always a ray of sunshine."

"Well now, we can't have you growing fat and content." Francis grinned. "Now go on. Get Torvin what he needs to keep us safe."

Micah nodded and rose to leave.

Once outside, he headed around to the back and grabbed the leads for the horses. Opening the swinging gate into their pasture, Micah gently guided Clyde and Noric together and hooked the straps to them. *Francis may be a curious man, but he certainly knows how to train his horses.* The pair followed calmly as Micah led them back up the main road to Frederic's shop.

By then, the sun had risen to its full height in the sky, soaking the world in warmth long missed in the days of dreary rain. Along the way, Micah scarfed down the bread he'd taken at breakfast, knowing that was all he was likely to get before supper.

As Micah rounded the corner of the workshop, he saw Torvin and a group of men waiting with the wagon pulled out and ready to go. Torvin looked over and motioned for a couple of the men to harness the horses.

"Thank you, Micah," Torvin said warmly. "We'll be on our way as quick as we can."

"I'm coming as well," Micah added, much to Torvin's surprise. "You have enough to worry about without watching your backs."

"I certainly won't turn down the offer. The men will breathe easier knowing we've got a good warrior with us." Torvin turned to the group as they finished hooking up Clyde and Noric. "All right, you lot! Let's head out!"

Matthias and Frederic opened the gate wide as the company passed through, with Torvin at the lead and his great ax swung over his shoulder. As the gate shut behind them, Micah grasped the pouch at his side and growled under his breath.

"Something wrong, Micah?" Cole asked anxiously.

"Forgot more ammo for my pistol," he muttered, berating himself for not checking first.

Cole shrugged. "With some luck, you won't have anything to worry about."

Elowë, let it be so, Micah silently pleaded.

They slowly made their way down the steep and winding road from Fairhollow, moving out onto the plains, where it continued along the border of Binthir Forest. The towering pines remained an ominous sight, even in the day's brightness. A dreary gloom lurked in the deep shadows cast under their lofty branches.

"We'll head farther down the road before cutting in," Torvin called from the front.

Apart from the dusty gravel crunching under scores of boots and wheels, everything was silent. A crow called out from a solitary tree in the field beside them. It was obvious the men were nervous. Few of them ever left the protective walls of their sanctuary. With the dark forest on one side and the barren plains on the other, Micah felt small and exposed in the vastness of the space.

To distract himself, he turned to Cole. "So, is Mark looking after the crops?"

"Aye," Cole responded, shaking out of his anxious trance. "He'll be fine. Might 'ave a lot to learn still, but he's getting there."

"He's certainly growing into a strong young man."

"Yes indeed," Cole proudly replied. "He's got a good set of arms and a quick mind. He's already taking to lessons I never learned at his age. A good sign."

"An extra hand working the land doesn't hurt either."

"Very true," he said with a brief laugh.

"And how's Sadi? Does she enjoy working with Rila and Marian?"

"She seems to like it," Cole remarked. After a moment, his voice turned somber. "Sadi's doing well enough, I reckon, but she's been quieter lately. At first, I figured it was just part of her growing older, but... I'm not so sure anymore." His brow furrowed.

"Kara." Cole's voice stuck for a moment in his throat. "Kara's... disappearance weighs heavy on her."

"I can only imagine," said Micah with a pang of sympathy.

"It's been tough, without her mother. She misses her. There's so much she needed Kara to teach her, and there's little I can do to fill that," Cole continued wistfully. "I just wish we knew. I wish we knew what happened."

"We all do. Along with everyone else who vanished."

Cole shook his head bleakly. They continued on in the quietness of the world; the silence broken only by the stomp of boots.

"This looks like the spot!" Torvin bellowed. "This way, lads!"

Torvin turned towards the forest as he led the wagon up a small slope. As they approached, a natural clearing filled with weeds and young saplings appeared on the edge of the pines, a good place to set up for trimming felled trees. The musky scent of pine filled Micah's nose as the group trudged into the open space.

The wagon circled around, and the men spread out, passing axes out of the back. Already in his element, Torvin studied the surrounding trees. His years of experience meant he would only accept the best the woods had to offer, no matter how patient he had to be in his quest to discover the healthiest pines.

As Torvin slowly moved from tree to tree, Micah's eyes drifted past him into the maze that was Binthir Forest. The lack of undergrowth in the dense pine was unsettling. Only a carpet of dead needles spread into the gloom. Eventually, the space between trees disappeared as the multitude of gnarled trunks fused together in the shadows, their depths shrouded in mystery. The longer he stared into the darkness, the more unnerving it became.

There is something... wrong with these woods. There were no sounds beyond the ones the men made. Not even the birds called out. Micah's mind immediately shifted to Gerar and his group. *I've made a terrible mistake sending them out here.*

"Ah!" Torvin exclaimed triumphantly. He cut a small mark into a tree with his ax.

"You there! This one is yours." He called over a handful of the men to explain the proper way to cut the pine before continuing his inspections. Torvin repeated the process with the rest of the men, lining them all up on several trees to collect. Soon, the clearing was buzzing with the sound of axes hammering away at the resilient trunks. As they worked, Micah paced the perimeter of the clearing, watching the woods for any sign of life, or worse, the sickly blue haze of the Mist. The woods were silent, save an occasional crow, Binthir's once plentiful deer and smaller critters long since ousted by the Mist's encroaching dangers.

Time slowly rolled by as the men continued cutting. He glanced briefly at one group, nervously sizing up their tree from different angles and unsure of where to begin, before Torvin finally came over to show them. As Micah returned to the watch, his heart stopped. For a moment, he caught the glimpse of glowing eyes staring from the shadowy void.

"Timber!"

The first tree shuddered, then cracked magnificently as it plummeted into the clearing. As the pine's massive weight smashed into the ground with deafening fury, the air vibrated in Micah's ears, startling a slew of birds into the sky as they fled to safety.

He jerked his head back to where he saw the eyes.

Nothing.

My mind's playing tricks on me.

Almost immediately, another man called out, and a second pine collided with the earth in thunderous splendor. In short manner, all the trees had fallen, and Torvin busily directed them in trimming the branches to prepare the trunks for travel. The wagon could only haul so much at a time, so the entire group worked to transfer as many trimmed logs into the wagon as it could handle. It would take at least two trips to transport all the materials back to town.

"Alright, first group, take the cart back and dump the load near the breach in the wall," Torvin commanded. "The men there should help you unload, but remember, it doesn't need to be pretty. Just keep 'em intact. We'll trim the rest of these beauties for the second round." He flowed through the trunks, directing the mass of men like a master.

As the first load headed out of the clearing, Micah looked up and noticed the sun had begun its descent. It would be a race to get everything back before they lost their precious light.

The men took turns hacking the hardy branches off the remaining trees and dragging the remains into a pile. Even the branches were useful. Strong branches made excellent bars for doors or windows, and the pine needles and sap could plug holes where the Mist might seep in.

Micah continued his solitary, and uneventful, watch until the wagon returned and the men loaded the second round. It had taken a long time to unload the first haul and return, costing daylight. As the group loaded the wagon up with as much as the poor horses could bear, Torvin swore loudly.

"That's it. We can't take any more," he shouted, frustrated. "We'll have to make a third trip. That's all there is to it." The men muttered nervously among themselves. They all saw the sun sinking lower in the distance, and no one wanted to be there when it was gone.

The second load left the clearing as quickly as it could, and the men shuffled closer to the center of the enclosure. The ominous presence of the woods seemed to grow with each passing moment.

"We should forget the rest and leave," Cole muttered, kicking a rock. "You know it as well as I do."

"It's a risk, yes," said Micah, "but we need this to keep Fairhollow safe. Everyone depends on us."

"It's too quiet. And those shadows are getting darker." Cole gestured to the foreboding gloom.

Hours seemed to pass as they waited for the wagon to return. The sky turned red in the setting sun, and shadows grew in the clearing itself, the towering pines blocking the comforting rays. The men fell silent, everyone huddled and watching the forest. Then, faintly, the crunch of gravel rose beyond the hill.

"They're back!"

In a flurry, everyone was up, grabbing any branches and remaining wood to throw into the wagon as quick as humanly possible.

The wagon rolled into the space and circled as men carelessly tossed the materials in.

"Steady, steady," Torvin admonished.

With the heavy logs gone, loading the remnants proved a quicker task. Everyone, including Clyde and Noric, was glad for that.

In the blink of an eye, the meadow dropped into obscurity as the sun lost its ability to pierce the trees.

"Move out!" Torvin called, flinging the last of the wood into the back. The men scrambled to pick up their axes and scanned for any missed pieces in the gathering dark. Suddenly, a restless nicker from Noric startled Micah. Both horses were uneasy, shifting about in fear.

"Whoa now," Torvin cried, trying to pacify them.

"In the trees!"

A man pointed straight ahead into a dim grove of pines. Micah tilted his head to get an angle to what the man was looking at. Then he saw them.

The glowing eyes.

A menacing growl emanated from the shadows. The man gasped, freezing in fear as Micah cautiously stepped forward.

"Back away slowly," he quietly commanded. The man's eyes never left the piercing yellow ones boring into him. Step by step, he retreated from the angry creature.

Snap.

The man looked down, startled by the broken branch. The growl turned into a snarl. A massive blur of black rushed out of the trees. With a hand already on his pistol, Micah whipped it out, aiming for the beast. The man screamed in terror as the blur bore down upon him.

BOOM!

The gunshot echoed in the clearing as sparks flew from the barrel. The man tumbled back as the blur faltered, crumpling to the ground mere inches in front of him.

Everything stopped as silence invaded. The man looked up, breathing a shaky sigh of relief before collapsing on the ground. Micah holstered his pistol before helping him to his wobbly feet.

"Th–th–thank you," he stammered.

"It's alright. Grab your ax. Let's get out of here."

A group of men rushed over to steady the man as Micah pulled his pistol back out and began reloading. As he did, he glimpsed down at the mysterious creature.

A timber wolf. Large, but not unusual. Yet, it was shocking it would attack such a large group of people. He looked closer at the corpse. Patches of fur were completely missing. Its ribs were clearly visible under its stretched skin.

It was alone, starving. Even for an apex predator, Binthir Forest had become unforgiving.

Torvin made his way over. "Good shot, Micah. Boy, am I glad you came," he chuckled, patting him on the back.

"Me too."

Torvin bent down to inspect the wolf. "This fella was in rough shape. See the bite marks where the fur is missing?" He pointed to various injuries on the body. "This pup was in a pretty wicked fight. It'd have to be something fierce to leave this kind of damage."

"A bear, maybe?" Micah suggested.

"Unlikely. The wounds don't line up."

His stomach dropped as they looked at each other. They both knew what this wolf had seen. He let out a trembling breath as Torvin nodded.

"Aye. No doubt about it. Looks like even the timber wolves don't get along with their Misty friends," said Torvin quietly.

Micah shuddered, shoving thoughts of the monsters lurking in the Mist out of his mind. "I think I've had enough for one day," he concluded.

"You and me both."

Torvin resumed his place at the front of the line, motioning the group out of the forest. Once they were back on the road, bathed in the dying light of the day, everyone's relief was palpable. The journey home was a quicker one, all the men eager to return to safety.

As they passed the small bend of the river and began climbing the hill towards Fairhollow, Micah heard Halvid shout from the wall for the gate to open. He turned back, staring into the darkness behind him, the last rays of the sun blocked by the village walls.

Elowë, keep Gerar, Tala, and Hamill safe.

Chapter 6
Training

Elisa was snuggled on the couch as Micah entered, a warm cup of tea clasped in her hands as she watched the last of the day give way to a calm night beyond the window of the sitting room. Her soft dark hair was pulled into a cascading fall over her shoulder. Her slender features cast inviting shadows behind her as she looked out. He stood there, captivated, savoring the beauty of the moment.

She turned to him. "Is everything okay?"

He smiled. "Just enjoying the view."

Elisa gave a playful grin. Micah walked over and took a seat on the leather-bound couch, wrapping her in his arms as she leaned into him. For a moment, they simply were. Content in their silent embrace. She turned and kissed him lightly before resuming her stare out the window.

"Did you see Samuel with that goat today?" she asked with a giggle. "I swear he thought it was the greatest war horse in history."

Micah laughed quietly, not wanting to wake him. "An adorable sight. He'll be riding a real horse soon enough. Next time we go to market, I'll check with the Hovens. I think they had a dam about to give birth. Samuel would love growing up with a little foal of his own."

Elisa smiled. "Anyone would. As long as you promise not to take him on some wild adventure!"

"On my honor," he replied with a chuckle. "I think we both know those days are long past."

They were quiet a moment longer. Micah relaxed, holding her close and breathing in her familiar scent.

A knock at the door broke the stillness. They both turned, surprised at such a late visitor. Micah extracted himself from the couch and moved to answer it. He swung open the door to find a young man standing on the porch. His light metallic armor bore the insignia of the Guard.

"Good evening, sir. Forgive my late appearance," he stumbled quickly with a hasty salute. "I had intended to arrive much earlier, but the heavy rains farther south delayed me."

"Not at all," Micah responded. "Come in."

The man wiped off his feet and walked inside, standing awkwardly in the entry space. Micah motioned him into the sitting room and shut the door. His polished boots clacked loudly against the bare floor as he made his way to a simple wooden chair.

"Elisa, would you mind fetching a drink for our guest?" Micah politely asked.

"Certainly." She smiled. "Water? Tea? I think we also may have a little ale, mister...?"

"Perentius," the young soldier offered eagerly. "Just tea, thank you."

As she headed into the kitchen, Micah took a seat on the edge of the couch nearest to Perentius.

"To what do we owe this pleasure?"

"Right, my apologies," he stammered. "I should've started with that."

"You're doing fine, Perentius. How long have you served in the Guard?"

"Only a few months," he responded humbly. "This is my first assignment. I admit, I was a little nervous when they asked me to deliver a message to the Warden of the West."

Micah laughed. "A loftier title than befits the man. I was just as much a soldier as yourself. Even as warden, I had many superiors I still reported to."

"Yes, sir," Perentius replied. "But you remain famous among the men. Your bravery and charisma in commanding your soldiers at such a young age, still sets the bar for ambitious captains."

"I'm humbled," he responded, nodding. "I was but an adventurous fool when I joined the Guard, looking to further my travels."

"That's why I joined too," said Perentius eagerly. "Getting to travel the breadth of Karthmoor is thrilling."

"Indeed. So, what message did your captain send with you?"

"Right, sorry. The message, er, order comes from higher, actually."

"Order?" Micah repeated, his curiosity piqued.

"The Conclave," he continued nervously, "has requested your presence at the council in Starkhaven. They require your expertise in defining a course of action in response to the Anderfall invasion."

Elisa returned to the room with drinks in hand.

"Expertise," Micah mused. "Their incursion into Karthmoor is certainly a concern, but I've retired from my duties. I no longer have access to the reports and movements of the Guard. I fear I would be of little use to the Conclave."

"*Yes, sir,*" *Perentius said respectfully.* "*I know only that they want you there in their deliberations. The Warden-Commander himself issued the message on the Conclave's behalf.*"

"*Berien asked for you?*" *Elisa chimed in.*

"*He knew how important truly retiring from the Guard was to me when I left,*" *Micah added.* "*Berien wouldn't ask unless it was serious.*"

"*The general mood towards the conflict is quite dim 'round the barracks,*" *Perentius offered. Micah sat back, thoughts crowding his head.*

"*How soon do they expect a response?*"

"*My orders are to return immediately with your answer, sir,*" *he answered.* "*Though it sounded like they didn't expect it to be a choice.*"

"*Old habits die hard, I suppose.*" *Micah was silent a moment longer before directing his gaze back to Perentius.* "*Tell them I'll be there. I'll make my way to Starkhaven the day after tomorrow.*"

"*Thank you, sir.*" *He nodded.* "*I suppose I should be off then.*"

They all stood, and Perentius saluted. "*Thank you for the hospitality, ma'am.*" *He nodded to Elisa, then headed to the door. As he opened it to leave, he abruptly paused and turned back.*

"*Sir, if I may,*" *he added,* "*why did you leave the Guard?*"

Micah glanced towards Elisa as she looked at him, curious. "*Some things are more important than excitement and glory.*"

"*I see. Thank you again, sir. Godspeed.*" *With that, he marched back towards his horse, his armor clinking as he vanished in the dark.*

—◦—

The patter of light rain against the window roused Micah from his dreams. He sighed. *Sounds like yesterday was only a brief reprieve.*

He slowly opened his eyes, rubbing the sleep away. Stretching, his body felt oddly sore. Then he remembered the encounter with the wolf. *The adrenaline of the moment must have been stronger than I thought.*

Micah hurried through his morning routine, returning to the shelter of the tavern after a thorough wetting. From the room's smell, the prior night's leftovers of chicken and porridge made up the meal Delvin had set for the morning. He ate quickly with a plan to head to the storehouse and find more ammunition. *Something I should've done yesterday,* he silently reprimanded himself. Merrick came in shortly after, tagging along behind a group of townsfolk. He sat down at the table as Micah nodded in greeting.

"Blasted weather continues to slow us down," Merrick tiredly muttered, running a hand through his wet hair. "We'll be lucky to make any actual progress today if this keeps up."

Micah bobbed his head in sleepy assent.

"The sky has to dry up sometime. Maybe we'll catch a break."

Merrick grunted and began picking at his bread and stirring the lukewarm broth. Micah finished eating and offered a quick goodbye before heading back out into the rain.

He hurriedly turned north, heading to the old two-story house that sat a building up from the tavern. The exterior was in rough shape, pieces of its timbered frame and roof broken by hard storms and winds. The poor construction of the place meant it was susceptible to the noxious Mist through its various gaps and openings. Instead of attempting to plug all the gaps and openings, the original inhabitants had moved into another home, and the interior was repurposed into a storehouse for imperishable supplies.

Micah unlocked the rusty door, and it creaked open. Shafts of light spilled through holes in the walls and roof, along with a steady drip of rain. A deep, musty smell hung in the air. He walked into the dank house, under a landing on the floor above, and opened the locked door to his right. This central room was the most protected, a good place to store the powder for their guns along with other moisture-sensitive items. He rummaged through a box of bullets, scooping a handful into the pouch at his side, then grabbed a couple of small boxes of powder. As he searched, Micah made a note of their remaining store. Even with its small size, the space was feeling emptier. Boxes of shot were disappearing, though perhaps not as quickly now that they had been relying on the more easily replaced bows and arrows. A small collection of spare pistols and muskets poked out of an open crate against the wall.

Micah finished his inspection and locked the room. The rest of the house was dark and quiet, beyond a dribble of water in the corner.

Drip.

He paused for a moment, captivated by the monotonous trickle as a memory flashed across his mind.

The soft peal of a hammer as his grandfather patched the hole in the roof of their little cabin, his mother carrying past a load of soaked blankets towards the line to dry.

"Nail, my son," his grandfather called from the ladder as Micah's youthful hand felt around in the rough pouch for a piece of iron.

"Why not?" Micah asked eagerly, stretching his lanky arm to hand it up. "Landin's father told him how his great grandfather

was a general in the rebellion. I promised I'd tell him about mine too!"

"Because," he rasped between blows against the shingles, "it is old history, son. Better it's left forgotten." His grandfather wiped his wrinkled brow and descended.

"Why though? I want to know what he was like. Or even what your grandfather, Beran, was like."

He turned, raising a bushy, gray brow. "Now, where did you hear that name?"

Micah fidgeted, scrambling for an excuse. "A letter. In my father's old belongings."

"Hmm." His grandfather studied him with a look of sadness, and something else, in his aging eyes. "It is not that simple, Micah. Nothing about our family is."

"But you knew him, right?"

"Aye, though, it was long ago." His gaze drifted across the golden sea of wheat, rustling in the breeze. "My grandfather Beran was... unique. He had a restless soul, always seeking."

"Seeking what?" Micah asked.

His grandfather grumbled under his breath before another coughing fit overtook him. "Ah," he finally wheezed, "here comes your mother. Go on now. Show her a kindness and fetch the next load, will you?"

Micah sighed and plodded into the shadows of the house.
Drip.

Micah shook his head, tearing his gaze away from the interminable splash in the corner.

I should check on Matthias while I'm out. He left the locked house behind and strolled quickly towards Fairhollow's entrance.

The light rain had slowed to a dreary drizzle as he approached the muddy area inside the gate. Frederic was already hard at work, hammering away on something near the forge. Micah shielded his eyes from the haze as he looked up at the wall. On a day like that, men manning the gate were immensely thankful for the modest awning Torvin had built atop their post. He climbed the ladder up into the roost with Matthias.

"Morning, Micah," Matthias said, his voice cool and collected as Micah stood.

"Morning. Any sign of Gerar's group?"

"Not yet. Kells reported nothing during the night, either."

"Hmm."

"It's only been a day since they left. Give it more time," Matthias offered. With the rain preventing much of the daily work, the day was guaranteed to be an agonizing wait.

Micah climbed back down and headed for shelter near Frederic's forge while deciding what he could still accomplish.

"Hello, Micah," Frederic welcomed as he took a break from his work. "Enjoying the weather?"

"As if," scoffed Micah. "This rain really hampers our progress."

"I might have a suggestion for you, if you're interested," said Frederic. Micah looked at him questioningly.

"Torvin left the wagon in the old shack behind Hamill's place last night," he began, "which motivated me to clear some space out in the workshop. If you want to help finish that, it would be an excellent area for sparring."

Micah immediately perked up. "That's a great idea. There's a handful of villagers who've been wanting to learn how to defend themselves, and Halvid has shown interest in joining the defenders. I just haven't had time to devote to training any of them."

"Let me finish this piece I'm working on, and we can get started," Frederic responded.

"I can go grab some men while you do that," he offered. "More hands mean we'll clear the space faster."

Frederic nodded. "Sounds like a plan."

Micah left the forge, heading to the tavern to see if any of the villagers were passing the day at its counters. His guess was good, as the place was quite full. After filling them in on the plan, several agreed to go grab the others, and everyone split up, much to Maven's displeasure at the loss of paying customers. Micah quickly headed out the door to find Halvid.

Halvid lived near the fields, across from Rila and Tala's house. While a good man, Halvid never married and had an annoying propensity for hibernating the day away, especially when it was raining. Hopefully, some training and responsibility would change that.

Micah approached his modest, dripping house and knocked loudly. No response.

He knocked again. Still nothing.

He reached for the wrought iron door handle and found it unlocked. Micah let himself in to find Halvid passed out in his bed, snoring heavily.

"Morning, sunshine!" he shouted, slapping the boot dangling from the covers.

"Huh? Whosnat?" Halvid groggily stammered. He rubbed his eyes, looking sleepily towards the end of the bed where Micah stood.

"Micah!" he exclaimed, yawning. "Don'tcha know better than to a wake a man enjoying his sleep?"

Micah chuckled. "And you're a man with plenty of it. Now up with you. You wanted to join the defenders, no?"

That shook him awake.

"Yessir, absolutely," he shouted.

"Well, today's the day. We're getting a space at Frederic's ready for training. Come join us when you're presentable."

"Yessir!" Halvid cried, clambering out of bed. "I'll be there in a jiffy."

Satisfied he'd properly woken him, Micah left the house and headed back towards Frederic's. The drizzle returned to a steady rain, transforming the dirt road into a muddy mess. As he reached the doors of the workshop, the rattle of metal filled the air alongside the smell of musty junk and hay.

"Put that over there! That piece goes with those. Just toss that one out back!" He heard Frederic shout as he directed the men burrowing through the heaps.

The workshop was a blur of activity as years of scrap collected by Alvin and Frederic were slowly organized. Some pieces were carefully grouped and transported to the loft above the main floor, while others found their place in the old horse stalls along one side of the barn. Everything else, rusted or useless, they threw into a great mound gathering outside the shop, evicted from its dry home. Halvid stumbled in from the rain shortly after.

Within a few hours, the group had cleared most of the workshop, leaving plenty of space to practice. With the rain showing no signs of abating, the commotion at Frederic's drew a small crowd of curious children and aggravated wives wondering where their husbands had disappeared to.

"Alright, men!" Micah shouted, grabbing their attention. "You've all showed interest in learning the art of combat. The days in which we find ourselves no doubt prove the value of self-defense. Fairhollow may have its valiant defenders, but never forget: you are its last line of defense. It is up to you to lead your families, sacrificing everything for them, even your own life, should Elowë will it."

The group stood straighter, a grim determination strengthening their focus.

"Frederic has provided several practice swords over there. Grab one and return to me."

The group distributed the dull wooden swords before falling back in line.

"To begin, spread out and take a moment to move the sword around. Swing hard, but steady. Get a feel for the weight of the weapon. Notice where the balance sits." After a moment filled with the whistle of wood singing through the air, Micah called them back.

"Halvid, join me at the front," he commanded. Halvid stepped out of the line, and they faced each other. The rest of the group looked on in eager anticipation.

"The most important techniques to learn are those of defense. To strike at your opponent's weaknesses, you must first learn to shield your own. Like so." Focusing back on Halvid, Micah continued, "Halvid, place your feet like mine. Notice the spacing." Micah nodded as the man imitated him. "While there are countless variations, a handful of simple movements form the base of any good defense. For example, should I swing in from the side, turn your sword like this."

Slowly, he moved Halvid through the motions, teaching his mind and muscles the movements of battle. The rest of the men looked on, soaking up every detail. Several imitated the movements along the sides as he instructed Halvid.

"Now, those are some basics of how to move, but until you face a situation where you must use them, your body is unlikely to remember. You must train your limbs to recall them, should the time come."

Halvid planted the tip of his wooden sword in the dirt, resting against it like a crutch. In a flash, Micah flicked it up with his own, and Halvid stumbled in surprise.

"Guard up, Halvid. Let's test your memory," Micah challenged. Raising his weapon, Micah slashed lightly at his side. Halvid reacted quickly, the dull thud of wood echoing inside the shop as he deflected the blow with ease.

"Very good. Now, a bit harder."

Micah swung quickly from above, his practice sword racing towards the man's head. Halvid raised his own, blocking the blow. Immediately, Micah unleashed a second strike, cutting up from his left. Halvid parried, if awkwardly.

"Again!"

Micah swiped from the right, and Halvid blocked more confidently. Micah smiled. *He's learning.*

He switched to the left, closing in on Halvid's other side before he could shift focus. Halvid's stumbling block blunted the forceful swing, but it left him exposed as Micah hammered his sword down on the flailing blade, the blow knocking it from his hand.

"Don't focus on defending a single spot. Your opponent will come from every angle he can think of. Be ready to move and meet him. Let's try again," said Micah.

The rainy afternoon wore on as they continued sparring. Once Halvid had a better feel for the blade, Micah broke them up into pairs to duel one another. He moved around as the clatter of wood filled the air, examining each man and giving instruction where needed. The group began awkwardly, everyone nervous to face his neighbor. Yet, all eventually settled into a serious effort.

It's progress, thought Micah. *Sure, they may not be soldier material yet, but they're showing promise. With a couple more sessions under their belts, they'll be well on their way.*

Eventually, Matthias found his way in to the workshop as the men continued practicing.

Micah glanced over at the doorway. *I must have lost track of time if Merrick already switched him.* He finished showing Cole how to deflect a jab and then made his way over.

"No sign of Gerar yet," Matthias reported.

"Right. Tomorrow then."

"They're looking good." Matthias gestured towards the group. "Still swinging like they're wielding a hoe, but they'll learn."

"They could use some pointers," Micah said, welcoming the help of an experienced soldier.

"You didn't grow soft in your command, did you?" Matthias smirked.

"I think we can safely lay that concern to rest."

The two of them wove back through the crowd of spectators, little boys and girls cheering on their fathers.

As the sunlight faded behind the stormy clouds, torches were lit to brighten the workshop. They continued a while longer before calling it a day.

Micah summoned them all to the center as they finished. "Good work, everyone. I saw significant progress here. We'll make sword masters out of you yet!" A handful of hearty laughs erupted as the men slapped each other on the back. "We'll do this again the next time our normal tasks are rained out. Until then, if you have questions or some free time, come find me. We can see about getting some short personal sessions in here and there. Thanks, everyone."

As the chattering crowd filed out into the drizzle, Lisra slipped through the throng towards Micah.

"They look good, Micah," she politely said.

"Thank you," he graciously responded. "Give me a few more sessions, and there won't be an untrained hand in Fairhollow."

"We'd be better for it, in times like these," she somberly replied. "I only wish Kelso were still here to join them."

Micah's expression softened as he nodded. An attack had claimed the life of her husband, Kelso, not long after Micah had arrived in Fairhollow.

"I'm sorry, Lisra. I wish so too," he murmured. "I'm sure he would have been a quick learner."

"He always had a cunning mind," she recalled fondly. "Still, I have a favor to ask."

"Of course."

"Without Kelso, I only have you and the other defenders for protection. Most of the other women in Fairhollow also rely completely on your defenders to keep us safe. But what if we had something to boost our confidence?"

Micah raised a curious eyebrow.

"Train us as well," Lisra passionately pleaded. "The mothers and children old enough to carry the responsibility. We don't need to be on the front lines, but we need a fighting chance."

He honestly hadn't considered the thought. Everyone in Fairhollow—with the exception of a few Guard-trained defenders—were farmers. Civilians. His training of the men was merely a response to the dire situation.

Still, a basic understanding of self-defense could be invaluable for everyone.

"You make a good point, Lisra," Micah began cautiously. "We don't have the luxury of living in peaceful times, and some training might save a life." Lisra brightened. "But you don't want martial training like I've shown here today. You want something more practical. If you end up in a fight in your own home, the rules of war go out the window. For that, I actually have a better trainer in mind for you."

"I see your point," Lisra said, predictably confused, "but what do you mean, exactly?"

"You need to learn to fight using whatever is at hand, and that likely won't be a longsword. For real, practical training, we need Tala."

"*Tala?*" Lisra sputtered. "That wild thing of a girl? What does she know about protecting a family?"

"There's more to it than that," he explained. "You need to know how to make anything a weapon, anything that can protect you and your children. I don't know of anyone more resourceful than her. She's a survival genius, inventing weapons and tools on the fly with whatever she can find. I once watched her use a wooden skewer and a rock she'd pulled out of the ground to wound a bear and send it running."

Lisra's incredulity lessened somewhat.

"Trust me, if anyone can teach you to be a resourceful fighter, it's Tala," Micah said emphatically.

"Alright," Lisra conceded. "I'll trust you, Micah Stormcrown. So, when can we have her start? I know for a fact there's already a group of women who would be ready tomorrow."

"Tala is still away hunting with Gerar. Once she's back, I'll discuss the idea with her. She'll need time to come up with a training plan, but I'm sure we can get something started soon."

"Very well. Let me know as soon as she's ready."

Lisra turned to leave the workshop. She stopped at the door, a cascade of drizzle falling behind her in the growing darkness.

"Thank you, Micah," she murmured. "It won't bring Kelso back, but it means I can give myself a fighting chance. For him." Lisra disappeared into the haze as he stared after her, alone in the glowing torchlight.

The day may not have begun as he had hoped, but they'd made the most of it. And perhaps there were more ways to strengthen the village than he thought. Micah mulled over Lisra's last words and chuckled.

And still a lot I have to learn.

He put out the torches and closed up the workshop to head to Delvin's and grab a quick meal before calling it a night. Merrick looked back from his post, giving a wave as Micah slammed the shop door shut. *At least I don't have to stick it out in the rain tonight.*

Micah trudged through the cooling drizzle, focusing on the inviting lights of the tavern ahead.

CHAPTER 7
THE MERCHANT

Bright sunlight streamed through the dirty window of the bedroom, falling across Micah's face and tugging him from sleep. He sat up, wide eyed.

I've overslept! Gerar has to be back. Hopefully, I haven't missed it.

He quickly strapped on his weapons and boots and rushed out the battered door.

The sky held only a few wispy clouds, a much better sign than the day before. Instead of heading to the tavern, he steered towards the gate, hoping Matthias had good news. Micah wound his way through the crowd of farmers heading down the main road to the fields for their morning chores. In the distance, a horse gave an excited cry.

"Mornin', Micah!"

He turned to see Beirand walking down the path.

"Morning, Beirand. Where are you headed today?"

"The fields, of course." Beirand hadn't worked the fields in years, a decade probably.

"Oh?" said Micah casually.

"Aye, Marian mentioned Lia is feelin' a little better but has been missin' a good bowl of carrot stew somethin' fierce. I offered to collect some from her part of the field," Beirand explained proudly.

"Good on you," he responded, pleasantly surprised at Beirand's helpful attitude. "Lia will love that."

"Aye. Anything I can do to help!" Beirand exclaimed as he continued his stroll after the rest of the villagers.

Well. Anything's possible today.

The square near the gate had quieted with everyone off to their chores, other than the customary peal of Frederic's hammer.

"Any news, Matthias?" Micah called up to Matthias as he paced on the wall above the gate.

"Morning, Micah. Running a little late today, I see," he called back. "No news yet. I'll send word as soon as I spot them."

"Thanks."

It's still early. Give it time.

He figured he might as well head to the tavern and see if there were any leftovers from breakfast.

"Hello there, Micah!" Delvin boomed as he entered through the low door. "There may be a smidgen of bread left. Oh! And a bit of cheese, fresh from Coraline's goat."

The cheese was an unexpected treat. Dairy was hard to come by, and the few goats the townspeople had were poor producers. As Micah leaned back, enjoying the warm tea Maven set out, Rila came in and took a seat beside him.

"Good morning, Rila," said Micah. "No tasks for Marian yet?"

"Hello," she replied, pulling off her leather satchel and placing it on the seatback. "Not yet. Marian was taking her sweet time getting around today. She also wanted some time alone to pray."

"So, you headed to the tavern? Tsk, tsk," he teased.

"Frederic mentioned he saw you head this way. I was wondering if you'd heard anything from Tala."

Micah shook his head. "Not yet. It's still early in the day, though. I'm sure they'll be back soon."

"You're right. I'm sure they're on their way," she agreed, though her worried look said otherwise.

"Tala knows how to fend for herself. If anyone can survive a trip through Binthir Forest, it's your sister," he said, attempting to console her.

"I know, but I still worry. Tala's the only family I have left." Her face dipped, laced with sorrow. Micah's heart ached for her. Both of them had lost so much at such a young age.

As he finished the tea, Micah tried to change the topic.

"So, was your trip to the river successful? I never got the chance to ask."

Rila looked up, pleased. "Yes! It had been a while since either Marian or I had gone, and there were plenty of new plants. I almost had to ask Hamill to carry my bag back because it was so full."

"How did Hamill do as an escort? He didn't up and leave you, did he?" he asked innocently.

"Not at all. Hamill was the perfect gentleman. He even dug out a bunch of the roots I needed. He offered to walk me back, but I knew he needed to catch up to Tala and Gerar," Rila answered happily. "It was wonderful having him along."

"I'm glad. From the look of him as you left, I'd say he enjoyed it, too."

Rila's face turned bright red as a playful smile crossed Micah's face.

"I—I should check on Lia," Rila stammered. "For Marian. She probably needs more tonic. Maybe I should stop by there first. Marian's, that is, not Lia's. For the tonic. Anyway, I'll see you later." Rila grabbed her bag, rushed across the room, and out the slamming door, her face still flushed. Micah chuckled as he returned his cup to the bar where Maven stood, scowling.

"What did you say to our young Rila?" Maven demanded. "What happened?"

He shrugged. "Young love."

Maven relaxed and started laughing. "Lord knows we could use more of that."

"Thanks for the tea, Maven," Micah said, inclining his head.

"Anytime." She was still chuckling quietly as he shut the creaking door.

Micah drifted through the remainder of the morning, passing from chore to chore, his mind focused on Gerar's group.

Surely they'd be back by now.

Progress on the wall remained slow, the heavy rain having muddied the trench for the new logs, adding to the difficulty. Still, the men were making quick work preparing the fresh logs for placement. Much of the extra scrap and branches from the pines had already flowed into the village itself, where citizens were busy putting it to good use. From fresh stacks of firewood to sturdy bars over exposed windows, the signs of new supplies were everywhere. Merrick was confident they would finish the wall by the next day, barring any downturns in the weather. The sooner that was finished, the better.

Many of the new crops down in the fields were coming in strong; a good sign they'd have an abundance of vegetables soon. Coraline's and Lisra's flocks would have a number of new chicks in the coming weeks. Yet, even with all the good signs, Micah's anxiety remained.

Much of the afternoon passed slowly as he gave Merrick a break on the wall repairs. The men were working hard, hoping to finish by sundown, but it was realistically improbable. Moving the great, muddy timbers proved a tedious task. As the afternoon sun reached the point where its descent became obvious, Micah worried they still wouldn't hear anything from Gerar. It would be late soon, and if they didn't reach Fairhollow in time, they'd have to find a place to shelter for the night.

The ground shook as a large blast echoed in the clearing. The men had dropped a trunk just as they'd straightened it up, shaking Micah from his thoughts.

"Careful!" someone angrily shouted.

"Take it slow," he called, walking over. "I can switch in if someone needs a breather."

As they lifted again, a small voice called out.

"Micah!"

He turned to see Mark running towards them.

"Micah!" he called again.

"Hello, Mark," Micah said as the boy stumbled to a stop. "What's the matter?"

Mark bent over, catching his breath, then looked up. "Matthias sent me. There's something on the road. He said it looks like a wagon!"

A wagon? Who in Aldaria could that be?

"Excellent job. Thank you for delivering the message."

The boy beamed proudly before running back towards town.

"Torvin, can you cover?" Micah shouted over to him.

"Aye!" Torvin hollered back.

Unwilling to waste any time, he retrieved his weapons from where he'd left them and dashed towards the gate.

The square was a mess of activity as Micah arrived. Pockets of villagers were shuffling about in curiosity and excitement.

"What do you see?" someone called to Matthias.

"Is it Hamill?" came another.

"Someone said there was a wagon!" yet another villager answered.

"A dragon?"

"No! A *wagon!*"

Micah wove his way through the swarms of people towards the ladder to Matthias' perch. As he climbed up, the soldier jumped back.

"Sorry," Matthias apologized, relaxing. "I don't know how many times I've had to yell for someone to get down."

"No problem. So, what's the commotion?"

"Take a look." He pointed towards the forest.

Micah fixed his eyes on the road as it wound its way beside the forest to the south. Far in the distance, something was moving. Too big to be a person. Its faint outline resembled a wagon being pulled by horses, but it was hard to tell.

"It sure looks like a wagon," Micah commented. "That was your take?"

"Aye," Matthias confirmed. "It's moving at an even pace. Doesn't seem to be in any hurry. I can't tell how many people are with it."

"What do you see, Micah?" a voice called out, Frederic from the sound of it. Micah turned to face the expectant crowd.

"It's still a long way off," he began, "but it does appear to be a wagon."

Whispers of excitement shot through the crowd.

"Could it be Gerar's group?" someone yelled.

"It's possible they found something on their trip, but it would be unlikely," he answered. "We will keep watching as it draws closer. If there's any risk to the village, Matthias will sound the bell."

The crowd devolved into a frenzy as they debated what the mysterious object could be.

"What I wouldn't give to have grabbed my spyglass," Micah muttered, thinking back to his old farm.

"It won't be long before I can make it out," Matthias assured him. "I'm already positive there's a single horse drawing the cart."

"I'll wait with you."

Together, they watched the tiny blur inch its way towards them as the sun continued its decline. The wagon would reach the gate before sundown, that much was certain.

"There's at least two people in it," Matthias observed. "A driver and passenger in the front. There's a mass of stuff behind them, but I can't make out what."

Micah nodded, trusting in Matthias' sharp sight.

"Wait, more people. Someone shifted in the back. Looks like maybe four people, including the front two."

Maybe a family? It'd been ages since they'd seen anyone from the outside world, but perhaps a straggling family had decided to head towards Fairhollow.

"Definitely four people," Matthias stated confidently. "Some kind of cargo with them. Maybe bags and some boxes. They don't look heavily armed. No gleams from metal armor or the like."

A moment passed.

"It's Tala!" Matthias sputtered.

"What?" Micah gaped, incredulous.

"The passenger. It's Tala. She's riding next to a man I don't recognize. Dark skin, darker than Hamill's. Almost black. I can't tell for sure, but I'm guessing Gerar and Hamill are the ones in the back," he said excitedly. An instant later, he confirmed it. "It's definitely the three of them. Plus, someone new. Must've run into a traveler on their way back."

A man below noticed the commotion. "What is it?" he called.

The crowd went quiet again.

"We can see Gerar, Tala, and Hamill in a wagon," Micah announced. "There's a traveler with them."

"A traveler!" an excited shout rose from the townsfolk. The crowd instantly became louder as they discussed the new revelation. Farmers on their way back from the fields, curious where the rest of the town had vanished to, slowly found their way to the square.

"Still can't tell what the cargo is. Definitely some boxes and what looks like large sacks. I'd swear I saw antlers sticking out from underneath one," Matthias added.

Soon, the cart was at the bottom of the hill leading to the village.

"Open the gate!" Matthias hollered. Eager hands moved to unbar and swing the doors open.

As the wagon drew near, Tala waved up to them from her seat.

"Welcome back!" said Micah, leaning against the rail. "Looks like you made a friend!"

"Micah!" Tala called back joyfully. "It's good to be home!"

"Make way! Make way, you lot!" Francis shouted from the crowd below.

The villagers reluctantly separated, moving next to the buildings and giving space for the wagon to enter. The dark-skinned man beside Tala appeared nervous, unsure of what to make of everything.

"Good work, Matthias," Micah thanked the faithful watchman.

He nodded as Micah descended into the crowd. The newcomers had captured everyone's attention as they gossiped and stretched for a better view.

As Micah pushed his way through, Gerar and Hamill climbed out from the back, stepping over a huge mound of bags. Both of them looked unharmed.

"Micah!" Gerar called triumphantly.

"Welcome back." Micah grasped his friend's arm. "This wasn't quite the return I expected." He nodded towards the wagon filled with curiosities.

Gerar laughed. "Nor ours, but you'll be happy to know Beirand was right. We found the herd. Near Poorman's Pond to boot."

"Good on him. So how did it go?"

He smiled. "Come and see."

They walked closer to the back of the loaded wagon. The heavy bags piled in the back were the very ones Hamill had grabbed before leaving Fairhollow. All of them stuffed to the brim with fresh elk meat. Below the sacks lay the corpse of a huge elk, ready for cleaning.

"We would've taken care of that one, except Hamill nicked it with an arrow, and it got away the first time. We cut our losses and stuck to cleaning the ones we had, but lo-and-behold, we stumbled onto the poor devil on our way back. It was in a sad state but made a pleasant addition to the rest."

"And our other new friend here?" Micah quietly added, eyeing the strange traveler.

"We'd chased the elk to the edge of the forest," Gerar explained. "Met him at the crossroads just south of the pond, where he just so happened to be passing by as we did. Quite a surprise for all of us."

"I imagine."

"He offered to help us back to Fairhollow in return for lodging and some supplies for the road," Gerar continued. "Seemed like a reasonable trade. I figured we could use some news from beyond our walls."

"Excellent job," said Micah, patting him on the back. "This is huge. Couldn't have asked for better."

Gerar gave a satisfied nod and glanced towards the gathered villagers. "Looks like we've got plenty of hands ready to help unload. We'll need to get it to Delvin's to cure the lot quick. I hope his storehouse is big enough," he replied with a grin.

"Yes, but first, let's welcome this traveler."

They walked around the wagon to where Tala was busy talking to the newcomer. The pair turned around as Micah and Gerar approached.

"Micah!" Tala rushed up and threw her arms around him. "It's so good to see you!"

"Welcome back!" he said with a laugh. "We missed you all. I'm so proud of you."

She beamed happily before stepping back.

"Micah," she began, gesturing towards the man, "this is Asher. Asher, this is Micah Stormcrown. He leads our defenders."

"Welcome, Asher." Micah stretched out his hand.

"Greetings, serah Micah," said Asher in a rich, curious accent. "I am humbled by your town's welcoming." Asher's appearance, from his black skin and short black hair and beard, to his fine, shimmering amber clothes, spoke of an exotic and foreign world.

"Move aside, move aside!"

Francis and Marian quickly made their way forward to join the exchange.

"Asher, this is Francis, our leading elder, and Marian, our town healer," said Micah, "and this is Asher…"

"A simple merchant," Asher finished as he shook each of their hands. "I gratefully receive the hospitality of your warm town. It is a bright spark of light in my many dark journeys."

"Welcome, Asher," Francis rasped. "Fairhollow is a small village, but as long as you come in friendship, we welcome you with open arms."

"Thank you, elder Francis," Asher humbly responded in his deep voice. Francis smiled faintly, clearly satiated by Asher's generous words.

"We appreciate your helping our hunters," Micah added. "The load would've been impossible without you."

"Of course, and I imagine it needs to be processed quickly. Please, lady Tala is most welcome to move my cart to wherever you need it."

"Thank you, Asher," Tala chirped before climbing back into the seat. "I'll move this over to Delvin's."

"Aye! This way," came Delvin's loud voice from the crowd. He escorted Tala away from the square and towards the empty tavern in the distance.

Asher turned to Micah. "Serah Micah, I have but one request."

"Of course."

"I am most happy to contribute as I can during my stay, but I must insist my other cargo not be disturbed. It must arrive safe and untouched to its owners," he cryptically finished.

"Understood. I'll ensure that your privacy with your own property is respected."

"Thank you, serah Micah," he said warmly.

As the sun reached its end, hues of orange and red streaked across the sky. The crowd slowly dispersed towards their homes, though many headed down the road to finish discussing the day's exciting events at the tavern.

"We have a couple houses in which you can stay," Micah offered, "though Delvin also has a few rooms at the tavern that may be in better shape. Whichever you'd prefer."

"Is there somewhere to keep my wagon out of the rain?" Asher questioned.

"We'll move it into Frederic's workshop once the game is unloaded." Micah gestured towards the building.

"Very well," Asher replied in his unmistakable voice. "I feel I would enjoy a room at your tavern. It would give me an opportunity to interact more with your people."

"I'll walk over with you," Gerar offered. "We'll see about getting a room set up for you upstairs."

"Thank you, serah Gerar."

As the two of them headed towards the tavern, Micah spotted Hamill talking with a group of villagers lingering in the square. As Micah approached, Hamill bade them farewell and turned to greet him.

"Good work," Micah told him. "It was a wise move being as prepared as you were."

Hamill nodded, obviously pleased with their success.

"We were still overzealous in our hunt," he said with a frown. "Our excitement at the find caused us to down too many of the noble creatures. Were it not for Asher, I would have regretted slaying the ones we would've had to abandon."

"But it all turned out in the end. The town will feast for weeks!"

He grinned. "No doubt. It's good to be home. It was hard leaving, even for only a few days."

"I know. I wouldn't have asked unless it was important."

Hamill nodded. "This is a big day for Fairhollow, but really it was big for me too. I think leaving made me realize what, and who, was really important to me."

Micah smirked. "Go on, go find her."

"Her?" said Hamill coyly, raising his brow.

"Rila."

"Ah." He awkwardly coughed, rubbing the back of his neck. Even with his dark skin, Micah could see his face turning red. "Was I that obvious?"

Micah laughed. "Only to me. I know you both pretty well. I think Rila has been aching to see you since your trip." Hamill's face immediately brightened.

"Go on," he repeated. As Hamill turned to dash away, Micah firmly grabbed his arm. "But Hamill," he added protectively, "just remember. She's been through enough. Treat her well. Be the man she needs you to be."

The tanner nodded, his face turning serious. "On my honor. She's worthy of nothing less." He strode away, bearing the charge set before him.

He's a good man. Young, but mature for his years. Micah was relieved to see, even in days as bleak as theirs, Rila might have a wonderful future ahead of her.

He watched Hamill pause in front of the tavern before the tanner turned down the slope towards Rila and Tala's house. Then Micah followed, heading for Delvin's open door as the curious crowd bustled in. It was sure to be a lively night.

Chapter 8
Whispers

The place was packed. Conversations and laughter filled the room, drowning out one another as Fairhollow's thirsty denizens continued to file into the tavern. The smell of ale, cooked meat, and sweaty farmers hung in the smoky air. The building was always busy, but now it was a scene of near calamity. Delvin and Maven were a flurry of busyness, Maven dashing from table to table, filling mugs and clearing trays of empty plates and glasses. Micah swore Delvin's hands never left the spigots of his massive ale barrels.

He rushed to claim a table in the corner overlooked in the chaos. Maven eventually made her way over, wiping her hands on the fold of her apron.

"Anything in particular, Micah?" she asked, clearly flustered.

"Just an ale, when you get a chance. Thank you, Maven." She rushed off to the next table, shoving her way through the jostling crowd. Micah scooted closer to his table. *This is one battle I'd prefer to avoid.*

Out of the corner of his eye, Micah noticed Gerar and Asher appear at the bottom of the stairs.

Hopefully, Gerar got everything situated for our guest before the place became a madhouse. Micah waved to them, but it was a moment before Gerar spied his hand over the multitude of bodies in the dark, hazy atmosphere. The two slowly made their way through the clusters of people. More than one curious head turned to watch Asher pass.

"Can you believe this place?" Gerar shouted over the clamor.

"There's been more news today than we've had in months," Micah shouted back. "Should've known this would happen." They each grabbed a seat before greedy hands stole them away to other tables. Maven returned with Micah's drink and took their order as well.

"I've got tonight," said Micah, tossing Maven enough coin to cover everyone. Gerar nodded in appreciation.

"I have seen many large cities," Asher observed, "with many people. But never have I seen a tavern as lively as this!"

Gerar smirked. "You've come on an unusual night, trust me."

"So, Asher," Micah began, "where do you hail from?"

"For this trip? Or rather, where is my home?"

"Either. I don't remember the last time we had a merchant travel through."

"Ah, well," Asher breathed. "My current journey has led me from the vast deserts of Araphon to your humble island as I seek its end in Greenwatch."

"Araphon?" Micah gasped. "Then you've come from Edros!"

"Indeed. A tough voyage. There are precious few ships willing to make the trip across the Fallow Strait. Most prefer staying near the coast. I was blessed to encounter one set on reaching Karthport."

"I'm surprised there are any ships active at all," said Gerar, crossing his arms. "Are the nations of Edros faring better than Karthmoor?"

"Hmm." Asher rubbed his frazzled beard. "I would not say better. All nations, from hardy Karthmoor to the lands of the Hamid Empire, suffer under the growing grip of the deadly Mist. Much of the north and west has fallen under its shroud. There are, however, pockets of resistance. Some peoples were more prepared than their neighbors, but many live in a state not unlike your own."

"Surely the Hamid Empire still fights?" Micah inquired. "Archon Valerius is a tough old wolf."

"Yes." Asher turned to him. "The Archon retains much power. But the Empire is weakened and stretched thin. Its provinces grow restless. With its neighbors in chaos, trade has become scarce, a hard blow to the Empire. Though under Valerius, its military might is growing once more. Its forces fight the Mist as they can to maintain order, but even its mages cannot contain the curse forever."

"Magic, pah," Gerar spat. "As if little tricks could save them."

Micah shifted awkwardly in his seat.

"What about Araphon then? I assume you left there recently?" Micah continued.

"It is a fascinating nation," Asher rumbled. "Its deserts are oddly comforting to me. The Mist tends to avoid the warmth of such places, but even so, it does not forsake a promising target. No mere heat has prevented the Mist from infesting Araphon's shimmering cities. It is truly proof the Mist is an unnatural curse, likely arcane in origin."

"It certainly feels unnatural," said Micah, "but I've never heard of magic like it. Who or what could've conjured something this destructive?"

Asher shrugged. "I have not met one who can answer this. But for it to threaten the Empire itself, the source must be powerful beyond imagining."

Micah sat back, pondering the wealth of information. None of them had realized just how all-encompassing this disaster was.

If the Mist has crossed over to the continent of Edros, seeping into its multitude of nations, where hasn't it gone?

"What about the southern nations? Has the Mist spread that far?" Gerar questioned.

"There are a few rumored to be unaffected still," Asher conceded. "Though that is likely to change. Refugees from northern nations press into their borders. If anything, that is likely to attract the Mist more quickly, given how it seems drawn to inhabited places. My homeland of Neboa is a small place, stretched to its limits by huddled masses seeking peace. It would be numbered among those the Mist has not reached."

"Yet, you left its safety," Micah observed. "It takes a courageous man to do that."

Asher laughed, a deep rumbling laugh.

"Courageous or foolish. Many moons have I wrestled with which one I am." He took a drink of ale after Maven returned with their mugs. "A most curious drink," he remarked, observing the amber liquid. "Very much unlike the wines of Araphon. Ah, but to your point. I left many years ago, seeking my fortune in trade. I was lucky enough to discover I had a skill for antiquities early on. Something nobles from every court enjoy."

"There're still nobles with the time to collect such trinkets?" Gerar scoffed, baffled.

Asher shrugged. "Not many. Instead, I have plied my trade elsewhere, seeking new avenues of business. With the arrival of the Mist, magical artifacts became of prime importance to many attempting to unravel its secrets."

"I suppose I see the connection, but Asher," said Micah, leaning onto the table in the growing gloom, "I've explored the wide reaches of Karthmoor and beyond, even to the Anderfalls. Nothing I saw helps make sense of this curse. Magical or otherwise."

Asher drew closer, his face hovering over the dying candle in the center of the table.

"Perhaps there are still secrets out there to unravel, serah Micah," Asher answered, his dark eyes gleaming. "There are many who look to shine a light on this accursed riddle. Some who are getting closer."

"Closer? How so?"

"I cannot say more," he abruptly replied. "It would betray the trust of my employers. But perhaps to assuage your spirits, take comfort in this: there are powerful forces at work in Edros, my friends. And they view something on your island of utmost importance in solving the mystery of the Mist."

Asher leaned back, taking another swig of ale as Gerar and Micah looked at each other in bewilderment.

Important? Karthmoor?

Karthmoor was but a backwater island compared to the vast nations of Edros. Even its peoples' faith, once shared by many, was now considered foolish in their wizened ways.

What on earth could they want with us?

"So, someone is close to an answer?" Micah concluded cautiously.

"I cannot say," Asher admitted with a slight frown beneath his beard. "Not because I do not want to, but because I honestly do not know, serah. But I know they are working on it. My employment furthers their goal. I only *feel* they are getting close. Inasmuch as my exchanges with them offer insight."

"I see. So, your journey to Greenwatch…?"

"Furthers their goal," he finished. "Beyond that, I cannot say."

Greenwatch lay on the island's western shore, quite a distance from Fairhollow. It was a relief to know there were survivors there, but what interest could the world have in it?

As Micah's mind calmed, he noticed the tavern was emptying. *More time must have passed than I realized.*

Gerar yawned across from him. Asher also appeared worn out from his travels.

"It's late," Micah observed. "We should all get some rest." They both nodded in assent.

"Thank you for speaking with us, Asher," he continued. "Your knowledge is invaluable to our solitary town."

"It is my pleasure, serah Micah," his exotic accent rumbled. "Anything I can do to be of assistance. It is the least I can offer for your hospitality."

"Thank you, gentleman," Gerar drowsily inserted. "I believe with that, I best turn in for the night."

"I, as well," Asher added. They all stood from the table and shook hands. "Good night, my friends." Asher bowed slightly before climbing the worn wooden stairs to his room.

Gerar and Micah headed for the tavern door and gave an appreciative wave to Delvin and Maven near the counter. Delvin nodded back before pouring another round for the rowdy group in front of him.

Out on the street, they separated, shuffling towards their houses. In the lonely dark of night, Micah pondered the ominous words of their guest.

What could be here that's so important?

Chapter 9

Iluvan

"Do you have to go?"

Elisa gazed at him longingly, her small figure pressed against the doorframe of the bedroom. Micah was hurriedly filling a travel sack with clothes and notes, important ones he had made during his adventuring days.

"Samuel is going to be so confused. We've only just settled down here."

"What can I do?" he said with a hint of exasperation. "The Conclave has summoned me. I can't just ignore the request of the highest power in Karthmoor."

"I know," said Elisa, trembling. "I know you can't. And I understand this is important. Berien wouldn't have asked otherwise. But you have a family too, love. We need you."

His hands stopped mid-reach. Micah relaxed, moving over to her. His arms wrapped around her back, feeling the curve of her body pressed into his. He looked into her somber eyes, her pale face covered with concern.

"I don't want to, but I must."

Her gaze dropped, and she placed her hand on his chest. Micah's eyes came to rest on the silvery shard tied to the simple cord around her neck. A present he'd given her after one of his long journeys into the unknown.

"Let him sleep tonight. I'll explain it to him in the morning," Micah offered. Elisa gave a slight nod. He gently touched her chin, raising her face. "I love you."

"I love you too," she whispered.

His dream shifted, and Micah was standing on their porch. The morning sun was beginning its bright ascent as Samuel dashed outside laughing, ready to explore the farm.

"Hold on, son," Micah called out. "I need to speak to you for a moment."

He politely waddled back as Micah bent down.

"Dada has to leave for a trip tomorrow."

"A trip?" Samuel asked, confused. "Where?"

"A big city. Starkhaven."

"Can me and Mama come?"

"I'm afraid not," Micah sadly answered. "I need you and Mama to take care of our home while I'm away."

"Why do you have to go, Dada?"

The question echoed in Micah's head, unanswered, as his dream flashed forward again.

Clouds filled the sky, lit by morning light. The day was warm, bright, but the thickening clouds could bring afternoon rain.

"I've let Jonas know I'll be away for a while," he told Elisa. "He or one of his sons will check on you regularly. If you need anything, he'll help."

"Jonas is a good man," Elisa murmured, looking him over from head to toe. It had been a long time since he'd worn his trav-

eling gear. A lengthy trip from Aringoth to Starkhaven awaited him.

"Be safe," she finished. "Come home soon."

"I will."

They embraced for a long moment, Samuel grasping at the folds of her dress.

"I love you," Elisa whispered.

"I love you too." Micah kissed her longingly, feeling the warmth of her lips, not knowing the kiss would be their last.

She reached behind her neck, undoing the crystal necklace. He looked at her, confused, as she handed it to him.

"Something to remind you of home. Of us," she simply answered. Micah nodded, tying it around his own neck before kissing her again.

He bent down to look Samuel in the eyes.

"Be good for your mother," he gently commanded. "Look after her."

"Yes, Dada," Samuel mumbled in his small voice. "I love you."

"I love you too." Micah covered him in a warm hug, kissed the top of his head, then slowly trudged down the steps towards his horse, saddled and waiting.

Micah climbed into the stirrups, directing him towards the path away from their farm. Looking back, he gazed pensively towards his family. Elisa raised her hand goodbye. Samuel clutched her dress again, holding back tears.

Micah's heart fluttered, and his breath caught in his throat, pushing back his own tears. He'd left everything to be with his family, but it seemed even now, he couldn't escape the world.

Step by step, he moved farther away until he was beyond the fence, plodding down the road toward Jonas' farm and the journey ahead.

He was already homesick.

Micah sat up, sobbing. It felt so real. Too real. The memories invading his innocent dreams taunted him with feelings he couldn't contain.

Why do I have to relive these images over and over again?

For a moment, he swore he smelled the sweet scent of Elisa. Her skin washed clean with lavender soap, a hint of cinnamon from a day in the kitchen. It was intoxicating.

He fell back into bed, consumed with despair.

Creator, he silently prayed, *why did I leave? I should have been there for them!*

Suddenly, there was a knock at the door, wrenching him away from his grief, but also the tender memories of his family.

I have others I must protect.

Fighting the weakness in his bones, Micah rose from the bed, grabbed his shirt, and walked stiffly to the door. He opened its rusty hinges to find Gerar standing outside, arms folded over his loose cotton tunic.

"You look like hell, Micah," he said flatly.

"I feel like it, and not from the ale last night."

"Everything alright?" Gerar asked, concerned.

"I'll be fine." He trusted Gerar with his life, but the failures were too personal this time. "What's the news?"

"Everything's calm so far," said Gerar, still eyeing him. "Merrick is about to finish repairing the breach. Figured you might want to be there for it."

Micah straightened. "Definitely. I'll be there shortly."

Gerar nodded. "I need to make a stop by the tavern and make sure Delvin and Tala didn't have any issues securing our game. After that, I figured I'd give Asher a tour of the place. We can start at the breach. Hopefully, it'll be the only one he ever sees."

"I'm sure he'd like that. He's already proven an invaluable source of information. Whatever we can do to keep him happy."

"Aye," Gerar agreed. "See you at the wall." He turned and wound his way back up the grassy path from the house.

Micah returned to the dingy bathroom to make himself presentable before grabbing the rest of his gear.

Leaving the lonely, ramshackle house, he traced the same path as Gerar out to the main road, taking a quick detour past the gate to check on Matthias as the warm sun rose over the trees of Binthir in the distance.

"Morning, Matthias!" Micah called up at the rough-hewn perch. "Any news today?"

"Nothing so far," the watchman responded, his peppery hair poking over the rail. "You'll know if that changes."

We could use the calm today, thought Micah. He would feel a lot better once the wall was finally sealed.

He slipped around Frederic's shop and through the grassy space leading towards the northern wall. As he neared the site, Micah saw there was already a small group of villagers gathered, expectantly watching the men moving the last of the logs into place. Only a few more remained.

As Micah joined the crowd, he spotted Francis standing near the front and made his way over next to him.

"Good morning, Francis," said Micah. "Here to watch the finishing touches?"

The old man nodded, his wrinkled frown never leaving the timbers. "Indeed. We all will sleep much sounder knowing the wall is at full strength. At least until there's another attack. Not like it does much to stop the actual Mist."

Micah smirked. "Always chipper. At least we don't have to worry about monsters or predators finding their way in."

"Very true," he said. "And now we'll have some more hands free to pitch in on other projects."

"Did I miss it?" came a panting voice from behind. Micah turned around to see Delvin's large frame bent over to catch his breath, his stained apron nearly touching the dirt.

He chuckled. "Not yet. They're close, though."

They waited patiently, looking on as the men continued to move the great trunks into position. Piece by piece, they slowly built. Each time they set a new log, a flurry of activity followed as they lashed the new pine to its neighbors, sealing it with additional planks of wood and tough bands of heavy leather and rope prepared by Hamill. As the sun inched higher, the gap displaying the outside world narrowed to the span of a single tree.

"Alright, lads!" Merrick called. "This is it! At your word, Torvin."

"You heard the man!" Torvin bellowed. "Move with all your might! For Elowë, our families, our hardy Fairhollow! And a belly full of ale once this blasted trunk is moved!"

The crowd cheered as the final group slowly inched the upright log towards its hole. A couple of men stood outside the wall, guiding it into place as the others pushed.

"Steady, a little to the right," Torvin directed.

The onlookers fell silent, eagerly watching the shuddering spire.

The great pine teetered on the edge, rubbing against the trunks on either side with a terrific groan. Torvin grabbed a shovel and began pressing at the base, trying to coax it over the ledge.

"It's moving!" one man outside the wall called. In a blur, the last bit of dirt crumbled, and the tree slammed into the hole, stuck solidly by the trunks on its left and right.

The crowd erupted, clapping and whistling as the men threw up their arms in triumph.

The breach was finally closed.

"Tie it up!" Merrick shouted through his cupped hands. "Nail those bits together. As strong as we can make it!"

The men rushed back to work with renewed energy, eager to finish the last piece of the job. Torvin climbed back up the scaffolding and shouted for the men outside to come around through the gate.

"A magnificent sight," Asher's exotic voice chimed from behind. Micah turned to see him and Gerar smiling along with the crowd. "You are very lucky to have the resources you do. The walls from the pine forest are an inspired defense."

"They were our master woodsman's idea," Micah answered modestly. "Without Torvin, we wouldn't be here."

"A fortunate thing," Asher rumbled. "Though even with walls, it takes many to maintain a sanctuary as well as this. Many others are not so fortunate."

Micah nodded soberly, knowing he'd likely seen the fate of those who were ill-equipped. "So, does Gerar have the rest of your day planned out?"

"I believe I am well looked after." Asher smiled. "There are many things I wish to see before I leave."

"Make sure he takes you by Marian's before midday. I hear she's planning to have a batch of her famous blueberry bread ready by then."

"This sounds intriguing," said Asher, turning to Gerar excitedly. "Berries in a bread? Such strange cuisine you northerners have."

Gerar laughed. "We'll certainly make a stop, but first, let me show you Frederic's forge. He has quite the layout for a smith."

As they walked away, Micah looked back towards the wall where the men were making quick work. They would finish within the hour. Then he turned to Delvin with a grin.

"I hope you saved a cask."

Delvin's boisterous laugh escaped him. "Now what sort of barkeep would I be if I hadn't planned for this? The men are free to drink to their hearts' content today. It's the least I can do in exchange for keeping us safe."

"Good man. Careful though, if they drain too much, we'll have to pull out the corn crop just so you can restock your brews."

"Ha!" Delvin laughed again before heading back towards the tavern.

Micah watched the men work for a while longer, their efforts growing harder as the heat of the day grew. After glancing at the sun's place in the sky, he figured he had some time to kill before switching places with Matthias on watch. Micah decided to grab a quick meal, curious to see if Delvin was already serving up new elk-inspired dishes.

Walking into the tavern, he was surprised to see Gerar and Asher inside at a table. He figured they'd still be off touring Fairhollow.

"Lookin' for a bite to eat?" Delvin called from behind the bar. "We've got a nice potato soup over at the fire."

Micah sighed. *There go my hopes of a meaty midday meal.*

He reluctantly grabbed a bowl and joined Gerar and Asher. As he sat, he realized why they had sequestered themselves in the gloomy tavern. Gerar had snagged a good bit of Marian's blueberry bread for the both of them. The warm, delicious scent made Micah's lunch all the more disappointing.

"You have a fascinating town," Asher exclaimed as he finished a bite of bread, "and I find myself thoroughly enjoying your unusual fare!"

"I don't suppose you saved any for your valiant leader?" pleaded Micah. Gerar laughed and passed over a small chunk. The scent of warm bread and blueberries rolled past him. It'd been a long time since Marian had made any, but it was still just as sweet as Micah remembered.

"So, did you get the full tour, then?" Micah inquired between bites.

"I believe we saw most of the town this morning," Asher replied. "The tannery serah Hamill runs is captivating. The smell was like those of Neboa, but your hides and leathers differ greatly from my homeland. I would, however, appreciate a second visit to young master Frederic's forge. I would enjoy a chance to inspect it more closely."

"Certainly," said Gerar. "We can head there once we finish."

"I'll join you," Micah offered. "I have to replace Matthias, anyway."

Asher beamed. "Wonderful!"

They scarfed down the rest of the rich blueberry bread as fast as they could while still savoring its sweet, juicy flavor, before heading back out into the sun. From the weather to the finished wall repairs, the day was off to an excellent start.

As they neared the shop, Micah heard Frederic hammering away. The smith caught sight of them as they rounded the corner to the opening of the forge area and paused from his work.

"Hello again, Asher and Gerar. Micah." Frederic smiled. "Back for a demonstration? I have plenty of axes to mend from all the work our repair crew has been doing."

"I imagine so," Micah replied. "We certainly appreciate all the effort you put into keeping the repairs going."

"Of course," said Frederic humbly. He stepped out of the dark space and into the square to join them.

"Serah Frederic, if I may," Asher began, "this forge seems... unusual for your charming village. Was it built locally?"

"Actually, no," said Frederic, obviously surprised by the question. So was Micah. He hadn't ever pondered the origin of the forge. "Our original blacksmith, Alvin, had this imported from Edros. Unfortunately, I don't recall the nation that produced it."

Asher nodded. "I thought as much. I have seen others very like it in the great cities I have journeyed through."

"Is that so?" replied Frederic, eager curiosity stirring in his voice.

"Yes, I..." Asher glanced towards the workshop. "No!"

Micah swerved around and peered into the open doors. Inside, a young boy, only a few years of age, sat atop Asher's wagon. It was Bergi, Lisra's son.

Bergi's attention was fixed on a large, mysterious box made of a metal Micah couldn't identify. Its dark, grainy texture appeared to be of foreign make.

"Bergi!" Micah shouted. "Get down from there!"

Too late. The boy had already opened the clasp on the front. He lifted the lid; to what, Micah could not tell. His hands shot inside and pulled out a sinister-looking black crystal, nearly the length of a short sword, but no thicker than the handle of Frederic's hammer.

Suddenly, a gust of energy blasted through the square, echoing in Micah's skull. He watched in horror as Bergi flew backwards out of the wagon like a rag doll. The force caused him to drop the crystal back into the box, and the lid fell shut with a clang.

"No!" Asher cried again as he ran towards the wagon, his colorful cloak flailing. They all chased after him.

Inside the workshop, a strange sensation prickled the back of Micah's neck, causing his hair to stand on end. A dangerous energy hung in the gloom.

"Bergi!" Gerar cried as he reached for the boy. Bergi appeared dazed, unable to move as Gerar lifted him from the dusty ground. He stood Bergi up, the small boy wobbling on the floor, and looked him over. "Are you okay, son?"

Bergi burst into tears, clearly confused as to what had just happened. Gerar picked him up.

"The boy will be fine," Asher grumbled. "There should be no lasting effects beyond the slight shock he likely received."

"I'll return him to his mother," Frederic offered. Gerar passed him over, and Frederic quickly left the shop.

"What was that, Asher?" Micah softly demanded, wondering what danger the strange foreigner had brought to their village.

"Have you not seen them before?" he asked incredulously.

Asher slowly reopened the box, revealing an extensive collection of dazzling crystals. Most glowed with a beautiful silvery blue hue that danced on the surface of the container. Yet, mixed in with those were a few as black as night. As his gaze lingered on them, a tingle of dread stirred inside Micah. The crystals were familiar, but he couldn't place why.

"They are iluvan," said Asher. "Powerful beacons of arcane energy, scavenged from mighty works now crumbling within the fallen cities of Araphon and beyond."

Micah jumped at the epiphany.

"Iluvan," Gerar breathed, "as in the same object behind the incredible devices from Edros?"

"Indeed," Asher quietly confirmed.

"Wait a moment. Was that why you were asking about Frederic's forge?" Micah asked.

He nodded. "Serah Frederic's forge, crafted in those faraway lands, is but a tiny product of the mystery that is the iluvan."

"Alvin once mentioned the hefty price he paid for his forge," Gerar mused. "He said magic helped power its inner workings. I thought it was just some wash he bought into."

"Your man Alvin did not lie," Asher replied. "Deep within the forge, you will find a type of magic: a crystal filled with much power. A small iluvan, quietly humming along, assisting its master in his daily craft."

"Incredible." Micah stared in amazement.

"Incredible as it may be," said Asher with a frown, "each iluvan carries great risk. A risk the young child has just unleashed on your unsuspecting village. There is a reason I asked for my cargo not to be disturbed." Asher quickly shut the chest, and the dancing light from within vanished.

Micah's stomach dropped. "What do you mean?"

"In our conversation last night, I hinted at the connection. There is something that binds the iluvan and the Mist together," Asher slowly continued. "Something I cannot explain. You have seen the black iluvan the child awakened." He gestured towards the box. "Its unique calling, its terrible power, draws the deathly fog towards it."

"Wait. You don't mean…"

"It will come. Soon."

Micah stared at Asher, his mind unwilling to accept his dire words.

"We have to prepare," Gerar interjected.

"I will aid your people as I can," offered Asher, "but I am no warrior."

Micah glanced at Gerar. "Ready the men." They turned to leave as Asher continued to stare at his wagon, lost in thought.

As they passed in front of Frederic's forge, Gerar grabbed Micah's shoulder, his face contorted with worry.

"I think Francis' family may have had one," said Gerar nervously. Micah looked at him, puzzled.

"A black iluvan. I was only a boy then, before I'd grown and left to join the Guard," Gerar explained. "A day burned into my memory. There was a commotion at his family's house. Smoke pouring out of the cellar as people came running. I couldn't see everything, but I remember a group of men led by Francis taking some object out of the house, wrapped in thick cloth. I followed them to the old well near the town hall and watched them throw the thing in, rags and all. There was a glimmer of black as it fell." He grew silent for a moment.

"Micah, that well has been dry ever since," said Gerar quietly. "They boarded it up soon after. I was too afraid in my youth to get any closer."

"You've never mentioned this before."

He shrugged. "It never seemed important. It happened decades ago."

"Fair enough. I imagine the iluvan crystals are older than we think. Edros has had them a long time, if the stories are to be trusted. Still, it's a good idea to confront Francis about this. After the defenses are ready."

Gerar nodded in assent.

There was no time to waste.

CHAPTER 10
THE MIST

"I'll round up everyone who's off duty," said Gerar.

"And I'll find those that aren't," Micah finished.

Gerar ran in a full sprint towards the center of town while Micah turned and bolted over to Matthias on his perch atop the gate.

"Matthias!" The sentry turned around and looked down over the rail. "Be on guard. We have Mist incoming!"

The color drained from his weathered face.

"At your word, Warden." He saluted.

Micah raced along the wall, making an entire circle around Fairhollow and stopping at the small lookout posts where a handful of defenders watched the fields beyond. Each post was similar to the one at the gate, and their occupants reacted with the same grim response as Matthias. The small number of manned lookouts always made Micah nervous. They'd have to fill each vacant post quickly if they were going to be prepared.

As he reached the men repairing the northern wall, Micah was relieved to see they'd finished with the wall itself. Cleaning up the debris was all that remained.

With the men on duty warned, he rushed to grab Hamill. Micah had placed Hamill in charge of securing homes, as he knew the village as well as anyone. He ran back to the center of town and headed towards the square. Hamill's shop sat south of the road leading to the gate, near Frederic's.

Micah threw open the door, causing Hamill to jump up from a rack holding a fresh elk hide.

"What in Aldaria?" he exclaimed. "Micah, what's wrong?"

"The Mist," Micah panted. "Not sure when, but it's certain to come. We need the safe houses secured. Now."

"I'm on it," said Hamill earnestly, tossing his stained apron onto a small stand beside the rack and heading for the door.

"Merrick already marked the most secure houses with red paint near the doors," Micah called after him. "Most should be near the center of town."

"Thanks." Hamill sprinted down the road towards the tavern.

Assuming Gerar had found most of the defenders, Micah set a course towards the storehouse.

By then, the whole town had heard the news. Most of the daily work had stopped as parents ran to collect their children or lock up their animals. Many were busy searching for the nearest safe house to help Hamill board up and plug any holes that could let the noxious Mist seep in.

The dusty road outside the storehouse was a flurry of activity, and Gerar appeared to have everything well in hand by the time Micah arrived. Men hurriedly passed rifles, pistols, and bows through the entrance to the others waiting outside. Gerar was busy assigning positions to the men as they received weapons and ammunitions. Frederic rushed up with a cart full of swords, axes, and shields, returned to full strength after the previous assault.

The afternoon wore on as preparations continued. The sound of hammers filled the air as villagers strengthened the wooden defenses. Families were busy filling buckets with hay from the field or mud from the pond to plug up any windy holes in the houses, the chore's messiness a thankful distraction for the smaller children. At her tiny home, Marian was busy readying for any injured defenders, with Rila vigorously assisting, both of them organizing bandages and salves for easy access.

"Your people are resilient," Asher observed as he joined Micah near the tavern. "I have not seen a group as united as Fairhollow in the protection of their homes."

"We've had a lot of practice," he sadly replied.

Time passed quickly, and as the sun set, Fairhollow settled into an uneasy silence. The streets were desolate. The last of the men lit torches, placing them throughout the village. Fire seemed to be the only thing the Mist would avoid, though it wasn't a perfect defense.

Nearly everyone was already in a safe house or stationed on the walls. Fear blanketed the town as they waited to hear if Matthias would ring the alarm bell. Micah always hated that moment. The calm before a battle you couldn't escape. He despised it even more so when it was an enemy you could barely face.

As the sun sank behind the western wall, he joined Matthias on the gate lookout. The poor man hadn't left his post the entire day, and he was already looking tired.

In front of them, Binthir Forest appeared quiet. No sign of the Mist. Matthias shuffled uneasily as his eyes darted across the landscape, looking for any sign of disturbance.

"There hasn't been so much as a stray crow in that direction all day," he muttered. "Something's wrong. I feel it."

"We're ready."

A moment longer. The sun behind them had reached the far horizon as a large, round moon strengthened in the clear, fading sky.

"There."

Micah's head jerked back towards the woods. Something was different. The shadows were... hazier.

They held their breaths. Then, like a silent specter heralding an inescapable doom, the haze brightened. Its wispy tendrils slowly solidified as the dark blur changed from black to gray, then to a pale, sickly blue.

The Mist.

Matthias reached for the small metal bell suspended from the awning and throttled the cord.

Clang! Clang! Clang!

The town echoed with its piercing wail, summoning every person to face their fate. Somewhere behind a locked door, a child faintly cried before being shushed by a fearful mother.

The Mist rose high into the trees, its trail spilling out beyond the road to the south and the fields to the north. The fearsome cloud swallowed everything in obscurity. Its progress was slow, but the killing fog would be upon the walls in minutes. Micah pushed away his dread, focusing on thoughts of his friends hidden in the dark houses below.

Elowë, protect us.

A door slammed somewhere behind Micah. Startled, he scrambled down to check. As he passed the tavern, heading towards the town hall, Rila exited Marian's garden in front of him.

"Rila!" Micah shouted, holding up his hands to stop her. "Get back inside!"

"I left my bag at the house. We need its ingredients!" She was determined to pass him. Micah clenched his teeth.

"Then go, go!" he growled. "And get back inside immediately. It's almost here!" Rila dashed down the road as he turned back towards the gate.

On the way, Tala appeared, a bow strung across her back and a musket in hand.

"Everyone's in place," she reported. "No sign of the Mist from any other direction."

"Good. Head up to your spot on the tavern. If anything gets in, I need you calling out locations."

Tala nodded and sprinted towards the building.

The sun had vanished beyond the horizon. Only faint trails of light remained behind an embankment of clouds in the distance.

"It's at the wall!" Matthias called from his perch. The great beams of wood were tight, but already Micah could see faint wisps of the Mist seeping in. Thankful for his own immunity, he scaled the ladder back up to Matthias.

Beyond the wall, the entire landscape had transformed into a sea of rolling, ominous fog. Only the tips of Binthir's trees were visible as the column of Mist made its way up the hill towards Fairhollow. The first tendrils of Mist washed lazily over the top of the trunks, spilling onto the ground below as the Mist grew taller. It wouldn't be long before it overwhelmed their sturdy defenses.

They stood there, silent. Unable to stop the advancing cloud as it grew stronger. The Mist reached so high in front of them now that the forest had disappeared, the last of the light of day fleeing along with it.

Then, a long, mournful howl pierced the night, chilling the blood in Micah's veins.

Creator, not again.

More howls answered the call.

Matthias shivered next to him. "So much for avoiding that," he grumbled.

As Mist enveloped their world, a dark shape bounded towards the wall, obscured by the haze. Howls continued in the distance, spreading out in every direction. As the blur came into view, its hideous shape sharpened.

Mist Wolves.

Patchy gray-brown fur covered its long, thin body, reflecting a diseased look that betrayed the beast's incredible strength. Its long snout flared open, revealing rows of dagger-sharp teeth. As it approached the gate, it slowed its four-legged vaunt to stare up at them. Huge black rings of bare, crusty skin encircled small beady eyes that scowled at the men in rage as pointed ears lay flat against its bony skull.

The monster rose, standing on its two back legs, appearing almost human-like. It was easily half a man taller than the tallest person in Fairhollow. Long, vicious claws dangled at the ends of its ugly arms, gleaming in the faint light. The beast walked a couple of steps closer, a terrifying growl burning with displeasure at their existence.

These horrors were not of this world.

It paused, sniffing in their direction. Matthias clutched his rifle closer as Micah drew his pistol from his side.

Without warning, the Wolf dashed towards the wall with inhuman speed and jumped. It scrabbled at the wood, shearing long strips from the outer bark. Finding no purchase on the smooth wall, it dropped to the ground, backing away with a sinister snarl.

Matthias raised his musket, taking aim at the Mist Wolf's head. It was smart enough to realize what was about to happen and tensed. Matthias feinted, and the beast lunged to the right. With lightning-fast reflexes, Matthias traced the monster's path.

The barrel of his rifle erupted as the bullet hit its target between the eyes. A momentary whimper sent it crashing to the ground, lifeless.

"Not fast enough," Matthias growled.

"Nice shot."

A scream rang out from behind, jerking Micah's gaze towards Fairhollow. He tumbled down the ladder and raced towards town, unsure of where it came from. The Mist was so thick in the square now he could barely see his hand in front of his face, forcing him to slow down. Luckily, the dense fog lessened into a drifting smog as he passed the torches by the blacksmith's shop. At the crossroads in front of the tavern, Micah ran into Hamill, the tanner wielding a sword and a torch.

"Where?" Hamill breathed.

"Over there!" Tala shouted from her perch, pointing down the southern road. "I can't see them, but that's the direction!"

Together they raced off, glancing at the houses as they ran. The ones beyond the center of town were unnervingly dark, empty. Most everyone was sheltering in the safe houses closer to the old town hall.

The scream came again in front of them, muffled as if inside a building. Mixed with it, Micah heard a series of angry yelps and thuds.

A Wolf is inside the perimeter!

They moved cautiously, the Mist growing thicker the farther they went from town. As Micah approached the end of the houses, he finally spotted the Wolf pounding away at the door to Rila and Tala's house.

Rila!

"Hey!" Hamill shouted angrily.

The creature swerved its menacing head around, ugly, blackened eyes locking onto them. Micah raised his pistol, aiming for the monster. A paralyzing howl emanated from the beast as it dropped onto four legs and charged.

BOOM!

The blast scattered the Mist near the weapon. The Mist Wolf flinched but continued barreling down the street. Hamill raised his sword. At the last moment, it jumped into the air, a row of gleaming claws screaming death as it plummeted towards him. Hamill jumped to the right, the beast missing him by a hairsbreadth. It landed heavily, blood dripping from its front leg where Micah's shot hit. Its weakened reaction gave Hamill enough time to recover and deliver a blow of his own.

Yet, with amazing speed, it swiped its massive hand at him, howling in anger. Hamill brushed it away with a heavy stroke of his sword, leaving the Wolf exposed. He plunged forward, stabbing the creature just as it prepared to lunge again. An anguished cry escaped its slavering jaws before it fell, pulling Hamill's sword with it.

Micah walked over and place a hand on Hamill's shoulder as he bent over, panting. Hamill retrieved his sword, wiping it on the dewy grass and sheathing it before they approached the house.

"Rila," Micah called softly, "it's Micah and Hamill. You're safe now."

There was rustling at the door as something heavy was pulled away.

"Quick!" she shouted from inside. "We need help!"

Hamill moved closer with his torch, light spilling through the frame as the door inched open. The first thing Micah noticed as he peered into the gloom was a horrible trail of blood. At its end, his eyes stopped on Asher, the merchant sprawled on the floor as Beirand pressed a tattered blanket onto his chest. Beirand was bleeding from a slash on his arm, though not heavily. Rila's face appeared beside the door, covered in tears and terror.

"Thank Elowë!" she cried as Hamill pushed his way inside. She threw her arms around him as Hamill caught her with his free hand.

"Micah!" She moved to hug him.

"What happened?" he asked in a worried voice.

"It was all my fault." Rila trembled, fresh tears gathering in her eyes. "I thought I could make it back to Marian's, but by the time I found my bag and headed out the door, the Mist was everywhere. Something rustled between the houses, and I started running back home, but it heard me. I screamed, and that's when Asher and Beirand came running out of a house." Hamill moved closer, throwing his arm around her to calm her nerves.

"All he had was a stick of wood," she gestured to Asher, "but he threw himself between me and the Wolf. It cut him right across the chest. That's when Beirand started throwing rocks. I don't think it'd noticed Beirand yet—he startled it. We were able to get inside, but not before it reached through the door and cut Beirand too." Micah bent down to Asher. His breath was shallow, sweat drenching his face, but he was alive.

"Micah," he whispered weakly, "you must..." The merchant slumped back, unconscious.

"We have to get him to Marian," Micah commanded. "Rila, do you have any torches?" She dashed to a back room and returned with a single stick. Hamill lit it using his. "Beirand?"

"It's only a scratch," he wheezed. "I'll live."

Micah nodded. His esteem for the poor man continued to grow.

"We have to go, quickly," Hamill urged. He handed his torch over to Beirand, and together, he and Micah moved Asher onto a sturdy-looking comforter. With Beirand in the lead, the five of them left the house, Hamill and Micah carrying Asher on the blanket as Rila watched the rear with the second torch.

They moved painfully slowly with Asher's weight, the Mist parting around them as it reacted to the torches.

"We're almost there," Beirand mumbled. More howls sounded in the distance. Occasionally, a rifle echoed as defenders took shots at the swarming beasts. As they neared Marian's, a new howl called out, much nearer than those outside the walls.

"They've definitely found a way in," Micah whispered. "Hurry!"

Beirand knocked rapidly on Marian's door.

"Asher's injured," he called quietly. "Let us in!"

A muffled grating creaked from the other side as someone unbarred the door. Marian herself opened it, looking small and frail. An expression of worry mixed with determination adorned her weathered face. She motioned them inside.

As Rila filed in, Cole and Mark shut the door, moving a large, heavy dresser in front of it and latching a bar of solid wood down over the frame as well.

"Lay him here." Marian pointed to a long, empty table in the center of the room as Sadi laid out a blanket. A solitary candle flickered against the far wall, the only light in the dim room. Marian immediately went to work, rubbing a strange, gooey substance on Asher's bleeding wounds before covering them in soft, absorbent cloth.

"Rila," she calmly commanded, "the bag."

"Yes."

Micah hadn't even noticed Rila sling her ingredient satchel on as they left. Rila quickly pulled out a handful of fresh-scented leaves and moved to a side table filled with a multitude of utensils for crafting Marian's healing tinctures.

"Will he survive?" Micah asked Marian nervously.

"I will do what I can," she simply replied. He nodded, knowing Asher's fate was now beyond his control.

Micah turned to Hamill. "We have to find that Wolf."

He nodded, and Cole unbarred the door again. Rila left her work, coming over to Hamill and wrapping her arms around him.

"Thank you," she said, kissing his cheek.

"I'll be back," whispered Hamill, gazing at her. She nodded, then returned to preparing the salves.

They left Marian's as quickly as they could, hoping to avoid drawing attention as the depths of the Mist swallowed them.

Chapter 11
Invaders

THE MIST GREW HEAVIER as they neared the tavern. Some of the torches placed in the ground had gone out, and Micah was immediately grateful he had taken Rila's. A howl rose from the north, echoing inside the village walls, and they dashed down the road.

"Rah!" someone bellowed from the row of houses across from them. Shuffling through a tight alley, they staggered out into the street to the sight of two large shapes flitting through the swirling Mist.

It was Torvin. Even with his massive size, the Mist Wolf stood taller still. Torvin faced the beast with a gleaming ax in hand, fearless. Its growl turned into a hateful snarl as it lunged towards the woodsman. He caught its outstretched claws on his ax, stopping the Wolf in its tracks as it tried to force him down under its colossal weight. Torvin grunted, his powerful arms trembling as he threw the monster to the side. It hit the ground, hard. Instead of trying to raise his ax, Torvin quickly brought his heavy boot down on the beast's outstretched hand. Micah heard the awful crack of bone as the Wolf howled in pain.

With blinding speed, it swiped its other claws at Torvin, tearing into his pants as he jumped out of reach. The beast rose, its terrible growl filled with pain and fury, and leapt again, its good hand outstretched and mouth opened with frightening teeth. Torvin's ax found its hind leg as it sailed past him, and the Wolf fell to the ground with another cry of pained rage.

"No more!" Torvin shouted. Bounding to its side, he raised his ax, crashing it down on the beast's neck before it could recover.

Silence.

Torvin stepped back, wheezing. As he spied Micah in the wispy fog, he waved and started towards them. The lumberjack stumbled, swearing as he caught himself. Micah raced forward to help steady him as he clutched at his leg.

"Bad?" asked Micah.

"A fair scratch," he gruffly answered with a chuckle.

"Let's get to the storehouse."

With Hamill in front, they made the short walk down the road to the old house. Micah tossed Hamill the key, and they stumbled inside after him. Torvin collapsed in a rickety, wooden chair in the corner as they all caught their breaths.

"There's at least one more," Torvin puffed as he recovered. "Gerar and a few others headed for the fields to find it."

"Right. We have to find the source." Micah attempted to calm his mind and make sense of everything. "We stationed men evenly on every side of Fairhollow," he mused, "but there aren't any lookout points near the western edge of the pond. Maybe we missed something there."

"We should at least check it out," Hamill concurred.

"Then what are we waiting for?" demanded Torvin in his blunt tone. He lifted himself from the chair, groaning in pain.

"Not you," Micah ordered, pushing him back down. "You're injured. Stay put until we can get you to Marian."

Torvin scowled. "I'm not some fussy child you can just leave behind," he angrily retorted.

"No, but in your state, you'll only get yourself hurt worse, or killed," said Micah pointedly. "Stay here. Find something to bind up your leg and watch the supplies. We may need them, but we definitely need *you* to stay alive."

"Don't take too long, will ya?" he grumbled, settling back into the rickety chair.

Hamill gave him a light shove. "Don't fall asleep."

Hamill passed the storehouse key to Torvin as he and Micah exited the building. Around them, the dark night rang with intermittent gunfire and howls as the defenders sporadically tried to fend off the beasts.

Micah and Hamill left the buildings of town and headed towards the herb garden and pond; the Mist solidifying into an opaque wall with every step. Even their torches barely scattered the air. Its eerie, heavy presence pressed in, smothering them.

Micah moved slowly, unsure of his footing in the darkness. After a few paces, he nearly collided with the low fence that ran around the herb garden. At least he had a point of reference. He felt his way around, moving towards what should have been the outer wall.

After a moment, the Mist lessened. His field of view grew to where he spotted the wall looming ahead.

"Found it," Micah muttered.

A heavy scrabbling rose from his right. Micah drew his sword as Hamill raised his own. A single claw appeared over the wall, not a stone's throw away. Then another.

With blinding speed, a Mist Wolf launched itself over the logs and onto the grassy ground. As it stood, the beast locked its beady eyes on Micah, its bared fangs releasing an awful howl that sent a shiver of fear through him.

Micah charged, sword raised. The monster switched to two legs, prepared to meet his shimmering steel with its deadly claws. He unleashed a powerful stroke, cutting from the left. The monster swung its enormous fist, the clash of steel echoing against its hardened claws. It swiped its other hand with gleaming claws at his shoulder. Micah ducked as five razor-sharp blades whistled above him. The beast immediately moved, hoping to stab its other claws down into him. Nowhere to run, he rolled forward, passing through the Wolf's massive legs. Surprised, the beast turned slowly, buying enough time to counter. Micah's blade shimmered in the faint light, cutting a deep wound across its back.

The Wolf howled in agony, stumbling away. It whipped around, the horrible black rings around its eyes contorted in rage. This time, it jumped with claws aimed at his chest. Micah rolled to the side, swinging his sword as it passed. The sharpened edge found its mark along the terror's powerful thigh. Roaring in pain, it turned again, slashing viciously. Micah jumped back, narrowly avoiding its deadly swipe. The Wolf scrambled to its feet and charged, snarling with arms outstretched in a killing embrace. He swung wildly, striking its arm, and it reared back, howling. With only a moment to react, he plunged his sword deep into its chest, cutting off the terrible howl as the beast fell lifeless to the ground.

One more defeated. Micah stopped to catch his shaky breath, blood pounding in his head.

"This has to be the spot," he gasped. "We have to see how they're getting over."

"I'll grab the nearest lookout and a ladder," Hamill offered. He sprinted away to the south, disappearing into the Mist, leaving Micah alone.

The space turned frighteningly silent, only himself and the body of the Mist Wolf. He stared into the Mist surrounding him, wondering what other monsters could be lurking just beyond his sight. Micah eyed the beast's corpse warily, afraid it might rise to continue their battle.

In the momentary calm, he sheathed his blade and reloaded his pistol, keeping it out, just in case. The bright moon cast spooky beams of light through the shimmering Mist as the echo of musket shots and howls continued in the distance.

After what felt like hours with his nerves on edge, he heard feet thumping through the grass. Out of the fog, the light of Hamill's torch reappeared, along with the lookout. The two of them were carrying the large ladder from his post.

"Tolsten," Micah breathed. "Am I glad to see you two."

The man grinned. "I see your friend wasn't the best of company." Tolsten was one of the most experienced defenders. His curly red hair and beard made him easy to spot. Though he was young and had a remarkable talent for sarcasm, no one doubted his skill as he had trained under one of the most famous blade masters of the Karthmoor Guard.

"He was certainly grumpy," Micah replied. "Now let's get that ladder in place."

A small board jutted out of the wall not far from the spot the Wolf had appeared, perfect for leaning the ladder against. They gently propped it against the wall, then turned to stare at one another.

"So... Who wants to peek into the unknown?" asked Hamill awkwardly.

"I rather like my head," Tolsten flatly stated. "Unless you think these fiery locks are going to scare them away."

"I'll look," Micah sighed, passing his torch to Tolsten. "But if I don't come back, don't leave Tolsten in charge."

"Oi!"

Step by step, Micah crawled his way up the ladder, tightly gripping his pistol. A dreadful silence hung in the air. All other sounds seemed muffled, distant. As he neared the top, he took a deep breath.

Hopefully, not my last.

He cautiously peeked over.

Nothing but swirling Mist.

Micah raised a little higher. Tilting his eyes downward, he could faintly make out the dark earth through the foggy air.

"Careful now," Tolsten whispered as Micah edged farther.

Holding his breath, Micah leaned over the wall to check the ground directly beneath it. At first, he saw nothing. The Mist was too thick to make anything out. Then a slight breeze pushed it aside. At the bottom of the wall, in a bizarre sight, a massive boulder rested against the wooden wall.

Where on earth did that come from?

The defenders checked the outer wall regularly, just like the interior. Surely one of their inspections would have reported that. Unless... Micah's stomach knotted in fear.

What if the Wolves are getting smarter?

"There's a boulder against the wall," he softly called down to them.

"A boulder?" said Hamill incredulously.

"You mean they're using a great bloody rock to get in?" Tolsten added, his mouth gaping.

"Get men over here to watch this spot immediately. It's too dangerous to move it now. Hamill, find Gerar's or Merrick's group. Bring extra ladders from Torvin's house. Tolsten, switch me spots."

"Aye," Hamill quickly responded before disappearing into the Mist.

Tolsten shrugged. "If you insist."

As Micah started to move, a low growl emanated from the gloom beyond the wall. He froze, searching wildly for the source, his pistol raised. There was a sudden shift in the drifting fog, and a Mist Wolf filed out of the dark, silently padding closer on its four legs, glaring at him.

He climbed to where he could aim his weapon over the jagged wall, drawing the beast nearer. Its aggressive nature sensed prey, and it drew near enough to pounce, hoping to snatch Micah in its piercing claws. Just before it sprang, he pointed the pistol towards the creature, and its easy leap turned into a retreat as it scampered away.

Micah fired. The explosion sliced through the Mist as the bullet chased its target. The Wolf moved amazingly fast, dodging the killing blow, but the shot still managed to find the beast's side. It yelped in pain and stumbled away into the obscuring Mist.

"Quick! Before it returns!"

Micah slid down the ladder as Tolsten prepared his rifle and scrambled up.

Minutes passed. The area outside the wall remained quiet. Micah reloaded his pistol, anticipating a counterattack, but nothing appeared.

Tolsten relaxed slightly, still scanning the area for any sign of movement. From the ground, Micah alternated between watching the foggy village behind him and Tolsten atop the ladder. After a short time, he heard footsteps again from the direction of town.

"This way!" he heard Hamill call. A group of men burst through the fog led by Hamill's torch. Merrick appeared beside him, breathing hard and covered in sweat and grime. The men immediately began raising more ladders near the area as Hamill directed them.

"Where do we stand?" Micah asked Merrick.

"There were at least two Wolves roaming the western and southern edges of town," he reported. "Gerar's group cornered one in the corn, but they were having trouble flushing it out. He didn't want to risk sending men in after it."

"Right. Patience will pay off."

"We split up and tracked down the other. Found it near the safe house just south of the town hall. The creature likely smelled people and was looking for a way in," Merrick continued. "It put up a good fight. Took a nick out of Halvid's arm on a lucky swipe but left an opening for the other men to take it down fast."

"Good job. Where is Halvid now?"

"He'll be fine," Merrick answered gruffly. "Rila was seeing to him."

"Any word on Asher?" Micah asked.

"Other than he looked awful? No, Marian had her full attention on him. He wasn't conscious."

"Hmm." Asher's act of bravery, though commendable, would be a dark stain on Fairhollow if an innocent guest were to be slain within their walls.

Merrick's men were already climbing their way up as Micah turned back around. At least they wouldn't have to worry about any more Wolves getting in that way.

"We should find Gerar. Make sure that last Mist Wolf is taken care of," Micah said.

With his men assigned, Merrick joined Hamill and Micah as they raced along the wall, heading for the fields at the opposite end of town. With any luck, Gerar's group would still be there.

Even with torches, the Mist forced them to slow their pace several times as it thickened in the dark space along the wall. Dodging rocks and other obstacles, they eventually left the smattering of houses on the left, and the land widened into a grassy field. Out of the gloom, Micah heard the three horses tearing up their pasture, consumed with fear. Beyond its fence, a faint twinkle of light appeared through the Mist where Gerar's group paced around the cornfield.

Merrick and Hamill fanned out as they approached. Half a dozen torches glistened around the field, evenly spaced, as the defenders watched for any disturbance in the crop.

"Micah!" Gerar hailed as he spotted them. He looked exhausted but unharmed.

"This the last one?" Micah gestured towards the tall stalks rustling in the faint breeze.

"It would seem," he replied. "Tala hasn't spotted anything else from the tavern. I had a few men sweep the rest of the village, but they turned up nothing."

"Let's finish this then," said Micah adamantly.

Gerar saluted. "By your command."

"I'll go in. Just be ready."

"If you're sure," he said, a hint of concern in his voice. "Watch your back."

Micah handed him the torch. Staring at the ominous fronds, he took a deep breath, then plunged into the waving field.

In an instant, Micah was in an entirely different world, silent and unnerving. The walls of silky stalks shielded the interior from the light of the defenders' torches. Only the faint moonlight above shimmered off the moving corn, tossing jagged shadows around him.

Something rustled several lengths ahead, and he froze, struggling to pinpoint the location. Micah unsheathed his sword, raising the polished blade.

His blood pounded in his ears, sweat building on his forehead.

He took a step. Then another. He swore he heard a faint moan.

Another step.

Another.

Crack!

A fallen stalk broke under Micah's boot. A low, terrifying growl sounded not an arm's length ahead. Micah roared, swinging his blade and decapitating an arc of defenseless corn. The monster shuffled away, roughly shoving the stalks apart as it retreated.

Micah yelled again, stomping after the beast. Suddenly, the massive creature knocked aside a row of corn as it reared to its hind legs, casting a nightmarish silhouette against the stalks in the moonlight. The Wolf cried out, a defiant, vengeful howl, its unnatural height towering over him. The men shouted beyond the field.

Micah bellowed back at the creature, charging with his sword held high. It swung a fist of glistening claws through the thick growth. Micah brushed the hand away with his sword, thrusting forward. The blade connected with something, and the Wolf snarled in anger. Unable to maneuver, it fell back, crashing through the fragile plants. Micah raced after it, yelling in pursuit.

The beast burst out across the field, racing straight towards a group of men. They cried out in surprise, raising iron swords and shields. The Wolf slowed, realizing there were too many to take on, but before it could locate an avenue of escape, Micah shouted again, and it turned to face him.

He collided with its rough chest, sword outstretched, knocking the Wolf off its feet. With a heavy thump, they collapsed in a bloody, muddy mess in front of the defenders. Foul, musty fur pressed against Micah's face, suffocating him. Shakily, he rose to his feet and looked down at his kill. The Wolf was silent, its rage-filled eyes extinguished.

"Micah!" Merrick dashed around the corner of the field towards him. "That was a heck of a thing!"

"We're safe," Micah wheezed, leaning over as his body succumbed to the effects of the nerve-breaking chase.

"Aye," he said, rubbing his tousled hair.

"The Mist is clearing!" a man shouted from the wall. Micah realized the incessant howls of the Mist Wolves were growing fainter, retreating towards Binthir Forest. The Mist around the cornfield began to lessen, its leeching tendrils extracting itself from the land.

Micah motioned to the men. "Back to town."

The group headed up the main road towards the village, its buildings still wrapped in dark but dissipating Mist. Micah sighed. *It's finally ending.*

A woman's scream pierced the night.

His head swerved to the left, locating the shadowy timbers of a safe house. The defenders rushed for the rickety door as a cloud of Mist withdrew from its scarred, wooden frame, rolling back towards the eastern wall.

"Open up!" Micah yelled, banging on the door.

"Quick!" a man called from inside. The groan of wood followed the sound of a heavy bar lifting from the door as barricades were moved away. The wail of a crying woman echoed beyond the shuffling.

An older man flung the door open as Gerar and Micah rushed in, scanning the entry.

"The bedroom!" the man cried, pointing. They dashed to the back. As Micah reached the doorway, a hideous swath of Mist swept past, escaping through a chipped corner of the window in the hall. Inside the room, Bolli lay motionless on the floor. His wife, Emina, was on her knees, rocking his head in her lap.

"No!" she cried, tears streaming down her face. Micah knelt next to her, wrapping her in his arms.

He sat there, holding Emina as she wept, feeling numb to the world as emotions overwhelmed him.

"Matthias reports the Mist has cleared the eastern wall," said Merrick quietly, entering the house. "It's over."

"It's never over," Micah muttered, bowing his head.

Elowë, forgive his sins and bring Bolli to a place of everlasting peace. For those of us left, deliver us from this nightmare.

CHAPTER 12
ELDER SECRETS

A SUNNY MORNING.

Birds sang busily to one another through the clear, breezy sky above Binthir Forest. Men and women set off on their morning walk to the fields below, lost in conversation. You would never have known that but a few hours before, Fairhollow was swarming with bloodthirsty monsters bent on killing every one of them.

Micah paced nervously outside of Marian's house. The packed room left no space for well-wishers or anxious Guardsmen.

Tala walked up, her face covered with exhaustion from the night before. "Any word?"

"Nothing."

She shook her head thoughtfully, strands of long, golden hair flowing around her shoulders. "Asher's strong," said Tala encouragingly, "and Marian's the best healer on Karthmoor. He'll make it."

"I hope so," Micah murmured. "It's bad enough we lost Bolli, but to lose Asher, a guest we opened our village to. That I promised safety to..." His mind flashed back to Bolli, sprawled across Emina and him. Cold, lifeless flesh. Then, it was Asher's. A lump rose in Micah's throat alongside guilt.

Tala firmly grabbed his arm, forcing him to stop and look at her.

"He'll make it. You just have to trust."

"Elowë? Or Marian?"

She gave a grim smirk. "Both."

He jumped as the door to Marian's creaked open, and Rila stepped out.

"How is he?" Micah demanded.

"Still asleep," Rila calmly answered.

"Will he make it? Can we see him? Did he say anything?"

Rila folded her arms. A stern look on her youthful face immediately silenced him.

"His wounds are deep, Micah. It's taken all of Marian's skill to staunch the bleeding and start mending them. He awakened briefly early this morning, but not long enough to talk. And no visitors until she says he's ready. Marian wants his mind to focus fully on healing."

Micah grunted in resignation, his heart still heavy.

"Asher is resilient," she offered gently. "Give it time."

"You sound like your sister," he grumbled with a small smile, "but I get it. Just let me know as soon as there's any change."

"Of course." The door thumped shut as Rila quickly slipped back inside.

"Gerar asked me to cover your morning routine," said Tala, a hint of curiosity in her voice. "He asked you to meet him at Frederic's workshop."

"Thank you," Micah replied, wondering what Gerar had in store.

As she walked away, he called after her, "Tala!" She turned around. "You were incredible last night. We couldn't have done it without you."

She smiled, giving a satisfied nod before striding on.

Still pondering Gerar's request, Micah headed past Frederic's forge to the open workshop beyond. Across the square, men were busy all along the walls, inspecting every inch for new weaknesses after the night's assault.

Inside the gloomy shop, Gerar stood with his back to Micah, staring at Asher's wagon and lost in thought.

"Morning, Gerar," Micah called, jolting him from his reverie.

"Good morning," he murmured, shaking away his haggard gaze. "Thanks for coming."

"I was wondering what you wanted to see me for, but now I think I know why."

"Indeed." He rubbed his beard. "We need answers. Something to help us solve the madness we find ourselves in again and again."

"Answers Francis may hold the key to," Micah finished.

"Exactly."

"What are we waiting for?"

They strolled past the square, making their way towards Francis' house on the outskirts of town. They turned off the dusty main road and onto the narrow, grassy path connecting his house and Micah's to the village. The ancient brick and timber structure slid into view as Micah rounded a squat log house covered in fresh claw marks. Beyond the stately, weathered home, Clyde and Noric were back to their happy selves, oblivious to the fact that they were lucky to avoid becoming

Wolf food hours before. Asher's majestic steed grazed calmly beside his new friends.

Gerar knocked loudly as Micah climbed onto the porch.

"A moment!" Francis shuffled inside, muttering to himself as he neared the door. The worn wood squeaked open, revealing a gnarled, exhausted face. Francis peered at them with a tinge of agitation.

"What do you want, gentleman?" he asked bluntly.

"Answers to a riddle you can help us solve," answered Gerar.

"And what riddle would that be? I find silly games distasteful," Francis sourly replied.

"One that began thirty years ago," said Gerar, "when your father died."

A dark shadow crossed Francis' face.

"Hmm." His brow furrowed. Whether in thought or anger, Micah couldn't tell. But a hint of fear glimmered in his gray eyes. "You'd best come in."

They crossed through the foyer of bare plaster walls and made their way to the pair of wooden armchairs in his dim, dusty sitting room. Faint sunlight filtered in through a grimy window overlooking the porch. The large house was uncomfortably silent as Micah glanced around at the odd assortment of antique furniture and decorations resting in the corners. Francis shut the door and took a seat in his customary leather chair.

"So," he said gruffly.

"The well," Gerar demanded. "What happened?"

Francis raised a brow before he rasped, "I'm surprised you remember. You were but a small boy."

"That day rocked the entire town. I saw it with my own eyes."

"I'd wager you saw less than you presume," Francis grouchily retorted. "Unless you happened to be in our cellar that day."

"So, it was the cellar," muttered Gerar. "Tell us the whole story."

Francis frowned.

"Whatever happened then might be the key to saving Fairhollow now," Micah added. "We're not here to implicate you."

Francis sighed, a heavy, worn-out breath. He rubbed his head, leaning with the weight of a time-wrought burden carried for decades in silent agony.

Francis cleared his throat. "My father was a decent man. Respectable. A simple farmer perhaps, but well off and of some importance in the circles of Fairhollow." He shifted anxiously in his chair. "But Mother always said his damned fascination with exotic trinkets would be the death of us. In the end, it was the death of him, and him alone." He paused, hesitant to bring the secrets and shame of a dark past into the light.

"Go on," said Micah gently. "What kind of trinkets?"

"Neither of you were alive when we first heard the news from Edros. And even we were slow to hear it. Men were calling it the greatest discovery in the history of Aldaria. Said it would revolutionize life as we knew it. Maybe it did. But all it brought to my family was death and misery."

Francis coughed. "Nearly ninety years ago, word spread like wildfire that excavations in the Hamid Empire had discovered a magical crystal filled with energy that could be tapped by wizards and specially designed machines. Entire cities ran off the curious things. Lights, workshops, transportation—everything.

"But it was rare. Expensive, you see. The Archon had a monopoly on the supply and charged whatever he pleased to sell the crystals to other nations." Francis' voice slowly became more serious.

"But it eventually made its way around. Edros was practically teeming with the stuff by the time news reached our little village. My father, being the man he was, simply had to own a piece of it. Some contraption he could show off and impress the well-to-do of Fairhollow and beyond. So what did he buy?" Francis growled, shaking his head in disgust. "A bloody ice chest. A great box filled with frozen air powered by one of those blasted crystals. Air colder than any cellar south of Frostharbor. The thing simply enthralled my father."

"So that was why," Gerar interrupted, his eyes wide. "Why people were always remarking how important your father was. Why villagers would always bring the choicest meats and produce to him. They were using his cellar!"

The old man nodded. "The very one. Farmers for miles around brought items they couldn't keep fresh to my father. He stored hundreds of pounds of goods in that cellar-turned-ice-cave. Charged people for it too. Made a tidy profit after recouping the fortune he paid for the blasted thing. Only his luck didn't last. The merchant he bought the thing from never mentioned the risk that came with the crystal." Francis turned from them slightly. Sorrow hung on his shoulders, and a whisper of pain echoed in his voice.

"They aren't stable," he said, trembling. "At least not the ones used the way his was. Over time, I watched the shiny blue light it gave begin to fade. A darker color started rising inside it. But for my father, nothing could be wrong with his damnable trinket. Oh no! It was the picture of perfection. How could it not be, after all he'd given for it?" Francis let out a shaky sigh, resting his arms on his legs as he fumed. After a moment, he slowly sat back up.

"The accursed thing exploded. Right in his face as he was fiddling with it that dark morning. I felt the blast shake these very walls. Mother and I ran downstairs, sure it had to have been his precious toy. We weren't expecting to find him there though, his burned body..." Francis' bony frame shivered as he shook away the images. "It killed him instantly. No doubt about it." He paused for a moment.

"The blast caught the cellar wall on fire. I rushed to put it out with water Mother had drawn for washing laundry that morning as the neighbors came running. The cursed crystal was laying there on the ground, perfectly intact. Except the color had completely changed. Its fading blue had transformed to pure black—horrible to look at. In the chaos, it rolled against another wall, which burst into flames. We fought to put that one out too. I knew we had to get rid of the thing.

"I grabbed some dirty blankets and threw them in the tub. Once I was sure they were drenched, I rounded up some other men, and we carefully wrapped the shard in the soaking cloth, the wicked thing hissing as we did. We didn't have long.

"We rushed it out of the house, but I had no idea what to do. The only thing I could think of was water. So we ran to the well, throwing it in, blankets and all. It hit the surface with a gush of steam. The steaming eventually stopped, but I could see it had done something to the well. I couldn't tell the rest of the town what happened, but I also couldn't let it hurt anyone else. So, I sealed it up, creating some excuse about a diseased animal falling in and poisoning it. For whatever reason, people believed me."

Micah sat back, overwhelmed by his horrific story.

"The well remains that way, even to this day," Francis finished. "It's not something I'm proud of. Certainly not something I want my family's legacy trampled on because of."

"Of course," Micah told him. "You have our word."

Francis nodded, relieved.

"If I learned anything in my long, winding life, it would be this: never trust that crystal. It is altogether evil. Anything it touches will only bring destruction."

The room went quiet, all of them lost in a flood of thoughts. To think, all the attacks, the Mist, the chaos...

What if his father's crystal was the cause of it all? Micah shuddered at the thought. He couldn't place the blame on Francis, though. How could he have known all those years ago what would happen?

We have to get rid of it, once and for all.

"Thank you, Francis," said Micah as he leaned forward. "This is vital to keeping Fairhollow safe."

"I have your promise? For my family?"

"I swear it."

He nodded, satisfied with Micah's answer.

Gerar and Micah rose to leave, and Francis walked them out. He closed the door without so much as a farewell. Micah was sure their conversation had dug up old bones he'd thought long forgotten.

"You didn't mention Frederic's forge," Gerar observed as they trudged down the steps.

"Probably not the best topic to discuss with our troubled elder."

"So, what's the plan?"

"It has to go. His father's crystal," said Micah. "It can't stay in Fairhollow. Neither can Asher's chest, for that matter. I say we put the crystal from the well with the ones in the chest."

Gerar shook his head. "Agreed, but where do they go? Who's going to take them?"

Micah paused as they reached the road. "We need to talk to Asher again."

"Right. In the meantime, I'll head to Frederic's. See if he's got any tools we can use to fish that crystal out of the old well. Maybe see about getting that iluvan out of Alvin's forge, too."

"I'll see if there's been any change in Asher," he offered.

They split up outside the tavern. Micah hurried over to Marian's house and knocked lightly on the door. Rila peeked out, then opened it wider as she recognized him and smiled.

"You have good timing. He just woke a few minutes ago. He's been begging to talk with you."

Micah entered the house, uncertain of what to expect.

Asher was still lying on the pine table in the center of the dark room. Fresh bandages encased much of his torso. His breathing remained shallow but steady, and weakness paled his dark skin.

As Micah approached the table, Asher's eyes fluttered open. His expression brightened as Micah sat down beside him.

"Micah," he exclaimed weakly. "You came."

"How are you, my friend?" Micah asked warmly, grasping his unsteady hand.

"I have been better." He chuckled before coughing. "I would say worse too, but I fear that would be a lie."

Micah smiled. *At least he hasn't lost his sense of humor.*

"I must speak with you, Micah," Asher whispered urgently. "There is little time."

"We fought off the Wolves. The Mist is gone."

"It will return," he said flatly, "and more frequently, until the source is moved far enough away."

"The iluvan, you mean."

He coughed again. "Yes. They must go."

"Asher, you're in no state to travel," Micah gently told him.

"This I know," he said, a deep sadness filling his dark eyes. "I have brought great pain upon your village."

"You couldn't have known."

"But I know the risks of the iluvan," he finished.

Micah fell silent, unwilling to cause him more distress.

"We may have found another. Inside Fairhollow," he finally offered.

Asher's eyebrows rose in surprise.

"A black iluvan, buried decades ago."

"Mmm," Asher mused, "a strange mystery. The black ones call out to the Mist, draw it near what it would otherwise ignore. This could be connected to the struggle of your people."

"What do we do with it?"

"Normal means cannot safely destroy it. If you wish to keep Fairhollow secure, it must be taken far from here," he breathed. "Place it carefully with mine—do not touch it! Handle it only with thick gloves or coverings."

"Then what?"

"Beyond Fairhollow they must go. To Greenwatch," Asher directed, panting.

"But Asher, you yourself just agreed you can't—"

"I was not speaking of me," he interrupted, hard eyes boring into Micah, "but of you."

"Me? Go to Greenwatch?" stammered Micah. "I can't–I can't leave Fairhollow. There are defenders to organize, repairs to coordinate, men to train... Innocent people to protect!"

"Serah Micah," Asher wheezed. "You have fought many battles in your life. Traveled many places. Seen horrors your peaceful village need never encounter. You have braved the Mist. Moreover, you are immune to its murderous effects."

Micah leaned back, letting his words hammer into him.

"If you wish to keep your beloved town safe, you must do this task. It falls to you."

His plea rang with truth. Uncomfortable, but wholly true, nonetheless. Micah had spent many youthful years exploring the northern world. Many years honing his skills in the art of battle in the Guard. He was well-prepared, but he was also responsible for the safety of dozens.

"Go." Asher weakly cleared his throat. "Retrieve your black iluvan. Think on my words. Return when you are ready."

"Get some rest," Micah told him, before bidding Asher farewell and exiting the small, dim house. Back on the street, his mind raced.

What do I do? Is there no one else? Could Fairhollow survive?

"Micah!"

Micah turned to see Gerar rushing towards him from Frederic's shop. "Frederic had these lying around. Figured they'd be good for scooping that iluvan out of the well." He passed a set of large hooks and several lengths of rope to Micah.

"I also grabbed these." Gerar pulled two pairs of heavy leather gloves from his waist. The gloves, resistant to the heat of the blacksmith's forge, would be perfect for transporting the dangerous shard.

Together, they made the quick jog to the old well in the empty green behind the town hall. Few houses in that area remained occupied after the fire that destroyed the town hall, and the villagers had moved closer together. A vibrant moss covered the stone walls of the well, with some blocks crumbled away as years of weathering took their toll. Worn boards covered its top, nailed into the mortar of the walls. Someone had clearly continued to replace the boards as older ones wore out, though it had been some time since anyone tended to them.

Micah found a solid-looking plank of wood by a nearby structure and tried to pry the cover off the well. The rusty nails squeaked in protest, resisting the effort to reveal the dark secrets they protected. Gerar grabbed another board, and together, the nails slowly loosened. Then, with a great pop, the cover flew into the air, sending them both stumbling. Gerar shoved the wooden seal away as Micah gazed into the murky depths.

A haze of foul-smelling dust rose from the shaft, agitated by the fresh breeze invading the space. The well had clearly been dry for some time. Strange flora clung to the walls, various mushrooms and vines seeking whatever purchase they could as they reveled in the gloomy pit. Micah squinted, trying to make sense of the shadows concealing the base of the well.

"There." Gerar pointed. A nearly imperceptible glimmer sparkled in the depths. The fearsome shard generated a dark glow, a malevolent light displacing the surrounding shadows. Oddly enough, the crystal had remained on top of the soil. Nothing, not even mold, grew near the accursed thing.

Micah and Gerar pulled out the hooks, tying one rope to the end of each, before slowly lowering them into the gloom. The weighty metal thumped solidly against the ground at the bottom. With painstaking effort, they worked the hooks towards the rounded shard, attempting to slide them under its smooth surface. After several failed attempts, Micah managed to slip his under as Gerar's hook held the other end of the shard in place.

The movement provided just enough momentum for Gerar to slip the other hook quickly under as well.

"Easy now," said Micah. Inch by inch, they pulled the iluvan towards them, careful not to outpace each other and risk losing their hold. As it rose from the depths, sunlight hit the crystal for the first time in years, its smoky surface shimmering ominously. Still using the hooks, they hoisted the load out of the well, lowering it onto the dusty road. Micah slipped on the blacksmith's gloves, then bent down and gingerly placed a finger on the perilous shard.

Nothing.

Satisfied, he gripped the end in his hand. The crystal remained calm.

Micah grabbed the length of it with both hands before standing.

"Watch it," Gerar warned nervously. He led them back towards the workshop, both of them eager to deposit the dangerous rock in Asher's box.

"Get back now!" Gerar shouted, as a group of farmers approached the crossroads near the tavern. The onlookers jumped away, gawking at the sight as the pair rushed past.

Back inside the workshop, Gerar flung the chest open. Dancing rays of silvery blue illuminated the room. Micah warily lowered the iluvan onto its siblings, afraid of causing another blast like poor Bergi. The crystals remained calm.

"What about the forge?" he asked as he closed the chest.

"We already removed it. Frederic yanked the thing out of the contraption with his bare hands before I'd even finished speaking." Gerar grinned. "I was afraid he'd cause another episode, but the blue iluvan didn't seem to react to his touch. Maybe it's safer than the black ones?"

"Maybe."

"So, what now?"

"Asher said to take them away. Get them to his employer in Greenwatch," Micah answered, hoping to avoid the rest of their discussion. Clearly, that was not going to happen.

"*Greenwatch?*" Gerar exclaimed. "Who in Aldaria is going to get them there? Certainly not him."

Micah paused before quietly answering, "He asked me to go."

Shock crossed Gerar's furrowed face before turning into a thoughtful look.

"It makes sense," he admitted with a small shrug.

"How does me leaving Fairhollow make sense?" Micah scoffed, astounded at his friend's sudden change.

"You're more traveled than all of Fairhollow combined, except for Asher," he explained. "Adventuring is in your blood. Plus, you're one heck of a warrior. There's a reason you rose to the rank of warden so quickly. If anyone could survive a journey across the Mist-filled wilds of Karthmoor, it's you."

Micah furiously shook his head. "What about the village? Who's going to lead the men if I'm gone?"

"Not to beat my own chest"—Gerar chuckled—"but I know how to command men. You've also got Merrick, Matthias, and Tolsten, all highly skilled Guardsmen, to lean on. Give us Torvin and Francis, and we'll fill any gaps made by your departure."

"You're serious, aren't you?" he asked, astonished.

"I am. You know the risks, Micah. Either the iluvan stay until we're overwhelmed, or someone carries them far away, taking the Mist with them. But if you send just any eager man, chances are he won't get five miles from Fairhollow."

Micah aimlessly kicked at the ground, mulling over his words. Deep down, he knew Gerar and Asher were right.

"Very well. I'll do it."

CHAPTER 13

A HARD FAREWELL

THE NEXT DAY WAS a flurry of activity. Micah bundled his belongings quickly and carried them out of the sad, old house he'd called home for the past several weeks. Something told him he'd miss its musty, timbered halls and scratchy bed once rocks became his sleeping companions. The sun glared in the late morning sky. Warmer weather seemed to be holding.

Micah set out for Frederic's workshop, thankful he hadn't hoarded belongings to weigh down his pack. Everyone greeted him as he passed, anxious glances covering their faces. News of his departure had spread like wildfire once Delvin found out.

Arriving at the shop, Micah tossed his belongings in the back of Asher's wagon. It would be slow going with the old cart, but the load was too large to strap onto a horse. He laid his pistol in the front seat, leaving his trusty sword fastened to his side. The goal was to leave by midday, giving him a good span of light to cover some distance as he set out for Greenwatch.

After exiting the workshop, Micah made his way over to the tavern for a quick meal.

My last one in Fairhollow, he thought wistfully.

He opened the door into the dim, cozy room, and Delvin turned from his work behind the bar, wiping his hands.

"Welcome, Micah!" he shouted. "Need a little somethin' for the road?"

"Just enough to tide me over for now, thanks."

Delvin hustled over, smiling sadly.

"We'll miss ya something fierce," he began, his deep voice unusually quiet, "but we'll make sure you go with plenty of help." Delvin set a hearty vegetable stew and fresh bread in front of Micah. "Go on and eat. While you're gettin' ready, I'll have a stock of freshly cured meat sent to your wagon. It may get a little dull, but you won't have to worry about food for a good, long while."

"Thanks, Delvin. That means a lot," said Micah humbly.

Delvin nodded and exited the rear door of the tavern, heading to his storage shack.

Micah scarfed down the stew, hoping to make time to visit Asher and a few others before leaving.

Back outside, several people were mulling about on the road, an odd occurrence on a perfect day for tending the fields. Brushing past them, he headed to Marian's house. Inside, Asher remained restricted to the table, though blankets and pillows had been brought in to make his rest more comfortable. Asher raised his head and smiled as Micah slipped into the shadowy room.

"How are you today, Asher?" Micah asked as he greeted him.

"Every day brings improvement," Asher responded. "Today is another such day." His breathing was more relaxed and stronger than before. While the bandages around his chest looked fearsome, his face was calm, only twinging in pain with sudden movements.

"You will leave soon then, yes?" Asher questioned.

"Within the hour."

Asher nodded, thoughtful. "This is a brave thing you will do; I am most grateful. Remember, when you arrive in Greenwatch, seek out a man by the name of Tomas. I was to transfer the shipment to him."

"Tomas, okay." Micah made a mental note.

"I have one last request of you, serah Micah, if you will indulge me."

"What is it?"

"You must take my wagon, that much is certain. Now I also ask you to take Edoran, my valiant steed."

Micah had planned on asking Francis for Clyde or Noric, not wanting to burden Asher further.

"Without your horse or wagon, you'll make a poor merchant," Micah teased.

Asher laughed before it transformed into an aching cough.

"Ah, I fear my merchant days may be behind me," said Asher quietly. "The dangers prove too great for my aging body."

Micah raised a brow in surprise. "What will you do?"

"In my brief time among your people, I find myself inspired by their kindness and courage," Asher explained. "They have taken care of me well. More so than I deserve, considering the danger I placed them in. In return, I would like to offer my skills and services to Fairhollow. I wish to stay, should your people be gracious enough to accept."

"They'll be honored to count you among them," Micah answered, stunned.

Asher nodded with satisfaction. "Then what remains in my cart, I offer to you. Do what you will with the wagon once you reach Greenwatch, but I ask that you return Edoran to his rightful stature. The poor beast was gifted to me after his master was slain in a skirmish. He is a war horse, bred for the dangers of battle. May his skills serve you well on your journey."

"I'm honored," he quietly replied. "I will look after him with respect."

Asher beamed proudly. "Now go, Micah. Face your task with valor. May your god watch over you." Micah shook his hand, feeling Asher's strength slowly returning, and left the house. It was nearly time he left.

Micah walked somberly towards the gate, his heart aching for the people and memories he was leaving behind. Faces passed through his mind as he dwelt on each of them.

As Micah looked up, the sight of the dusty square startled him. From end to end, the people of Fairhollow lined the sides, the entire village coming to send him off. The crowd cheered, and his breath stuck in his throat as his eyes threatened to water.

Rila and Tala were the first to approach as he reached the square. They stood with sad smiles on their youthful faces beside the wagon, loaded and ready, with Edoran calmly waiting.

"Rila, Tala." Micah nodded at each of them. They reached in, throwing a warm hug around him.

"We'll miss you," said Rila sadly.

"I'll miss you too," Micah chokingly began. "I never told you two this, but you've become like daughters to me. I know I can never replace your parents, but you gave me a chance to help you grow, helping heal my own grief, too."

"You looked out for us when we had no one." Tala smiled.

"And gave us the support to become who we are," Rila finished. "I'd say that kind of love makes you just as much family as Mom and Dad were." Micah embraced each of them again, kissing the tops of their golden heads.

If every parting is like this, I swear, I'm not going to last.

As the girls backed away, Halvid, Frederic, and Torvin stepped forward.

"How does it look?" Micah asked, pretending to rub dirt out of his eye.

"The wagon is sturdy," Torvin rumbled. "She'll serve you well."

"Micah." Frederic pulled a cloth from behind him. "I've been working on this for a while now. For you." He lifted the pale fabric, revealing a magnificently crafted hunting knife. Symbols of the ancient language flickered across the tempered blade. Small carvings of bounding deer, roaming wolves, and birds in flight adorned the flowing wooden handle. It was an incredible gift.

"Thank you," Micah replied, stunned, as Frederic passed it to him. Micah shook the men's hands, and Marian took their place.

"Micah," she said in her warm, friendly tone.

"Marian." He nodded. "Thank you for everything. I'll miss your wisdom and guidance deeply."

"Fairhollow will miss your presence. Before you go, I wish to offer a prayer for your journey." She gripped Micah's hands in her frail fingers as they bowed their heads.

"Elowë, Father of All," she began, "we praise you for the blessing you gave us in Micah. You sent a protector for your people when it was so desperately needed. As one step in his path ends and the next begins, we ask that you watch over him. Guide his wanderings, Lord, and use the might you've given him to be a blessing and shield for others. May he always find strength in your care."

"Thank you," he said quietly as Marian returned to the crowd.

Last of all, Gerar, Merrick, and Tolsten approached.

"Everything set?" Micah asked.

"Looks like you've got plenty of supplies to make it to Greenwatch," answered Gerar, looking over the wagon.

He shook his head. "Not me. Fairhollow. Did the morning inspections report anything? No more boulders lying against the walls? What about repairs for the weapons?"

"It's all well in hand," Merrick chuckled. "You needn't worry about us, Micah."

"Now get going," Tolsten teased. "There'll be no light left at this rate, and you'll be stuck here, sittin' on yer rump 'til the sun comes up." Micah laughed and gave each man a gruff hug. All of them saluted.

"The Guard may be no more," Gerar declared, "but you will always be our Warden, Micah Stormcrown."

Micah left his men and climbed into the wagon. Looking around, his heart swelled with pride and longing. A sea of friends and family waved back.

"Open the gate!" Matthias called from his post.

A group of men swung the shuddering gate wide, the opening beckoning onwards. Micah glanced over and saw Francis nodding his head in encouragement, his wise eyes pushing him on. Rila and Tala stood near, tears on their faces as they waved. The rest of the men waved their own farewells across from them.

Deep breath.

Micah cracked the reins, and Edoran sprang forward. Slowly, he drew past the crowd, sailing away from their familiar, comforting faces. Matthias gazed down, the weathered soldier steadying his rifle against the floor and saluting, as Micah passed under the gate. In a fleeting whisper of a moment, he found himself beyond the walls of Fairhollow. The gate gently closed behind Micah, shutting out the noise of the crowd.

Suddenly, he was alone.

The vast fields and forest lay in front of him. There was no going home this time. No family to escape to. The world spread endlessly before him, adventure calling on unknown winds.

At least I have Edoran, he thought to himself, brushing the fears from his heart.

CHAPTER 14
THE ROAD LESS TRAVELED

A BRIGHT SUN GLISTENED off vast towers of stone. Hues of gray, white, and silver sparkled from their dazzling heights. Micah had been to Starkhaven before, but the sight always took his breath away. Karthmoor's capital city was a sprawling masterpiece, the work of generations of planners, masons, and woodworkers. The dizzying heights of its many buildings dwarfed everything else the people of their island nation had constructed.

Micah urged his horse forward, plunging into the crowded streets. Exotic vendors called to passing citizens, hawking trinkets and curiosities from mysterious lands. A strange mixture of aromas filled the air as spice traders, butchers, bakers, and apothecaries lined the busy roads. His senses were overwhelmed by it all.

The seat of power on Karthmoor lay near the center of the city. Tar'auth Ben, the Tower of Minds in the ancient language, housed the chambers where the Conclave debated the future of the island deep within its majestic walls. Micah dismounted his horse at the stables near the mass of stairs leading to its entrance. Brushing the dust of the trail off as best he could, he scaled the stairs two at a time, already late. Micah strode across marbled floors, his boots echoing obnoxiously in the towering stone corridors. Grand columns and chiseled statues of figures in elaborate robes flanked the hall.

In the entryway to the council chambers, Berien paced anxiously.

"Micah!" he exclaimed as relief flooded his face.

"Warden-Commander Berien." Micah saluted. "Forgive my delay."

"Not at all." Berien waved dismissively, quickly embracing his arm. "It was a hard journey, I imagine. How is Elisa?"

Micah smiled. "She's well, and Samuel is growing into a strong, young boy."

"Ah." Berien grinned. "Little Samuel was but a swaddled infant when last I saw them. It's been too long."

"Indeed."

"Well then. Shall we?"

Berien pushed open the massive, oaken doors to the chamber. Inside, the room was awash in a din of voices. Rows of men and women sat in stands of carved stone lining the circular room, peering down at the central floor below.

"Order!" A man banged a gavel from a podium in the stands. Micah followed Berien into the center, and they took a seat near the platform wall.

"There's been no consensus on a course of action," Berien whispered. "Maybe your testimony today will change that."

"Let us first summon Governor Beckett of Greenwatch," the man on the platform called.

"Speaker Olan, in case you didn't recognize him," Berien whispered again. "The years haven't been favorable."

Two men appeared wheeling a bizarre-looking cluster of crystal, nearly as tall as a person, into the center of the chamber. One side of the silvery blue stone was chiseled and smoothed into a fine sheet of sparkling reflections. A swirling fog danced inside it, like Micah was looking into a watery or smoky world beyond.

A mage stood and gently touched the stone. The surface rippled, coiling in on itself like a rushing whirlpool. Suddenly, a person appeared in the crystalline mirror. An older man, dressed in an extravagant vest and shirt with ruffled sleeves, carried an air of seriousness as he held his arms behind him. The mirror sharpened to where Micah could see an ornately decorated room with richly paneled walls behind the man.

"Governor Beckett," Berien explained. "The Conclave promoted him after Governor Larius passed."

"Welcome, Governor Beckett," Speaker Olan called out. "What is the report from the western province?"

"Thank you, Speaker," Beckett boomed from the strange device. "I am honored to address the Conclave, though I wish I came bearing better news."

He cleared his throat. "To be short, Frostharbor is no longer under our control. Our scouts confirmed the city has surrendered to the Anderfalls. Smaller villages in the area have sent no word, and so we assume they are under their influence as well. Farshore to the south reports a significant increase in invaders landing on the peninsula. Their walls are strong, but the city cannot hold out much longer. So far, Greenwatch remains untouched. Likely, the Anderfalls hope to capture the outlying towns before closing in."

"What of their movements deeper into Karthmoor?" Speaker Olan questioned.

Berien stood. "Honorable Speaker, our scouts report that the Anderfall armies are contained to the coastal regions. They have not solidified into a force ready to press eastward yet without exposing their flank."

"Thank you, Warden-Commander." The Speaker nodded as Berien returned to his seat. Olan turned back to Governor Beckett's figure in the arcane mirror. "Have the Anderfalls made any demands? Given any reasons for this outrage?" he angrily asked.

"No messengers have been sent to Greenwatch," Beckett answered. "Nor was any reason given to those defending Farshore or Frostharbor. They were unprovoked, and we received no communications from their solitary isles leading up to the incursion."

"Thank you," said Speaker Olan. "Unless the Conclave has any additional questions, Governor Beckett, you are dismissed."

The Governor bowed within the curious mirror before the picture began to distort. Its surface spun, returning to a swirling state. The room filled with a cacophony of whispering as members of the council debated amongst themselves.

"Order!" Speaker Olan called again, banging his gavel. As the chamber quieted, he cleared his throat.

"Warden-Commander, you have been called here today to help us understand this threat. Please, address the council."

Berien stood and walked to the center of the room where he saluted the Conclave.

"Honorable members of the Conclave, Governor Beckett's report is wholly accurate in that the Guard has found no evidence of any acts of provocation, intentional or accidental. However, the customs of our westward neighbors remain... elusive, at best." Berien paused.

"In order to combat this threat, we must understand who we face. To understand who we face, we require someone who knows *the Anderfalls—its people, its culture, the nation itself. To that end, I present to you Micah Stormcrown, the former Warden of the Western Province. His experience exploring and interacting with the natives of the Anderfalls provides us with a unique insight into our enigmatic invaders." He motioned for Micah to rise.*

Micah nervously touched Elisa's pendant around his neck, slowly rising from his seat. Micah walked awkwardly across the empty floor of the council chamber, every eye watching as he replaced Berien in the center.

"Welcome, Warden Stormcrown." Speaker Olan nodded. "Your service to Karthmoor brings you honor. The Conclave asks that you share any information you collected during your travels to the Anderfalls."

Micah saluted, his mind racing as he tried to build a cohesive summary of everything he remembered from his time amongst the Anderfall people.

"Respected members of the Conclave," He trembled before taking a deep breath. "I have journeyed across many spaces of the northern world in my brief time upon this earth. I was fortunate enough for Elowë to bless me with the strength and courage to do so in my youth, and then to use that knowledge to defend our nation.

"In all my years of travel and adventure, no land remained as foreign and mysterious as the Anderfalls."

Micah stepped forward, more confident.

"The Anderfalls are a proud people—tough, unyielding. They make a hard living on their harsh, frigid islands, most either as farmers or warriors."

"What of their leaders? Who governs the isles?" someone called from the stands.

"Their governance consists of a collection of chieftains, each ruling their own hold across the islands," he answered. "From among them, a Jarl, or king, is chosen to speak for the Anderfalls. Jarls are granted authority to make treaties, direct trade, and call for war, among other powers. However, a majority of the chieftains must agree before engaging in conflict beyond their territories.

"How the chieftains are selected remained unclear during my voyage, but their rule is absolute. They dictate the laws of the land, which citizens must obey. The Jarl has only minimal power to overrule them. They are in constant struggle between themselves for more power and land. It is a delicate game with deadly results, should one fail to heed the dance.

"Honor is the foundation of Anderfall's culture. It is a grievous thing to insult an Anderfall warrior, and they will demand a duel to the death to resolve the matter. They hold little stock in material gifts or goodwill, honoring feats of strength or courage above all else."

"If they are placated with honorable acts," the Speaker mused, "then what has Karthmoor done to show dishonor?"

Micah paused, thinking.

"A terrible insult would have had to be made against their nation, Jarl, or chieftains, for the Anderfalls to invade. Something so egregious that a majority of their leaders would agree to war," he slowly concluded. "Nothing leads me to believe the chieftains would band together and share a common goal for anything less."

"What, then, would insult them and kindle their anger?"

"A difficult question," Micah admitted. "The source of their anger and pride was always fickle to me, never knowing what would be negatively construed. But Karthmoor has little interaction with the Anderfalls. I recall no merchants or citizens trav-

eling there. Without such relations, I humbly admit before this council, I do not know what has provoked them."

The room fell uncomfortably silent. The members sat, pondering his words, poring over their notes.

"Thank you, Warden Stormcrown." The Speaker quietly dismissed him to his seat.

"This makes no sense." A member across from the Speaker rose. "They were never provoked. We must send a delegation to the Jarl and demand an answer for this invasion!"

"A delegation?" another shouted, incredulous. "We're at war! The Anderfalls started this fight. It's our responsibility to finish it!"

The room descended into chaos. Members of the Conclave shouting at each other as the deafening volume exploded. Speaker Olan hammered his gavel to no avail. Berien sat, arms crossed, as he shook his head. Micah let his head fall back against the wall.

What had he done?

❦

Micah rubbed his eyes and groaned before tossing again in his sleeping sack. The sun hadn't even broken the horizon, but the ground tormented him with persistent prods from inconsiderate rocks. He tiredly sighed. *Might as well get up.*

It was a chilly morning, but the sky was clear. A good sign for traveling. The dense evergreens surrounding the makeshift campsite swayed gently in the breeze as the chirps of stirring birds reached his ears. Micah's first night on the road to Greenwatch was an adjustment but thankfully, without danger. The grove provided just enough space to conceal all of his belongings, allowing a safe, if restless, night. The transition to sleeping on the ground in the wilderness would definitely be tough after living with a soft bed inside the walls of Fairhollow.

Micah picked at a loaf of bread Delvin had sent for breakfast, but wasn't overly hungry. There was still a long road left to Greenwatch.

If I'm going to cover some distance today, I'd better get started.

He packed up his gear, dumping it in the back of the wagon before seeing to Edoran. His brown mane glistened in the morning sun as he grazed contentedly on the thick grass surrounding the copse of trees. It was clear Asher had taken excellent care of the powerful war horse. Micah undid the reins from the branch and led him back to the wagon.

After one last look around the clearing, Micah jumped into the seat and sent them off toward the wide, dusty trail leading west from Fairhollow. He'd made decent time the day before, giving him hope he would cross the Silvenar River before sundown. He knew from experience that the road became more rugged on the western side of the river as it passed through the forested hills and mountains bordering Karthmoor's western coast.

The dirt road remained completely barren. Few discernible traces of travelers like himself remained on the trail, evidence it'd been quite some time since anyone had come that direction. Though there were no signs of the Mist in the immediate area, Micah cautiously watched the horizon, looking for any disturbance.

His movement along the road was unsettling. Hours rolled past with no signs of life other than the occasional bird. An ominous feeling gripped the land, the earth itself exuding a silent fear of the curse it bore. In the vastness of the grassy plains, he felt conspicuously alone, as if he was the only person left in the world. A last survivor of an unknown catastrophe, though the fields and trees wore no signs of the destruction.

In the quiet solitude, Micah's thoughts drifted to Fairhollow. He imagined Gerar and Merrick moving through the daily routines. Men and women working the fields as their children played nearby. An evening at Delvin's filled with laughter and good drinks. All the life he had known for the past couple of years outside of the Mist's relentless assaults. Next, his mind returned to the thoughts that had consumed his dreamworld those past several nights. The dull ache as he lingered on sweet memories of Elisa and Samuel only increased his loneliness. Micah reached up and grasped the cool crystal around his neck.

Something to remind you of home. Of us.

The silvery necklace felt alive, quietly giving him a confidence to brush away the doubts and grief creeping into his reverie. Micah shook the thoughts from his head, focusing back on the road and watching Edoran press steadily onward.

By late afternoon, the gentle, rolling plains gave way to hilly forests broken briefly by grassy fields, an indicator he must be close to the Silvenar. Before long, he could hear the soft sound of rushing water coming from a collection of falls.

At least it's a change in scenery.

As he rounded a bend in the road next to a rocky cliff, the river finally came into view.

The Silvenar was the largest river in Karthmoor. Many smaller streams fed its wide, swift current as it wound from Lake Hemeth, far to the north, to Karthmoor's southern coast.

The cobblestone bridge before Micah appeared to be in poor shape. Years of neglect had allowed portions to deteriorate, sending pieces of its once sturdy path into the dark waters. The short waterfalls just past the bridge roared as the flow rose into the air and spilled over the precipice. Stony points of rock jutted out along its lip.

Micah brought Edoran to a stop and climbed down, inspecting the bridge on foot. The northern half of the bridge appeared to be in better shape. No gaps or supports had given away, yet, but it would still be a risk sending a full wagon over. He paused, mulling over the options. The next nearest crossing was Varan's Lodge, a small farming settlement about a day's journey south. Adding two more days to his trip meant increasing the chance of running into the Mist or other dangers that now inhabited the island.

He growled in frustration, staring at the weathered bridge. The last thing he wanted was to be caught in the open by a pack of Mist Wolves. He decided to risk it.

Micah jumped back into the wagon, starting with Edoran at a slow pace and avoiding any sudden movements. The stallion remained remarkably calm, obeying his measured, steady pace as they passed unnervingly close to the open pits in the bridge. A single glimpse at the rushing water below forced Micah to look away and focus on the dry land ahead of him. *Almost there.*

CRACK!

A loud rumble rocked the bridge as the wagon passed over a weakened section. The mortar between the stones shattered in a deafening sound as he urged Edoran forward. A chunk of rock crumbled into the swift current below, threatening to take the wagon with it.

Faster! Micah whipped Edoran into a run, desperately aiming for solid ground. In a moment, they reached it, and the rumbling of the bridge subsided.

Thank you, Elowë. He silently looked up to the heavens. *Next time, I'm finding another route.*

With the cart safely on the other side of the Silvenar, he calmed his beating heart and inspected the terrain. Rocky hills and fields bordered the road as it continued its westward march. Soon enough, it would turn north, leading all the way to the city of Greenwatch.

With the sun beginning to set, Micah refilled his water skin at the river and started looking for a suitable spot to shelter for the night. Luckily, there was still no sign of the Mist, or anything, really. Farther down the road, he spied a stony outcropping with a grove of leafy trees and undergrowth not far from the edge of a small forest. A promising spot to camp.

Directing the wagon off the trail, he bounced over rough weeds towards the trees. Suddenly, a small yelp cried out from the thicket. Micah grasped his pistol, ready for some terror to spring forth. Instead, a young fox dashed from the grove, fleeing to the forest beyond. With a sigh of relief, he guided Edoran into the copse and found a small clearing nestled at the foot of the cliff. *It'll do.*

Micah climbed down and detached the wagon, giving Edoran space to graze as he unloaded his equipment. Afterwards, he gathered a small pile of dead brush, hoping to get a fire going and make a hearty stew with some of the meat Delvin had sent. Micah grabbed the flint from his satchel and crouched beside the kindling. Whether it was the breeze or plain bad luck, the fire refused to start.

"Come on," he muttered as the sun sank lower. The kindling continued its defiance. He tossed the flint away, frustrated. Micah stood, attempting to calm his mind and recall a long-forgotten training.

Before rising in the ranks of the Guard, he had served as a Protector. To most, Protectors were little more than common soldiers, but their training came with a well-kept secret, making them invaluable as scouts or lone agents. In the dangerous wilds of the Mist, he realized that knowledge might just hold the key to his survival.

Stilling his thoughts, Micah reached deep into his mind, searching for a spark he'd buried long ago. Would it still be there?

At first, nothing. Just a swirl of feelings and memories. Then, a momentary sensation before the spark vanished. He'd felt it.

Micah retraced the path, finding a barrier enclosing a deep corner of his consciousness. The instant his mind touched it, the veil strengthened, denying him entrance. Micah pressed harder, the effort straining his will after so many years of disuse. Gradually, the barrier weakened. Then, in a momentary flash, he was through. A powerful force flooded his body, and he gasped as if his adrenaline was racing. His focus sharpened to a razor's edge as he stretched out a trembling arm.

A flicker of flame leapt from his fingertips, striking the brush. Micah staggered back, shocked at the amount of effort it had taken as the strength drained from his limbs. He felt as if he'd just spent the afternoon hauling rocks on his farm. It had been years since he'd used magic. The meager knowledge he'd learned as a Protector had dwindled, but at least he knew the ability was still there. It just needed practice.

Micah sat down, watching the flames come to life, and pondered what he had just done. Magic was inherent to their world, of course, though few were born with the ability to wield it. The dangers and mystery of its nature often frightened the common citizen. As such, communities often shunned or even exiled those who showed signs of arcane talent. Some met unfortunate ends, unable to control the consuming power. Others abused it, fueling the distrust even as they incurred the wrath of peacekeepers, or worse, vengeful townsfolk. Still, some magic wielders eventually found their way to sanctuaries or schools dedicated to teaching them control, such as the Hillmarch Academy. The rest, like himself, were identified early by the Guard and enlisted as Protectors, quietly using their powers in the service of Karthmoor to defend the very ones who feared them.

Micah had never revealed his scant abilities to anyone save a handful of Guardsmen he'd served with and Elisa, nor had he much need for his limited knowledge after retiring from the Guard. The people of Fairhollow would've likely banished him as soon as they discovered his magic had they known. And after so much time among them, thoughts of his magic had faded into the obscure corners of his mind, replaced with more pressing matters. While he was grateful for the ability now, he knew he'd have to be mindful of its use to avoid the wrath of suspicious townsfolk.

With a steady flame building, Micah filled his small cooking pot with water, elk meat, and a pinch of curious spices from a box in Asher's wares. As soon as the stew bubbled, he eagerly filled a bowl, sitting back to relish the rich flavor. The tender meat mixed wonderfully with the sharp, spicy taste of the exotic seasonings, providing an exquisite meal for a weary traveler. He watched as the dwindling sun gave way to the dark night, enjoying the quiet moment. Twisting shadows danced off the trees and rocky wall of the meadow. The crackling fire, chirping crickets, and stamping of Edoran brought a swath of memories flooding back. A glimpse of the simple joy he had found in his days of youthful adventuring. It'd been too long since he had rested in that peace. It felt right.

Micah watched the dying flames a moment longer, then crawled into his sleeping sack, staring up at the clear night sky and the twinkling stars. Gerar was right. As much as he missed Fairhollow, this was his calling and strength. He silently smiled.

Use it as you will, Elowë.

CHAPTER 15

GREENWOOD

A FEARFUL CRY FROM Edoran jolted Micah awake. The sky was still dark, cool air collecting dew on the grass in the clearing. Though there wasn't any sign of the sun, he could feel dawn approaching.

Edoran snorted again, shifting nervously near his tree. Something was wrong. Micah unsheathed his sword, quietly rising from his sleeping sack. With only the faint moonlight, he could barely make out the edges of the campsite. The fire pit held a faint glow, its deep embers bereft of strength. He scrabbled around for his flint and struck the remaining kindling. It caught, slowly spreading its light along with shifting shadows across the clearing. The trees were quiet.

Micah rummaged around, throwing everything back in the wagon in case he needed to make a quick escape. Edoran let out another worried neigh, sure to attract any danger lurking beyond Micah's sight. He moved over to the horse, patting its neck to soothe the poor beast.

"Shh, shh," he whispered, eyeing the gloom between the rustling branches. Edoran calmed enough for Micah to guide him to the wagon and hook him up. He trusted Edoran's instincts—if something was prowling nearby, he'd rather leave and avoid a confrontation.

With everything loaded, Micah made his way towards the wooden seat. Just as he was about to climb up, a growl sounded from the far edge of the clearing. Edoran cried in terror, nearly bucking the wagon hitch. Micah brandished his sword, his eyes darting along the tree line.

A fearsome-looking timber wolf prowled out of the dark. Unlike the one the logging crew had encountered in Binthir Forest, this beast was strong and healthy. Its sleek gray coat glistened in the dim firelight. Another growl emanated from behind it. Micah's other hand grasped for his pistol as a second wolf padded threateningly into the clearing a small length away. Micah aimed the barrel at it while pointing his sword at the first, the beasts drawing closer. His body tensed, fear rising. He was outnumbered. He inched towards the wagon as they advanced, the second wolf silently trying to flank him as the first bore down, its piercing yellow eyes locked on him.

In a blink, the growls transformed into terrifying barks, and the first wolf dashed towards Micah. He whipped his pistol around, aiming for the dark blur as it launched into the air.

BOOM!

A flash of light erupted. His shot connected, sending the wolf tumbling to the ground. The second wolf pounced before he could react. The weight of the massive beast crashed into him, knocking the weapons out of his hands as the pair collapsed in a whirling heap. Micah gripped its powerful neck with his hands, straining to keep its snapping jaws away, slobber spraying his face. Sharp claws dug into his clothes, ripping a gash in his leather coat as they struggled in the dirt.

Micah kicked wildly at the creature's rear, trying to throw it off as it convulsed. Luckily, his boot found purchase on one of its hind legs. He lashed out with a fierce kick, and the wolf stumbled off balance. Free from its vicious teeth, Micah shoved the wolf away, rolling from underneath its crushing weight.

He grasped for Frederic's hunting knife at his side as he staggered to his knees. The wolf recovered, lunging again, and Micah swung the blade, scoring a cut across its snout. It jerked back with a yelp, and he thrusted again, aiming for its ribs. The wolf swiped, claws scraping against his skull just as the knife connected, burying in its furry hide.

With a yelp of surprise, the wolf crashed to the ground. Micah collapsed, breathing wildly.

Shooting pain pulsed from the top of Micah's head where the claws landed. He reached up and found a trickle of blood in his hair. He groaned, rising from the dirt and stumbling towards the wagon. The cut wasn't deep, but each touch sent a jolt of pain across his scalp. He rinsed out the wound with his waterskin and pressed a cloth against it.

Micah attempted to pacify frantic Edoran while nursing his throbbing head. The steed eventually calmed, satisfied the danger had passed for the moment. With the cloth still pressed into his tangled hair, Micah clambered into the wagon seat and guided Edoran quickly back out into the open air.

A faint glimmer of light was dawning on the horizon as they reached the road. Looking to the south, Micah's gut twisted in fear. A bank of sickly blue Mist tumbled slowly over the hills near the forest, approaching the grove he had just left. There was no time to lose.

He whipped Edoran into a trot, rushing along the road as it wound north. As the dawning sun added more light to the world, Micah glanced back, relieved to see their pace was putting distance between the wagon and the Mist. At least the accursed fog moved slowly.

Not willing to risk a second encounter, he pressed on, making only brief stops to give Edoran a moment of rest. As the sun rose higher, the terrain became more mountainous. The gentle hills and forests surrounding the smooth, easy road steadily transformed into tall, rocky cliffs. The dusty trail turned to winding gravel. Edoran strained to pull the load up a particularly steep stretch of gray cliffs leading to a pass in the rocky peaks. Micah scanned the land below as they reached the top. In the distance, a smooth, rolling blanket of Mist completely engulfed the land. With any luck, the range of mountains would slow its progress.

Micah guided Edoran towards the narrow pass, well worn by a multitude of travelers in ages past. Jagged walls of weathered stone loomed above the wagon as they creaked through the silent gap. Near the end of the confined space, a vast scene spread out in front of him. In contrast to the bleak, gray passage, the rich emerald of a massive forest sprawled as far as the eye could see, reaching endlessly to the west and north. On its eastern edge, the Silvenar glimmered faintly as it wound its way past the mountains.

The Greenwood.

Directly ahead, the road snaked its way down from the heights, disappearing into the maze of trees. Micah glanced at the sky full of heavy gray clouds.

Hopefully, they'll relent from drenching us.

He tugged at the reins, moving Edoran slowly down the steep hills towards the forest. Somewhere on the other side of the Greenwood lay their destination.

Brush and weeds slowly claimed the barren, rocky slopes as he pressed on. Lush, green ferns and short, leafy trees overtook the open surfaces closer to the forest's edge. The air became cool and wet, the ground and foliage laden with the moisture of a fresh rain. A chorus of birds sang happily from the Greenwood, oblivious to the danger that lurked beyond the mountains to the south.

The wide gravel road transformed into a damp, muddy trail as it guided the wagon into the depths of the vibrant woods. Under the cover of soaring oaks, maples, and beeches, the forest swarmed with life unlike anything Micah had experienced since the Mist invaded. Gray squirrels darted from tree to tree, chasing one another through the branches above. Rabbits scampered away as the squeaking wagon approached. Twice he caught glimpses of deer grazing in the undergrowth with their young. After years of sparse, sickly wildlife, the Greenwood felt like another world. Micah wondered if perhaps the mountainous ranges that bordered its southern and northern edges had prevented the expansive Mist from entering its depths. He relaxed, drinking in the peaceful scenery as they plodded softly along the dirt trail.

Hours rolled by as the sights of the Greenwood continued. They passed a few babbling streams making their way towards the Silvenar, schools of fish visible in their clear depths as curious long-legged waterfowl watched for an easy meal. At one point, Micah stopped, giving Edoran a long break beside an eddy in a stream, and took the opportunity to wash off the grime of the road. He enjoyed a small midday meal along its bank, using the time to refill the spare water skins and inspect the wagon.

The Greenwood held only a smattering of settlements throughout its leafy confines. From his brief travels, Micah recalled no formal villages, only sporadic houses of hermits and lumberjacks. Few looked to make a living in its damp, wooded depths, save those harvesting its ancient timbers or looking for a quiet life away from the cares of the world.

I wonder if anyone still survives here?

Back on the road, the clouds finally reached capacity, sending a steady drip through the thick canopy above. Thankfully, the leafy roof prevented the heavier rain from reaching the forest floor. A soft rumble of thunder echoed through the trees as the small storm passed overhead. Micah guessed at the time to be mid-afternoon, but the impenetrable roof and overcast sky shrouded the sun from view.

A woman's scream pierced the woods, shocking him from the serenity.

Micah straightened and reached for his pistol. The maze of trunks prevented him from locating the source, or even its direction, though it seemed to come from ahead. Going a bit farther, he brought Edoran to a stop and climbed down. Using what little tracking skills he had, Micah inspected the vegetation, searching for signs of movement. In the damp, muddy ground, he discovered a small set of footprints leading deeper into the brush. The petite shoe could certainly have been a woman's. With no other signs, he cautiously followed their route. The forest became oddly silent, and the woman's voice did not return.

As the road disappeared behind the wall of trees, Micah found another set of prints in a muddy clearing. Large boot prints, unlike the dainty prints from before.

A bandit? He moved carefully in their direction.

Immediately, a lazy tendril of Mist rolled from behind a cluster of trees, and he froze. Swerving his head around, Micah scanned for any sign that Mist Wolves were waiting to spring. The forest remained ominously still.

He crept towards the deathly fog, clutching his pistol tighter. Beyond the trees, Micah found another small clearing. The air was thick with swirling Mist. Hugging the nearest tree, he inched forward.

A branch snapped in the Mist.

Warily, Micah tilted his head around the mossy bark and peered into the meadow, blood pounding in his veins. The haze blocking his view shifted, revealing the outline of a man standing in the center, his back towards Micah. Micah drew a sharp breath, shocked to see another living soul.

He peeked out again. The man bent down, inspecting something in the tall grass. Though the Mist obscured many of his features, Micah noticed his short black hair and that he appeared to be in good shape. His clothes were odd, however. Unlike the familiar clothing of Karthmoor. Some sort of armor, mostly black leather with bits of metal and scale, covered him from the neck down. A wicked-looking sword, thin and shimmering like darkened obsidian before curving to a thickened point, rested in a sheath strapped to his side. Everything about the man was foreign.

"I know you're there," his deep, aggressive voice called out. "Reveal yourself."

Micah took a breath, blood pounding, and stepped out from his hiding spot. The man slowly turned, rising to face him. He was slightly older than Micah, though still relatively young. A thin, neatly groomed beard covered his face, coming to a point at his chin. He scowled, narrowing his dark eyes as he sized Micah up. A hand rested threateningly on his dangerous blade.

"Identify yourself," the man calmly demanded, a hint of warning behind his words.

"Micah," he said curtly, holstering his pistol. "And you?" The man studied him a moment longer.

"Garrin." He walked closer, though still leaving a comfortable distance between them.

"Do you not fear the danger around you, Micah?" he asked in a soft, menacing tone.

"I know the dangers of the Mist," replied Micah, "and the monsters it brings."

"Indeed?"

"What about you?" he asked defensively. "What are you doing here?"

Garrin fell quiet again, like he was thinking about how much to say.

"Odd that you would seek it out," he began. "As for me, I do not need to fear the Mist. It doesn't keep me from my task."

"Task?"

"Yet, the Mist hasn't taken you," he observed, ignoring Micah's question. "I wonder..."

An odd feeling crept over Micah. A strange, invading power washing over his skin and passing through his mind.

He has magic! Micah grasped for memories of Protector training to shield his thoughts from the mage, desperately attempting to erect a barrier around his consciousness.

"Most curious," Garrin coolly remarked. "I had not thought to find a wielder of magic in this forest, though your attempts are pitifully weak." How he sensed Micah's effort was beyond him. "Relent from your struggle," the mage commanded. "You cannot best me."

A powerful force crushed the feeble barrier around Micah's mind and he gasped as it was ripped away. A foreign, painful presence invaded his thoughts—searching, probing his mind for... something.

Pain shot through Micah's skull as Garrin bluntly shoved through memories, both old and new. Powerless to stop the assault, Micah's consciousness withdrew, attempting to hold the fraying ends of his identity together. It seemed an eternity before Garrin finally extracted himself. As quickly as it began, the imposing presence lifted, and the pain began to recede, granting Micah relief from the shocking strength of the dark mage's mind.

How had he done that?

"My, my," said Garrin with a sneer. "You are quite the surprise, Micah *Stormcrown*."

How did he know my last name?

"You are indeed immune to the deadly Mist and have seen many of its beasts. Though far less than you realize," he continued. "And I wonder how much you truly know of yourself."

"What was that?" Micah wheezed as he struggled to lift his head. "What did you do to me?"

"I left no lasting harm," answered Garrin quietly. "My abilities far exceed your own. Your experiences are certainly... enlightening as to the world I now find myself in, however. I thank you for that."

"What do you mean?"

"You need not concern yourself, Stormcrown," he hissed.

"Just who are you?" Micah yelled at the frightening man. Garrin smirked at his helplessness.

"One looking to cleanse your pitiful world of the terrors you cower from. You think Mist Wolves are the greatest danger the Mist brings?" he scoffed. "Your lands are young and naïve. You have not tasted the full power of the curse. Not yet."

Micah's mind swirled with confusion. *He's speaking in riddles.* Fuming, he glanced towards the spot in the clearing where he'd first seen the man.

A body. The woman who screamed.

Micah gasped. "What did you do?" Garrin's brow twitched, acknowledging the source of the question.

"Nothing the curse hadn't already done," he said dismissively. "She was the one I came to find. Only the Mist found us first." Then, in a chilling voice, "She won't be a danger any longer."

"What do you mean?"

He laughed, a dark, sinister laugh, before his eyes renewed their hostility towards Micah. "You are blind, Micah Stormcrown. Yet, in time, you will see. Maybe then, with your eyes open, you'll be of some use to us."

"Us?" Micah asked, bewildered, scanning the clearing.

Garrin sighed. "I tire of this. Return to your treasure and complete the mission set before you. We'll meet again soon enough."

"Explain yourself!" Micah shouted, stepping towards him.

Garrin held up his hand. Micah rushed to close off his mind from another probe. Instead, a pale, swirling energy formed around Garrin's palm. Instantly, an invisible force smashed into his chest, sending Micah flying through the air. He collided with a tree, the breath knocked from his lungs.

"Begone, Stormcrown!" Garrin commanded, his voice filled with rage. "Do not test my mercy."

Micah staggered up, backing away from the powerful mage. He took one last look at the woman, realizing there was nothing he could do. She looked young, normal. How was she a danger?

Micah shot a final, furious scowl at Garrin and turned, shoving his way back through the brush. He felt utterly humiliated. He had led dozens of men in battle, fought unnamed creatures, and protected entire villages from unnatural horrors. Yet, here he was, tossed around like a rag doll and his mind infiltrated by a simple man with a fancy sword.

Maybe not so simple, he sulked, nursing his pride.

Crashing out of the foliage and onto the road, Micah stomped back to the wagon. He slumped back into the seat, steering Edoran onto the path. As much as he hated it, Garrin was right—he had his own task to complete. Maybe Greenwatch would hold some answers to understanding just who the mage was.

⎯⎯◆◯◆⎯⎯

The rest of the day passed quickly, though Micah no longer enjoyed the sights of the Greenwood, thanks to his dour mood. As the sun set beyond the sheltering trees, he made camp in a clearing just off the road. He was asleep in seconds, exhausted from a day of riding and the intense encounter with the dangerous mage.

The next morning, Micah rose early, hurriedly packing his gear back into the wagon. He was ready to put the lush surroundings of the woods behind him as thoughts of the city crept into his mind. Micah had first been through Greenwatch years ago when he was still adventuring in his youth. He'd sought passage to the Anderfalls in its ports and was lucky enough to find a lone sailor willing to risk the voyage. He was a salty, weathered old man, though there had been a certain likability to him.

But of the city itself, Micah recalled very little of interest, neither from then nor his time in the Guard. The streets were lined with sturdy, stone-built houses, many with multiple floors and clean exteriors that suggested there was a fair amount of wealth to be found in the city. There was only a single massive tavern to accommodate the bustling port. Micah had stopped at its gloomy bar briefly in his search for a shipmaster.

Whoever this Tomas fellow is, likely someone there will know of him.

Who was he really, though, Micah wondered. Was he one of the mysterious figures looking to end the Mist, as Asher had hinted, or just another middleman in a vast network of hidden faces and secret powers?

The road passed over a section of small brooks and bridges before Micah noticed a growing light in the distance, like that at the end of a tunnel. As he drew closer, the encompassing branches above lessened, allowing hints of the clear sky. For a moment, he caught sight of the vast mountains ahead, the range bordering the northern end of the Greenwood. He was almost through.

As Micah broke out from under the massive trees, the ground transformed into a terrain similar to the forest's southern border. Hardy plants and prickly trees vied for soft soil on the rocky cliffs at the base of the mountains. The fertile undergrowth of the Greenwood was quickly replaced with stony outcroppings and boulders as the path turned sharply right. Luckily for Edoran, there was no steep slope to climb here. The road wound its way around the base of the mountain range, hugging its side before entering the plains leading to Greenwatch.

The energy of the forest was still heavy on Micah as they left its sheltered depths, but the environment had changed dramatically. Without the cover of the woods, all signs of animal life vanished. Among the rocky slopes and crags, few birds called out except for an occasional hawk. The world regained its ominous tone, saturated with the dire effects of the Mist.

At least the sky was clear, and the sun was bright.

The afternoon wore on as the road traveled east. After several hours, the bumpy path slowly made a turn to the north, signaling the end of the protective wall surrounding the Greenwood. Micah took one last glance back at the rich, green carpet laid out behind him, miles of trees swaying in the breeze of the dying day, before pressing forward and focusing his eyes on the desolate view that awaited.

As the day neared its end, Micah finally caught sight of the grassy plains. Greenwatch wasn't far now. Yet, judging by the location of the sun, it would be late in the night by the time he reached the gates, which would be closed, leaving him exposed to dangers in the open fields. Instead, he settled on searching for a place to rest for the evening before exchanging the sheltered bluffs for the dusty trail below.

A few moments later, Micah spied a large outcropping of rock jutting from a towering cliff. A space large enough for the wagon lay protected by the overhang, almost like an airy cave. He steered Edoran into the space. The ground was rough, with only a smattering of coarse grass. Any trees or solid wood were nowhere to be found, meaning no fire.

I guess neither of us will eat well tonight, he thought. *Still, at least we're shielded from any weather and predators lurking beyond the mountain.*

Micah unhitched Edoran and spread out his gear for the night. They had made good progress that day. The next, they would finally reach Greenwatch. He walked to the edge of the clearing, watching the fading sun dance off the rocky landscape.

Elowë, bring us safely to Greenwatch, he silently prayed, *and then speedily back to Fairhollow. Home.*

CHAPTER 16
THE LONELY CITY

MICAH ROSE JUST AS the morning light broke over the peaks of the mountains. The world was quiet, a slight fog filtering through the sleepy crags. Today, his strange journey would end, and he'd finally be rid of his treacherous cargo.

Micah smiled. At least Edoran was ready to go, too. Evidently, the poor beast wasn't enjoying the sparse accommodations.

With the wagon ready, he returned to the rocky road leading down a gentle slope to the open fields. It was a quick jaunt to the city, less than half a day. As the sun passed over the top of the endless range behind Micah, the trail changed from bumpy gravel to a wide dusty road, heading west northwest towards Greenwatch.

The fields resembled those near Fairhollow—an endless sea of coarse, wild grasslands billowing in the chilly morning breeze. The only sign of life appeared when a lone crow rose out of the weeds, its solitary call searching for companionship that had long since fled the encroaching dangers. As time passed, the harsh grass turned into patchy fields, the first hint of civilization in days. However, these fields had long since been abandoned. Weeds and spiky grass had overtaken their rich soil, the owners having fled to the safety of Greenwatch's walls, or perhaps worse. As Micah surveyed the bleak span of forgotten farmland, sadness filled his heart. Once upon a time, fields like these were bustling with farmers and farmhands, lovingly tending to rows upon rows of crops. Their work brought meals to people throughout Karthmoor. Now the Mist had ruined this peaceful land, corrupting its purpose. Like Fairhollow, the barren plains had been forever changed.

Gradually, the fields showed signs of cultivation. Sparse crops appeared, proof some farmers were still operating, even if only on a small scale. As Micah reached the top of a small hill, he spotted a shape in the distance. The thin dirt road converged with a dark, blurry mass on the western horizon.

Greenwatch.

He ushered Edoran on, ready to reach his goal and, hopefully, a good meal and a warm bed. Towering walls of large stone blocks sharpened as they came into view, a sight which put Fairhollow's makeshift defenses to shame. Drawing even closer, Micah noticed the wide, wooden gates were shut. Long gashes marred its once-pristine insignia—a large oak tree atop a jutting rock. Normally, that would have been an odd sign in the middle of the day, but considering the times, it seemed only practical. At that distance, the great stones fortifying the city appeared solid and immovable, but many bore large scratch marks. Others were missing entire chunks. Clearly, powerful forces had assaulted the city.

As Micah passed rows of new wheat and potatoes nearer to the city, he spied farmers sporadically tending the fields. Occasionally, a soldier in variegated armor appeared, patrolling the fields and watching for any signs of danger beyond the swaying harvest. Many of the laborers looked up from their work, the shock of seeing a traveler plain on their dirty, downcast faces. Micah quickly drew near to the gate, the watchman above following his approach.

"Who goes there?" the defender shouted down, a musket gripped tightly in his hands. He was young, with a scraggly beard and head of shaggy, rust-colored hair, along with a general look of exhaustion.

"I'm Micah Stormcrown of Fairhollow. I have a delivery for Tomas, a resident of your great city," Micah answered back.

"A delivery?" he mocked, scowling. "Of what? Silver cutlery? Fine jewels? Scented perfume?"

Micah stifled a scowl, pushing aside his annoyance. "I cannot say. It's a private package for him."

"No one comes to Greenwatch, certainly no merchants," the man retorted, "and you make for a dangerous-looking merchant at that."

"What's going on here?" a voice called from the wall.

"Sir!" The watchman turned around with a salute. A second man appeared, leaning over the edge of the rampart. He was older, a little beyond Micah's age. Long, dark hair hung over his weathered face as he looked down with a frown. Guarded eyes slowly passed over Micah's cart. Although the stone wall blocked most of him, Micah could tell the man wore the scaled officer's armor of the Karthmoor Guard.

"Who comes to Greenwatch, traveler? And how in Elowë's name have you survived?" the officer calmly asked.

"Micah Stormcrown, a protector of the village of Fairhollow, sent to deliver a private package to Tomas, a resident of your city."

"Stormcrown?" The man straightened in surprise. "As in Warden Stormcrown?"

"Formerly, yes."

"I apologize then, sir." The officer nodded. Then, turning around, he shouted, "Open the gates!"

The great wooden gates slowly opened, creaking in protest. Micah prodded Edoran through the opening into a modest plaza inside the entrance. Beyond it, a cobblestone street lined with homes ran due west before terminating at a market square in the distance.

The man in Guard armor, along with the watchman, descended a row of stairs at the edge of the plaza, making their way towards the wagon as Micah disembarked. Curious citizens in faded tunics and cotton dresses appeared along the sidewalks, groups of men and women whispering and pointing at the rare sight.

"Welcome to Greenwatch, Warden Stormcrown." The officer saluted. "We're honored to receive such a renowned guest, sir."

"I'm grateful." Micah saluted back. "But remember, I'm retired. My Guard days are long behind me."

The man smiled. "Even so. You're always a Guard, sir, and you far outrank any of the soldiers here."

"Some of the western garrison survives?" he asked, excited.

"Some, though we've lost many. Forgive my manners. I'm Captain Logan, interim leader of the Greenwatch garrison. This is Rawls, one of our best watchmen." He motioned to the other man Micah had seen on the wall.

"Sir," Rawls began with a salute, "Please forgive my outburst. If I'd known..."

Micah waved his hand. "No need. You're all under a lot of stress." Turning back to Logan, he asked, "You said you were the interim leader?"

"You may recall the western garrison was formerly led by Colonel Clovis. Unfortunately, he was slain in an ambush several months back."

"So, the command falls to you."

"Under normal circumstances," replied Logan. "But these are strange times, and our governess has her own ideas on how to defend the city." He looked down the main road at the gathering crowd.

Governess? Last Micah knew, Governor Beckett was presiding over Greenwatch.

"Speaking of which, it's my duty to escort you to her. Rawls will see your wagon moved to the stables and your horse taken care of."

Micah nodded. "Of course."

"Follow me, please." Logan motioned toward the street as Rawls led Edoran and the wagon away. The crowd parted, shuffling towards the narrow sidewalks as the pair stepped onto the cobblestone. As they passed row after row of houses, Micah couldn't help but notice their condition. Many of them were quite grand. Beautiful craftsmanship decorated the timber framing of some, while others were built of fascinating hues of stone. Their slanted shingled roofs towered over the road. Yet, for all their meticulous detail, the signs of wear and deterioration were present on nearly every structure. Loose shutters and windowsills creaked in the faint breeze. Several of the stone houses had missing sections, the blocks loosening over time and crumbling off their frame.

"We've seen better days," Logan remarked, noticing his inspections. "We're under almost constant attack, leaving little time for routine upkeep on everything from family homes to infrastructure. Our exterior defenses are top priority. All spare materials are directed towards patching our fortifications."

Micah nodded sadly. "I understand. In Fairhollow we erected palisade walls. Any new timber we brought in from Binthir Forest went there first, before the remnants were sent to the houses."

"Hard times indeed," he quietly concurred.

The cobblestone diverged as they arrived at the town square. It was a wide space of large tiled stones; its edges ringed with more timbered homes and shops. Identical streets bordered the square, with branching roads spreading out in the cardinal directions. The middle of the square contained a chaotic maze of street vendors and carts, many of which were barren, the demand for luxury goods or trinkets having long since disappeared. In the center of it all stood a solitary statue of a soldier in gleaming plate armor, sword in hand, watching the southern horizon. From his time in the Guard, Micah recognized it as a memorial to the valiant men who gave their lives in Karthmoor's struggle for independence from the Hamid Empire in the distant past.

Logan ushered him through the maze of stalls, curious eyes staring as he passed. For an open market, the square was oddly quiet, the normal shouts of vendors enticing passing residents subdued below their normal volume. The looks on the faces around Micah were heavy with exhaustion, a hint of despair masked faintly with grim determination. Their heartache recalled that of dozens of friends back home. All people, though leagues apart, seemed to share in the same troubles, just as Asher had said.

At the opposite end of the square, the cobblestone continued a short distance before ending at a large, gated mansion. They hurried down the street, passing more rows of homes and side streets before arriving outside the mansion's wrought-iron gate. The smell of salt filled the moist air as waves crashed in the distance.

"This is Farhaven Manor." Logan gestured. "It's been the home of Greenwatch's governors for generations."

A wild tangle of gardens overgrown in their neglect surrounded the stately building. Ornate stonework and carvings adorned the mansion's exterior and balconies, many of their sharp angles worn down by years of harsh weather blowing in from the Ander Sea. A tired, faded spirit hung over the area, the same feeling echoed in its citizens.

Logan led Micah through the creaking gate and up a flight of stone steps to the gnarled entrance. As he ushered him in and shut the door, Micah was quickly engulfed in gloom. There were no lights burning inside the grand entryway, only scant daylight filtering in through the windows behind him. Ahead, he saw two sets of stairs leading to the floor above, a rich, dark carpet flowing upward between gilded rails that twisted in a delicate and fascinating design. A large, crystalline chandelier hung silently from the molded ceiling, its multitude of lights extinguished. Between the stairways along the plastered wall, a large pair of white doors, as well as smaller ones near the foot of the stairs, hid additional rooms and halls from view.

"This way." Logan beckoned. He pulled the golden latch on one of the central doors, and light spilled into the entry. The next area was a large, warmly lit hall decorated with countless paintings and sculptures. Towering marble columns with twisting vines reached all the way to the ceiling, another story above them. A walkway ran around the perimeter of the second floor, displaying more murals and works of art. Iron chandeliers and sconces flickered with candlelight, bathing the room in their glow. A plush train of rug flowed from the painted doors to an identical set at the opposite end, where a pair of serious-looking sentries stood guard.

As they walked across the hall, Micah marveled at the artwork. There were countless portraits of men and women, all dressed in extravagant finery and dresses, with serious expressions. Some wore Guard formal attire.

"A history of Greenwatch's leaders," Logan explained. "Below each, you'll find a plaque with important events or contributions each made to our city. A way to never forget where we come from and what our forbearers sacrificed." As they reached the opposite end, the guards saluted. Logan saluted back before opening the door.

As Micah walked through, he nearly collided with another man. Micah looked up, startled by his massive size. His scarred face and arms were covered in harsh blue markings, their angled patterns signifying some exotic purpose. Dark red hair tied back in a weaving tail covered his head, and a similarly large beard ended with a curious knot. Heavy chain armor interspersed with rich furs covered his legs and chest. A cloak of the same fur lay across his wide shoulders. His thick, iron boots clanged loudly against the tiled floor as he took a step forward. His hands tensed, ready to grasp the massive battleaxe strapped to his back.

An Anderfall warrior! Micah stepped back and placed a hand on his sword.

"Just a traveler, Hogrom," said Logan quickly from behind. "We're here to see the governess." Hogrom squinted at Micah for a moment longer before relaxing, slightly.

"Pass," he gruffly declared and stepped aside.

Looking beyond the imposing warrior, Micah discovered a span of columns continuing across the empty room. Though the chamber was smaller than the previous, a massive bay of windows towering at the far end lent additional depth to the space. Outside, an endless sea of blue rolled far below in the bright light of the day. A simple throne of chiseled rock rested below the center of the wall of glass where a woman with gray hair, exquisitely styled, sat patiently in the seat. A silken dress covered her from shoulder to toe, its design and material hinting at immense wealth. Expensive gold jewelry adorned her neck and fingers, each probably worth more than a farmer's decade of earnings. Her weathered and serious face never left Micah as he approached. Piercing eyes slowly passed over him, attempting to ascertain his purpose.

A second Anderfall warrior stood beside her throne, his garb similar to Hogrom's, though his dark hair was loose around his face with a single, braided strand on one side. A thick, short beard covered his strong jaw.

Logan moved in front of Micah, bowing respectfully before the woman.

"Lady Mira," he announced, "I present Micah Stormcrown, former Warden of the West and defender of Karthmoor. He comes with a delivery from distant Fairhollow for one of our citizens." He then turned to Micah. "Warden Stormcrown, this is Lady Mira, Governess of Greenwatch and leader of our people."

Micah stepped forward and gave his own respectful bow to the governess.

"Welcome to our humble city, Warden," said Lady Mira, her voice tinged with years of wisdom. "Your name is well known here."

"You'll have to forgive me," he replied. "I did not know Greenwatch had a new leader."

"You were familiar with my husband, Governor Beckett, I imagine."

"Yes, though I didn't have the pleasure of meeting him in person. I learned of him and of his bravery during the... Anderfall incident." Micah glanced briefly at the warrior standing next to her.

"Indeed, my husband was a valiant man," she murmured, her eyes softening. "Though we were unprepared for the arrival of the Mist. The monsters of the curse claimed his life not long after it appeared."

Micah bowed his head. "My deepest apologies. He will be remembered for his courage and leadership."

"No doubt," said Lady Mira. "After his passing, and with communications to the Conclave cut off, I was left to fill the role of leadership. We have had our issues, though I like to think we have fared better than many others."

"It looks like Greenwatch is still strong," said Micah approvingly. "It'll be welcome news in Fairhollow. We could use some hope."

"I had not thought the smaller villages capable of surviving," she replied, bending forward in her seat. "It is good to know our people are resilient."

A moment passed in the empty room.

"Speaking of your village," Lady Mira continued, "what errand brings you this far?"

"I came on behalf of a merchant who stopped in Fairhollow," Micah began. "He was traveling from Edros with a shipment for one of your citizens, Tomas."

Her eyebrow jumped at the mention of his name.

"Do you know him?"

"Only by extension. His employers are under my protection. Deliver whatever it is they have requested as soon as possible."

"His employers?" Micah asked, burning with curiosity.

"It is not my knowledge to give," she curtly responded. "As long as their work does not endanger my city, I will uphold the bargain my husband made. Should they find you worthy, perhaps they will reveal more."

He conceded, not wanting to insult his new host. "Do you know where I can find Tomas?"

"I do not, but speak with Teigan, our tavern keeper. He usually knows the comings and goings of our various citizens."

"Thank you."

"Well then," she said, smoothing her dress, "unless there is something further to discuss, I have other items I must attend to."

"Of course. Thank you for your time, Lady Mira."

"And you for your assistance." She nodded. "Greenwatch is open to you, Warden Stormcrown. I ask only that you lend your help wherever your expertise can strengthen us. Your experience could be vital to our survival."

Logan returned to Micah's side, and they both bowed before exiting the room.

As they walked back through the gallery hall, Logan turned to him. "She's right in that Teigan can likely point you to your man. I don't know this Tomas fellow, but everyone passes through his tavern at one point or another. He'll know him. I can accompany you there, if you'd like."

"Sure," Micah agreed. "It sounds like my delivery is important to the governess, as well."

"If it involves her researchers, well... Only defending Greenwatch is higher in priority to her," said Logan.

"Researchers? What do you know?"

Logan shrugged. "Only rumors. Story is Governor Beckett made a deal with a group of mages to provide shelter, hidden away from prying eyes in Starkhaven. They paid Greenwatch a pretty sum—likely the governor got his cut too." They passed through the gloomy foyer, exiting back onto the cobblestone street.

"But what they're doing or researching, I haven't the faintest clue," Logan continued as they headed towards the town square. "Even as captain of the guard, I have no idea where they're located because it isn't in official records. Honestly, it hasn't been a priority for me to step on the governess' toes over this. I've had more important troubles."

"I understand. Protecting the city from the Mist is a never-ending task."

As they reached the northern edge of the square, Logan led Micah towards a dim storefront that Micah recalled was the tavern. Suddenly, a boy with shaggy, dirty hair and worn clothes pulled on the back of his shirt. Micah spun around. The boy looked to be about thirteen or fourteen.

"Sir, are you really from the outside?" the boy asked excitedly.

Micah smiled. "I am. You can call me Micah."

"I'm Darian. Rawls said you came from outside, but everyone thought it was a joke."

"Leave the man alone, Darian." Logan scolded him. "Shouldn't you be at the bakery?"

Darian stepped back, looking embarrassed. "Master Winslow sent me to fetch some supplies, but they weren't ready yet," he answered.

"Well, go check again. If he trusted you with an errand, make sure you keep that trust."

"Yes, sir." Darian dashed away, disappearing into the sprawling market. Logan shook his head and sighed as he watched the boy vanish.

"That boy is nothing but trouble. It was good of Winslow to take him in, but he still spends all his days out on the street."

Micah raised a brow. "He's an orphan?"

"Aye, parents were killed in an ambush during the harvest last year," Logan explained. "Whole pack of Mist Wolves. Terrible ordeal. The boy lived for months on his own in his parents' house or in the alleys. Got into trouble for stealing food from several of the merchants but always managed to escape. Eventually, enough of them complained that Lady Mira was ready to arrest the lad, except Winslow found him first. Offered him shelter, meals, and a job at his bakery if Darian would give up stealing. The boy agreed, though it hasn't tempered his inclination to roam the streets."

Turning back to the tavern, a faint glow emanated from its dark, dusty windows. The muffled din of shouts and laughter could be heard even in the busy street. Logan pushed open the heavy wooden door, and the clamor spilled into the road. Inside, the tavern was a jostling mess of tables and patrons, the crowded room filled with noise, smoke, and the smell of ale. The space was massive compared to Delvin's modest enterprise. An immense square of counters sat in the middle, a large chandelier fashioned out of deer and elk antlers suspended above. In the middle of it all, two men were busy passing mugs and refilling the glasses of impatient drinkers.

Logan and Micah maneuvered their way across the room towards the bar. Chairs scraped loudly on the wooden floor as they squeezed through the gloom. Several patrons called out to Logan, and he waved back, his voice drowned out by a sea of guests and the occasional drinking song. It might have been dark times, but that appeared to only be a boon to the tavern business.

As they reached the bar, a stocky middle-aged man with frazzled hair and bushy sideburns made his way to them, continuing to hand out drinks as he came.

"Welcome, Captain!" he shouted above the noise, "and welcome, Warden! We're mighty honored to have you in our humble establishment."

"Word travels fast here," Micah observed, shaking the man's ale-soaked hand as he laughed.

"I may serve the finest drinks in the western province, but information is my true business. The name's Teigan, but you can call me Teig. Proprietor of the Seagull's Roost. What can I get you, gentlemen?"

"Two of your finest ales and a room for our guest," said Logan, leaning against the bar. "Plus, some information."

Teig nodded. "Comin' right up. I'll have Percy prepare a room upstairs." He turned around to the other bartender while still pouring a couple of drinks. Percy nodded and finished serving the patrons in front of him before heading towards a set of stairs along the far wall. Teig returned a moment later with two overflowing mugs of ale, a rich scent wafting from their depths. Micah took a quick swig of the stout brew.

This would give Delvin a run for his money.

"So," said Teig after refilling the mugs of the men around them, "what can I help you with?"

"I'm looking for a man by the name of Tomas," Micah loudly replied over the noisy bar. A nervous look crossed Teig's face.

"The mages, eh?" Teig rubbed his neck. "Normally, I'd charge for that sort of information, but I'll give you this one. Maybe it'll help Greenwatch." He motioned to an empty table a good distance from the rest of the rowdy patrons. The three took their seats as Teig began.

"There's only one Tomas I know in Greenwatch. He comes in occasionally for a drink but always alone. Seems normal enough, but I always get a strange feeling around him—and not just because he's a mage," Teig's voice dropped to a whisper. "I get the sense he's waiting for someone."

"Probably Asher," Micah murmured to himself. "Do you know where I can find him?"

Teig shook his head. "That I don't. The fellow always seems to just disappear. Your best chance is to catch him here. It's been a while since I've seen him, so he's likely to show up soon. Usually, he comes late afternoon, right before the evening crowd makes their way in."

Micah nodded, grateful for the insight.

"I'm sorry I don't have more information for you," Teig finished, frowning. "Those mages are an odd bunch. Most folk want nothing to do with magic or that sort of thing. If they want to stay out of sight, people 'round here are more than happy to forget about 'em."

Micah shook Teig's hand, and he returned to the bar.

"I guess it's a waiting game," he said to Logan.

"Seems as much, and unfortunately, I need to return to my duties. Unless there's anything else I can do to help?"

"No, thank you. I can manage." Micah shook his hand as well, and Logan rose to leave.

"If you do learn any more about the mages, I'd be interested to know," Logan added. "The more I think about it, the more uncomfortable I am not knowing who exactly is living inside our walls. Just don't raise the ire of Lady Mira, if you would."

Micah nodded. "I'll be careful. Thanks, Logan."

The captain made his way across the raucous room and disappeared outside. Micah settled back, finishing his ale. Before long, Percy returned from upstairs and made his way over to the table.

"Your room is ready whenever you need it," he said, handing Micah a small metal key. "Second door on the left at the top. Let me know if you need anything else."

Micah thanked him, and he returned to assisting Teig at the bar. Micah figured he had at least an hour or two before Tomas arrived. He finished his ale and left the noisy tavern.

By the position of the sun, he reckoned there was plenty of time to check on Edoran and the wagon. Back near the gate, Micah quickly located the stable where he found Edoran contentedly grazing on fresh hay in his stall. The wagon was parked under an awning next to the stable, its contents untouched. He checked the small lock Frederic had placed on the iluvan chest, verifying it was secure before grabbing some of his gear to take back to his room.

After shuffling up the tavern's narrow stairwell, Micah came to the rickety door of his new lodgings. Inside, the room was small but cozy. A simple pine dresser sat next to a matching short table and chair along one side. A long, soft bed stretched against the other. It would be nice to enjoy the comforts of a real mattress again. He dropped his gear and headed back to the bar.

As Micah took a seat at the table from earlier, it appeared the room had cleared a little, the midday patrons having grudgingly returned to their work. Teig brought over another ale as Micah settled in to wait.

The hours passed slowly in the dim room. Each time the tavern door opened, Micah jumped, hoping his contact had arrived. However, each time, Teig simply glanced over and shook his head. A warm drowsiness gradually washed over him as the afternoon waned.

No more ale, Micah silently declared, not wanting to miss Tomas entirely.

Soon after, the outside world appeared again as a cloaked man slipped through the door, a hood drawn over his face. A peculiar feeling shook Micah from his dozing. Teig turned to him and nodded.

It's him.

Tomas moved quietly along the edge of the tavern, taking a seat at a shadowy table in the far corner with a perfect view of the room. Micah rose from the table, slowly heading over.

The mage's gaze immediately locked onto him. From the faint glow of the candle on the table, Micah could make out a long, thin face within the hood. A dark, pointed beard rested above his chest and deep brown eyes flashed warily in the flickering light. His arms were folded across a thin torso, a strange tan robe covering his features. Compared to the rest of the patrons, he looked starkly out of place. Micah stopped in front of his table.

"Yes?" he said bluntly.

"Tomas?"

The mage shifted in his seat with a defensive glare before shrugging with a hint of suspicion. "Perhaps. I don't know you, however."

"Micah Stormcrown. You look like you're waiting for someone."

His eyebrows flickered in surprise before he quickly concealed it.

"I recognize your name, but no games, Warden," he bristled. "State your purpose."

"I have a shipment for you. One that the merchant, Asher, was to deliver before he was injured," Micah explained.

Tomas' brow furrowed.

"If what you say is true, this is highly unusual," said Tomas cautiously. "The delivery is the first in a very long time. Regardless, our merchants are expected to remain confidential. If Asher has broken that trust, there will be... unpleasant consequences." He paused for a moment. "I'm surprised he entrusted this journey to you."

"Asher revealed nothing of your organization," Micah quickly added. "And the contents of your chest were kept confidential beyond myself and a trusted friend."

"Hmm." Tomas rubbed his beard. "Unfortunate, though we may overlook this mistake if what you say about his actions is true. Where is the chest now?"

"Still in Asher's wagon, which I've brought. I can take you to it or move it to wherever you require."

"No need. We know where it will be kept," he mysteriously responded. "My associates will collect it." From within the folds of his robe, Tomas pulled out a heavy bag of coin and passed it to Micah. "This would've been the merchant's payment, though it appears to belong to you now. We appreciate your... assistance." Tomas pushed back his chair and turned towards the door.

"What will you do with the iluvan?"

Tomas froze. He whipped around, his dark eyes flashing. "Do not speak of the contents," he hissed. "It is no concern of yours."

"Lady Mira requested my support in keeping Greenwatch safe," Micah retorted. "I know the dangers of your shipment, especially the black ones. They're a threat to everyone here."

His eyes widened in momentary surprise. "You may grasp at strands of truth," he slowly warned, "but you do not understand the reality of our research."

"Then help me to."

"That is not for me to decide. The authority lies with Lady Mira and the director. If the governess believes you could be an asset in our work, she will confer with my leaders. Otherwise, our business is finished."

Tomas wheeled around and strode across the room. As the tavern door slammed behind him, Micah scrambled to follow. He dashed into the street, looking around wildly. Tomas was nowhere to be found.

Teig wasn't kidding when he said the man vanishes.

Micah raced to the stables, hoping to catch Tomas' associates. He arrived within minutes of leaving the tavern, rushing to inspect the wagon. He immediately discovered Asher's curious chest had disappeared.

How had he moved so quickly?

With his suspicions growing and no other leads, Micah's only option was to speak with Lady Mira again. He knew he may have finished his task, but the safety of hundreds could be at stake.

Leaving the stables, Micah noticed the daylight was fading rapidly. He would have to wait until morning for an audience with the governess. He grudgingly made his way back to the tavern, attempting to calm his worries with the sights of Green-watch. At least there was a warm meal and a soft bed ahead.

CHAPTER 17
THE REQUEST

LIGHT SPILLED THROUGH THE window of Micah's small bedroom above the tavern as the sun broke over the horizon. He was already up, busily dressing and gathering his things. He hoped to catch the governess first thing before her day invariably filled with distractions.

With his gear ready, Micah rushed downstairs, grabbing a small breakfast of bread and porridge from Teig before heading out into the chilly morning air. The sky was cloudy, the smell of the sea heavy on the breeze. A flock of seagulls darted above, calling out as they headed west towards the harbor. He pulled his leather coat closer and crossed the street after a wagon filled with grain bags passed.

The roads were swarming with citizens making their way to work. Micah passed a mob of groggy men and women in worn, dusty clothes, shuffling down the cobblestone street towards the city gate and fields beyond. In contrast, another group of mostly men with warm, knitted caps and coats headed in the opposite direction, the dockworkers and sailors preparing for another day along the ocean. Micah wove his way through the busy streets, heading for Farhaven Manor.

Inside the silent mansion, he returned to the gallery hall. The two soldiers were still posted outside the throne room and saluted as Micah approached.

"Warden, sir," one of them addressed him, "the governess has asked not to be disturbed."

"It's important to the security of Greenwatch," Micah urged.

The guard looked hesitantly at his counterpart.

"I'll take full responsibility," Micah added.

"Very well," he said slowly. "As you will, sir."

Micah passed through the doors into the dim throne room. The space was empty except for the unnamed Anderfall warrior from before, standing patiently near the wall of glass. Micah crossed the room as the warrior watched him, silent.

"I need to speak with the governess."

The warrior remained mute and completely still. His intimidating face blank.

Micah stared back, expecting an answer he refused to utter. Just when he was about to give up, the warrior finally spoke.

"She is not here," came his deep voice.

"Can you let her know?" Micah politely asked.

"No."

"What do you mean, no?"

"She is not here," he repeated.

"Can you find her?"

"No."

"Why not?" Micah challenged, his frustration building.

"I am not a messenger," he said matter-of-factly.

Micah stared at him, struggling to understand his foreign mind.

"Who can I send then?" Micah relented.

After a moment, the Anderfall answered, "Yourself."

"Me? Why me?"

"You are a messenger." His face remained serious, but Micah swore he glimpsed humor in his eyes.

"A messenger?" he repeated, baffled.

The warrior was still for a second, then shifted slightly. "You deliver things, do you not?"

"I brought that delivery to Greenwatch, sure, but that doesn't make me a messenger," Micah argued.

"I do not see the difference."

He sighed, annoyed. "Then I suppose I'll go wander the manor."

As Micah started to walk away, the Anderfall spoke again. "She will return. Soon."

Micah stopped, gritting his teeth.

Why couldn't we have just started with that?

"Fine."

The warrior proved correct. After a few moments, a door on the side of the room opened as the governess and her other Anderfall bodyguard entered.

"Warden Stormcrown," she said. "Is there something you wish to discuss?"

Micah gave a small bow. "There is. It's important to Greenwatch's safety."

"You have my full attention then," Lady Mira replied as she took her seat.

"The mages in your city. Do you know what they are working on or what... materials they are requesting?"

"If I did, I could not say," she answered cautiously. "As it is, I truly have little insight into the details, only a vague explanation from their leader. Given your actions and deeds within the Guard, I trust you enough to share my knowledge." She dismissed her two guards, and they disappeared through the doors behind him.

"My husband originally offered the mages sanctuary for reasons unknown to me. This was before the Mist. I believe they were hiding from rival factions looking to steal their secrets," Lady Mira explained. "But once the Mist arrived, their purpose shifted. I know only that they are now studying the Mist, looking for ways to counteract it."

"Their research may pose a risk to the city," he responded. "I would ask to speak with their leader."

"Do you have evidence of such a risk?" Lady Mira demanded, leaning forward.

"Only the delivery I made. The contents of the chest they requested has the potential to draw the Mist."

"What were the contents?" Her voice and eyes hardened.

"Iluvan crystals."

"Iluvan?" she repeated, confused. "I'm afraid I do not see the connection. Iluvan crystals have been used for decades, including some throughout Greenwatch. How are they related to the Mist?"

"It's only certain ones," Micah explained. "The crystals can become corrupted, turning black and dangerous to the touch. These corrupted iluvan seem to draw the Mist."

Lady Mira sat back, deep in thought.

"There are scattered stories of accidents involving iluvan, but I am not aware of any issues in my city," she replied. "Do you believe these... black iluvan, were included in the mages' shipment?"

"I know for a fact they were."

"I see." She sighed, rubbing her brow.

"You have placed me in a difficult position, Warden," Lady Mira eventually began again. "I have a full assurance from the mages that their work is harmless and one day could provide a defense against the Mist. Yet you are telling me the opposite."

She was quiet for a moment, weighing the options in her mind. The only sound in the room was the faint crash of waves below.

"Very well," she concluded. "I will discuss the matter with them myself. I will also request you be allowed to speak with them after our conversation. Perhaps I have been naïve in my trust, believing my husband knew the entirety of the risk. Your investigation may shed some light on the situation."

"Investigation?"

"You may not report to me as part of the Guard, but I would like to officially request your service."

"I am willing to help however I can," Micah offered.

"Then I charge you, Warden, with ascertaining the truth behind these researchers," she commanded. "Uncover their true motives and goals, anything they may have kept from me, along with any risks they pose to my city. Inform me of your findings, with full detail, so I may lead my people in confidence."

Micah nodded. "As you wish."

"Excellent." She gave a small smile. "I will notify you of the outcome of our meeting. You should have an answer by midday."

Micah bowed again and took his leave. The Anderfall warriors returned as he exited, their threatening presence towering over him as they passed. With his business momentarily concluded, Micah left the manor, heading for the town square.

Instead of returning to the tavern, however, he decided to pass the time wandering the maze of streets in the sprawling city.

Micah passed dozens of shops and residences along the southern road from the square, its cobbled path eventually turning west as it sloped towards the harbor. Several of the buildings looked abandoned, their cracked windows and battered doors boarded up to deter inquisitive souls. His leisurely stroll ultimately ended at the top of a wide stairwell, its large stone balcony overlooking the harbor. A dozen ships were moored along the docks, captains shouting orders as deckhands moved loads of barrels and gear. Micah watched the sight for some time, enjoying the sea breeze of the cloudy day, the sound of the waves, and the call of gulls. It had been many years since he had lived near the coast. The view was fresh, invigorating.

After his rest, Micah retraced his steps up the winding main road towards town. Not far from the square, a delicious smell wafted through the air. The scent of warm bread and cinnamon filled his nose as he spotted the open door to a well-lit bakery.

This must be Winslow's shop, Micah thought as he stopped, weighing whether to buy one of the enticing sweets. *Yep.*

Inside, a variety of breads, rolls, and cakes adorned the shelves. A table in the center was piled high with an assortment of fresh cinnamon rolls and breakfast pastries, the source of the smell that had drawn him in.

"They're the best on Karthmoor," a small voice proclaimed. He turned around to find Darian, the boy from the road.

"Are they now?" said Micah with a grin. "What would you recommend, then?"

"Well..." The boy rubbed his chin, trying to appear professional. "The blueberry muffins are excellent, a specialty of Master Winslow's wife. However, I would go with the cinnamon rolls. I discovered an extra store of sugar in one of the old warehouses, so they're dripping in delicious frosting."

"A rare find indeed."

"I'm not a good baker," Darian admitted, "but I'm the best at finding things. Master Winslow wanted to make a batch, but it wasn't until I stumbled on the sack and brought it back that he was able to." A hint of pride filled the boy's voice as he spoke.

"Sounds like you make for a valuable assistant."

Darian beamed at the compliment.

"Would you like one?" he asked enthusiastically.

"Sure."

Darian dashed behind the counter, rummaging for a plate and utensils, as Micah took a seat at a small table near the window. The boy stopped at the display of treats, scouring for the most promising candidate. He gave a satisfied hum, plucking one from near the top before placing it on the plate and delivering it to Micah.

"Here you are, sir!" he said.

Micah tossed him a few coins, and his eyes widened at the tip. As Micah took a bite, Darian watched in eager expectation. Micah's mouth filled with the warm, sweet taste. Sugary cinnamon and gooey bread melting together in perfection. He gave a sigh of approval, and Darian grinned in triumph. It had been a long time since Micah had tasted such a delightful luxury. He motioned for Darian to take a seat.

"So, how do you like working at the bakery?" he asked as he enjoyed the roll.

"It's really great!" Darian answered earnestly. "Master Winslow's teaching me to make some of the simpler things and letting me put them out. I'm not as quick as he'd like, but he's a nice man. He doesn't like when I wander the streets, but I try to help by finding things for the shop."

"The streets are a hard place to live. It's good you've found a place here."

His bright face turned somber. "My momma and papa were killed by the Mist," he quietly replied. "I was on my own before Master Winslow took me in. I don't want to go back to living out there, but I still like to have adventures."

"I can understand that." Micah smiled. "I did a lot of adventuring when I was young. Just barely an adult, not many years older than you."

"I bet you saw lots of neat places!" said Darian, wiggling with excitement. "What kinds of people did you meet? Were there monsters? What about trolls or dragons?"

Micah laughed at his fervor.

"I met all sorts of people throughout many lands and saw many monsters. No dragons, I'm afraid, but a handful of trolls, certainly. I did my best to avoid those."

"That's good," he breathed. "Captain Logan says they're the most dangerous creatures on Karthmoor. I asked him if dragons were more dangerous, but he said they don't exist."

Micah grinned. "Captain Logan is a smart man, and most people will tell you dragons are just the stuff of stories. But Aldaria is a big place, with lands we've never been to. You never know what might call those home."

"I want to be the first to see them all!" Darian declared.

He chuckled. "Perhaps one day you will, but be patient. Grow strong with Winslow's help and then you'll be ready to face the world when you come of age."

"I will." Darian nodded with determination. Looking at him, Micah saw his own dreams and passion reflected in his youth.

That familiar thrill of discovery so clearly mirrored by the boy. It was encouraging to see another so willing to join the crusade that had defined his early life.

Micah finished the cinnamon roll, and Darian cleared the table, returning to his duties. Through the clouds outside, Micah judged the time to be near midday, the morning successfully passed after his stop at the bakery. With Darian distracted by a new customer, Micah rose to head for the tavern in the hope Lady Mira had already sent someone there to retrieve him. Instead, as he reached the bakery door, a massive shape blocked his exit.

It was the frustrating warrior from the manor.

"Looking for me?" Micah asked pointedly, crossing his arms.

"Yes," the Anderfall gruffly answered.

"I thought you weren't a messenger."

He frowned. "I am not. I serve as the governess directs."

"But she sent you?"

"Yes."

"Sounds like a messenger to me." Micah grinned.

The warrior continued to frown, but refused to be baited. "I am to accompany you to the mages," he explained.

"Accompany? Does she expect trouble?"

"I requested it."

"You requested it?" The shock was obvious in Micah's voice. "Why?"

"You are known to the Anderfalls," the warrior replied in his deep voice. "I am curious to see how the Warden of the West handles the warlocks."

"I'm known? What do you mean?"

He was silent for a moment.

"My clan knew the stories of your time on Endwaith. Of the Hunt of the Sharpclaw beside Clan Grimloth. When you became the leader of your warriors, many wished to test their strength against yours, though our chieftains denied them permission."

Micah wracked his brain, trying to remember what event the foreign warrior was describing. The name Endwaith was completely unknown to him, though he recalled visiting a Clan Grimloth while in the Anderfalls.

"I vaguely remember a hunt with Grimloth," he slowly began. "A massive bear had been preying on their flocks, so large they believed it was a demon. One of their warriors actually struck the killing blow, however."

"Even so," the Anderfall concluded, "you proved outsiders could show honor. You remained a... fascination for many young initiates to Clan Grimloth."

Micah marveled for a moment, stunned by the impact he'd left. *I had no idea my voyage made such a mark.*

"I'm humbled," he said, unsure of what to say.

"I am to accompany you to the warlocks," the warrior repeated after a moment. "When you are prepared."

"I'm ready, though, one question."

He looked at Micah with a quizzical expression.

"Do I get to know your name?"

"Kelj."

"I'm honored by our meeting, *knaerlck* Kelj." Micah placed his right fist across his left shoulder, the customary sign of a warrior's greeting in the Anderfalls.

"You remember." Kelj nodded in approval. "That is good. I am honored, knaerlck Stormcrown." He returned the gesture.

With that, he wheeled around and strode into the street. Micah followed quickly behind, trying to match his enormous stride.

Kelj led him back to the center of Greenwatch, turning towards Farhaven Manor.

Does the governess house them inside the manor? Micah wondered as they approached the gate.

Instead of heading up the stairs to the entrance, however, Kelj turned left, facing the tangled gardens. He pulled a torch from his belt and lit it from the lamppost on the street corner. Then he brushed aside the sprawling branches of towering shrubs and disappeared into the chaotic garden.

Micah shoved his way through the brush and tumbled onto a narrow dirt path. Limbs and weeds pressed in on every side, filling the air with the smell of decay and disuse. The colossal growth immediately darkened the light of the cloudy day. The jungle maze was like a dark, unsettling new world, the sounds of Greenwatch blocked by the thick, musty foliage.

Kelj plowed through the overgrowth, following the curious trail in the sea of faded green. Before long, the path widened, emptying into a small courtyard. An old stone fountain rising from the center stood dry, filled with vines and moss.

Kelj moved around the fountain to a spot where the path vanished again in a new tangle of shrubs. Micah chased after him, fearful of losing the warrior in the maze of plants. Several paces in, Kelj abruptly stopped.

An odd stone structure appeared beyond the foliage. Its exterior reminded Micah of an ornate mausoleum, completely out of place in a manor garden. Its thick stone door was shut tight. Kelj rummaged through the folds of the fur covering his shoulders and produced an ancient-looking key. He stepped forward, inserting the scraping metal into a small opening in the rock face. An audible crack sounded as he turned it. Kelj pushed against the ancient stone. For a moment, it refused to budge before finally giving way with a loud rumble. Kelj growled as he shoved the door aside, its massive weight fighting every inch.

Surely the mages don't use this route every time.

The stone swung open, revealing a darkened pit as dust spilled out into the dim light. Kelj motioned for him to lead.

"If you insist." Micah shrugged, unsure of what to expect. He faintly discerned a set of stairs only a few steps into the crypt. A handful of torches rested in a small barrel near the door. Micah grabbed one and lit it using Kelj's, took a deep breath, and then slowly entered the shadowy chamber.

CHAPTER 18
SHADOWS UNDER GREENWATCH

Micah's boots echoed awkwardly off the stone stairs as he descended the cramped space. The steps abruptly ended, replaced by a thin tunnel path. The chiseled stone of the mausoleum quickly gave way to dirt and rock, the underground path stretching into the blackness beyond the reach of their torches.

We must be below Farhaven Manor, he realized.

The dark, musty tunnel maintained a gentle downward slope as they trekked forward. Its winding path soon had Micah lost as to where he was in relation to the surface. Eerie rock walls seemed to press in as they descended deeper into the earth. Thankfully, the ceiling remained high enough for Micah to stand comfortably. Kelj was not so fortunate.

"Where are we headed, Kelj?" Micah asked the silent Anderfall behind him.

"I cannot say."

"Can't or won't?" he challenged.

"I cannot say because I do not know," said Kelj gruffly. "The governess only revealed where to begin."

"What is this place, then?"

"These tunnels pass under the breadth of the city. Escape passages for your rulers, should the need arise," he answered. "This one leads to the warlocks."

"So, there are others?" Micah replied, surprised.

"And other entrances," he added. "Well hidden."

Their hike continued, the endless shaft filing ever onward in the black void. An uneasy, tomb-like feeling settled over Micah. Only the sound of their muffled steps in the soft dirt echoed in the silence. The twisting trail remained unbroken; none of the other passages Kelj had mentioned connected to cause confusion.

After what felt like hours in the persistent dark, a faint light appeared beyond a curve in the path.

The surface? That can't be right. We haven't been going up.

As he moved closer, Micah realized the light emanated with a subdued, bluish hue, not the bright warmth of day. The sound of waves rose ahead. The air felt fresher, a dampness heavy on it. Moments later, they rounded a corner, and he found himself staring into a vast domed cavern. Soaring rock walls curved to where brilliant stalactites loomed above. A large pool of ocean spilled into the cave, the light of the sun beyond glowing faintly in the water as it passed through a small gap in the rock wall, too low for a boat to traverse. With the additional light, Micah's eyes adjusted, taking in the monumental span of the cavern.

Peering across the waves, he noticed the faint glow of torch-light dotting the far wall, where the rock had been excavated by unknown hands. A large, carved staircase, visible in the new light, led to a magnificent edifice with towering, bronze-hued metal doors that were sealed shut.

This must be where the mages are hiding.

They passed along the wide ledge ringing the cavern pool, heading for the structure. As they reached the ground in front of it, one of the doors screeched open, and the silhouette of a robed figure appeared, obscured by light from within.

"Welcome to our sanctuary, Warden Stormcrown," a low but familiar voice called out over the crashing waves of the cove. Tomas stood at the top of the steps, a guarded look on his face. Micah sensed Kelj tense next to him as he eyed the enigmatic mage. They climbed the wide stairs towards him. At the top, Tomas motioned them through the metal doors. Their size was enormous, even compared to Kelj's impressive height.

Inside, the sight of a large hall greeted Micah. Bright tapestries adorned with the symbol of a white hand with a star in its palm covered rows of high, stone pillars. Rich rugs blanketed the wide, polished floor. An array of halls and doorways branched off in every direction, hinting at the structure's immense size.

"Welcome to Underhaven," said Tomas from behind him. "Perhaps not the official name, but it seemed fitting, considering our location in relation to the manor above."

Micah nodded, thankful to have some semblance of bearing again.

Tomas led them across the lofty hall and into a smaller passage. Bright torches lined the corridor between solid wood doors along one side. As they walked through the silent space, Micah caught a glimpse of a sprawling room beyond a partially open door. A host of researchers were spread out across the floor, studying strange obelisks of pale stone and darkened glass that lined the walls, each taller than a man. The front of some were swung open, like an upright chest. Their unnatural appearance and design were unlike anything he had ever seen. As curiosity slowed his stride, the door abruptly shut.

"This way, please," Tomas called impatiently. The rest of the ancient doors remained closed as Micah chased after him, each concealing unspeakable mysteries from eyes looking to unravel their nameless secrets.

At the corridor's end, Tomas ushered them through the final door and into a small office lined with overflowing bookcases. A large, beautifully crafted desk sat near the far end, littered with an assortment of trinkets and arcane tools. The room was warm and cozy, a healthy fire burning in the carved stone fireplace to Micah's left. A woman stood near the desk, her back to them as they entered.

"Director." Tomas bowed as she turned around. The woman was middle-aged. The pale skin under her slender gray and blue robe showed hints of wrinkles, suggesting years spent in the study of magical arts. Dark, black hair was pulled into a tidy bun atop her head. Her narrow eyes had a curious slant to them, giving her a distinctly foreign appearance.

"Micah Stormcrown." She nodded. "Lady Mira speaks highly of you and your prior accomplishments. We're honored to receive such a distinguished guest to Underhaven."

"Thank you," he replied, unsure how to begin. "I realize this is probably quite unusual."

"You are correct, though we live in unusual times," she agreed, folding her hands behind her. "I'm Director Mai. Head researcher of the Heraldan Collective in Greenwatch and Master Sorceress of the Collective at large, though that will mean little to you."

"The Heraldan Collective?"

"Did Lady Mira not even reveal our name?" said Director Mai, incredulous. "I suppose I shouldn't be surprised. The governess has a distinct lack of enthusiasm for magical study, unlike her husband. Our request for privacy seems to have implied burying our existence outright."

"Perhaps you can enlighten me then."

The director nodded as she cleared her throat. "I cannot say more than what my predecessor explained to Governor Beckett when the original agreement was struck, but I will be as open as possible in the interest of... mutual cooperation," she began. "The Heraldan Collective is an organization of mages spanning the breadth of Edros in an effort to obtain, study, and unlock the secrets of magical artifacts scattered throughout our world. Our particular chapter was sent to Karthmoor decades ago, tasked by our master wizards with studying a singularly difficult and enigmatic technology that had been discovered many years before."

"Iluvan?"

"Not precisely," Director Mai answered, "though the iluvan are intricately connected. No, the focus on the iluvan came much later, once the Mist arrived, and a link between the arcane devices and the iluvan was discovered. The pressing dangers of the Mist encouraged a shifting of priorities, for the time being." Mai walked towards the door. "If you will follow me."

The director led them back to one of the closed doors they had passed in the hall. She pulled a large ring of keys from her waist and unlocked it with a dull click. Inside, no torches or sconces lit the small room, though the walls glowed brightly, illuminated by a dazzling blue light. Rows of heavy, oaken tables were filled with shards of iluvan, some held in strange metallic contraptions, while others lay exposed on stone trays and wooden containers. A couple of mages were busy at work, intently focused on iluvan crystals suspended by glass stands that magnified their crystalline features. One woman maintained a small flame from her hand underneath a crystal that reacted to the magic, intensifying its glow.

"This is our primary research lab," Director Mai explained as they entered. "It is through the hard work and dedication of our researchers and Ilumancers that we continue to unravel the mysteries behind the iluvan."

Micah glanced at Mai quizzically. "Ilumancers?"

"Mages with the ability to channel the power of iluvan without the use of devices," she explained. "They are quite rare. Only a couple among us possess the ability, but it is invaluable. Their connections to iluvan have provided the Collective much insight, including the dangerous link between it and the Mist. How the Mist is drawn to the darker crystals, the black iluvan."

"Then you know the danger this research places Greenwatch in," Micah pressed.

"We are fully aware of the threat," she retorted, "and we take every precaution when interacting with black iluvan to avoid triggering a beacon, as we call it. In any event, our research is primarily confined to natural iluvan, which has shown no indications of drawing the Mist."

"Then why continue to bring in black iluvan?"

"The source of our shipments does not inquire as to our specific needs. We simply work with whatever materials are sent."

Micah began to speak, but she quickly cut him off. "As I said, our research is less focused on black iluvan and more so on its sibling's practical applications."

"So, what else are shipments like Asher's used for?"

Mai shifted uneasily. "As I said before, the iluvan was not our original focus of study, nor is it our only directive. Before the Mist arrived, our previous director was tasked by the Archmage himself with studying a unique technology that could potentially alter the course of history. A device so powerful and with so many possibilities that it was sent here, to Greenwatch, far from prying eyes in Edros. In exchange for shelter and secrecy, Governor Beckett was generously compensated for his hospitality," Mai cautiously answered.

"And what is this technology?" Micah continued. "Was the governor aware of it?"

"In part, though sworn to secrecy with an unbreakable vow woven between him and my predecessor with arcane power," she said. "When our former director left and Lady Mira became the new governess, I renewed the pledge with her. Though in our current circumstances, I fear the risk of our secret being exposed is less immediate than the threat of the Mist."

"I'm here on the governess' behalf," Micah explained. "Anything you can tell me to put her mind at ease will only help your cause."

"I am aware of your role," she grumbled, "and I will show you our current work on the devices. The governess has already approved the general goal of our research. Perhaps this will assuage her. As her envoy, I expect you will keep this confidential. For her sake."

"Of course," said Micah, his curiosity burning.

Director Mai led them out of the iluvan room and farther down the hall. She stopped at another door, fiddling for the key.

Was this the open door from before?

As she unlocked the latch, Micah recognized he was looking back into the large chamber filled with the curious obelisks. Mai ushered them in, down a small set of stairs, and into the center of the room. A dozen researchers turned, eyeing them nervously.

"These are the apex of our work in Greenwatch." Mai slowly gestured. "Every ounce of sweat, every sleepless night. All of it is for unlocking the secrets these pods hold."

"What are they?" Micah asked, peering closer at the one near him.

Its odd, silvery-white exterior was polished smooth like fine marble, the stone glimmering in the light of the iron chandeliers. The device stood slightly taller than Kelj, its back cut at sharp angles and even sides that ended with a gap near the front, hinting at the device's ability to open. The stone slowly curved across the front, giving way to dark, smoky glass that adorned the top half like a strange window. A matching stone handle protruded from below the glass. Inside, the device appeared empty, more stone cut at an incline, a single slab large enough for a person to recline on. A metal grate near the bottom of the outside glowed with a silvery-blue light from within.

"A mystery no mind has been able to unravel for several lifetimes," Mai mused. "We call them time pods. In conjunction with natural iluvan, they have the ability, theoretically, to suspend a person in infinite stasis, placing them in a sort of slumber where they are kept alive for years—perhaps centuries or longer. The length of the stasis is correlated with the strength of the iluvan, hence a need to replace weaker crystals. In any event, the power of these time pods is unlike anything we've ever seen."

Micah's mind raced, considering the possibilities. "Amazing. And these were all found somewhere in Edros?"

"Actually, no," she confessed. "These pods were constructed by mages from the Collective years ago and brought to Karthmoor. Their design was inferred from the original time pod that was discovered. Though, where the original came from and where it is, I honestly cannot say. It was before my time and not something I was granted to know. Perhaps our former director had access to the information."

"So, the first researchers brought them?"

"Yes, and some came with Marinaya, the previous director. Additional ones came slowly through hired merchants, much like our iluvan today."

"The Collective can build them but don't understand them?"

Mai gave a short laugh. "Ironic, no? A network of the greatest minds in all of Aldaria, and the best we can do is imitate the real thing. From what little information we were given, the design was difficult, but not impossible, to replicate. But as to how it actually functions, our wizards are at a loss. We still don't fully understand the nature of the iluvan and its relationship to the device. Iluvan, for all its useful applications, remains an enigmatic force. Indeed, it was just but a few years ago that a third type of iluvan was discovered."

"A third type?" Micah echoed, curious.

She shrugged. "I'm not surprised you haven't heard. Iluvan is widely used but rarely understood. Before the Mist, researchers in western Edros discovered what they called 'white iluvan' within a lot they were excavating. Whereas natural and black iluvan already contain a store of energy that varies in size, it is said white iluvan is void of such power. Instead, it has the unique ability to absorb and store energy for later use."

"Really?" Micah's hand unconsciously reached for the keepsake around his neck, hidden under his shirt.

"If you believe the rumors. The extreme rarity of white iluvan makes it difficult to confirm, but its potential uses are immensely intriguing. Just think how the ability to store and replenish vast amounts of energy on demand could revolutionize how we view magical application!"

He nodded, not knowing what else to say.

"Unfortunately, we have none here, and that is beyond the scope of our work," Mai finished wistfully. "Instead, we have focused on bringing in more natural iluvan to further our current studies. And as the Mist has grown, these pods have revealed another important use."

Micah glanced over and noticed Kelj inspecting a pod. Suddenly, Kelj recoiled in surprise before lunging forward, cupping his hands around his eyes to peer into its depths.

"There are people in these pods, Warden!" Kelj hollered. "Greenwatch citizens." Micah swerved to Mai, furious.

"Explain yourself. Now."

"We do not harm anyone," said Director Mai slowly. "We are here to help these people."

"You failed to mention you were testing the pods on innocents. What have you done to them?" he demanded, his hand sliding towards his sword.

She quickly shook her head. "Please, Warden, let me explain. Some of these men and women have come voluntarily. Others were rescued from the Mist."

"What do you mean?"

"All of them, every one of these souls, are what we call Mist-marked. Perhaps you have encountered such people?" Mai said as Micah crossed his arms. "They are ordinary individuals who no doubt want to live simple lives. But for whatever reason, they are targeted by the Mist. The accursed fog would kill them instantly, should it reach them."

"I'm aware that the Mist targets certain people," he grumbled. His mind flashed back to Bolli, collapsed in the arms of his grieving wife. "But we could never determine a pattern. How have you identified the Mist-marked? And why put them in time pods?"

"I cannot reveal how they are identified," she adamantly replied. "Doing so could place these people in even more danger. Needless to say, the knowledge came from a source far away that nearly proved our undoing. Had the source possessed the patience to interrogate the unfortunate souls who brought us this ability, they most certainly would have discovered our location in Greenwatch. I ask that you keep this secret, for the sake of these innocent ones."

"If what you say is true, I will," said Micah, relenting, though still suspicious. "So, what about the time pods?"

"In studying the pods, we discovered they are also impervious to the Mist," the director explained. "It cannot penetrate the seal around the device, ensuring the occupant is secure. Ordinary means can, with great force, break the pod, but the Mist itself cannot enter."

"So, these people..."

"Were identified as Mist-marked and placed within the pods for their protection. Many were identified early and given the choice of entering. Most quickly agreed. Those who didn't were free to leave, knowing the risk it entailed."

"And the others who weren't approached?" Micah challenged.

Mai sighed, rubbing her hands.

"The chaos of Mist attacks leaves little room for... finesse. There have been occasions during an attack where a

Mist-marked individual, in immediate danger, is... relocated to Underhaven. For their own protection."

"With no say in the matter? That sounds like kidnapping to me," he retorted, clenching his fist.

"We take every precaution to ensure the individuals here are safe and comfortable. We only wish to help them."

"How? They can't stay like this forever! Surely they have families and people wondering where they are."

"Many do. The Mist is a terrible curse on everyone," Mai somberly answered. "It is our goal to find a cure for Mist-marked souls. An entire group within the Collective here is dedicated to learning how to remove the target placed on these innocents so they can return to their lives without the added danger."

"You gave them no choice!" Kelj shouted as he stormed over, bearing down on Mai. "I know this man." He gestured to a pod along the far wall. "He would have fought to the last breath to protect his family. Like a true warrior and not hiding. Instead, he vanished. *You* took him." Anger seethed from Kelj as his towering eyes bore into the quaking mage.

"It's for his own protection," Mai squeaked in a small voice. "Without us, he would be dead and his family without protection. As it is, he is safe, and his existence gives us another point of research, moving us closer to a cure."

"His family is already without protection because of you!" Kelj roared. "They believe him to be a coward who abandoned them. There is no honor in your actions."

Mai's voice found a new agitated strength. "We are trying to help these people!"

"You do not bring help. You are dangerous, dishonored warlocks guilty of man-stealing. The governess is right to question your place among her people. Greenwatch will not suffer such an outrage," he fumed. Mai's own infuriated face immediately filled with horror.

"Please, for the sake of these people, don't reveal our work," she begged. "Inform the governess, of course, but the citizens of Greenwatch can never know of this. The world already distrusts magic. They'll never understand we're doing this to protect them."

"They are right for thinking so," Kelj growled.

"Enough!" Micah shouted, moving between them.

"Warden Micah, please," Director Mai pleadingly turned to him. "This must remain confidential. The governess has a right to know, but remember what I said. There are many powers at work in Edros. Some who wish to destroy the very people you want to help. And they'll destroy anyone, including us, to get to them. Our work must remain secret for these innocents to survive."

Micah paused, letting her argument sink in.

"I will consider your words," he said hesitantly, "and I will report to the governess. She'll decide what happens."

Mai stepped back, the look of worry still apparent on her face, though resigned.

"I understand, and I see there is nothing further I can say to satisfy your doubts. We will await her word."

Director Mai motioned for Tomas, and he stepped forward to escort them back to the entrance. Filing back into the hallway, Micah could feel the wrath emanating from Kelj. Were it not for his service to the governess, Micah could only imagine how he would have seen fit to carry out justice on the Mist-markeds' behalf.

They quickly returned to the main hall, clusters of mages eyeing them warily as they headed for the wide, bronze doors. The doors opened swiftly, and Kelj and Micah soon found themselves back in the massive cavern, the roaring waves flowing vigorously into the cove. Without a word, Kelj lit his torch from a sconce and stomped towards the tunnel to the Farhaven gardens.

"Kelj, wait!" Micah called after him.

At the far side of the cavern, the Anderfall paused, giving Micah a chance to catch up.

"What was that?" he panted.

"They are lying villains!" Kelj thundered, his deep voice booming over the waves. "Their twisted powers will only end in evil whispered by devils from beyond. Stealing men is only the beginning. They should have been slain long ago."

"I don't understand. I don't exactly trust them, but I can see their reasoning. Where is this hatred of mages coming from?"

"Magic is the work of demons," Kelj coldly answered. "It brings nothing but death and destruction. Treacherous warlocks like those are the cause of our curse. They will be the downfall of every nation, just as it was with my homeland."

"What do you mean? You think mages started the Mist? What's happened to the Anderfalls?"

Kelj wheeled around with furious eyes. "That is not your concern," he growled. "Cease with your questioning."

"I meant no disrespect. I only wish to understand."

Kelj relaxed slightly.

"As it always is with foolish outsiders," he muttered. "I will lead you to the governess. Our ways part there."

They moved at a speedy pace back through the silent tunnel, the air filled with a tense awkwardness.

The return trip passed quickly as Micah mulled over the events in Underhaven. Instead of answers, he felt only new questions rising over the Collective and their research. Another tangle to unravel. Nothing involving the Mist was ever simple.

Soon, they found themselves back at the stone mausoleum. Kelj roughly shoved the door open, letting in a stream of light as he trudged into the garden. Micah breathed deeply, thankful to be back in the fresher air. They pressed their way through the overgrowth, seeking an escape from the tangled vines. Micah sighed.

No doubt an eventful meeting lay ahead.

CHAPTER 19
UNINVITED GUESTS

THE SUN WAS NEARING the horizon as Micah and Kelj crashed out of the garden and back onto the path to Farhaven Manor. Kelj mounted the stairs, two at a time, racing towards the large entrance. Micah followed closely at his heels as they passed through the gloomy entry and gallery hall. Not pausing for a moment, Kelj breezed past the guards stationed outside the governess' throne room, throwing the door open. Inside, Lady Mira was seated with Hogrom at her side. Another person stood before her, obscured by the dying light beyond the glass wall.

"We certainly appreciate any offer of support," said Lady Mira, "though I will need to confer with him first once he—" The governess looked up at their arrival, and the figure turned.

Micah froze.

Garrin.

A sly grin formed below his cold, calculating eyes.

"Welcome back, Warden," Lady Mira greeted. "We were just discussing you. Your companion here seems most gracious."

"Companion?" repeated Micah, attempting to conceal his confusion.

"I am but a humble assistant," said Garrin, laughing oddly. "Happy to help our brave warden. I'm lucky I found you again so quickly."

"Indeed," Lady Mira interjected. "Garrin relayed the frightening tale of the Mist encounter in the Greenwood that separated the two of you. Your actions were indeed heroic."

Micah was completely baffled now. "I–that's not—"

"He was indeed very brave, my lady," Garrin added. "Which is why we're now both here."

"Yes, as I was saying, we are happy to receive more assistance," the governess continued, "and perhaps with your approval, Warden, we can now discuss your investigation."

Garrin perked up, and Micah hesitated, carefully choosing his words.

"Certainly. Though I would recommend we speak privately first due to its... unique nature."

Lady Mira raised a suspicious eyebrow. "Very well."

Hogrom headed towards the gallery hall as she focused back on Garrin. "We will continue our discussion once this matter is concluded. Thank you, Garrin."

He gave a curt bow before abruptly turning. Garrin scowled at Micah as he passed, striding quickly for the exit. The door shut, and the room filled with silence.

"So then." She leaned forward with her hands clasped, elbows resting on the armrests. "What did you learn?"

"A great deal," Micah began, trying to refocus. "Much of it is very unexpected."

He laid out in detail everything he could remember from Underhaven. Kelj interjected along the way, adding information he observed that Micah had not. When the story came to the time pods and missing citizens, the governess' brow furrowed.

"How many people?" she asked after a deep breath.

"A dozen or so," Micah answered. "There were plenty of empty pods, easily enough to double their occupants."

"And they are our citizens?" She looked at Kelj.

"Some," Kelj gruffly replied. "There were faces I did not recognize."

Lady Mira sat back, rubbing her temples in frustration.

"I anticipated some complications, but this…" She sighed. "It is a delicate situation. By your report, innocent citizens of our city are being held by a powerful group of mages. Yet, by their own words, the actions taken were done so out of compassion. Even if it left countless families without answers as to whether their loved ones still live."

"I cannot speak to their judgment," Micah responded, "but I don't believe the Mist-marked have been mistreated. They appeared healthy. As if they were simply sleeping."

"But still captive to the warlocks and their devices," Kelj bitterly added. The room dropped into an uneasy stillness as Lady Mira pondered the predicament. Several minutes passed with no obvious answers rising from the mire of confusion. As Micah's mind started to wander, he was pulled back into the present when the governess finally spoke.

"I thank you both for this information. It is invaluable in terms of protecting the interests of Greenwatch," Lady Mira slowly concluded. "Director Mai must answer for this personally. No more hiding behind vague promises. A panel of my most trusted advisors will be present to weigh the implications of her choices. We will judge whether the treatment of these people is deserving of punishment."

"I will bring her immediately," Kelj offered. The governess shook her head.

"Not yet. I must summon my advisors and discuss the situation. The director will be brought before us once we are prepared."

Kelj bowed with a tinge of frustration.

"Before you are dismissed, Warden," Lady Mira continued, "do I have your approval to include your assistant in these matters?"

Micah paused, unsure of how to approach the subject, given the risks surrounding the man in question.

"He's not my assistant," he flatly admitted, "though I have met him before." The governess looked at him questioningly.

"Go on."

"I stumbled across him in the Greenwood on my journey here," Micah explained, relaying their encounter in the clearing with the body of the young woman.

"Regardless of his words, the man is dangerous," he warned. "His abilities proved that. I don't know what his goal is, but I don't trust him."

Lady Mira nodded. "He arrived most humbly and personably. Likely an attempt to lower our guard. If he is a mage guilty of murder, he will be tried for his crimes. Though, with the Mist and other circumstances present in your encounter, it would be difficult to prove."

She thought for a moment before finishing, "For now, I will ask Hogrom to keep an eye on the man. Perhaps his intentions will come to light."

Micah nodded. "Very well. He will be a slippery one to follow."

"Hogrom may be large, but the Anderfall people are excellent hunters. I have confidence in his skills. As for our other matter, I would like you to find Captain Logan and Arland, the Administrator of Greenwatch. I will require both advisors. Arland is likely at his office near—"

Suddenly, the doors burst open, and Logan rushed into the chamber.

"Captain, excellent timing," she greeted before noticing his flushed appearance. "What's wrong?"

"The Mist," he gasped, collecting his breath. Micah's stomach dropped as the familiar weight of fear swept the room. Lady Mira turned white as she attempted to regain her composure.

"We will discuss the mages later," she said hurriedly. "Warden, Kelj, go with the captain and secure the city."

"Yes, my lady." Kelj bowed.

"Were Hogrom and another man still in the gallery when you arrived?" she asked Logan.

"Yes, though the man left quickly when I mentioned the Mist. Hogrom is already heading to the wall." Another knot of worry formed within Micah, wondering where Garrin had disappeared to.

There's nothing I can do about that now, though.

"I see. On your way, then," the governess commanded. "Defend our people. The Creator give you strength."

The three of them dashed out of the room, the walls painted red in the dying sun.

Protect us all, he silently prayed.

Chapter 20
Siege

Daylight had nearly vanished as Micah, Kelj, and Logan barreled down the cobblestone towards the main gate. People were swarming everywhere, crying out in confusion as families rushed for cover. Stalls and carts lay overturned in the marketplace as the three sprinted past, dodging scattered sacks and crates along with frightened men and women. The sound of crying children and the clang of bells echoed in the street as they neared the gate. Doors and shutters slammed as citizens sealed their homes from the deadly Mist.

They rushed up the staircase leading onto the high stone wall. Scores of men in patchwork armor lined the battlements, each with a musket in hand, staring into the lands beyond. Micah followed their gaze and instantly met a wall of sickly, white-blue Mist covering the fields. Its size defied words. Even with several fields still between it and Greenwatch, the Mist loomed monstrously high, blocking out the sight of the mountains to the south with its solid mass. Its width concealed every feature of the landscape, making it seem as if the city was the only place left in existence. Micah stood there in fear and awe as the mighty cloud drifted towards him, feeling as insignificant as a grain of sand before the tide.

"It won't be long." Rawls stood at the same post where Micah had first seen him when he entered Greenwatch. His knuckles were white, tightly gripping the rifle in his hands.

"We're ready," Logan declared. "Were the drainage grates sealed?"

"Yes, sir!" a man replied.

Logan walked over to a long chest near a set of barrels above the gate and pulled out a worn rifle. He tossed one to Micah and another to Kelj. Micah loaded it with powder and shot from a case beside the chest while glancing at their imminent doom.

"You've faced Mist Wolves before?" Logan asked grimly.

"Aye."

"What about the rest?"

"Rest of what?"

Logan started to respond when another man cried out.

"Wolves!"

They rushed to the edge of the rampart, watching as more fields were swallowed by the Mist. Dozens of Mist Wolves raced out of the haze towards the walls, their bizarre, lean bodies dashing through rows of wheat on their powerful legs. Several of the men panicked, shooting wildly at the approaching beasts. Their bullets landed with most of the monsters still out of range.

"Steady!" Logan rebuked. The Wolves rushed closer, eyeing the sturdy barrier, looking for weaknesses. In the blink of an eye, they crashed upon the stone, clawing at it with horrible, razor-sharp talons. The ground transformed into a sea of swirling fur as the air filled with blood-chilling shrieks and howls. A few beasts found crumbled bits of rock, clambering above their brethren and growling in rage at the defenders still high above them.

"Now!"

The wall erupted in a deafening blast as countless rifles fired into the swarming creatures. A chorus of Wolves cried out in pain, and the horde retreated, unable to breach the impervious stone. A handful of vile, gangly corpses lay where fortunate shots claimed their victims. The defenders cheered, but the victory was short-lived.

As the Mist reached the last field and the gleam of sunlight faded, a new swarm of Wolves joined the vanguard. What were dozens now looked like hundreds as their furious yelps and growls drowned out the men. The defenders fumbled to reload in the growing gloom as the Wolves anxiously paced just out of range.

"Our walls themselves are strong, but there are several weaknesses," Logan explained quickly. "The gate is sturdy but old. An easier target than the stone. There's also a handful of small drainage grates on the northern end where attacks have gotten through before. We've reinforced them, but it's still a weak point."

"So, don't expect them to just keep throwing themselves at the wall?" said Micah dryly.

"Aye. When the Mist reaches us, they tend to get more creative. Not sure why."

Several torchbearers raced along the wall, lighting braziers evenly spaced along the battlements. The height of the defenses limited the range of the light, though the outlines of the terrifying creatures still roamed below.

"It begins," murmured Kelj, his eyes gleaming.

The Mist finally cleared the last field and washed against Greenwatch, its wicked tendrils lapping at their feet. The mass of fires momentarily halted the thick Mist, but it quickly diverted around and above the flames. Its unnatural movement only increased the eeriness of its imposing presence.

The next Micah knew, the Wolves scattered, their cries fading into the distance as they spread out along the wall. As the Mist tumbled into the city, a horrible snarling rose as the sound of scraping wood filled the air.

"The gate!" Logan shouted.

A mob of men pushed towards the gatehouse, leaning over the parapet to get an angle on the enemies below. Muskets sporadically fired into the haze, followed by an occasional yelp. A wisp of Mist dissipated in front of Micah, providing a clear line on a group clawing furiously at the corner of the gate. He raised his musket and fired. Through the smoke, he saw one Wolf crumple, only for another to take its place.

"Archers!" Logan bellowed.

A handful of men in light leather armor moved forward with bows in hand. The rest of the defenders withdrew from the edge. The archers pulled arrows from their quivers, their tips covered in a curious cloth, before dipping them into an open barrel of liquid beside the gatehouse. Micah made the connection just as the man nearest to him held his up to a torch. The tip burst into flame as he quickly nocked the arrow on the bow. With a flash of light, the multitude of flaming arrows raced downward, scattering the Mist and piercing the horde of Wolves. Howls of anguish rang out as they erupted in confusion and scattered in the Mist, their burning hides drifting away in the swirling fog. Riflemen lined up shots on the remaining Wolves, the rift in the Mist rapidly closing.

"Fire all!" Logan cried.

Gleaming barrels flashed brilliantly in the dark, bullets racing towards the murderous beasts. Raging growls turned to fearful yelps as more Wolves fell, the stragglers retreating into the Misty gloom. The men again shouted in triumph, their voices ringing across the wall.

A menacing roar echoed from deep within the void.

The cheering men subsided, valiant faces turning to dread as they rushed back to their places.

Another roar.

"Logan..." called Micah nervously.

"Kelj, find Carlin," said Logan hurriedly. The warrior raced down the stairs, disappearing into the Mist.

Logan turned to Micah, his face full of concern in the flickering flames.

"So, when I said the rest of them..." He chuckled uneasily. "I guess you're about to find out."

A third roar sounded. Closer.

The cries of Mist Wolves faded as they paced beyond sight, waiting. The sound of massive stomping feet filled the darkness. It pounded towards the gate, the formless threat drawing closer.

The noises ceased.

A heavy, angry breath rose from within the Mist. The sheer volume was unnaturally loud as Micah's mind vainly attempted to guess at what immense monster lay hidden in the dark.

An archer shot a lone arrow from the gatehouse into the void, its faint glow illuminating the cloud of Mist. As the light raced away, the silhouette of a hulking creature appeared, mere paces from the wall. The enormous monster stood almost as high as the massive gate itself.

"Mist Troll!" Logan cried.

The Troll roared, a terrible rage-filled roar, as it charged the gate. The ground vibrated under its colossal weight. Micah caught a glimpse of leathery pale gray skin and a small, deformed head in the torchlight as it barreled towards them. Piercing, beady eyes scowled angrily at their existence as it bared its jagged teeth and snarled. A new fear rose within Micah as he stared at the twisted monster.

It slammed into the gate at full speed, shaking the length of the battlements. Huge fists pounded into the ancient wood, each blow sending a rumble through the gatehouse. Men fired wildly, their bullets glancing off the monster's thick skin. A few arrows found purchase in its wide back and shoulders, their flames quickly extinguished as the Troll growled at their pricks.

The gate shuddered under the Troll's weight. Men below rushed to bolster the oaken barrier with more braces, angling thick wooden beams against the ground as it trembled ominously. From the ramparts, Micah could see the shapes of Mist Wolves creeping back towards the wall, the chilling creatures barking in excitement.

The monster raised its massive fist, punching with unstoppable might. A frightening crack echoed from the gate. It reared again.

Another crack.

"It won't hold!" a man called from the street. Defenders fired hopelessly at the looming beast, praying for something, anything, to stop the siege.

The Troll lurched back, gathering all its power for a final, mighty blow.

"Kill it!" screamed Logan.

The monster roared, bashing its shoulder into the weakened gate. Its beaten wood crumbled beneath the behemoth, spraying the men with a cloud of splinters. The Troll bashed again, sending the pulverized remains into the road with an outstretched arm.

"The wall is breached!" Logan shouted. "Defenders, to the streets!"

The men below jabbed vainly at the towering creature with pikes and pitiful wooden poles. One swipe of its monstrous arm shattered their weapons and sent one poor soul flying across the street. He slammed into a house before collapsing in a heap on the ground. The Troll lumbered past the entrance, heading for the center of town as fumbling defenders tried to halt its advance. Outside the city, the cries of Mist Wolves grew louder, the horde racing towards the open gap.

Micah and Logan clambered down the stairs just as a multitude of Wolves invaded Greenwatch, dashing into the streets and vanishing in the swirling Mist.

"Find those Wolves!" Logan commanded a group of defenders arriving from the southern wall. They split up, teams of men racing off into the night after them.

Without warning, a snarl sounded from behind. Micah twisted around to a Wolf charging through the gate towards him. Rows of pointed teeth were opened wide below its sunken, rage-filled eyes. Instinctively, he raised his musket, aiming for the creature.

BOOM!

The shot connected with the Mist Wolf as it leapt into the air, sending its sickly brown body slamming into the ground.

More defenders rushed from the wall, dozens filling the space where the splintered gate stood ajar, in an attempt to stem the flow of Wolves into the city.

A roar from the city pulled Micah's attention away. The Troll continued to rampage closer to the square. Huge chunks of houses littered the cobblestone street where it had swung its massive fists into buildings.

"I'll handle the gate if you can stop that thing," Logan shouted.

"Right, no problem at all."

Logan grinned before rushing to help the defenders. Micah took a deep breath and sprinted down the road through the swirling Mist.

By the time he reached it, the Troll had entered the market square, smashing feeble carts beneath its massive feet. More defenders had arrived, jabbing spears and pikes at the beast, with little avail. It turned to the northern road, swiping at the men and ripping weapons from their hands. More than a few men were sent flying across the open space, landing roughly among the debris. If he was going to stop this creature, it had to be now.

With the Troll's back to Micah, he drew his sword and charged. He slashed forcefully at the back of its knees, its flexible hide splitting open as the blade connected. The monster roared in pain and stumbled forward, nearly crushing a group of men as it caught itself with thick, hideous arms. Its grotesque face contorted in rage as its hideous eyes locked onto Micah.

Uh oh.

The Troll rose, pounding across the cobblestone with its hand outstretched. He rolled away as it lunged, ugly fingers thicker than his legs snapping closed where Micah had been standing only a moment before. The beast studied its hand, confused, before searching for him again.

"This way!"

Kelj stood near the corner of the northern street, waving through the hazy Mist.

Micah raced towards the warrior, the Troll roaring in protest as its prey fled. The Troll lurched after him, its long stride quickly gaining on the quaking ground. Kelj disappeared down a wide side alley, and Micah swerved after him. The Troll smashed into the house on the corner as it turned, spraying boards and stone into the street. Men shouted angrily as they followed the chase. Several smaller alleys flashed by. Just ahead, the lane widened briefly into a small grassy space, and Kelj abruptly turned again. Right before he reached the turn, Micah leapt over a gleaming chain snaking along the ground through a tiny path between houses.

As Micah reached the alley, he glanced back right in time to see the chain spring to life. It snapped into the air, sending the Troll tumbling to the ground as its legs caught on the trap. Several men cried out as it dragged them out of the gap, still clinging to the chain.

"Now!" Kelj shouted.

A rain of arrows poured onto the Troll from the rooftops. It howled in agony as dozens of stings sank into its exposed flesh. Then, the door of the house across from them opened. A stout, grizzled man confidently stepped forth. Below his perfectly bald head, a thick, bushy beard tumbled across his chest. Heavy chain mail with dark metal plates covered his body as he raised a wide-barreled rifle.

The blast of his gun reverberated off the houses as it erupted in a cone of fire. The monster roared in pain, shards of metal and shrapnel cutting across its shoulders and face and lodging in the creature's hide. It sprang up, wildly swiping at the man and rubbing its bleeding face. The warrior dropped the blunderbuss and pulled a wicked-looking battle axe from his back. To Micah's surprise, he noticed Kelj had snuck behind the beast. The Anderfall silently swiped his own axe at the same area Micah had attacked.

The Troll howled again and fell to its knees before crashing into the ground with a loud thud. With the beast weakened, the other man closed in. The Troll swiped groggily at him, missing. The man swung at its passing wrist, landing another blow, and the Troll recoiled in pain. Without stopping, the man leapt to the beast's neck, bringing his axe down with a mighty yell. The menacing roar turned to silence.

Men cheered as the two warriors coolly extricated themselves from the ugly mess, meeting in front of it.

"You make for good Troll bait, Warden." The gruff warrior chuckled.

"Good thinking with that trap," Micah panted.

"Well done, Battlemaster," Kelj congratulated him.

"Battlemaster?" echoed Micah. He hadn't thought to meet another officer in Greenwatch.

"Aye, Battlemaster Carlin of the Frostharbor garrison," the man replied. "Never thought I'd say it, but it's good to see a superior officer, sir."

"Even if he's worn out Troll bait?" asked Micah, grinning. "How'd you arrive in Greenwatch?"

"It's a long story, but the short of it is I escaped Frostharbor right before Kelj and Hogrom did, shortly after the Mist arrived," Carlin explained. "My garrison was wiped out by monsters, and I knew Greenwatch had to be warned. I'm sure Kelj can relay his own gripping tale once we're out of this."

"Right." As curious as he was to know the story behind the three warriors, the threat of Mist Wolves still roamed Greenwatch.

"Several of the Wolves headed towards the abandoned warehouses. Split up and find them!" Carlin commanded the men. Then he raced off with one group as Kelj and Micah ran down another alleyway. Without the deafening roar of the Troll, chilling howls filled the air, reverberating off the buildings.

They burst onto a street, thankful to be out of the tight space. Micah paused, listening for the nearest cry. After a moment, a solitary howl called out from beyond a large, worn structure ahead. Then another. A third.

A boy's scream pierced the night.

Blood drained from Micah's face as they sprinted towards the sound. The barks and howls moved away, hidden somewhere beyond rows of buildings and dilapidated shacks. Boarded ruins quickly replaced the quaint brick houses of the city center as they headed north, desperately trying to locate the Wolves on the muddy road.

They rushed down another short alleyway, spilling onto a wider lane of crumbling warehouses. Without warning, the pack tumbled out of another alley at the far end, wildly sprinting towards a wall surrounding of one of the larger buildings. As Micah and Kelj chased after them, the sound of cracking wood erupted from the warehouse. Micah rounded the stone wall to find the warehouse doors blown completely off their hinges. They rushed into the shadows, weapons ready.

The warehouse was dark and cramped. Piles of beaten crates towered throughout the murky space. Moonlight and pockets of Mist filtered in through the collapsing roof high above them.

Given the layers of dust and debris, it was clear the building hadn't been used in a long time.

A heavy box crashed to the floor somewhere, and a Wolf snarled, shaking the eerie silence. More growls sprang from other points in the room as the beasts felt their way towards the sound. Kelj and Micah slowly crept forward, peering around corners in the maze of cargo. At a fork in the path, they split up, Kelj heading left as Micah headed right, a row of crates covered in heavy tarps between them.

Within moments, a Wolf stumbled out from behind a row of shelving onto the path. Its ferocious face was focused on the other direction as it paused, sniffing. The Mist Wolf detected Micah's scent immediately, swinging its gray, patchy body around in his direction. Nowhere to hide, Micah rushed forward with a yell, his sword flashing in the pale light. The beast's beady black eyes hardened, the hideous dark circles around them contorting in anger. It rose to its hind legs, lifting a fist of deadly, gleaming claws, ready to strike.

Only he was faster.

Just as the creature prepared to swing, Micah's sword connected. The blade plunged into its scratchy fur; the force sending the Wolf into a shelf piled with small crates. Its rusted bars gave way, sending a wave of wood and metal into the row behind it. The warehouse shook with a deafening roar as several rows of narrowly spaced shelves collided, falling like dominoes.

The other two Wolves howled in surprise, shoving their way towards the noise as Micah fled the clutter. He wove desperately through the maze, completely losing his place as he carved an awkward path towards the far wall of the warehouse.

Micah turned a corner and, without thinking, found himself at a dead-end. Large, heavy crates were piled high in neat order, walling in the space. Only a small crevice remained between two columns, too small to squeeze through. An odd wardrobe-like cabinet sat in a corner against the boxes. He turned around, preparing to face the Wolves closing in.

Suddenly, a muffled thump emanated from the wardrobe. Micah stepped back to its worn doors and flung them open. A small voice screamed in terror, and Micah jumped, stumbling back from the cupboard.

Darian.

"What are you doing here?" Micah hissed. "Why aren't you at the bakery?"

"I was exploring. I–I got scared," he stammered.

A tower of boxes collapsed nearby.

"Hide. Hide!" Micah slammed the closet shut, the clicking of claws on stone drawing closer. He pressed himself into the corner of the crates as the monsters sprinted past, only for one to lock eyes with him. It let out a howl of delight as they circled back to the enclosure.

The Wolf on Micah's right stood slightly taller than the other. Unlike the other Mist Wolves he'd encountered, its gray fur was healthy and thick. Bright black rings encircled its hateful eyes. Long, pointed claws dangled from its elongated arms. The other Wolf was covered in typical, patchy brown fur. It quivered as its own deadly talons flexed with excitement. Even though the path was wide, he was completely blocked by the two Wolves. They rose to their hind legs, drawing closer while Micah stepped towards the center with his sword raised. Drool fell from their vicious, snarling mouths.

The gray one moved as if to lunge, and Micah flinched. The other sprang forward, closing the gap with lightning speed. Micah tripped backwards, unable to recover as its claws barely sailed past him, their tips ripping through his sleeve. Burning pain shot through his arm. Luckily, he moved far enough that the rest of the Wolf missed, only to crash into the closet behind him.

The wardrobe tumbled forward, splitting open on the ground and sending Darian tumbling in surprise. The beast roared in delight.

"No!"

Micah swung at the brown Wolf as it prepared to shred the boy with razor-sharp claws. The blade's sharpened edge sliced its arm, and the beast yelped in anger, turning back to him. He clambered to his feet, pressing against a stack of boxes on the far side as the two Wolves bore down on him.

"Hey!" A lump of wood thumped the brown one on the head. It reared back, confused.

"Over here!" Darian shouted.

"Darian, no!"

The Wolf snarled and barreled towards the small boy.

Then Darian disappeared, and the Wolf collided with the tower of boxes.

The crevice! Micah grinned at Darian's cunning.

Then the pillars groaned. The lead Wolf paused, distracted by the awful sound. Micah quickly realized the collision had fractured the bottom crates. The towers wavered, swaying under their own colossal weight.

Uh oh.

In an instant, the bottom gave way with a magnificent crack. The massive towers came crashing down, pulling neighboring stacks with them into a sea of chaos. Micah dashed towards the exit, fleeing the avalanche closing over his head. The smaller Wolf cried in fear, instantly swallowed by the destruction. With splinters pelting his back, Micah leapt out of the space, debris tumbling barely a handsbreadth from him.

"Too close," he wheezed.

He clambered to his feet, searching wildly for Darian.

"Micah!" Darian shouted from beyond the mess.

"I'm coming!"

A wrathful growl rose from somewhere to Micah's left. Darian screamed, followed by the Wolf's horrible barking. Micah rushed in their direction, climbing over the wreckage that spilled into the adjacent row. Ahead of him, he heard the Wolf giving chase.

"Warden!" Kelj bellowed from behind.

Micah rounded the last row of crates at the warehouse's end, just in time to watch Darian swing an odd panel of stone shut. The gray Wolf smashed into it, sealing the wall with an echoing thud.

"Over here!" Micah angrily shouted at the Wolf. It turned around, fixing its furious eyes on him. The beast charged, howling in rage at his survival. Forceful claws clashed with steel as they collapsed in a tangled mess near the shelves of crates. The Wolf reared back with a vicious growl as it swiped again. Micah narrowly deflected a set of claws as it swung with its other hand. He grasped for a thin box on the shelf and raised it, the killing blow obliterating the defenseless wood. He hurled the remaining splinter at its face, a pointed edge catching the tip of its nose. The Wolf yelped as the wood cut its sensitive flesh.

The momentary pause gave Micah just enough of an opening to roll away from the beast, its jaws snapping an inch from his leg. As he tried to stand, it swiped again, only to rear back in anguish. Its confident growl turned into a pained whine. It whisked around, revealing a small throwing axe buried in its hide.

Kelj stood at the end of the row, his gleaming battle axe in hand.

"Face me, beast!" he roared.

Blinded by rage, it charged Kelj. The tips of its sharpened claws clicked furiously against the stone floor as the distance rapidly shrank. The Wolf pounced, rows of dagger-like teeth opened wide, ready to sink into the warrior's flesh. At the last possible second, Kelj deftly stepped aside, the Wolf sailing harmlessly past. As it landed, Kelj planted a heavy blow with his fist into the Wolf's face. Its head jerked downward from the force, the Wolf's snarl abruptly silenced as stars danced in its head.

"That the best you can do, Wolf?" Kelj taunted.

The Wolf howled in fury, shaking the pain from its head as it slashed with its claws. Kelj reached out, catching its wrist in his own massive hand before kicking the beast in its ribs with his reinforced boot. The Wolf gasped, falling to the ground. In a flurry of motion, Kelj gripped his axe with both hands, bringing its shimmering edge down on the beast.

The whimpering growls ceased.

Kelj stepped back, cleaning the blade of his axe in the Wolf's fur, before striding over to Micah.

"I'm glad you're on our side," Micah remarked.

Kelj grunted in satisfaction. "Where is the boy?"

He pointed to the warehouse wall. "He disappeared over there."

Beyond a worn torch ring, the wall was solid stone. While normally someone wouldn't have given it a thought, compared to the rest of the wooden warehouse, the back wall seemed oddly out of place.

"This isn't part of the exterior wall of Greenwatch, is it?" Micah wondered aloud.

"No," Kelj replied. "Something else must be on the other side."

Micah felt around the icy surface, searching for anything that might hint at an opening. Outside the warehouse, the howls of approaching Wolves grew louder.

"Quickly," Kelj urged.

Micah angrily punched the wall. There was nothing.

The howls drew closer.

With no other guesses, he inspected the torch ring. Once upon a time, a wooden torch likely sat in the hole, though it had been ages since. Micah reached up and tugged at the ring. Nothing. He gripped the ring in his hand, twisting it to the right. To his surprise, it moved.

A faint click emanated from the wall.

Suddenly, an entire section popped forward, a cloud of dust releasing from the tiny movement. The crack allowed just enough space to wedge his fingers in. Ancient hinges shrieked in protest as Micah pulled at the stone door until it swung wide enough for a person to squeeze through.

What in Aldaria?

Howls erupted from the far end of the warehouse, pulling Micah's attention towards the crates.

"Go," Kelj commanded.

"And leave you to face them alone?" he argued. "You're crazy!"

"You will need safe passage back, and the boy may be in danger. I will deal with the beasts. Now go!"

Micah growled in frustration, shoving his way through the hidden entrance. Kelj heaved the stone closed, sealing him in. A faint light glowed from beyond a stone staircase leading into the gloom.

Nowhere to go but down.

Chapter 21
Firewalkers

A solitary torch burned at the bottom of the rocky stairs.

Someone lit this. Recently.

Another light danced farther in, and Micah headed in its direction. The dirt tunnel wound on, shadowed and obscured, save for the occasional torchlight. After a steep slope, he found himself in a wide, low-ceilinged grotto. More tunnels branched off from the thoroughfare, vanishing into darkness.

This must be another section of passages under Greenwatch, he realized, thinking back to Underhaven.

At the far end of the murky hall sat a lone torch, guiding his path.

"Follow the lights," came a faint, but familiar, call.

"Where are you?" Darian's small voice echoed in the passage.

"Darian!" Micah broke into a run.

The wide exchange transformed back into a cramped passage, twisting deeper into the gloom. Before long, he noticed the path slowly rising again. Micah passed torch after torch, but Darian was nowhere to be found.

The slope ended at a rough set of stairs hewn into the rock and soil. Micah lunged up the steps and found himself in a natural cave. Two torches burned at the end, casting shadows across a stone and mortar wall enclosing the cavern's mouth. A door of thick, carved stone sat slightly ajar in its center, a strange glow and wisps of Mist seeping into the cave. He cautiously approached the opening, unsure of what lay beyond.

As Micah peeked around it, the light of an immense fire reflected off a thick ring of trees, scattering the Mist in the clearing. He returned his sword to its scabbard and reached for his pistol before stepping outside. It took a moment for his eyes to adjust to the peculiar sight.

He was standing in a large clearing in a grove of oak trees. The Mist was thick within the boughs, twisting and turning on itself. Within the grove, it swirled angrily, engulfing the entire area except for a wide ring of fire that blazed in the center, preventing the Mist from entering. Micah shielded his eyes from the flames, attempting to make sense of the scene. There were shapes in the fire.

His breath caught in his throat.

Garrin and Darian.

Inside the flames, Garrin roughly gripped Darian, his arm crooked around the boy's neck. Darian struggled hopelessly under the mage's overwhelming strength.

"Micah Stormcrown!" Garrin shouted gleefully over the crackling inferno. "Welcome. Took your precious time arriving at our little party, didn't you?"

Fury rose in his gut. "Release the boy, Garrin! He's innocent!"

"Innocent, is he?" Garrin asked ominously. "No, I imagine you would rather I keep him here, with me." He smiled wickedly, squeezing tighter as Darian gasped for air.

"He's just a boy," Micah fumed, clenching his fist. "He hasn't hurt anyone!"

"Just like the woman," Garrin scoffed. "Brave Micah, riding to the rescue, even as he has no idea the chaos he will unleash."

Darian gave a panicked cry, choking as he clawed feebly at Garrin's arm.

"Let. Him. GO!"

"You have no clue what dangers have befallen your world, do you?" Garrin continued, astonished. "You are still blind."

The circle of flames relaxed slightly, the Mist groping hungrily.

"But I will make you see."

Garrin's fire vanished. In a blink, the Mist rushed into the circle as he tossed Darian towards it.

"No!"

The Mist swarmed Darian, completely obscuring him from sight as the boy screamed in terror.

"Darian!" Micah cried, rushing forward. Garrin laughed, raising his hand. A wave of energy blasted Micah off his feet, sending a daze of stars pulsing through his skull as he collided with the cold earth. He could only listen in horror as Darian's cries transformed into a terrible choking sound.

Suddenly, Micah was confused. The Mist's victims never had a chance to cry out before suffocating them.

Something was different.

The gasps slowly subsided as a deep, pained breathing took their place. The Mist was still too thick to see where the boy disappeared.

"Darian!" he called again.

The heavy, hoarse breathing continued.

Garrin stepped to Micah's side, dragging him to his feet by his shirt. He spun Micah around to where Darian had vanished.

"Witness the true horror of the Mist, Stormcrown," he coldly commanded.

The thick fog began to dissipate, a large, dark shape slowly taking form. Larger than Darian.

Instantly, Micah knew where he'd heard that breathing before.

Where the energetic boy who loved adventure had sat rested the terrible outline of a Mist Wolf.

Its brown fur was thick, healthy. The Wolf hunched on its knees, its razor-sharp claws outstretched on the dampening grass to support itself. Its normally small, raging eyes were closed in their black circles, unusually relaxed.

"Darian?" Micah whispered. He stepped forward, crouching in front of the beast. It didn't move.

"Darian, it's me. It's Micah. Darian?"

The Wolf opened its beady eyes wide, locking onto him in confusion.

"Darian, it's going to be okay. I'm here."

Its pupils contorted in rage. The Wolf reared back, releasing a soul-piercing howl towards the sky with arms outstretched.

Micah stumbled back in dismay.

It rose to its feet, snarling.

"Darian! Remember who you are!"

The Wolf took a step, raising a fist of deadly claws to annihilate him.

Micah's eyes widened. "No!"

A blast of fire erupted, flinging the Wolf across the clearing. Micah swerved around and saw Garrin, his hand outstretched.

"Darian!" Micah rushed over to the Wolf. A wicked burn covered the entirety of its chest, the fur smoldering furiously as the stench of charred hair and flesh met his nose. The Wolf was silent, its breath forever silenced.

"*You*," he raged, wheeling to Garrin, who watched him with a scowl. "You monster!"

"Do you see, Micah? Do you now see the true reality of the Mist?" he challenged, crossing his arms.

"He was just a boy! How could you be so *evil*?" Micah shouted, gripping his pistol until his knuckles turned white.

"Evil?" he pouted with feigned hurt. "Control your emotions, fool! The boy was a beast. The Mist does not lie."

"You could've saved him," Micah fumed. "We could have taken him away!"

"And done what? Waited until the Mist found him?" Garrin scoffed. "There's no cure, Micah, whatever your magical friends have told you. Becoming a Mist Wolf cannot be reversed."

How did he know about the mages?

"So you just execute him? Execute anyone you find?" Micah demanded, his anger boiling.

"You fail to see the bigger picture, Stormcrown," Garrin sighed, annoyed. "The Mist may follow black iluvan, but the true draw is the Mist-marked. Whether it kills the man or transforms him does not matter. The Mist remains as long as they do."

"So that's your goal," he realized, horrified. "The reason you killed that woman in the Greenwood."

"Do the woods not prove my point? The Greenwood is free of the taint. None of the Mist-marked live there. That land is safe because of my actions."

"You're nothing but a murderer," retorted Micah. "If it were up to you, no one would be alive to enjoy it."

Garrin's calm demeanor turned to fury.

"You're a naïve fool, Micah Stormcrown," he growled. "You have seen the truth but refuse to accept it. Still, you remain blind to the forces at work in the world. I thought perhaps you would aid us in ending the curse, but I see now that I was wrong."

"Aid us? What 'us'? Who are you working for?"

Garrin laughed at his ignorance.

"Our order once followed a great leader, until the Mist overcame my people," he replied, half to himself. "But those of us who survive will continue our campaign against it. The Firewalkers will drag you to victory, even if we have to sacrifice a thousand souls to achieve it."

The cracking of branches echoed from the trees. Micah spun around, afraid of what other monsters might rise from the Mist. Instead, three humans strode from the depths of the shadowed trunks.

Like Garrin, each of them wore dark, imposing armor. Leather and scale of the highest craftsmanship. A pale young man stepped into the clearing from Micah's left. Dark hair flowed to his shoulders. Cold, black eyes studied Micah from his long face. The second was a woman, older than the man, likely around Micah's age. A waterfall of fiery hair was pulled back behind her. Green eyes flashed in the strong moonlight, her jaw clenched in agitation. Her angled face would have been unusually attractive were it not for the steely ice of her demeanor. The last was a towering man with dark skin, much like

Asher's. His black hair was shaved to his head, with a thick, neatly groomed beard surrounding his mouth. His expression was almost unreadable, studying Micah with deep, reserved eyes as his hand rested on a dangerous-looking mace at his side.

Micah backed away as the three of them joined Garrin, facing him across the clearing. The space immediately felt smaller as Micah realized how pathetically outnumbered he was. *If they're all mages like Garrin, I'm lost.*

"Had all the fun without us, hmm?" the young man smirked at Garrin.

"Little Micah here grew impatient, and you took longer than expected," Garrin admonished with a growl.

"Our scent drew a pack of Wolves from the city. We were... delayed," the larger man coolly explained.

"More are likely to follow unless you covered your trail, Arksul," Garrin responded.

The dark-skinned man waved a dismissive hand. "We will be gone before they arrive."

"Enough of this," the woman snapped. "Did you obtain the information?"

Micah slowly inched his way back towards the cavern entrance.

"Not yet, Armeia," Garrin replied, turning to the woman. "We agreed to extend an offer first, did we not?"

"Given the evidence, I'd say your offer was rejected," the young man retorted.

"Perhaps," Garrin confessed, "but even you took some convincing, Hadrian. Maybe brave Micah is ready to reconsider."

The four of them turned their gaze back, and he froze.

"Well, Micah?" Garrin demanded.

"Wait a minute. What information?" Micah asked, bewildered.

"The results of your little journey," Garrin explained with faint annoyance. "Rest assured, we will correct your misguided magical friends, once we know their hiding place. They are weak, and their ridiculous attempts to play nice with Wolves are folly."

"But what if they can cure the Mist-marked? Won't the Mist disappear?" he offered, playing for time.

"Five hundred years of study by the greatest minds has proven that impossible," Garrin irritably replied.

"Five hund...?" Micah echoed. Garrin had to be mad. "The Mist appeared two years ago. What do you mean?"

Garrin ignored him. "Besides, the curse stretches farther than you imagine. Surely you can figure that out. Where do you think the Mist Troll came from?"

Micah thought back to the encounter. It was certainly unlike any creature he had ever seen, but there were similarities to the native trolls he had encountered.

"So, it affects all creatures?"

"I really *do* have to spell it out, don't I?" Garrin mocked. "Yes, little Micah, it does. The Mist affects all living things. More than your pathetic world realizes."

"So, then, who are the Firewalkers?"

"No more!" Armeia angrily interrupted. "He knows enough. He makes his choice. Now."

"Indeed," said Garrin. "You now know the truth of the Mist—its real danger. Our goal is to end it."

Micah took a small step back as Garrin continued, "This is your final offer. Join us or die."

Micah's pistol trembled in his hand beside his hip. He couldn't fight them all.

But maybe he could buy a chance to escape.

"I see your goal, Garrin, and I share it," he began slowly, gripping the pistol harder, "but I've also seen your methods. Whoever you are, whoever the Firewalkers are, your actions make you no better than the Mist. I would never join that."

Garrin's frown turned into a furious scowl.

"Then you're a fool, Micah Stormcrown," his quiet voice hissed.

"You'd betray the very people you claim to protect. Betray even Elowë himself!"

"The people are blind, as you are," Garrin growled. "And your god abandoned this world long ago. We are all that's left to stop the Mist."

Garrin's hands clenched in anger. "If you won't join us, I will take what secrets you've kept from me. Even in death, you will further our goals."

Micah furiously drew his pistol, except Garrin was quicker. His head erupted in pain as Garrin's mind invaded his own. Micah struggled to close off sections of his thoughts, feeble barriers smashed apart as Garrin ravaged his memories. Micah fell to his knees as the dark mage stabbed at his very being, the relentless power rending Micah's consciousness apart without the slightest hint of mercy. He was helpless in Garrin's killing grip.

Garrin paused as he alighted on the encounter with the mages under Greenwatch. Through their bizarre and painful connection, Micah felt a sense of surprise and rage wash over him as he replayed the memory of the time pod room, studying every detail of the meeting with Director Mai. Then, he slowly drifted through the rest of Micah's time in Underhaven, hesitating on a handful of details—the iluvan, the Mist-marked detection spell, the mention of the former Director—each moment sending bolts of excruciating pain through Micah's head as Garrin shoved through the fraying strands of his mind.

After he finished his examination of the Heraldan Collective, Garrin rushed through the remaining memories leading to their stand-off. Micah huddled there, shuddering under the weight of his torture.

"We have a new task," Garrin informed his companions. "The mages will need to wait."

He slowly turned back to where Micah lay feebly on the cold, damp grass. Micah gasped in agony as Garrin renewed his stranglehold on Micah's mind.

"You've been most... informative, Micah," Garrin sneered with a cold smile, tightening his grasp on Micah's defenseless thoughts, "but I'm afraid your usefulness has reached its end."

Garrin sauntered forward. Mist swirled around him, heralding death. Micah strained to lift his head, his eyes fluttering weakly as Garrin drew his obsidian sword.

"Farewell, Micah Stormcrown. May the Flame Eternal embrace your soul." He raised its black edge, gleaming in the moonlight.

Micah's last thread of consciousness bleakly held on, flickering between fear and peace, screaming out in terror of the life-drinking blade as curious memories of Elisa and Samuel danced in the shadows of his soul.

Micah surrendered, closing his eyes. *Take me home, Elowë.*

A blast ripped across the clearing.

Garrin's consuming presence vanished. The remaining pieces of Micah's mind rushed to mend themselves as he struggled to make sense of his surroundings.

Garrin had disappeared. Bolts of dazzling light hurtled across the clearing, casting an array of shadows in the trees.

As Micah's head regained its functions, he realized the ground where Garrin had stood in front of him had been obliterated. He quickly spotted Garrin retreating across the grassy space as his companions unleashed a torrent of fire and molten rock towards something behind Micah. He spun around on his knees to see two figures at the mouth of the cave.

"Micah! Run!" shouted Tomas' familiar voice.

Micah stood, his joints fumbling as he lurched towards them. Tomas and the other mage deflected the attacks, whizzing past Micah's head, grunting under the heavy blows. Garrin yelled in fury, aiming a raging inferno directly at him. With lightning-fast speed, Tomas unleashed a spear of rushing ice. The bolts collided in a violent clash, the bright light of the flames vanishing in a cloud of steam.

Without warning, a flurry of howls sounded from the far edge of the grove. Everyone paused, directing their attention to the trees. Garrin cursed loudly as a pack of Wolves raced out of the Mist towards them, drawn by the light and sound.

"Go!" Tomas commanded.

The three of them rushed into the cavern, their enemies distracted. Together, the mages heaved the stone door shut. As it closed, Micah watched the Firewalkers launch waves of flames at the marauding beasts.

The three dashed towards the tunnel entrance. At the opening, Tomas turned back and released a barrage of spells. A shower of colored bolts smashed into the sturdy rock, vicious flames of blue, green, and orange flashing in the dark space as they tore chunks of stone from the ceiling. The roof started to quake, the natural formations quickly weakening. All of a sudden, a mighty crack reverberated around the room. The roof collapsed in a deafening landslide, rubble flying in all directions and burying the entrance in a massive pile of rock and dirt.

They stopped briefly to catch their breaths as the thunderous sound subsided.

"Just to be safe," Tomas gasped.

"I was as good as dead," Micah breathed. "How did you even find me?"

Tomas' companion turned towards the sunken passage and summoned an orb of light, guiding them down into the gloomy abyss. The bouncing spark shone like a miniature sun in the cramped space, casting odd shadows on the jutting rock.

"When the siege started, several of our mages took to the streets, searching for anyone who might be targeted by the Mist," Tomas' voice echoed in the narrow tunnel. "Ferrald here was lucky enough to pick up on a Mist-marked and traced him to the warehouse where we found the governess' bodyguard fending off a pack of Mist Wolves."

"We would've been there quicker if it weren't for the accursed Wolves," Ferrald growled. "Those mindless beasts likely cost that poor soul's life."

"If it were only that simple," Micah muttered, unwilling to say more until his brain had fully processed the nightmarish events of the grove.

I should have been faster. Guilt mingled with fury as Darian's scared face and Garrin's menacing eyes filled his thoughts.

Tomas looked at him quizzically, and Micah quickly changed the subject.

"Is Kelj alright?" he asked.

"That Anderfall is an unnatural sight," said Tomas. "He probably could've defeated the whole pack on his own, but it would have cost him. As it is, he had only minor injuries. We offered to come after you while he kept watch."

"You have my thanks."

Tomas nodded. An uneasy silence filled the dreary passage, broken only by their soft steps in the dirt.

"Who were those mages?" Tomas asked quietly.

Micah shook his head. "Trouble. Whoever they are, they're looking for the Collective."

Even in the faint light, he saw the color drain from Tomas' face.

"Then they've come to finish it," the mage murmured. "I guess we couldn't hope to stay hidden forever."

"What are you saying?"

"The group who originally learned the Mist-marked spell. The ones who were murdered? Sounds like their killers have finally found the rest of us."

Micah's chest constricted with dread.

"And I led them here... I had no idea what Garrin was talking about in the Greenwood. He used me."

Tomas shook his head, lost in worry.

"We have to warn the director," he finally concluded, "and the governess. Those mages can't be allowed to enter the city."

"There's no time to waste," Micah replied. The three of them broke into a brisk jog, working their way back towards the warehouse entrance. At the large thoroughfare, the mages halted near one of the side tunnels. Micah turned to them with a questioning look.

"This is where we leave you, for now," Tomas explained. "It'll be quicker for us to return to Underhaven here."

Micah nodded. "I'll inform the governess and the captain about the Firewalkers."

"We'll find you once we've informed the director and reached a plan," Tomas finished.

"Tomas."

The mage looked back.

"I may not fully agree with what the Collective's done, but the Firewalkers are a threat to everyone. Greenwatch and the Collective will need each other for this."

He nodded somberly before vanishing, swallowed by the darkness. Micah grabbed a torch from the wall and hurried down the path.

As he climbed the rocky stairs to the wall of the warehouse, Micah spied a small lever near the hinges of the hidden door. The wall sprang to life as he pulled it, releasing the lock. Micah shoved the stone door open, nearly running into Kelj with his axe poised to strike.

"Warden!" he exclaimed, relaxing.

"It's okay," said Micah hurriedly. "What happened to your arm?"

Kelj looked down at the pale strip of cloth around his forearm. A thick splotch of blood had dyed a good portion of it.

He grunted. "It is nothing. One of the accursed Wolves got a lucky nip before it lost its head. Where is the boy?"

A bitter knot formed in Micah's stomach. "He's... gone."

"What happened?" Kelj bristled. "Where are the treacherous warlocks?"

"They took another tunnel back to Underhaven—"

"Curse my weakness," Kelj stormed. "I should not have trusted them. If they harmed that boy—"

"No, no," Micah quickly interrupted, "it wasn't them. But we have to find the governess. Now. I'll explain on the way."

Kelj nodded, his eyes flooded with questions.

Together, they rushed out of the warehouse and back to the empty streets.

CHAPTER 22
RIDDLES ON THE WALL

THE NIGHT AIR WAS cool as Micah and Kelj left the decaying warehouse district. Faint tendrils of Mist swirled along the edges of the abandoned roads and sidewalks. The cries of Wolves were fainter than before, only an occasional howl sounded above the crumbling roofs as they sprinted towards the center of Green-watch.

"Our defenders must be close to rooting out the Wolves," Kelj observed as they passed scores of dark, silent buildings. The moon shone faintly through wispy clouds and Mist, casting an eerie light in the quiet streets.

As they neared the inhabited section of Greenwatch, Micah finished relaying his encounter with the Firewalkers to Kelj. He held nothing back, revealing Darian's awful transformation as well as the Collective's fateful rescue. Micah began to more fully comprehend the nightmarish events as he relived his scrambled memories.

"Then the mages were not entirely dishonorable," Kelj groused. "Nonetheless, Lady Mira must know about the true danger of the Mist and these Firewalkers. Even her own citizens may be a threat."

Micah nodded. Everything he thought he knew about the Mist had changed. The Wolves weren't just monsters; they were people, just like him. He thought of Fairhollow and the raids. How many creatures had he fought? How many had been friends he knew? They were questions he didn't want answered.

Soon, they heard shouting ahead of them. Flickering streetlights appeared through the hazy Mist, signaling the edge of occupied buildings. A team of defenders rushed past, heading for a wide side street as Micah and Kelj entered the main thoroughfare to the square.

The marketplace was a flurry of activity. In the dwindling moon, Micah spotted Logan directing groups of guards as others rushed to carry heavy beams towards the gate.

"Still breathing?" Captain Logan called as he recognized them. "Haven't become Troll food yet?"

"Nearly." Micah smirked. "But we have a bigger issue."

"What could be bigger than a Mist Troll?" he asked, exasperated.

Micah quickly relayed his encounter with the Firewalkers.

"Never trust a mage," Logan muttered. "Very well. Hopefully, your collapsed tunnel was the only secret entrance into the city. The men have almost finished barricading the main gate. That should give them pause. The last of the Mist Wolves inside the city are also being dealt with. I'll send any available men to reinforce the gate and keep watch along the wall for any sign of these Firewalkers."

Micah nodded. "Right. We'll inform the governess."

Micah and Kelj continued along the western road towards Farhaven Manor. The commotion of the defenders diminished as they neared the governess' mansion. The palatial houses ringing the center of power in Greenwatch sat in ominous, Mist-filled silence, their occupants sequestered in fear, praying they outlasted the night. Kelj bounded up the steps to the manor, and Micah chased after him.

Inside, they found a string of guards, all prepared to defend the governess with their lives. Several gave a sigh of relief as they recognized Kelj, making a path for the pair to enter. They rushed through the gallery hall, bursting into the chamber where Lady Mira waited on her throne, Hogrom at her side.

"You've returned," she said tiredly as they approached.

In the faint torchlight, the governess appeared ready for anything, yet the signs of exhaustion weighed heavily as the night stretched on.

"The captain sent word that you and Battlemaster Carlin headed north after a pack of Wolves," Lady Mira continued. "I assume you were successful?"

"The Wolves are slain," Micah reported, "but I have grave news. Winslow's apprentice, Darian, was lost. And we have a new threat to Greenwatch."

"We grieve the loss of any life to this curse," she lamented. "What new danger has the Mist brought us?"

"An order of mages—the Firewalkers. They are responsible for Darian's death."

Micah swiftly repeated the events of his harrowing evening, taking care to recount the details of the encounter in the grove while staying his own grief and anger.

"After we escaped into the tunnel, we split up. Tomas took another route back to Underhaven," he finished. "They'll meet with us once the Collective has been warned."

Lady Mira sat back, resting her chin on her fingers as she shook her head.

"When I learned of my husband's dealing with the mages, I was skeptical. Their gold may have bought his goodwill, but were it not for his honor and memory, they would have been removed long ago," she said wistfully. "Perhaps if I had been less sentimental, we would not be in this predicament."

The room was silent, no one willing to address the governess' words.

"I said the director would answer for their taking of the Mist-marked, and she will. But for now, the Firewalkers are our common enemy. Greenwatch and the Heraldan Collective must stand together to fend off these killers," Lady Mira declared. "Once this menace is dealt with, we will re-discuss the Collective's research and methods. With the gruesome fate you witnessed tonight, I fear their research may have more importance than any of us realized."

Micah gave a slight bow. "As you say. Should I find the director?"

Lady Mira sighed. "No, I imagine the threat of destruction will bring Mai to the manor soon enough. Assist Captain Logan in fortifying the city. Kelj and Hogrom will accompany you. You may need their unique training."

He looked quizzically at Kelj, but the Anderfall remained stoic.

"Very well." Micah turned back to the governess. Hogrom stepped away and joined them before her throne. The three of them bowed, then quickly left the room. A contingent of guards in clinking armor replaced Hogrom as they exited the manor and headed for the city square.

The central exchange was still a mass of activity, but Logan was nowhere to be found.

"Likely at the gate," Micah concluded. The warriors silently nodded in agreement, and they strode towards the entrance. The moon was nearing the end of its path, dawn fast approaching. Around them, the sounds of Wolves had vanished—a good sign the city had returned to relative safety, though the billowing Mist remained.

As they approached the gate, Micah studied a handful of men laboring hard to seal the breach. The Troll's damage had rendered the splintered gate useless, but that hadn't prevented the resourceful defenders from repurposing its pieces. An assortment of beams, planks, and housing materials had been haphazardly furnished into a solid wall, sealing the gateway closed. Additional layers of supports and barricades filled the space, effectively sealing Greenwatch off from the outside world. If the Troll had found the gate difficult to breach, he could only imagine the challenge a reinforced solid wall would be.

"Micah!" Logan called down from the ramparts. Micah scrambled up the stairs, Kelj and Hogrom following close behind.

"We have visitors," he said with a worried frown beneath his tired eyes.

Anxiety flooded Micah's mind as Logan led Micah to the gatehouse. Beyond the wall, he caught sight of a wicked ring of fire, displacing the Mist in the distant fields.

The Firewalkers.

As Micah entered the building, a figure in a familiar tan robe turned to face him.

"You're quick," Micah exclaimed as Tomas pulled back his hood.

"Spend enough time with us, and you might learn your way around too," he said with a small smirk. "The director is on her way to Farhaven as we speak. A group of us have come to help stop the Firewalkers."

"The rest of his fellows are spread out along the battlement," Logan interjected, "ready for whatever springs from that blaze out there."

They piled out of the small gatehouse, joining the rest of the defenders. Micah watched as the restless men cast suspicious glances at the handful of mages spaced along the wall, unsure of whom to watch.

The howls of Mist Wolves had disappeared; only the swirling Mist still remained. Beyond the startling fire, a faint light glowed on the horizon. Micah quickly noticed that the impenetrable Mist from earlier had thinned dramatically, allowing him to see farther into the fields beyond the city. Dozens of Mist Wolves lay dead, whether killed by the defenders or the arriving Fire-walkers, he could not say.

"Micah Stormcrown!" a menacing voice bellowed from the inferno. The flames leapt aside as Garrin stepped through the ring, striding confidently towards the wall.

Micah moved onto a small balcony beside the gatehouse, nervously gripping his weathered pistol. Garrin stopped several paces from the wall and looked up. Even from here, in the dim glow of dawn, Micah could tell his midnight eyes were contorted in fury.

"Incredible that one so weak can cheat death so many times!" Garrin goaded. "How *have* you survived on this godforsaken island?"

"Begone, Garrin! The bravest warriors of Greenwatch stand against you."

"Is that so?" Garrin reached down, picking up a small rock in his glove. He playfully passed the rock between his fingers.

"Oh, no doubt they are the most battle-hardened men alive," he continued in sweet mockery, "considering any warriors of even a scrap of renown were slain by the Mist long ago."

Micah could feel Logan seething beside him.

Garrin's hand snapped out. With blinding speed, his tiny rock smashed into the wall. A section of the parapet exploded, showering the defenders with debris. The men shouted in confusion, a couple releasing arrows at Garrin. At the last moment, the projectiles unnaturally changed course, angling away from the dark mage and embedding harmlessly in the ground.

Garrin sneered at Micah. "They have no idea what real power is."

"They don't stand alone," Tomas boldly shouted. Garrin glanced at him in surprise.

"Well, well. The mage from the clearing. We would relish the chance to fully test your meddling powers."

The flames behind Garrin vanished as his three companions appeared. Each of them sat on a grim, dangerous-looking warhorse. A fourth waited patiently for its master.

"But that will have to wait for another day. Our business is elsewhere now, thanks to your brave warden."

Micah could feel faces turning to him, puzzled.

"Humor me, Micah," Garrin continued with disdain. "Why is it you fight for these people? Why waste your life trying to save this pathetic island?"

"This is my home. These are my people. As long as we survive, Karthmoor survives," he retorted, restraining his anger. "We fought for our independence from the Hamid Empire, carving a nation from nothing, with naught but our shared sweat and strength. We overcame wars, plagues, and disasters too numerous to recount. We *will* outlast the Mist. We *will* outlast you."

The men erupted in defiant cheers, rattling their weapons.

"They are not your people," said Garrin flatly, "any more than they are my people."

"I am a soldier of the Guard, the Warden of the West. You know nothing about me."

"On the contrary. I know you better than you do yourself," he ominously warned. "You forget, I've seen your memories, your life. Your blood runs deeper than foolish sentiments."

"What does that mean?" Micah scoffed.

"Have you never wondered about your past? Why your name, Stormcrown, is so unusual in this deplorable land?"

"My name?" he echoed. "What does that have to do with anything?"

"You carry a name older than you realize. Older than this tiny nation you call home, even," Garrin said as if recalling some memory. "Once a feared name, then"—his voice hardened—"one of betrayal."

"Away with your riddles! Tell me what you mean or begone!"

Garrin smiled at Micah's frustration before his expression turned to cold wrath. He clenched a fist at his side.

"Old it may be, but you are still the offspring of traitors. Of men sworn to preserve our home before they grew fat in their greed and wealth," Garrin pronounced. "Ousted for their betrayal. For their lies as we crumbled beneath the Mist." He paused, lingering on some mysterious knowledge.

"You are *Eldvenir*. Oathsworn." Garrin spat out the word like poison.

"I don't understand," said Micah, baffled. "Oathsworn?"

"You are the heir of a dead house," Garrin scornfully continued, his hatred visible. "Of an order charged with the safety and security of the most powerful nation this world has ever seen. An order that failed and whose hands are stained with the blood of thousands. You may not have lived during the Cataclysm, but you are the inheritor of all its disgrace."

Micah crossed his arms. "You're insane. None of that makes sense."

"Stormcrown," he continued irritably. "It cannot be denied."

His tone relaxed slightly. "The name is legend among the Firewalkers, even for an Eldvenir. Our orders may have debated one another before the Cataclysm, and shed each other's blood, but the Stormcrown name... Generations of valiant men solidified its weight. Before your ancestors were exiled, of course. Surviving only on the last graces of that name, I imagine."

The men around Micah whispered as his story built, their bewilderment joining with Micah's own as he struggled to dismiss Garrin's impassioned words. The Mist appeared but two years ago. Something that destructive couldn't have gone unnoticed in Edros for centuries, as he'd implied in the grove. And who were these Oathsworn? Garrin had to be mad; why else would he be so committed to his tale? But then again... what if he wasn't?

"Did you ever wonder why your grandfather avoided your family's heritage? Do not deny it!" Garrin snarled. "Or did you not ponder why you so quickly grasped magic as a Protector, weak as you were? Magic is woven into your family, as it has always been for our people."

Several of the defenders turned in shock as Garrin revealed Micah's secret. Micah's face burned under their penetrating stares.

"Honestly, Micah, had you devoted more attention to your studies, you might be as powerful as I am," he chided. Then, like a prophet proclaiming an inescapable fate, Garrin revealed his final pronouncement.

"We share a common blood, Micah Stormcrown. Across oceans and ages, fate has seen fit to reunite us. The last of the Firewalkers and the last Oathsworn. *We* are your people, Micah. Our home—your real home—lies far beyond this despicable island."

He left Micah rendered mute, dumbfounded. Unable to answer as Garrin's words tumbled like boulders in his spinning mind. Light grew in the distance, the Mist quietly vanishing as the sun neared the horizon.

"That can't be true," he finally stammered.

"I have never lied to you," said Garrin simply. "Search your thoughts, and you will feel the truth of my words. Perhaps if you'd accepted them sooner, you would have felt the weight of my offer in the grove. You could have redeemed the Stormcrown name."

"My answer would have remained the same," Micah quickly denied. "I don't care if I am the last Oathsworn. I still wouldn't join you."

"I assumed as much. Still." Garrin smirked. "Declaring you the 'last' Oathsworn is perhaps a slight exaggeration. Your time with the Collective was most... enlightening."

Another riddle.

"What do you mean?" Micah demanded. "Explain!"

Armeia's horse stepped forward, the woman clearly agitated.

"You've gained a second—no, a third chance, by my reckoning." Garrin laughed. "My, my, you *are* a lucky one. It seems you are spared execution once again. Furthermore, you will have your wish. We'll leave your pitiful city with its naïve mages. For now. That is the final mercy you will receive."

Garrin turned to join the other Firewalkers waiting anxiously in the charred field. Before he reached them, Garrin looked back, his gleaming eyes freezing Micah in place.

"Remember this, Stormcrown," he growled. "Should our paths cross again, should you meddle in our affairs, neither our shared blood nor your Oathsworn heritage will save you." Without another word, he leapt into his saddle.

"Answer me!"

As the sun greeted the land, the Firewalkers retreated, angling their horses east and racing off across the plain. Their shapes faded into the distance, vanishing in the glare of the coming day. Answers to the questions exploding in Micah's head dissipated like the breaking Mist, lost forever in Garrin's twisting speech.

"The Mist is gone!" a defender below shouted triumphantly, breaking the fragile silence. Men turned to each other, muttering as they cautiously watched the mages. And him.

"Let's... report to the governess," Logan awkwardly offered. Micah cast a final, fuming glance at Garrin's receding figure.

Together, they made their way down from the wall with Tomas, Kelj, and Hogrom and headed towards Farhaven Manor. The city below began to awaken in the bright morning light. With the all-clear cheerily sounding, residents joyfully returned to the streets, celebrating another day.

Greenwatch was safe. The Mist and the Firewalkers were gone. As much as Micah wanted to join in the jubilation, he couldn't. His entire existence had been shattered.

Who am I?

Chapter 23
Gathering Storm

"THE CARPENTERS WILL MOVE immediately to repair the gate, and the walls will be reinforced wherever possible," Logan concluded. "It was a hard fight, but numerous lessons were learned. We'll be more prepared for the next one. Whatever comes."

Tension hung over the governess' throne room as the group contemplated in anxious silence.

"Walls will not stop determined mages," said Director Mai coolly. "The beasts of the Mist may be thwarted by your physical barriers, but what of arcane defenses?"

"We've never faced hostile wizards before," Logan bristled. "How were the men supposed to be ready for *that*?"

"Enough," Lady Mira commanded. "Captain, your defense of the city is commendable, as are your plans. Director Mai, I wholeheartedly agree with your concerns. As such, I ask that you select a contingent of your most powerful battlemages to train alongside our other defenders."

"*What?*" The director's jaw nearly dropped to the floor.

"Your Collective has the expertise Captain Logan requires, and your presence and camaraderie among the men will go a long way towards mending the trust you and other mages have broken," Lady Mira replied with a hint of steel. "As your patron and governess, this is a request you would do well to accept."

"Of course, my lady." Mai nodded, masking her agitation. "I will identify those with the necessary experience and direct them to Captain Logan. I merely wish to caution the impact this could have on our efforts to understand the Mist."

"You mean your man-stealing," Kelj growled.

Mai shot a furious look at the towering warrior before the governess silenced the pair with a glance.

"Except for the immediate defense of the city, your research into a countermeasure against the Mist and a cure for the Mist-marked are our highest priorities. We must not allow any more of our citizens to be turned into agents of our destruction," Lady Mira directed. "Which brings us to my next point. There *will* be a discussion concerning your prior actions in obtaining subjects for your research. You are to remain here until the council convenes this afternoon."

The director's jaw clenched in indignation, but she remained quiet.

Lady Mira continued, "Given the dire circumstances of our situation, the Greenwatch Guard will coordinate with the Collective to organize a city-wide screening of all citizens to identify the remaining Mist-marked. The Collective is henceforth forbidden from approaching or harassing citizens in secrecy. All those carrying the curse are entitled to an explanation of the grievous fates that could await them, but are to be given the choice to join our efforts to find a cure. Those who refuse will be confined to a designated shelter within the unused section of Underhaven, overseen by officials selected by Administrator Arland. Their final option, regrettably, is expulsion from Greenwatch. Thus far, we have been blessed to have none of the Marked transform within the city walls. That is a record I aim to maintain."

"That is a fair compromise," Logan slowly concurred, "though the Guard will be hard-pressed to provide the manpower for all of these projects."

"I feared as much. Captain, you are hereby permitted to enlist volunteers to assist in carrying out these tasks," Lady Mira added. "Find any willing citizens able to responsibly bear this burden."

Logan saluted. "Yes, my lady." The room settled into an uneasy assent.

"Now"—the governess sighed—"if our pressing issues have been addressed, there is a final matter I wish to discuss."

"The Firewalkers?" Logan offered.

"Indeed. Karthmoor appears to have a new enemy, and a dangerous one at that. What is their goal?"

The room immediately fell silent, everyone hesitant to speak.

"Prior to the revelations at the wall, it would seem their primary objective was our annihilation," Director Mai quietly answered. "Tomas' theory is sound. They must be the ones behind the murder of our other researchers."

"Because of their work on the Mist-marked?" Micah ventured.

"Yes. Our people likely outlived their usefulness." Mai sadly shook her head. "I fear the origin of our ability to find the Mist-marked is derived from the Firewalkers, given not for our mission of a cure, but the alternate goal of hastening their attempts to exterminate the innocent. The power is unlike any magic used in Edros. The Firewalkers surely guard that secret jealously."

"Then why leave so quickly after finally discovering your location?" Lady Mira interrupted. "What is so important that they would leave their hidden knowledge exposed?"

"The time pods," Micah blurted. Everyone turned, surprised. Lady Mira sat back, gesturing for him to proceed.

"Garrin obsessed over that particular memory when he invaded my mind," he explained. "Something about the pods shocked him, filled him with rage."

"I'm amazed by your fortitude," Director Mai added respectfully. "Telekinesis is very rare and perilous. To have survived an invasion with your memories intact is a miraculous thing. Even more, your connection with the Firewalker's own mind is an invaluable resource."

"A vital clue, no doubt," Lady Mira agreed. "Though the exchange on the wall does hold some... concern." The governess' hard stare bore into him. "You had not revealed your abilities as a mage. A disquieting fact, in light of Garrin's other words."

Immediately, Micah felt the chamber turn cold. Those around him exuded an air of suspicion and wary distrust. Only the director appeared sympathetic.

"My magic was limited to the time I served the Karthmoor Guard," he asserted. "When I left the Guard, those skills remained behind, forgotten."

"As you say. Yet, something made you an object of fascination for these Firewalkers. Some commonality they believe you share with them." A cold edge crept into Lady Mira's voice. "Can we trust the information you offer?"

Micah paused, lost as to how to convince her of his innocence. The second his meager power was revealed, he became subject to the same prejudices the Collective endured. It was an awkward realization.

"Upon my honor, I stand as witness to his words."

Micah spun around, gaping, as Kelj stepped forward.

"You would offer this vow, *to a warlock?*" Hogrom choked.

"Honor is the highest virtue of your people," Lady Mira mused. "Am I correct in recognizing the significance of this?"

"An outsider will never fully grasp its gravity, but yes, your instinct is correct, Governess," Kelj rumbled. "My time with the warden leads me to trust his words."

Lady Mira's gaze flashed between them, contemplating.

"Very well, Warden," she relented. "Kelj has lent you his honor. Tell us everything. Anything that might shed light on the Firewalkers' cruel intentions."

Micah nodded slightly to Kelj, grateful for his testimony. He took a deep breath, then quickly recounted the events of the grove, relaying Garrin's nightmarish foray into his mind.

"Garrin returned several times to the encounter in the time pod room," he recalled, finishing his story. "As I said, he was shocked and angered by them, or something connected to them, but he was oddly uninterested in their ability. It was almost as if their existence didn't surprise him, but more so their presence in Underhaven."

"Perhaps the director can now explain what role her devices play in all of this." The governess turned as Mai shifted uncomfortably.

"I have little information to give beyond what's already been shared," Director Mai answered. "Their beginning was lost when the Collective's leadership beyond Karthmoor vanished. What little time we devoted to studying their composition before the Mist appeared revealed scant clues as to the pods' construction. We don't even know what some portions of them are made of. In all my research across Edros, they are definitively unique."

"There's no one?" Logan exclaimed, baffled. "No one in all of Edros who knows *anything* about them?"

The director hesitated, pondering what dwindling secrets she should reveal.

"Speak," Lady Mira instructed. "Anything to solve this mystery."

"The only other person who possibly knows more about them is Marinaya."

"The previous director in Greenwatch?" Micah asked.

Director Mai nodded. "Marinaya was instrumental in the Collective's research on Karthmoor. Her position as an advisor to Archon Valerius provided the connections to move our shipments quickly and without drawing attention. It also provided the means to finance our research and to persuade Governor Beckett of how much he stood to gain by welcoming us."

"So, they were the same," Lady Mira murmured, realization in her voice. "I thought it too strange to be a coincidence. The woman who created the pact with my husband never revealed her position beyond the Heraldan Collective, but I couldn't shake the feeling there was something distinctly Imperial about her."

An odd sense of fate pricked at Micah's neck. "You knew her too?"

"Indirectly. I was not a part of the meetings my husband held with the Collective. I learned of her only after his agreement had been struck. Within the circles of nobility, however, the name Marinaya was associated with an advisor of the Archon's. A position of influence within the Hamid Empire. She refused an order from Valerius and was stripped of her power, or so the rumors went," Lady Mira explained.

"Marinaya would recall a slightly different story, but you are correct in that they are one and the same. There is little point in denying that now," the director admitted.

"Is she here?" Micah asked, eager for answers.

"No," Mai replied. "There was a... disagreement with the Archmage, and she resigned. Marinaya left her position under Archon Valerius as well before joining the Hillmarch Academy as a resident scholar."

Micah's eyes brightened. "So, she's possibly still there? Assuming Hillmarch has fared as well as Greenwatch."

"There has been no word from the eastern province since the Mist began," Lady Mira cautioned. "We do not know what lies beyond the Silvenar."

"And we don't dare risk our remaining Guardsmen on a hopeless journey," Logan added.

"We're grasping in the dark," Director Mai argued. "The Collective will devote what we can towards better understanding the time pods, but without Marinaya, I cannot guarantee we'll reach a discovery before the Firewalkers locate their prize. They were ready to kill us all. Whatever they're looking for could be far, far worse."

The throne room erupted in argument, Logan and Mai shouting as the governess attempted to intervene. Micah stepped back from the fray, weighing the risks and dangers. The Firewalkers were looking for something. Something more dangerous than the loss of their precious knowledge and the Mist-marked. Yet, Marinaya might hold the key to understanding everything. Maybe even answers to Garrin's vague riddles, assuming Micah could survive a journey across the entire breadth of Karthmoor. It was a longshot, no doubt.

He stepped forward. "I will go."

The room fell silent, frustrated heads turning in surprise. A guard coughed awkwardly in the corner.

"Putting aside your abilities, your efforts on behalf of Greenwatch have been commendable, heroic even," Lady Mira offered. "We cannot afford to lose any of our defenders now. Not when the Mist attacks without warning."

"Now that the threat of Firewalkers lurks beyond our walls, I need every Guardsmen I've got, wardens with magic included," Logan concurred with a grin.

"With the Collective, you've got an army of defenders, both arcane and otherwise," Micah countered. "I've already crossed the span of your province. I know what awaits me. We must stop the Firewalkers before they find whatever it is they're after. And Marinaya might just hold the key."

The group faltered, looking to the governess for direction. She studied Micah with reserved eyes, her face expressionless. The quietness of the room only increased his anxiety.

Finally, Lady Mira nodded. "Very well."

"My lady!" Logan objected. "We can't send him out there! We're only just recovering. Without every defender—"

"Even with every Guard left on Karthmoor, we would still fall should these dark mages return with an even greater power," she reasoned. "We survived before Micah Stormcrown appeared, and we will continue to do so in his absence. In the meantime, we will pray his courage and unique skills bring him safely through this journey."

Logan halted with a stiff salute.

"Our enemies move swiftly," the governess declared. "Our warden must be swifter. Prepare his horse and gather provisions for him. Logan, have a scout retrieve the last reports from beyond our walls while everything is collected."

"Yes, my lady." Logan quickly left the room.

"Warden Stormcrown," she continued, turning to him again, "your service to me is at an end. I am grateful for the role you played in bringing truth to light in Greenwatch and for making allies out of a seemingly impossible situation."

Micah glimpsed at Director Mai, who slowly nodded in agreement.

"Even so, I ask that you do everything in your power to keep Greenwatch safe from the threat of these Firewalkers. The entire province, including Fairhollow, is in danger if they remain free to pursue their malevolent goal. End their campaign by whatever means necessary."

"As you say, my lady." Micah respectfully bowed.

"May Elowë guide your path," she finished, a hopeful look crossing her exhausted face.

Micah took his leave, exiting through the gallery hall and into the entryway. As he reached the manor doors, Director Mai called from behind.

"Wait! Hold a moment, Warden." He turned, wondering what else there was to discuss.

"There's something you should be aware of before you leave," said Mai hurriedly as she rushed over.

Her voice dropped to a nervous whisper. "I couldn't say more within the throne room. Too many ears. While I respect the governess, one loose tongue could cost me—us—everything."

"What do you mean?" Micah asked, alarm stirring.

"You're entering a dangerous game, Micah. As a fellow mage and friend to the Collective, you ought to know," she warned in a low voice. "You'll find Marinaya welcoming enough; she has a good heart. But her conscience cost her dearly."

"Her resignation?"

Mai nodded, her narrow eyes wide with fear. "It wasn't her choice. The Archmage," Director Mai whispered, casting a worried glance around the room. "He's alive. But even I don't know who it is. His, or her, identity isn't revealed, but previously, he always sent letters with each merchant. Signed with the Archmage's unique signature.

"The Archmage himself ordered the research on the time pods and made it our top priority to discover their limits. Except, not long after we moved to Greenwatch, our orders changed. The Archmage became obsessed with black iluvan, wanted us to map the entirety of its properties, including how it interfaced with time pods. He wanted to know how it would react under different stimuli. A simple enough study. Only then he demanded test subjects placed in the black pods. Marinaya refused, so he exiled her from the Collective."

Micah's eyes widened. "Which left you with the same choice. What did you do?"

"The Archmage has the ear of Archon Valerius. Marinaya was banished from the Empire, forced to remain on Karthmoor on the pain of death for the false charge of subversion. The rest of the Collective was ordered to execute her on sight if she returned. What else could I do but continue the tests?"

He gasped. "Mai..."

"The black pods were housed in our eastern enclave, near Harrowmont, to avoid any connection to Greenwatch," she continued, the dark truth spilling into the light. "None of the first subjects survived. When the Mist arrived and started killing the Mist-marked, the Archmage directed us to test them as well. That led our Harrowmont researchers to seek out a means to identify the Mist-marked, placing them in the path of the Firewalkers as we now know."

"All those people..." Micah shuddered.

"Micah, the researchers never got the chance to test the Mist-marked." Her voice filled with guilt and pain. "Right after they'd obtained the number of subjects needed, the enclave was obliterated. A single researcher escaped, passing a note to a merchant near Starkhaven before either the Mist or Firewalkers found him. All it said was, 'They are after us.'"

"And then?" He desperately wanted her gruesome story to end.

"We cut off all communication beyond Greenwatch. Soon, the messages and iluvan stopped arriving," Director Mai continued. "We assumed the rest of the Collective was consumed with problems created by the Mist. Without guidance from the master wizards, we started to turn on each other. So, I repurposed our goals. A shameful attempt to atone for what I'd done."

"And the black iluvan?"

"We stopped all research on it," Mai confessed. "We refocused on the natural shards and responsibly discovering the secrets of the time pods. Still, we'd discovered the pods' resistance to the Mist during the episodes with the black iluvan. Given the nature of the Mist-marked, we believed there was a chance to cure them of the curse. The time pods proved also to be a way to keep them safe as we worked towards that."

"You still reverted to kidnapping," he argued.

"I know, and I take full responsibility," Mai whispered urgently. "We shouldn't have fallen into that. We were just so focused on finding a cure as fast as possible. I knew the people of Greenwatch would never trust us if they learned the truth about our history on Karthmoor."

"If it weren't for the Mist, the Conclave would've tried you for your crimes," Micah coldly replied. "As it is, the governess has given you a second chance."

"I know, and for what it's worth, I still feel the horror and guilt over what I've done," Mai quietly admitted. Her normally dignified appearance contorted in regret. "But there's one last thing you should know. Your shipment of iluvan. There was a note."

That caught him off guard. "From the Archmage? Where?"

"The chests were specifically designed for iluvan. There's a hidden compartment in the bottom of each one where our directives are stored. You wouldn't ever know unless you knew what to look for."

"What did it say?" he asked apprehensively.

"Resume testing."

The words dropped like stones in Mai's hollow voice.

"You can't!" Micah exclaimed. "Mai, you can't follow that order. Any hint of treachery will throw this alliance into chaos, taking the city with it."

"I know." She swallowed nervously. "And I won't follow it. Our people are united behind this goal of a cure now. None of us could stomach that monstrousness again. The Collective can banish us to Karthmoor all they want. It's not like we're going anywhere." A small smirk crossed her face.

"You're making the right call," said Micah approvingly.

"Just be ready, Micah," the director sullenly replied. "There's no guarantee they'll leave us alone. Certainly not you if you draw their attention. The Archmage is out there. The Archon too. You hold to a valiant goal, but there are plenty of powers who have their own designs on the Mist. You'll need every bit of strength and cunning to survive their game."

Micah nodded. Another layer of danger added to the curious strands tying their fates together.

"If we had more time, I would happily offer to help grow your talents," Mai mused wistfully. "Should you have the chance, learn all you can from Marinaya. She is a powerful magician."

"I will, and thank you for the warning." Micah bade her farewell and left Farhaven Manor, pausing on the street below.

The gentle breeze teased wispy clouds in the morning sky above, the cheerful sight contrasted by the dark machinations of men below. A brief flash of his friends in Fairhollow crossed Micah's mind. A bittersweet recognition that his journey was far from finished.

Elowë, keep them safe.

Chapter 24
Parting Rumors

THE MOMENT MICAH STEPPED through the door of the Seagull's Roost, the boisterous laughter dissipated. An uncomfortable atmosphere settled over the tavern as the rowdy bunch recognized him. Around the bar, men slowly turned back to their drinks, their exchanges transforming into agitated mutterings and sidelong glances. Teig urgently beckoned to Micah from the counter in the center. Micah quickly maneuvered through the room's perimeter, avoiding the crowded tables of wary men.

"Warden Stormcrown." Teig nodded as he arrived. "Welcome back. I hate to do this, as you've done right by me. All of Greenwatch too, even if folks 'round here won't acknowledge it. But I'd suggest you collect your things and find a more hospitable location to lodge. I fear you'll find the patrons here rather... perturbed, on account of the rumors."

Micah hadn't expected word to travel so quickly. He cast a quick glimpse around the bar, fearful and saddened by the speed at which his circumstances had changed.

He shrugged. "I'm leaving Greenwatch, anyway. You've been an excellent host, Teig. I appreciate it."

Teig nodded in thanks as Micah hurried towards the stairs. In his small room, he haphazardly stuffed belongings back into his leather travel pack. After a brief survey of the space, Micah shut the door, returning to the bar downstairs and heading for the exit. Just before he reached the door, a large, burly man, clearly deep in his ale, leaned out from a table, blocking the way.

"Leaving so soon, mage?" he taunted. "Off to cast some spells? Don't burn down any of our houses now."

"I have no quarrel with you," Micah replied steadily. "Let me pass." His fists instinctively clenched, trembling.

"Oh, of course, your wizard-ness," he goaded as his comrades laughed. "I'm sure you have urgent, magicky business with your new friends beyond the wall."

"They're my enemy too," Micah argued. "Not all mages are the same. Most of them you'll ever meet are far better people than those fiends."

"Pah!" The man scowled angrily. "There's nothing good about wizards. Touting your haughty powers above the rest of us like we're dumb beasts. Worse, you can't even control them. Abusing people, destroying their lives and livelihoods for your own amusement. I don't see a difference. You, your pals hiding in our city, those Fire-wizards—You're all fiends in the end."

"Then you're an ignorant oaf," Micah retorted. "Out of my way."

"Gladly." He jerked back to the table. "And take your sorcerer friends with you!"

Micah glared at the drunken man as he stomped past, thrusting open the door and slamming it shut. An older man, passing by on the street and lost in a scrap of parchment, jumped in fright. Micah slowly cleared his head as he approached the square.

I'm sure that really improved their opinion, he sulked, reprimanding himself. Normally, he was in better control. *Apparently, I'm more sensitive to this subject than I realized.* Suddenly, Micah was aching to be back home, his real home before the Mist, with Elisa. The simple peace of the farm, his family, a humble life. All of that felt like a dream now.

How could a soldier, a mage, like me hope for that?

Micah shook the depressing thoughts from his mind, focusing on the road as he headed towards the gate.

At the stables, Logan stood hovering over a table covered in worn pages and hastily scrawled images. Kelj was beside him, pointing at one of the maps. Beyond them, Edoran waited patiently, refreshed and recently groomed. A finely stitched saddle filled with supplies rested on his back. Another large, dark-colored horse was tethered beside him.

"Micah," Logan greeted warmly. "We were wondering where you'd disappeared to."

"Just grabbing my things," Micah replied as he adjusted the pack. "Ran into a little altercation leaving the tavern."

Logan's brow furrowed. "It'll be a long time before people accept magic, for good reason, but it's regrettable they'd dismiss your service as warden and actions on our behalf so quickly. If there's ever been a mage the common folk should welcome, it's you," he said encouragingly.

"I appreciate the support," said Micah with a small smile.

"Now, Kelj here retrieved our final scouting reports," Logan began. "Unfortunately, it's been a long time since anyone has explored beyond the crop fields. The risk is simply too great when there's a city to protect."

Micah nodded. "I understand. Greenwatch is the priority. I know the path through the Greenwood is relatively safe, but it would add a large amount of time to the trip."

"Right," Logan agreed, shaking his long hair. "The quickest route is here." He pointed to a twisting line on the weathered map. "The Old North Road. Ol' North runs all the way to Hillmarch on the eastern shore. It'll take you through Bowman's Crossing first. The last communication we had with the Crossing was just after the Mist appeared. Folks had already begun evacuating during the Anderfall Invasion. The rest were moving towards Hillmarch or Starkhaven when it hit."

"Our chieftain sent scouts to Lake Hemeth before the Mist besieged Frostharbor," Kelj added. "They did not return."

"The north was a dangerous place even before the Mist, as I'm sure you're aware," Logan cautioned. "Lots of strange beasts and creatures roam the Frozen Wastes and wilds. There's no telling what kind of nightmares the Mist has created there."

"If we're going to beat the Firewalkers to Marinaya, I have to risk it," Micah concluded. "The north it is."

Logan nodded with a grave look on his tired face.

"Beyond the Crossing, everything else is completely outdated. Hazelcourt and Dorn would be your next stops, but it's unlikely they've fared any better. I'm afraid you'll be on your own until you reach Hillmarch."

"Not alone," Kelj interrupted.

Micah looked curiously at the towering warrior. Kelj stepped back from the table and turned to him, his curious blue markings wavering under a stoic frown.

"Knaerlck Stormcrown," he proclaimed, "I ask permission to accompany you."

"You want to come with me?" Micah stuttered in disbelief. "A mage traveling into who knows what?"

"A warlock you may be," Kelj gruffly answered, "but you have proven your honesty and bravery. My people forbid magic, but your actions reveal an honor we have not witnessed in the magic-cursed. I seek to complete your quest and increase my own honor and glory as your shield-brother."

"Shield-brother?" Micah repeated, puzzled.

"The Anderfall do not fight alone. Our warriors are bonded to one another, by solemn vow and the blood of their battles. By this, we are made shield-brothers."

"Then... Hogrom?"

"The importance of your quest outweighs all other concerns. I will leave one shield-brother for a time to join with you, but the original oath is not broken," Kelj explained. "I will be a shield-brother to both, joining us all as a shield-pact. Our armies are strongest when all men are joined by this common bond."

"Sounds like a high honor," Logan observed, crossing his arms. "No wonder the Anderfalls are such disciplined warriors."

"The governess has released me from her service," Kelj finished. "Only your word remains."

"I can see how much this means to you," said Micah humbly, "and you honor me with this offer. Knaerlck Kelj, I gladly accept your request."

Kelj nodded, clearly pleased. He drew his axe, resting its head on the ground between them and grasping Micah's forearm with his hand.

"By the strength of my axe, the honor of my ancestors, and the blood of our enemies, I pledge myself to you as shield-brother, Micah Stormcrown," Kelj vowed. "By our shared might, may we seek greater glory and higher honor in life and in death. Let all our deeds be done for this purpose, to the glory of the Allfather."

Micah repeated the pledge to Kelj, and he nodded in approval.

If I'm going to be riding off into the unknown, at least I'll have another warrior at my side.

"My horse, Coalfire, is saddled and ready," Kelj added. Above them, the morning sun was nearing its peak.

"There's no time to lose, then. Unless there's anything else?" Micah turned to Logan.

"That should be it. The horses are fed and packed. You'll find supplies for the road, including a fur cloak for the cold nights and a parchment with notes from our reports here," answered Logan, drumming the table. "Ultimately, success will depend on your speed and wit. This isn't the Karthmoor we all knew. It's the Mist's territory now."

Micah nodded, acutely aware of the dangers stalking beyond the safety of the high walls. Logan saluted, and Micah returned the gesture before shaking his hand in a final farewell.

"I hate to see the Warden of the West leave Greenwatch," said Logan, grinning grimly, "but if anyone is going to unravel the mysteries at work here, it's you. Good luck, sir."

"Thank you, Captain," Micah gratefully replied. "Keep the city safe. Elowë watch over you."

Micah and Kelj withdrew to the horses, untying the reins and climbing up. Micah could feel Edoran's impatience to get going, eager for wide spaces to stretch his legs. Logan walked them to the gate before mounting the stairs to the battlements. A host of men, busily deconstructing the solid barricade so the carpenters could repair the damage, jumped aside to give them space.

Passing under the high stone arch, Micah was overcome by an ache in his heart just as when he had left Fairhollow. The life of an explorer made parting a regular event. Still, through the tumult of the Mist, leaving another bastion of refuge cast a disheartening tone upon his departure.

Kelj eyed him oddly as Micah wistfully looked back at Greenwatch, Edoran carrying him slowly away.

At least there'll be some conversation to pass the time on this trip, he thought.

Kelj passed by without a word.

Or not.

High atop the city wall, Logan's lone figure watched them fade into the distance, his arm raised in farewell. Micah raised his own in reply before turning to face the empty fields ahead.

The road to Greenwatch had been a long and twisting journey.

A longer one awaited.

Chapter 25
Bowman's Crossing

By the third day, Micah was immensely grateful for Logan's foresight. The sky above had traded the dazzling, warm sun that had guided them from Greenwatch for a dreary overcast spouting an icy rain. The thick, bear fur cloak became his closest friend as Micah shivered in the cold northern winds. Kelj, however, seemed right in his element, neither stopping nor showing any reaction to the sudden drop in temperature as the Old North Road wound towards Lake Hemeth. Given the distance they had covered, Micah expected they would reach Bowman's Crossing by nightfall.

The land around them had transformed from the gentle grasslands of Greenwatch into rocky moors covered in hardy northern weeds. Small groves of towering pines dotted the land, broken occasionally by hills of weathered stone.

The chilling mist resumed, drenching poor Edoran as Micah huddled in his cloak. He only hoped someone still survived in the Crossing, ready to offer a warm shelter for the night. As the mist increased to a steady rain, Micah and Kelj paused under a jagged overhang of rock on a nearby hill. The horses took a rest, enjoying a quick graze and drink from the pooling water. The land was desolate, still. Only the sound of rain filled the air.

"This place, Bowman's Crossing," Kelj began, stroking his wet, tangled beard. "What do you know if it?"

Micah had passed through the Crossing, briefly, while visiting each of the western garrisons as warden. Though it'd been years, it was unlikely much had changed.

"I remember it as an unassuming lakeshore village," he answered. "Fishing is their main commodity, the livelihood of its people. It's small, with little of importance to the world at large."

"Similar to Frostharbor, then," Kelj concluded. "What else?"

Micah scoured his brain for any information he could recall.

"Perhaps the most unique feature of the Crossing is its wildlife. An odd assortment of waterfowl and creatures call Lake Hemeth home. Even stranger beasts from the Frozen Wastes are known to migrate into the area during the winter months," Micah added.

"The people are accustomed to this?" Kelj continued, interested.

"It's a part of daily life," Micah added, smiling. "The locals actually made a sport of catching and breeding the largest glowfrogs imaginable. I remember the contest from when I visited. This one angler had bred one the size of a calf!"

"Glowfrogs?" he questioned with a serious look. "What are glowfrogs?"

"Think of a common frog but much larger, anywhere from the size of your fist to a small pumpkin, with bluish green coloring," Micah explained. "Then, add a thin appendage dangling from their head, similar to a fishing pole with a tip that glows like a hundred fireflies. That's a glowfrog. You'll find them all around Lake Hemeth."

"This contest... Do they eat the largest one?"

Micah laughed. "Eat it? No! They keep the quirky things as pets. The biggest glowfrog receives a medal."

"Hmph. A senseless waste."

"I have heard a select group of nobles consider their glowing lures a delicacy," he offered, "though it's only rumor."

"At least some have a semblance of sense." Kelj shook his head as Micah stifled another laugh at his seriousness.

"We should keep moving if we want to reach Bowman's Crossing today," Micah finished, eyeing the gloomy sky. They hesitantly returned to the road as the drizzle continued.

By midafternoon, the rain thankfully subsided. The heavy clouds returned to a lighter shade after shedding their icy load. The horses picked up the pace, happy to be rid of the downpour, their hooves clicking on the pieces of the Old North Road that were still intact. Around them, the land remained unchanged, the inhospitable features free of any signs of man beyond the crumbling road. Lucky for them, the Mist also seemed to ignore the empty plains.

As the sun dipped towards the horizon, the road drifted up a hill, hidden by the slope and rocky mounds adorning it. Urging Edoran up, Micah was quickly greeted by the sight of the Silvenar River far below. From the crest of the hill, the road tumbled down at a winding angle, racing towards the river. Tracing the road's path, he spotted the Silvenar's wide mouth where it met Lake Hemeth. The buildings of Bowman's Crossing sat beside the delta, the first sign of civilization since leaving Greenwatch.

A narrow range of small mountains enclosed the basin beyond the village.

Micah pointed. "There it is. Bowman's Crossing."

"I do not see any lights," Kelj observed.

"The sun hasn't disappeared yet. We'll probably see them better once we're closer."

The road down the towering hill proved steep and treacherous. Rains and disuse had washed out whole chunks of the road, making the last stretch to the Crossing even longer. They finally reached the bottom as the path evened out near the riverbank, following the river's course north towards the village. As they drew nearer in the dusky light, the road broke away from the river, following a smoother trail over a large hill. At the top, Micah took in another sight of the village from a closer view. To his relief, several of the houses emitted a faint yellow glow, a good sign people remained. Hopefully, with large, cozy fires.

"There're lights," he sighed with relief. Kelj nodded.

"A welcome sign. Though, from here, I do not see anyone in the streets," Kelj replied.

"It's well past dinnertime," said Micah, brushing away his concern. "Everyone is likely getting ready to turn in for the night. We'd better hurry."

They nudged Edoran and Coalfire into a brisk pace, quickly covering the remaining span of road before it ended at a wide stone bridge over the Silvenar. Bowman's Crossing waited just beyond, wrapping along the southern shore of Lake Hemeth. As the road turned to cross the bridge, Micah finally caught a glimpse of the village streets, empty, as the light of day faded. A bright moon was rising in its place. From their spot beside the river, only a single wooden home on the edge of the village emitted the welcoming firelight through a half-opened door. The backs of houses blocked the rest of the village. They directed their horses across the bridge.

The moment Edoran's hooves hit the cobblestone, the light from the house vanished. They both halted, confused.

Micah turned to Kelj. "There was a light there, just now, right?"

"There was."

They cautiously pushed on, traversing the bridge and leaving the Old North Road to turn left into the Crossing. As they reached the street traveling through the center of the village, Micah saw nothing but dark homes, the lights from before nowhere to be found. Beyond the flow of the river, everything was completely silent.

"Something is not right," Kelj whispered fiercely. He drew the axe from his back.

"Maybe they're hiding?"

The eeriness of the empty village put Micah on full alert. They slowly plodded towards the center of town. None of the lights returned. A number of houses sat with front doors ajar, swinging ominously in the faint evening breeze. Their depths were shrouded in darkness. Nearly all the buildings showed signs of wear, the wooden exteriors and thatched roofs decaying from lack of upkeep. The sides of the road were littered with the remains of nets, barrels, and fishing gear. Tiny boats sat near the houses, splintering in the harsh elements.

"This place is abandoned," Kelj quietly concluded. "No one is here."

"Not for a long time, by the looks of it, but still. Where did those lights go?"

"I am not sure, but we should not linger."

"You're right. Something feels... wrong," Micah nervously concurred.

They swiftly turned the horses around, heading back to the Old North Road.

A gurgling growl echoed from behind them.

Edoran whined in fear, nearly throwing Micah from the seat as he tried to soothe him. Kelj wheeled around, searching for the source. Then, Micah noticed a light materializing from the house ahead of them. He drew his sword as the light inched towards the door.

"Kelj!" Micah hissed.

The warrior turned back, focusing on the glow.

To their surprise, a glowing orb bobbed through the opening.

"Wait. It's a glowfrog lure." Micah let out a sigh of relief.

"Do they normally reach that height?" Kelj slowly asked, watching the dancing light.

Micah looked again. The lure was dangling about where his shoulder sat, based on the weathered door.

"No..."

As the lure moved again, Kelj drew a sharp breath.

"That is not a glowfrog."

A gruesome, scaly creature leaned out of the house, wrapping its grotesque, webbed hand around the doorframe. Fingernail-like claws dug into the wood as its members gripped the warped structure. Its large, insect-like eyes were transfixed on Micah, their shifting depths glowing orange in the light of its lure. Two holes, like a fish's nose, quivered beneath its gaze as it breathed heavily. A wide mouth opened in a snarl, revealing rows of needle-like teeth as it let out another gurgling growl.

More glowing lights sprang into existence from the surrounding houses.

"Micah..."

The monster from the house stepped out of the frame, a set of webbed feet, much like its hands, softly plopping on the wooden porch. Its pale, lean body resembled a man, but the features were closer to an actual glowfrog. Upright, Micah judged it to be slightly bigger than a large dog. Ashen blue scales covered its entire frame, a hideous, bumpy hide triggering fear deep within him. It took a couple of steps before switching to four legs, crouching in vile mockery on the street.

A chorus of gurgling growls joined with the creature.

"We must move. Now!" said Kelj.

A different growl sprang from between the houses beside Micah. Before he could react, a force smashed into his side, shoving him from the saddle. Micah grasped at a hairy arm digging into his shoulder as he hit the ground, his sword spinning away in the dust.

Mist Wolves!

The Wolf snarled as it rose over Micah, attempting to get an angle with its vicious claws. He struggled to keep a grip on its powerful arm while fumbling for his blade. Kelj shouted, spurring Coalfire towards them. The beast opened its terrifying mouth, revealing rows of dagger-sharp teeth ready to sink into Micah's flesh.

It lunged, gaping fangs racing towards his face. Suddenly, its weight vanished. Micah peeked just in time to see Edoran's bucking legs send the Wolf careening down the street, the horse's wild panic narrowly saving him. Micah scrambled for his sword, grabbing his pistol in his other hand as he rose from the dusty ground.

The Mist Wolf recovered, regaining its feet. It spun around, locking onto Micah with a furious howl before it charged. Edoran screamed in terror as Micah raised his pistol, aiming for the Wolf's head. It lunged to the side, but there wasn't enough space between them for it to dodge completely.

BOOM!

The shot connected with the edge of the beast's chest, and it yelped in pain, stumbling to the ground. It snarled defiantly as it struggled to move. Micah raised his sword, ready to finish it.

Without warning, a sea of lights swarmed out of a large house behind the Wolf. More of the lake monsters. Micah backed away towards Edoran. Instead of attacking him, the creatures swarmed the injured Wolf. In a grisly flash, they converged on the beast, tearing into it with their terrible teeth. The Wolf howled in terror, disappearing beneath the mass of scaly monsters.

The remaining ones turned, eyeing Micah as he grabbed Edoran's reins.

"Micah!" Kelj shouted as he and Coalfire barreled towards him. His axe gleamed as he swung it into the group of lake monsters. A throaty, agonized cry resounded from the horde as they tumbled back.

Just as Micah moved to mount his horse, the lake monster from before rushed for him, scrabbling on its ugly legs. It launched into the air with a triumphant shriek, webbed hands outstretched with glistening claws and needle-teeth shining in its glow. Micah lurched back, dodging the creature as it sailed between him and Edoran. It hit the ground hard, growling in frustration as it swirled around. Micah slashed furiously with his blade, cracking through its scaly arm. A tinge of pale, luminous blood instantly welled from the wound. The beast shrieked in pain, collapsing as Micah clambered into the saddle.

The rest of the creatures swarmed after Micah, growling in fury.

"Move!"

Micah spurred Edoran into a frenzy, Kelj and Coalfire galloping ahead as they raced away from the village. More lake monsters poured out of the gloomy houses lining the street, the horde growing into a glowing sea as the riders sprinted for safety. They swerved back onto the Old North Road, racing away as a mass of angry croaks and growls protested their escape. They rode hard, barely looking back as their horses fled in terror from the river valley and back into the barren moors.

As the moon rose above, Micah finally pulled Edoran into a trot. "I think we're clear," he panted, scanning the dark, empty plain behind them. Through the heavy breaths of the horses, he heard Kelj attempting to calm Coalfire.

"I have never fought creatures so hideous," Kelj puffed. "What were those?"

"I have no idea. They must have come from the Mist. Maybe it transformed the villagers into those instead of Wolves?"

"Perhaps," Kelj pondered, "unless the village was abandoned before the Mist. They may be twisted shadows of nature's beasts."

"Glowfrogs from the lake, then?" Micah theorized. "They certainly resembled them, except much larger and, you know, terrifying."

"With the Mist Wolf being one of the last unlucky villagers," Kelj finished. "I feel that is the case."

"Lurkers are a good name for them," Micah decided. "I'll be happy to never see another of their creepy faces."

Kelj nodded emphatically.

They continued their trek under the black sky, casting continued glances over their shoulders, just in case.

"I believe I have found a glowfrog worthy of entering these contests," Kelj abruptly declared.

Micah stared at him, puzzled.

"And it would make for a far more thrilling event."

It took Micah a moment for it to click before he burst out laughing.

"Wait," Micah struggled between laughs, "did you just tell a joke? Do Anderfalls do that?"

"I do not understand this word, 'joke,'" he gruffly answered. "I simply seek to increase my honor."

Micah gawked at the strange warrior, unsure of what to say.

"But it would make for an amusing sight." A smirk played at the corner of the Anderfall's mouth.

Micah chuckled as Kelj spurred Coalfire ahead.

I guess Anderfalls have a sense of humor after all.

CHAPTER 26
THE ANDERFALL'S TALE

BERIEN QUIETLY OPENED THE doors into the council chamber, and he and Micah slipped into their seats, unnoticed. Above the marbled floor, the Conclave was already at a fever pitch, debates raging amongst the rows of men and women in regal attire.

Three days into the emergency meeting of the Conclave, and there was still no consensus among its members on how to address the Anderfall Invasion.

"Order!" Speaker Olan banged a gavel from the central platform. Slowly, the din receded as his repeated command echoed around the circular room.

"Sir," one attendant beside the crystalline mirror squeaked.

"Where is Governor Beckett?" Olan impatiently demanded. "His report is overdue."

"We—we are trying to raise him, Honorable Speaker," the attendant nervously stammered. "The mirrors are responding, but no one is answering on the other end." The misty swirls of the blue mirror continued, undisturbed.

"Keep trying!" the Speaker irritably commanded. The woman jumped back to the mirror in fright. "In the meantime, Warden-Commander Berien." He turned to them. "You've been quiet these past few days. What updates from our scouts?"

Berien rose from his seat and approached the center of the room as Micah glanced at the unsettled faces around him.

"My scouts report Anderfall reinforcements have joined the siege at Farshore, Honorable Speaker," he began. "Additional Guard regiments have been sent from Karthport to flank their armies. The scouts surveying occupied Frostharbor have yet to send their intelligence. My reconnaissance team is unusually late."

"Meaning?" the Speaker pressed.

"I cannot say," Berien respectfully replied. "The weather may be delaying their messenger's return, or they may have run into trouble."

"Anderfalls?"

"It is possible."

"Sir!" the mirror attendant exclaimed.

"What is it?" the Speaker grumbled.

"We're receiving a signal."

Slowly, the lazy fog of the mirror began to shimmer. It swirled inward, rushing like a flood of water as an image rose to the surface of the crystal.

The same room from the governor's mansion appeared, but the image was no longer upright. Instead, it was angled as if the mirror had tipped. A number of windows in the background were cracked or smashed. Somewhere beyond them, a smoky glow rose from the city. Without warning, a woman's scream pierced the room, magnified by the mirror's power. The entire Conclave jolted at the sound.

"Governor Beckett?" Speaker Olan shouted. Panicked voices and chaotic commotion sprang from the image. The faint sound of gunfire and battle drifted into the mansion. The fuzzy view of the city outside the mansion windows began to change into a hazy blur of bluish white, the outlines of buildings vanishing in the bizarre scene.

"Governor, are you there?" the Speaker called again.

A shadow passed over the crystalline image, blocking Micah's view. It quickly drew back, and the figure of a young soldier appeared, collapsed on his knees. The man was clearly frightened, a trickle of blood running down his cheek from a cut as his eyes scanned the mirror room in fear.

"Soldier!" Berien hollered. The man jumped at the noise before focusing on the mirror.

"I am Warden-Commander Berien, soldier," he commanded. "What is your situation?"

"S–s–sir!" The man gave a shaky salute. "We–we're under attack!"

"By whom? The Anderfalls?" Speaker Olan interjected.

The soldier shook his head frantically. "No, no, sir. I don't know what they are," he shrieked in a panicked pitch.

"Explain yourself, soldier—now!" Berien barked.

"A fog rolled in from the west. Off the sea and hills," he answered, quaking. "Then people just started collapsing. F–f–falling right where they stood!"

"You're not making any sense, soldier," Berien reprimanded him. "What's going on?"

"There's... things in the mist, sir!" he cried. "Monsters roaming the streets, killing everyone!"

Micah glanced at Berien with nervous confusion.

"Where is the governor, boy?" Olan demanded. "Is he safe?"

"Governor Beckett was returning from his morning hunt when the fog hit," the soldier stuttered. "A man from the wall said he's dead!"

"Where's Colonel Clovis?" Berien questioned. "Find him or whoever is in charge and bring him here!"

"Y–yes, sir," the soldier stumbled as he scrambled to his feet. The sound of cracking wood echoed from the mirror. The young soldier jumped in fear.

"No!" he yelped, backing out of view. A horrible snarling emanated from the hazy image.

"Soldier!" Berien called.

Something crashed, and the man screamed. The governor's mirror tumbled from its place as the sounds continued. Just as a long, wolf-like howl started to rise from the blackened image, a deafening crack split the air, and the mirror went silent. Its black picture swirled away, returning to the calm, smoky blue surface of the crystal.

The Conclave was utterly silent.

Berien strode to a messenger stationed near the entrance.

"Send word to the battalion in Karthport," he commanded. "I need all available cavalry rerouted to Greenwatch to reinforce the western garrison." The messenger saluted and raced from the room.

"What are we facing, Commander?" Speaker Olan quietly asked. "What have we just witnessed?"

"I have no explanation for you, Speaker," Berien confessed, "but something terrible is coming."

The room filled with fearful whispering as he faced the council, frozen in place.

Micah groggily opened his eyes. The sky above greeted him with gloomy clouds as a damp breeze wafted through the prickly trees in the chilly morning air. As he peeked out of the cozy sleeping sack covered with his warm fur cloak, he spied Kelj busily deconstructing the camp. Kelj glanced over as Micah sat and stretched, his back aching from a night-long campaign against menacing rocks.

A small pot sat over the remains of the fire in the center of the clearing. Micah grabbed a quick bowl of broth, looking out into the barren moors to the north. Somewhere beyond the endless prairie, sparse evergreens, and stony pillars, lay the Northern Wilds. A twisted expanse of foreboding wilderness inhabited by Karthmoor's most dangerous creatures. He could only imagine what horrors of the Mist now called it home.

After finishing his brief breakfast, Micah sleepily packed up his gear, returning the bundles to Edoran's saddlebags. Kelj was already mounted on Coalfire at the edge of the grove, waiting. Micah hopped onto Edoran to join him, and they returned to the crumbling road.

The path remained barren, any signs of life long since faded by the weather of the open plains. While it was odd to not catch a glimpse of deer or elk, at least the effects of the Mist also remained less apparent. Having a couple days between them and Bowman's Crossing had likewise relieved some of the tension, though the eerie silence of the land begged a wary attitude. Thankfully, the immediate area was void of Mist Wolves, Lurkers, and other nameless terrors, even as an occasional bank of Mist rose thinly from the moorlands.

As the sun rose somewhere above the hazy clouds, the Old North Road took a turn away from the north, bidding farewell to the empty moors as it steered towards the center of the island. Slowly, the bleak landscape transformed from rocky weeds to richer soil and lush grasses.

"What is that?" Kelj asked as they pressed on, peering at the object rising in the distance. A solitary peak pierced the horizon, rising to the clouds above. Thoughts of home instantly flooded Micah's aching heart.

"That would be Tar'auth Eld, the Tower of Oaths in the common tongue," he explained. "The tallest mountain on Karthmoor."

Kelj studied the view in awe as they gradually moved closer. "It is a fitting name," he rumbled. "A powerful, solemn sight."

"My home sat in the western hills below the mountain," Micah reminisced, "near Aringoth. It was a beautiful sight in the evening—the final rays of light shining across its peak."

"This was before Fairhollow, then. You had a family, yes?"

"Aye, my wife, Elisa, and son, Samuel," said he quietly, the pain morphing into guilt within his soul.

"Did you dwell there?" He pointed. "In that forest?"

"That would be the Forest of Midland," Micah answered, the massive wood springing into view as they climbed over a hill. "My farm sat on its western border. No one lives in Midland, though. The trees are cursed, if the tales are to be believed. It's said they move without being seen, trapping those who enter in an ever-shifting maze."

"Do you believe the tales?"

"I've briefly traveled through the edge of the forest, and it is a peculiar place. But cursed? I don't know. There's certainly a strange... presence to the wood."

"The road did not enter the Forest of Midland on the map," Kelj observed.

"Right. It runs along its edge towards Hazelcourt to the east. There's a good chance we'll reach the village before the day is over."

"Hopefully, with better results than the Crossing," Kelj muttered. Micah shuddered, reliving their close encounter with the Lurkers.

Near midday, the road finally reached the forest. Its ancient, gnarled trees towered above the billowing fields like an imposing wall of green, stretching endlessly in either direction, swaying in the gentle breeze. The trees were so thick, Micah caught only brief glimpses of its depths, shrouded in secrecy by the mysterious wood. Thrilling mysteries seemed to whisper from the musty timbers, beckoning his curious mind. He shook the spell from his limbs and refocused on the path ahead of them.

The road gently turned from the forest, gliding back to the east along the wooded expanse. In several places, massive roots burst from the ground, splitting the stone of the road as weighty branches provided shade from the warm sun peeking through the clouds.

"Looks like the forest has expanded," Micah commented, eyeing encroaching trees.

"Curious when so much else dies under the Mist curse," Kelj replied. "The wood feels strangely welcoming. I sense something in them. An echo of my homeland."

Micah raised a brow. "The Anderfalls in Midland?"

"I cannot say why," he mused, "but it reminds me of the wild depths of Reigmar."

They continued down the broken road, taking in the old, majestic forest.

"Kelj," Micah abruptly asked, "why did your people leave the Anderfalls?"

He hesitated. "You ask why my people invaded your homeland."

Micah shrugged. "Partially. There was so much confusion when the Mist appeared. We never learned what started the invasion."

Kelj rubbed his beard, gazing into the distance with solemn eyes.

"Your people are not our enemies," he finally said. "You have only the misfortune of being our closest neighbor."

"What do you mean?"

"You wonder where this Mist curse hails from. Your wise men and elders thought it to be from Edros, the great cities of heathen men. They are wrong."

"No one knows where it came from. How can you be sure?"

"Because it invaded my homeland first," Kelj answered sadly, "from beyond the Endless Sea."

A skeptical look crossed Micah's face. "No ship has ever returned from a voyage across the Endless Sea. It's called Endless for a reason—there's nothing out there."

Kelj frowned. "I know this. It does not change the fact that the Mist came from it."

Micah shook his head as he shifted in his saddle. "So, what happened?"

"There was no warning," Kelj recalled. "It was a normal day. Men and women, each waking to their daily chores, going about their lives as any other day on Reigmar.

"My clan controlled much of its eastern coast. The capital island did not receive reports of the Mist until boats from Endwaith were already piling on the western shore. Hundreds of commoners. Men, women, children. The elderly. Those of us who escorted the ships brought tales of a killing fog slaying our people. Air is not an enemy we could fight, and so our warriors retreated to the capital island.

"The Mist halted on Endwaith, giving Reigmar time to regroup and prepare, if that is possible. I see now it was harvesting the souls left behind, creating more of its monsters.

"We had more notice when the Mist finally crossed to Reigmar and northern islands. Even so, our valiant armies were of no use against the devil's curse. As it progressed towards my clan's territory, Mist Wolves appeared, giving us a target to slay, but providing no answers to stopping the Mist's advance."

"What did you do?" Micah asked, enthralled with horror.

Kelj paused, lost in thought, as he aimlessly scanned the empty horizon.

"We were in danger of losing the capital when Jarl Angvarn ordered all seaworthy ships loaded," he continued. "Our people would cross the Ander Sea, to Karthmoor, using your homeland to fortify a stronghold against the Mist in the hopes of outlasting the scourge. Our elders assumed the Mist would linger in the Anderfalls, taking longer to cross the open sea."

"Evacuating makes sense," Micah concluded, "but why not send the Conclave an emissary? Why lay siege to our western coast, knowing what's behind you?" Kelj's face darkened.

"Jarl Angvarn was an honorable leader, but his lack of resolve in facing the curse allowed his thinking to be clouded by fear and swayed by the most vocal chieftains." His frown deepened. "The most vocal being the most bloodthirsty. Several chieftains had long sought glory through conflict with the other nations, believing our might would cause the heathen kings to cower in fear. The Mist became a pretense for invading Karthmoor and increasing their own standing.

"These shameful men, these Dishonored, counseled that occupying your cities and repurposing its citizens for the coming battles would bolster our ability to combat the Mist. Karthmoor's existing defenses would lessen the cost of our own while your ignorant masses would become fodder, buying time to strengthen our position. Ultimately, the wiser voices of the Sylmach failed to overrule them. Rather than abandon our unity and weaken our people, we obeyed our Jarl and prepared for war. There would be no declaration, only a single surprise attack to hasten our victory.

"A vast array of vessels poured across the Ander Sea, the clans dividing into two armies bent on taking your cities of Frostharbor and Farshore. With your outlying towns pacified, we would then capture your western stronghold, Greenwatch, solidifying it as a sanctuary against the Mist."

"What of the rest of Karthmoor?" Micah questioned.

"The Jarl was unwilling to press farther into unknown lands without knowing how quickly the Mist would follow," Kelj answered. "He feared leaving our rear defenses exposed. Several of the Dishonored had other intentions, however. Were it not for the fierceness of the Mist, their designs on your nation would undoubtedly have been realized."

"The Anderfalls took Frostharbor. That was the last we knew before the Mist appeared, and everything turned to chaos."

"Mmm," Kelj rumbled. "Several of the clans, including mine, were tasked with the northern front. Frostharbor was a quick, decisive victory. There was much honor in our clans' strategy as it avoided unnecessary bloodshed, using the cover of night and ambush to overwhelm your warriors and force a surrender. The

Dishonored took a more aggressive approach to Farshore. The siege cost the Dishonored dearly."

Micah nodded. "Battlemaster Carlin mentioned you were at Frostharbor."

"I was," Kelj admitted, "and I performed my duty to my kin, though I admired your people's tenacity. Even while occupied, many refused to submit to our might. Your Guard fought valiantly. Regardless, they could not hope to overcome us. The captured were forced to assist in preparing the city for the Mist while we awaited word to march on Greenwatch."

"Only the Anderfalls never made it to Greenwatch." said Micah grimly.

Kelj rubbed his beard again, a sad look reflected in his eyes.

He sighed. "The Mist arrived faster than expected. We had thought the Anderfalls and wide sea would allow more time to prepare, but the accursed fog followed too closely. As the siege of Farshore dragged on, a straggling vessel from Reigmar arrived in Frostharbor. The Mist was coming. Soon.

"We were far from sealing Frostharbor from the Mist. Its weak defenses were ill-equipped to deal with the horrors of the curse. Still, we knew there could be no escape this time. We dug in, fortified what little we could. Our chieftains even released and armed your imprisoned Guardsmen. All of them were convinced it was some twisted trap; though, when the Mist arrived, their distrust quickly disappeared.

"The Mist came with a fury, slaying villagers by the dozen in the streets. Your people refused to comprehend our warnings and panicked. As swirling fog overtook the land, Mist horrors appeared, laying siege to the city we ourselves had taken. Mist Wolves and a handful of Trolls demolished our attempts to prevent their entry, spreading through the town overnight.

"Jarl Angvarn had crossed with the Dishonored to Farshore, and our leaders in Frostharbor were consumed with fear. The clans had nowhere to run and no orders to follow. Our mighty people were separated, confused by the unknown space and Mist. Easy prey for beasts lurking in the darkened streets. No doubt some were taken and transformed into the very Wolves who slew my shield-kin."

Micah gaped at the warrior. "How did you survive?"

"The Mist invaded quickly, but the battle lingered for days," Kelj replied. "Pockets of warriors resisted across the city. A pack of Wolves and a Mist Troll attacked the barracks my clan was using as a base. The Troll tore the building apart, beams and men tossed like children's dolls. Hogrom and I were all that survived. With our shield-pact slain, we headed to join the other groups throughout the city. Those closest to us had been wiped out before our arrival.

"Alone and with the sounds of battle fading at an ominous rate, Hogrom and I decided to leave Frostharbor. We escaped the walls, drawing the attention of only a few Wolves as the rest focused on the city center. As far as we knew, our only remaining kinsmen were the southern clans, and so we chose to retreat to Farshore.

"We hoped to find an end to the Mist once we were out in the wintry landscape, but the accursed fog never left us. With only a faint glimpse of the sun, we headed south. The Mist followed. Days passed as our journey continued.

"Our ignorance of the island led us to believe Greenwatch and Farshore would lie close to Frostharbor. In the shadowy Mist, we thought we had passed Greenwatch and come upon Farshore when the road led us to the walls of another city under attack. We assumed we had finally reached the other clans who were busy defending Farshore from the Mist." Kelj gave a small smirk, glancing at the forest.

"Like ignorant children, Hogrom and I blundered into Greenwatch, slaying Mist Wolves without hesitation as we called out for our kinsmen. At that point, your people did not care that we were foreigners, only that we were fighting the Mist. We assumed they were more warriors conscripted into Farshore's defense."

"You really had no idea?" Micah asked, incredulous.

He chuckled. "None at all. It was not until we were brought to your Colonel Clovis that we realized the men were not under Anderfall control, and that the city was not Farshore. We were bound and taken to the governess to answer for what magic we had unleashed on her city."

"Lady Mira thought the Anderfalls created the Mist?"

"She did, and I cannot fault her belief," Kelj answered. "Even as neighbors, our people understand little of one another. I could not expect her to know my people outlawed the practice of magic. What else could she think, after our invasion had so quickly taken your cities?"

"So, how did you go from prisoners of war to personal body-guards?" asked Micah in amazement.

"The governess eventually believed our words, trusting in our honesty, as we held nothing back about Frostharbor," he replied. "She revealed how Farshore had been lost to the Mist as well. With all our kin and clan killed or vanished, Hogrom and I were lost. It was impossible to return home, if there was even a home to return to. Our Jarl and chieftains had been slain, as had our shield-pact. All that remained was the Mist. If we were to avenge our people, our only option was to ally with yours to face the Mist curse. Thus, we came to serve Greenwatch, eventually earning positions as the governess' life-guardians." Kelj smiled. "Ironic, is it not? The invaders became its defenders."

He fell silent as his tale ended. Only the occasional call of a hawk echoed across the empty landscape. As trees passed unceasingly alongside Edoran, Micah pondered the harrowing journey Kelj had taken to reach this place with a newfound respect. While there was still much he struggled to understand of the warrior's ways, loss was something they both were well acquainted with. For now, that was enough.

CHAPTER 27
HAZELCOURT

THEY TREKKED ON IN silence, the afternoon sun passing overhead as a cool breeze pushed the clouds away. The rich grasslands rustled calmly on one side and the curious trees on the other. Micah and Kelj stopped briefly at a small brook where they rested and refilled their water skins after a short midday meal. The Old North Road stretched endlessly into the distance. Micah mulled over Garrin's riddles as they continued their ride, the journey and his answers moving frustratingly slow.

As the afternoon ended and the failing light signaled the evening's arrival, the gentle plains and forest abruptly sank into the horizon. Reaching the rocky overlook, Micah and Kelj found themselves gazing down a large slope where the grasslands and forest continued over another vast plain. Looking ahead, Micah spotted several wispy columns of smoke rising from a curious tendril of forest spilling over the road and onto the plains. Around it, the earth showed sign of cultivation.

"Hazelcourt?" Kelj asked as he studied the strange sight.

"It should be, but the trees aren't making any sense. Hazelcourt is a good distance away from the forest. And Midland should be on the complete other side of the road."

"It would seem the woods have grown."

"It can't be," said Micah, gawking. "I passed through Hazelcourt only a year before the Mist. There's no way the forest grew that quickly. Surely the townsfolk wouldn't let it take over the road."

Kelj shrugged as they headed towards the odd spectacle.

As they approached the outskirts of the growth, thick trees blocked any view of wherever the smoke was originating from. It was quickly apparent that it would be impossible to guide the horses through the dense vegetation. Thankfully, the road itself remained open; its stony path was curiously free of the choking foliage. Towering, twisting trees, their weathered branches swaying in the evening wind, covered the shadowy road like a great wooded tunnel.

"I guess... follow the trail?" Micah suggested. "Maybe there'll be a break closer to the village."

"Perhaps," Kelj replied with a hint of caution.

Hesitantly, Micah guided Edoran into the gloomy passage. The light of the fading sun promptly vanished in the thick canopy. Only scattered beams broke through the branches. The forest was completely still beyond the sound of hooves on the stony path. Imposing trees and moss-laden branches seemed to press in as they moved deeper. Old, musty air filled the space between the foliage, adding to the primitive aura of the wood.

"Micah!" Kelj abruptly whispered.

His gaze jerked away from the forest just as a man walked out of a break in the trees ahead, guiding a small cart. Upon spotting them, the man jumped in surprise before dropping the handles and rushing back into the gap. Micah motioned for Kelj to press forward. As they approached the spot, a faint light emanated from the shadowy path. A dirt trail led away from the Old North, quickly ending with the glow of fading sunlight and an escape from the dense woods. At the exit, someone had erected a set of tall, wooden barricades. A rough gate of thin trunks lashed together provided passage in and out of the forested tunnel. As they neared the structure, a man's head peeped over the coarse wall.

"Who goes there?" he shouted in a shrill voice. A worn leather cap covered his dusty, unkempt hair. His face was young, a smattering of youthful whiskers spouting from his chin. His wide eyes watched them warily.

"I'm Micah Stormcrown, and this is Kelj. We've come from Greenwatch seeking rest in Hazelcourt."

"Greenwatch?" the young man gaped. "That's impossible. No one could've survived out there, let alone traveled all the way from the western shore."

"I assure you my words are true, and either way, we're simple travelers. We mean no harm."

The man studied them with suspicion.

"Is this Hazelcourt?" Micah pressed.

The man paused, unsure of how much to say. "It... is," he relented. "What's left of it, anyways."

"What's going on here?" an irritated voice hollered from behind the barricade.

The young man whisked around, focusing on someone hidden from view. "Mayor Stern!" he exclaimed. "There are travelers at the wall."

"Travelers? Pah! Bandits more likely," the cranky man hollered.

"Wh–what do I do?" the man stuttered.

"Well, for starters," the mayor replied, "stop quaking like a frightened schoolgirl. Second, move aside so I can take a look at 'em." The young man rubbed his neck ashamedly, stepping down from the barricade.

The sound of heavy steps climbing the wood echoed through the tunnel as Micah stared at the empty barrier. A dark hat poked over the top as the mayor strained to see.

"Fetch a stool, Caspin!" he barked. The young man dashed off.

"Curse these high walls," the older man grumbled quietly. After a moment, the sound of rushing feet on the hard dirt returned. Micah heard Caspin climb up to the mayor, thumping a wooden stool onto the parapet.

"Now then," the mayor groused. "Let's see who's lurking out there."

A wrinkled face appeared above the rough defenses. A worn but expensive looking top hat covered wispy gray hair as the mayor strained to peer at them, squinting his dark eyes with distrust.

"Well, what do you want?" he gruffly called. A grizzled mustache wrinkled above his frowning mouth.

"We're seeking a brief rest on our journey to Hillmarch," Micah replied. "We mean no harm to your village."

"Hillmarch?" he asked incredulously. "Haven't you heard, man? There's no Hillmarch left."

Micah's gut twisted in dread. "What do you mean? What's happened to the city?"

The mayor rubbed his mustache, pondering. After a moment, he shrugged and waved his hand dismissively.

"Pah!" he spat. "Caspin, open the gate and let these lost men in. We'll have a proper talk."

Micah heard the sound of chains and bars scraping against the wall as Caspin struggled to undo the locks.

"Come now, boy," the mayor chided. "My grandmother could open this gate faster than you, and she's dead!"

"Yes, sir!" the young man abashedly replied.

The barricade door swung open, revealing Caspin's flustered face. His lanky form awkwardly moved aside as the portly mayor stepped forward. The mayor was a startlingly short man dressed in what was once exquisite formal wear, now covered in a patchwork attempt to maintain its worn fabric. He motioned them in, and they directed the horses through the small opening.

On the other side, the tunnel of trees evaporated, and the evening sunlight returned to the dusky sky. A vast clearing filled with modest cabin homes, dirt roads, and pens of animals sprawled before them. Villagers passed along the streets, pausing to marvel as newcomers entered the sheltered village.

"Now then," Mayor Stern said from behind Micah. "You can leave your horses at the stable there and follow me." He gestured to a tiny structure near the fence.

The old man quickly led them down the center road. Curious faces and a flood of whispers greeted them as citizens monitored their trek. To Micah's pleasant surprise, several groups of children raced between the houses, laughing, as parents shouted in scolding tones, calling them home for bed.

The mayor turned towards a wide house near the center of the village. A humble porch spanned the front of the log dwelling, where weathered rocking chairs creaked softly in the evening breeze. Its worn roof hung low over the entrance, low enough that Kelj had to duck to enter the house. Inside, a warm fire burned in the small stone fireplace, casting flickering shadows in the dim room. A modest set of rustic seats surrounded a small table in front of it. The cozy space was covered with various animal furs and a handful of tired paintings. A narrow doorway shrouded the rest of the mayor's dark home from view.

Mayor Stern crossed the creaking floor, taking a seat in front of the fire.

"Well?" he grumbled, motioning to the seats. They quickly moved to fill them.

"I'm Mayor Stern," he began, "the official representative of Hazelcourt. Who might you be?" He sat back, crossing his arms over his wide belly.

"I'm Micah Stormcrown, former Warden of the Guard," Micah answered, "and this is Kelj, defender of the Governess of Greenwatch. We're simple travelers on the Old North Road. We anticipated passing through your village but didn't expect to find Hazelcourt like this."

"You mean the forest." His round head bobbed knowingly.

"Yes." Micah nodded. "I don't recall Midland ever being this close to Hazelcourt."

"In a different time, you'd be right. It seems that with the world gone mad, the forest decided to join in." Mayor Stern cleared his throat. "Shortly before the Mist arrived, trees started sprouting at an unnatural pace in the fields between the village and Midland. Farmers would pull healthy saplings out of their crops one morning, only to have more appear the next dawn. Eventually, they couldn't keep up."

"Are the woods known for such feats?" Kelj interjected, fascinated.

"Not in the history of Hazelcourt. It must've been some nefarious magic," the mayor replied disgustedly. "Some mischievous wizard likely figured he'd get a laugh swallowing the town with a bunch of trees."

"You said this started before the Mist?" said Micah, gently corralling the exchange.

"Aye, maybe a month before the first travelers fled through," he groused. "We had to abandon the fields as the forest grew. Within a week, it'd reached the Ol' North. Then it kept growing towards Hazelcourt. Folks started getting mighty nervous as it drew closer. At that point, the entire town went out to cut back the growth, but hacking at the trees on this side of the road was like trying to cut steel. Only the strongest axes could even make a dent in the young trunks. Anything else shattered. Most of us who hadn't already done so resolved to flee the village as it reached the houses.

"Except, once it did, the trees stopped moving forward. Instead, they began growing *around* the village. Can you believe that?" The mayor laughed in disbelief.

"Within four weeks after it began, all of Hazelcourt was surrounded by a great wall of trees, completely impenetrable from the outside. The only route in or out was a narrow path along the Ol' North," he continued. "We soon learned the trees along that path could be trimmed back, letting us widen the opening enough to haul whatever carts and gear the farmers needed to tend to their crops. We're lucky that path remained. Without it, we would've been trapped in our homes, left to starve."

"And the trees simply stopped growing?" Kelj questioned, incredulous.

"Wouldn't you know it. Had to be magic—there's no other answer." Mayor Stern frowned. "Still, the woods have proven to be a reliable defense against the Mist. It doesn't seem to like the trees. Plus, we've heard monsters in the fog roaming beyond the village, but they've yet to find a way in."

"That's incredible," Micah remarked. "It's a relief to know other places are finding ways to survive."

"Indeed," said Mayor Stern curiously, "which brings me back to my question. You mentioned you hail from Greenwatch." He eyed Kelj with caution. "What madness caused you to set out for Hillmarch?"

"We're tasked with an important mission vital to the safety of the city," Micah evasively answered.

"Important, eh?" the mayor mused. "What sort of mission would cause two young men to leave the walls of the western capital and brave the dangers of the Mist?"

"We are searching for someone," Kelj replied bluntly.

"Who?"

"A resident of Hillmarch," Micah hesitantly revealed. "One of the scholars visiting the Academy."

"A mage, you mean," Mayor Stern bristled. "Unnatural folk. What on Elowë's good earth could you want with one of those treacherous wizards?"

"The Mist brought a spate of dangerous mysteries to our home. This scholar may have information that could stop a threat to Karthmoor."

"You speak in riddles like one of those magic-cursed devils," the crusty old man retorted. "What makes you think they'd help you? The Mist is clearly their fault."

"Even so, there's reason to believe this person could help save the lives of hundreds of people. We have to reach Hillmarch," Micah earnestly finished.

Mayor Stern leaned back, his bushy eyebrows furrowed in thought.

"Like I told you, Hillmarch is gone." He shook his head. "There's nothing for you there."

"What do you mean, gone?"

"I mean the Mist took the entire city. Endless packs of terrible monsters murdered every poor soul in the Eastern Jewel. Only a handful of survivors made it out." Micah's heart dropped, grieved at the thought of thousands of innocent lives cruelly taken by the evil curse.

"But some escaped?" he asked, grasping at hope.

"Some. Led by a group of mages, of all people," the mayor scoffed.

Micah's ray of hope blossomed. "From the Academy? Where are they now?"

The tired elder grumbled.

"Story is the mages led folks from Hillmarch to Dorn first, but the group was too much for the village to handle. Dorn tossed 'em out. Not that I blame them," the mayor griped. "Last we heard, the survivors had built a camp on the western shore of Long Lake, near the mouth of the Winding River. Now, there's a rumor that refugees from all over the island are making their way there, hoping the mages can shelter them from the Mist. Hogwash, if you ask me. Only a madman would seek help from that two-faced lot."

Micah glanced over at Kelj, who nodded.

"Thank you, Mayor Stern," said Micah graciously. "This information could be vital." With a nod of approval, his grouchy demeanor receded slightly.

The cabin door opened, and a middle-aged man entered the room dressed in rough, mud-stained clothing. A simple, dark beard adorned his weathered face below a head of tousled hair. From the look of him, Micah reckoned him to be a farmer from the area, his hands callused from years in the field, while his arms were strong and able. Mayor Stern nodded in welcome and motioned for him to join the group.

"This is Benrick," the mayor explained. "He'll show you to your rooms for the evening. Before you go, however, give me what news you have from the western province. I assume Greenwatch has fared better than the rest of us?"

"Life in Greenwatch is difficult, but its walls are thick, and its people are tough," Micah answered. "The Mist is a relentless force, but so far, they've been successful in keeping the worst of it from entering the city." He quickly recounted the state of the city, along with his travels throughout the western province. The mayor listened with keen interest as Micah recalled their encounter with the Lurkers of Bowman's Crossing and the journey to Hazelcourt.

"It would seem there are new dangers prowling beyond our fair village," he observed with concern, "but it is good to know there are still others out there. Perhaps one day, we'll be able to reconnect with Greenwatch and Fairhollow." Mayor Stern's gaze drifted away from them, deep in thought. After a moment, he snapped back.

"We aren't keen on outsiders here, but I appreciate your openness," he finished with only a modest hint of irritation.

"You've been most hospitable," said Micah warmly. "On our honor, we'll leave your peaceful village at first light." Mayor Stern grunted in satisfaction.

Benrick stood as they shook hands with the mayor. Turning away from the warm fire, Micah and Kelj followed as he led them back outside.

The sky was dark as Benrick guided them on a twisting route between buildings. The mass of curious villagers from before had vanished, families safely ensconced in their houses for the night. A serene aura filled the village as night descended, the towering trees of Midland rocking above like protective watchmen.

Benrick ushered them to a small log-framed house not far from the entrance to Hazelcourt. The inside was dark and musty, though clearly a family had once lived here. Small painted toys lay scattered in front of a quaint fireplace. The kitchen counter along the opposite wall was littered with dishes. Piles of plates and utensils were stacked haphazardly, as if their owners had abruptly left. An uneasy feeling crept over Micah.

"Don't mind the mess," Benrick quipped. "The family who lived here fled when the woods began surrounding Hazelcourt. Haven't heard from them since."

As Micah looked around the gloomy room, he couldn't help but imagine how terrified the couple must have been. Where did they go, trekking across the island with a young child? *Creator, let them be safe.*

"There're a couple of beds in the back rooms." Benrick pointed to the narrow hall beyond the living area. "Should be clean enough for a night, though no guarantees they're sizable." He looked up at Kelj awkwardly.

Micah shrugged and turned to face him. "Thank you, Benrick."

Benrick nodded. "Follow the road outside south when you get up in the morning. It'll lead you to the stable," he added. "If you need anything, I'm three houses down, on the other side of the road." With that, he left the house, the thin timber door slamming shut against the tired frame. The cabin felt even more desolate without another presence.

Kelj's boots thumped loudly across the dusty floor as he headed towards the hall. They found two doors across from one another in the narrow space, each revealing a small, cozy bedroom. Kelj turned, claiming what appeared to have been the parents' room. Wood-carved nightstands sat in the dark, gathering dust beside the wide bed. Even with its large size, it was obvious Kelj was in for an uncomfortable night.

Micah turned to his own, a tiny room littered with more wooden toys and a handful of little clothes scattered across the floor. He reached down, grasping a small, knitted sweater covered with dust. A memory of Samuel's first winter flashed into his mind.

His bright, smiling face glancing at Micah from across the snowy yard. His little nose turning red in the chilly air as his short legs vanished in the deep drift. Fresh snow sailing into the air, Samuel laughing wildly.

The scene filled Micah's heart with a desperate ache. He dropped the sweater, quickly leaving the room. Back in the main area, a rough, wooden couch rested against the wall near the fireplace.

It won't be comfy, but it's better than in there.

Sighing, he dropped his gear beside the couch and resigned himself to a sore wakening.

At least we're safe for the night.

Chapter 28
Out of the Woods

A ROOSTER'S CRY STARTLED Micah from his sleep. Faint beams of morning light filtered through the front windows, where wisps of dust danced in the dazzling rays. The musty smell of the cabin slowly returned as he rose from his makeshift bed. He heard Kelj shuffling around in his bedroom. Micah stretched and immediately felt his stiffness. It would be a rough day of riding.

Micah moved to the fireplace, gathering dry remnants of kindling and wood to heat a quick meal. He piled the stack of splintered logs and twigs on the charred stone and reached for his flint. Grasping the leathery pouch, he hesitated. Where once he wouldn't have even considered the thought, the cryptic words from Garrin now taunted his pride.

Had you devoted more attention to your studies, you might be as powerful as I am.

Garrin's chiding tone stoked the indignation in Micah's heart. *If I'm ever going to stand a chance against the Fire-walkers, I must become stronger.*

He shoved the flint back into his pack and returned to the blackened fireplace. Micah squatted in front of the cold stone, closing his eyes in an attempt to center himself. Aside from Kelj rustling his belongings together, the world was quiet. He took a deep breath, relaxing his body and emptying his swirling thoughts.

Micah reached into the void, searching for the barrier shrouding his untapped energy. This time, the path appeared more quickly as his mind recalled the way. A tingling sensation built as his consciousness focused on the spark, its deep power veiled behind the nameless barrier. As Micah pressed against the resistance, he sensed more time passing. Doubt quietly began to rise, causing his attempts to pierce the barrier to falter.

He was at the edge of surrender when his flailing pounding managed to find purchase. Micah gasped, raising a hand as his mind hammered against the weakness and released the spark. A flicker of flame shimmered from his outstretched palm. He exhaled wildly; the flicker exploding in a weak, chaotic tendril as it licked towards the fireplace. Luckily, the dry straw caught, and a small fire sprang into existence.

Then Micah noticed the smoking floorboard next to the hearth.

He swiped a worn cloth from the table and rushed to smother the wayward flame. Thankfully, the thick fabric resisted the fire's attempt to spread as he frantically stamped the wood. In moments, the fire was extinguished, leaving a charred groove in the ancient floor.

Micah collapsed on the floor, attempting to calm his mind as the magic's toll of energy drained from his body. Just knowing the path to summon the power clearly wouldn't be enough.

"A dangerous move."

Micah twisted around to find Kelj standing rigidly near the hall. His arms were crossed over his wide chest, his mouth pursed in disapproval.

"A shield-brother you may be, but I do not understand the cause for magic," he gruffly continued. "It is a treacherous curse, best left forgotten."

Micah stood, irritated and defensive.

"You saw how powerful Garrin was. How am I supposed to face him if I can't counter his magic?"

"Not by burning down a house," he retorted.

"I'll never learn to control it without practice."

"And this is how your Guard trained you? Lighting fireplaces?"

"Not exactly," Micah answered obstinately.

"So you will teach yourself, regardless of the risks?"

"Do you see another option?" he challenged.

"Abandon this foolish notion."

Micah snorted. "Besides that."

Kelj paused, his narrowed eyes distorting the blue marking across his cheek. "I do not agree with this path, but I understand your reasoning," he slowly admitted. "When a boy aspires to join the brotherhood of warriors among the Anderfalls, he first submits to the teaching of a knaerlck, our most honored and experienced warriors. As an initiate, they learn the art of war from their elders. To learn the art of magic, you must follow a similar path. An elder warlock must be found."

Micah relaxed slightly, considering his wisdom. "Director Mai suggested I learn what I can from Marinaya," he recalled, "but time isn't on our side. Unless she's willing to come with us, our mission has to come first."

Kelj nodded. "Another solution may present itself in time."

"Maybe," he morosely replied.

"Until then, I ask that you refrain from incinerating our shelters."

Micah grinned abashedly and shrugged.

With the fire going, Micah heated a simple porridge and grabbed a handful of dried elk meat from their supplies. After a quick breakfast, he and Kelj hoisted their packs and left the solitary house.

Outside, a handful of farmers were stirring, making their way towards the exit from Hazelcourt. Tired hands pulled carts piled with shovels, trowels, and rakes, ready to trim and collect whatever crops their owners were tending before the heat of the day arrived. The pair followed close behind a man with an empty cart, making their way along the dusty road. The towering trees of Midland cast long shadows over the squat cabins lining the street, broken only briefly by slender streaks of golden light filtering in from the early morning sun.

Soon they reached the narrow gate ushering a crowd of people into the forested tunnel and the outside world beyond. They squeezed through the throng of grumbling farmers, aiming for the stable along the wooded perimeter. Micah spotted Benrick speaking to an unknown defender near the barricade and waved.

At the stable, Edoran and Coalfire greeted them with obvious delight, relieved to see familiar faces in the strange enclosure. Micah and Kelj returned their gear to the saddlebags, doing one last inspection before guiding the horses out of the rickety stalls to join the group waiting to file through the shadowy exit.

As their turn approached, Benrick walked over to give his farewell. Compared to the drooping faces around them, he seemed unusually spirited.

"Truly men of your word." He smiled. "I trust your stay was pleasant enough."

"It was. We're grateful for your town's hospitality," Micah replied. "Please let Mayor Stern know we won't forget Hazelcourt's kindness."

Benrick nodded, pleased. "The mayor mentioned you were headed for the refugee camp," he added. "Avoid the Old North once you clear the forest. The last word from Dorn warned the road was covered with Mist-spawn. Angle southeast through the hills, and you should reach Long Lake. It's wild country, but I reckon it's safer than the more civilized areas."

"We appreciate the warning." Micah shook Benrick's hand before mounting Edoran as Kelj and Coalfire paced beside them. Turning back to the barricade, Micah gazed into the dark depths of Midland, readying himself to return to the chaotic world of the Mist. Kelj prodded his horse on, leading the way and disappearing into the rustling gloom of the trees. Micah quickly followed after him.

They plodded softly behind the sparse line of villagers making their way through the tunnel as it stretched to the stony remains of the Old North Road. At the fork, each one turned to the right, heading towards the fields they had seen the day before.

Micah paused, observing them faithfully returning to their daily work. Even in the chaos, life went on. Fields were plowed, the harvest was gathered, families were raised. Amidst all the pain and death, the simple chores of the ordinary and mundane whispered not all was yet lost. He marveled at their resolve.

Elowë, protect and strengthen these people.

Micah shook the musings from his mind and turned left, following Kelj along the Old North eastward. The road continued in the shadows, a near-solid wall of green guiding them ever onward in the soft creaking of branches. A couple of hours passed slowly in the unbroken solitude, the scenery around them unchanging, until a faint light eventually appeared ahead.

After a moment, Micah spied the exit from the forest tunnel, the clear light of day shining brightly against the dark of the woods. The horses sensed the wide land beyond as a fresh breeze wafted from the opening, and Edoran strode forward eagerly. As they neared the gap, Micah noticed a dark lump sprawled near the exit. His gut dropped as he recognized the shape.

A Mist Wolf.

He pulled his pistol from his side as Kelj removed the war axe from his back. Micah slowed Edoran into a cautious trot as they approached. Up close, he realized the beast was lifeless. He brought Edoran to a halt and dismounted, moving closer to the Wolf. Micah bent down, inspecting the corpse. Though he saw no gashes or holes from a fight, the body was contorted in unnatural angles, suggesting a significant amount of broken bones. Moving towards its head, he discovered a single wicked gash across the top, a trickle of dried blood flowing from its dented crown. Whatever had killed this Wolf, it must have been unbelievably strong to crush the beast's skull.

"Well?" Kelj asked as he apprehensively scanned the exit.

"It's dead. Killed by a blow to the head. Maybe a blunt weapon?" Micah guessed, surveying the creature.

"Hazelcourt was not under attack when we arrived," Kelj observed. "This kill looks fresh."

"Maybe it was someone else. Someone guarding the road?" He struggled to concoct a logical explanation for the monster's demise, but ultimately found himself at a loss.

"Whatever the cause, we best be wary," Kelj concluded. Micah quickly scrambled back onto Edoran, and they passed out of the sheltering forest, on guard against whatever dangers could be lurking just beyond its borders.

As their eyes adjusted to the growing light, the land around them revealed no further clues as to the Mist Wolf's demise. The gentle plains were devoid of life beyond the stalks of grass swaying in the midmorning breeze. Micah gazed across the horizon, taking in the endless sea as the borders of Midland receded.

"Looks like we've reached the end of the forest."

"Now we make our own path," Kelj eagerly declared.

Following Benrick's warning, they steered the horses off the worn, stone road and to the southeast, delving into the tall grasslands as the last evidence of human existence vanished in the golden weeds. High above, the sun continued its daily climb as the flat plains of the north transformed into the rolling green hills of the island's center.

Micah and Kelj were conspicuously alone in the unbroken swath of colored reeds. Nothing, not even a single tree, rose to defy the gently sloping fields below the clear, blue sky. As the day warmed, Micah grabbed the waterskin from his pack to cool his parched throat.

At the crest of a hill, Micah looked away to the north. His eyes landed on a thick bank of Mist swirling in the distance. His muscles tightened as he motioned to Kelj. They stopped, watching the wispy mass as it slowly tumbled across the empty plain. It was clear after a moment that the cloud had no interest in them as it drifted quietly away, heading for some unknown destination to the north. Kelj glanced at Micah, who shrugged. They angled hurriedly away, and Micah was immediately thankful for Benrick's warning to stay off the road.

The rest of the afternoon passed by, uneventful. The empty hills eventually began to show variation as rocky mounds jutted here and there, and short, leafy trees sporadically dotted the landscape. It wasn't long before they found themselves passing through groves of broad-leafed oaks and towering birches, providing intermittent relief from the bright sun of the plains.

As evening hues of orange, red, and pink streaked across the warm sky, Kelj discovered a small clearing nestled in a thick copse where they tiredly unsaddled the horses, sore from a full day of riding.

Kelj volunteered to make the fire—with flint, he added—while Micah grabbed their packs from the saddlebags. A handful of vegetables mixed with strips of meat made for a warm, delicious stew as Kelj added a curious mixture of spices from the Anderfalls. Once the meal was ready, Micah greedily consumed his bowl, starving after the meager hunk of stale bread he'd eaten earlier on the road. Contented, Micah sat back, savoring the lingering taste as the foreign spices flooded his senses. Kelj stood after finishing his and moved to check on the horses tied at the edge of the clearing. Micah watched the sky, enjoying the last of the fading light and the warmth of the fire. The clearing was peaceful, broken only by the occasional call of an owl somewhere in the distance.

"On your feet, Warden!" Kelj abruptly commanded. Micah staggered up, spinning awkwardly to face him. Kelj tossed a long, metal object at Micah, and he lunged to shield himself.

As his hand grasped the end, Micah realized it was a sword. The narrow blade was dulled almost to the point of being rounded.

"A sparring sword?" Micah watched as Kelj pulled a second from a sack on Coalfire.

"I have seen you fight the Mist, Micah Stormcrown, and named you knaerlck for your worthy deeds among my people," Kelj announced. "But there is one test that remains. Face me in battle, Warden of the West. Let us see if your skills match the words."

Kelj raised his blunted edge as they moved away from the campsite, circling one another like wary predators. With his sword poised, Micah quickly scanned his opponent, searching for weaknesses. Clearly, size and power were not on his side. The Anderfall towered over him, his brute strength a firm deterrent to frontal assaults. *If I'm going to beat him, it'll take every ounce of speed and dexterity I can muster.*

They paused, silently staring each other down as the fire crackled furiously. The clearing was quickly growing darker as the sunlight above the clearing weakened. Suddenly, a bird cried from the trees, and Micah shifted in surprise.

Kelj didn't waste a second.

In a blur, the warrior closed the gap between them with incredible speed, lashing out with his sword. Micah flicked his own with a swift jerk, pushing Kelj's blade away mere inches from his chest. Kelj recoiled, preparing another blow as Micah jumped back and recovered his footing.

Kelj lunged again, striking hard from above. In a flash, Micah swung to meet him, their weapons clashing in bitter protest. Unperturbed, Kelj recalculated, drawing back and swiping for his side. Micah deftly blocked his blow, pushing the blade away and making a light jab at his hip. With impressive speed, the gruff warrior parried the blow—barely.

It was enough to put him on the defensive. Micah unleashed a flurry of blows, their speedy assault pushing back the powerful veteran as he countered the barrage. His retreat provided just enough space for him to repel each blow, much to Micah's frustration.

Right as Kelj reached the forest edge, Micah lashed out with a final, powerful strike, hoping to push the warrior up against the wall of foliage. Instead, Kelj wildly deflected the sword, and Micah nearly crashed into him. His massive hand grasped Micah's wrist as they struggled to overpower each other, their swords clattering madly. Micah rapidly found himself being shoved back into the clearing, Kelj's grip digging into his skin. Options vanishing, Micah resorted to the only tactic he could see.

Micah relaxed his arm, dropping towards the ground as his hand wiggled free in the brief window. Kelj stumbled in surprise as Micah rolled around his bulky legs, rising quickly to his feet and scoring a hasty blow across Kelj's back. The Anderfall roared in frustration as the metal rapped against the leathered mail covering his torso. He whipped around, breathing hard.

"A clever move. Were you slower, I would have squashed your tiny size!" he growled.

"Good thing I'm quick then," Micah retorted.

Kelj laughed. "So it would seem." He lowered his blade and gave a slight bow.

"You have proven your mettle, knaerlck Stormcrown," Kelj declared. "I yield this match."

Micah nodded, accepting the hardened warrior's praise.

"Even so, I suggest we continue these spars. It will be good practice for when we next meet the treacherous Firewalkers."

"I agree. You're a challenging opponent, knaerlck Kelj."

He gave a small chuckle before collecting the swords and returning them to Coalfire.

Micah collapsed beside the fire again, exhausted from the fight. He gulped greedily from his waterskin, the cool liquid soothing his aching chest. Kelj joined him by the fire, dropping heavily to the ground. He softly grunted in pain as his back thumped against the smooth surface of a rock jutting from the grassy earth.

At least I won't be the only one feeling sore tomorrow.

INTO THE LABYRINTH

A COOL, GRAY SKY peered down as Micah woke from slumber. A breeze, heavy with rain, rattled through the trees of the grove as he stretched, rousing himself from the warmth of his sleeping sack. Rain would make for a miserable day of traveling across the open country. Micah said a desperate prayer for the clouds to relent from drenching them.

Once Kelj was up, they hurriedly packed the camp, hoping to cover some ground as the breeze grew stronger. As they rode out of the sheltered grove, the wind whipped harshly against the horses. Edoran flattened his ears, clearly unhappy with being forced into the gale.

They set out along the same route as before, blazing a winding trail as the rocky hills grew steeper, and the trees grew taller. Fortunately, the rain-laden clouds refrained from pouring, only subjecting them to an occasional misting. The rain and the brisk wind marked a sharp contrast from the unusually warm weather they had enjoyed before. Still, they were making good time.

As midday approached, the rocky crags guided them up a wide slope, where the peak presented them with a majestic view of the surrounding land. With a break in the rain, Micah scanned the horizon and spotted a faint, glimmering stretch of water to the east across a broken scene of forest and brown, weathered cliffs.

"There." He pointed. "That's Long Lake."

From their vantage point, Micah guessed them to be near the northern end of the lake, making the location of the camp somewhere south of them, according to the mayor's advice.

"Now to find the camp," Kelj replied.

Micah looked around, hoping to spot a trail through the maze of rock and trees. Nothing stood out.

"It'll be a challenge making our way to the Winding River through this labyrinth," Micah remarked.

Kelj silently observed the terrain. "Is there a way around? Or along the lakeshore?"

"Not that I'm aware of," he grumbled. "Much of the western shore of Long Lake is steep cliffs, and these crags spread all the way to Tar'auth Eld. It would take too long. We'll have to find a way through this mess."

Kelj nodded in assent, and they carefully made their way down, descending into the chaotic paths between the towering cliffs. At the base of the hill, Micah chose a narrow gap that seemed to travel at an angle along the lake. Edoran and Coalfire snorted nervously as the riders coaxed them into the tight passage, their thighs nearly rubbing sections of the rough stone.

After several minutes, the trail widened slightly and turned away from the lake, heading back to the west before transforming into a maddening channel of twists and turns. It wasn't long before both of them had completely lost their bearings below the sheer cliff sides and thick trees that blocked the cloudy sky above. Then, as if the path hadn't been unpleasant enough, Micah rounded a sharp corner and nearly collided with a high wall of rock.

Dead end.

He growled, frustrated.

"There was a side passage not far back," Kelj offered. "Perhaps that will continue on."

Micah cast a final furious scowl at the taunting rock face and plodded after him. Backtracking, they nearly overlooked the gap in their attempt to locate it, the diminutive opening causing the horses another bout of discomfort. Thankfully, the tight entrance proved brief. The channel soon widened enough so that they could easily ride alongside each other, providing a sense of relief—to them and the horses. Its gentle winding was bereft of any further gaps or trails, guiding them along its course as the day grew older.

Micah was starting to lose hope they would ever escape the maze when the ravine abruptly thinned and rose upwards. They filed out of the crevice, finding themselves in a fertile, though rocky, woodland. Micah guided Edoran to a small embankment, hoping to catch a glimpse of something, anything, to reorient himself. Unfortunately, still higher cliffs of imposing stone blocked any significant views of the world around them. At least from the opening, he was able to guess the position of the sun as the clouds finally dissipated. Micah returned to Kelj, picking a trail that led south through the towering oaks, maples, and pines.

It wasn't long before the route returned to the snaking paths between cliffs as it slowly descended again. Giant outcroppings of stone protruded over their heads as they passed underneath. Having solid surfaces of stone below, beside, and now above, only served to increase the claustrophobic feeling of the trail.

I'll be happy if I never visit this place again, Micah sulked.

Again, the enclosed tunnel was short-lived. The overhangs subsided, and the sky reappeared. Gradually, the path broadened as the sheer cliff walls grew to new heights.

They soon found themselves deep within a canyon of monumental size. Inside the mountainous walls, spires of tan stone and wide bluffs enclosed a plethora of trees and wild plants growing wherever they could find purchase in the rocky soil. Micah reflected solemnly on his own finiteness as they traveled along the colossal rift, undoubtedly created long before there was an inkling of his existence.

The flora grew thicker the farther they traveled into the canyon, bringing with it a sweet chorus of calls from a multitude of birds. Evidence of wildlife slowly appeared, an encouraging sign that the Mist had yet to conquer this area of the island. Even with his frustration at spending the day lost in a maze, Micah was cheered by the sights of squirrels, hawks, and even deer thriving within the shelter of that colossal place.

"Halt!"

The voice shook Micah from his reverie as he searched wildly for the source. Kelj jerked Coalfire to a stop, and the horse protested loudly.

"Another step, and a hundred men will open fire," it threatened.

Wonderful.

They dismounted, holding their hands above their heads.

A moment later, the bushes rustled along a slender ledge ahead of them. The ledge dipped down, joining to the canyon floor where a man in tattered clothing stumbled from the undergrowth. He gripped a long, battered musket tightly, eyeing them nervously.

"No sudden moves, strangers. Remove your weapons—slowly!—and lay them on the ground."

They cautiously complied. Micah undid the belt holding his blade, pistol, and his hunting knife, laying them at his feet. He glanced over, watching Kelj unload an impressive array of weaponry from the folds of his furred garments. A row of knives and hatchets tumbled to the ground before he gingerly placed his beloved war axe on top of them with a forlorn look.

Micah inspected the man as he waited for Kelj to finish. His scarred face was tired and caked with dirt, masking his grizzled age. His distrusting eyes betrayed a quiet fear. Both his weapon and cotton tunic were in poor condition, suggesting an untrained hand behind the rifle.

Another pair of men emerged from the bushes bordering the canyon trail. Like the first man, their gear was in similar shape as they hesitantly approached.

"Pack the weapons onto the horses," the man directed. He then turned back to them.

"You certainly don't look like refugees," he remarked suspiciously, examining their weapons. "I don't know what you want, but I can't let you leave. Aranaias will decide what to do with you."

"Who are you?" Micah asked. "And where exactly are you taking us?"

"I... I'm not at liberty to say," the man stammered. "It's for our protection. As are these."

He moved closer, handing each of them a long strip of thick, black cloth. Micah immediately felt anger emanating from Kelj, who slammed the cloth into the dirt.

"You shame those who come in peace," Kelj snarled. "No harm or even threats of harm have been given. It would be a stain on my honor to submit to your pitiful leading as I stumble about in darkness. No warrior of the Anderfalls will ever be cowed into such feebleness!"

The men stepped back, glancing nervously at one another. Micah quickly stepped between them.

"I'm a Warden of the Karthmoor Guard. We fight the same enemy," he hastily declared. "I promise upon my Guardsmen's Oath, your people will not be harmed."

While Micah couldn't tell if they believed him, the tension lessened.

"A grand gesture." The lead man nodded. "But unfortunately, the Guard holds little weight in the world today. Either take the blindfolds, or I'll do what I must." He raised his hand, signaling to unseen defenders. "I don't want to, but my family is at stake."

"Kelj." Micah turned. The tall warrior still furiously scowled at the mysterious men. "Do me this favor, or it all ends here. Take the blindfold, and I will lead. Will that satisfy your code?"

He continued to fume in silence.

"Were it not for the grave dangers facing us, I would tear them apart. I would be the last man they try to blind," he growled. "This once, I will accept your compromise. It shall not happen again."

He snatched the cloth from the dust, roughly yanking it around his eyes before his mind changed.

"Lead on then," Micah called to the man, tying his own cloth around his head. The world went black.

Micah felt a hand grab his wrist lightly, guiding it to a shoulder.

"Keep hold, and we'll guide you," the man directed. He felt Kelj's thick fingers grasp his own shoulder, trembling with fury. Slowly, the man moved forward, leading them into the unknown.

For a few moments, Micah could sense they were continuing straight, following what he knew to be the canyon as the sounds of the forest continued. Without his sight, the cries of circling hawks and chirping songbirds echoed through the chasm with added volume. Beyond the crunching of boots and the horses behind, the surrounding men remained silent.

Then the man turned, leading them along a new path. The ground rose and dipped, though Micah felt a gradual trend leading them up from the canyon floor.

"Careful now," the man warned. "There are a series of stone steps here."

They took every step warily, feeling for the edge of each bumpy stair. Eventually, they reached the top where the carved stone ended, and a trail of dirt and rock continued the winding upward climb.

The cool shade of the trees vanished, replaced by the faint warmth of the unseen sun. They trudged on in silence. At one point, Micah nearly lost his footing, his toes catching on a pothole in the trail. He felt Kelj tense as he recovered his balance. The man ahead muttered an apology.

Before long, the path quickly turned to their right, and the air shifted. Micah sensed shade covering them, either from more canyon walls or perhaps a section of trees, though it remained very quiet. The space felt small, enclosed.

"Just a moment," said the man. His shoulder disappeared as Micah heard him move forward. The sound of cracking rocks echoed from somewhere, like someone striking flint. After a moment, the man returned with what sounded like a crackling torch.

"We're heading into a tunnel," he informed Micah. "The ceiling is tall, and the path is wide enough that the horses will be fine. Stick close, though, there are some dangerous spots."

They set out again, Micah's hand firmly back on his shoulder as he led them into the cave. The moment they stepped into its mouth, Micah could feel the change. Cold air washed across his skin from the depths, and every sound was amplified by the enclosure. Behind them, the horses whined nervously as men gently tried to calm them. After several attempts, the creatures fitfully subsided, allowing their guides to coax them along the cavern path.

The dampness of the air, smelling stale and musty, clung to Micah's clothes as they descended into the cave. Somewhere, water dripped endlessly against cool stone. Each blind step proved treacherous as they shuffled along the slick, stony path. The faint dripping gradually became a trickle, then transformed into a dull roar reverberating against the murky walls. After a slight curve in the trail, the volume exploded, water pouring thunderously from somewhere near them into a large hollow below. The wet rock under Micah's feet became a wooden bridge, solidly built, and they crossed over the towering waterfall. He could only imagine the spectacular view and size as the booming sound drowned out the world.

As the deafening torrent faded, the trail began to rise, a warmer air blowing lazily towards Micah. The man led them out of the echoing chamber, back onto dry ground beyond the cavern. In the distance, Micah heard the commotion of people, the ringing of a hammer, and the bleating of goats.

"You can remove the blindfolds," the leader instructed.

Micah quickly yanked the cloth from his eyes, grimacing in the bright light. As his sight returned, he discovered they were standing on a wide outcropping that overlooked a large, rocky gorge. Dozens of caves lined the walls and floor of the valley. A handful of narrow paths led to the ones situated on ledges above. Far below, the vast ground sat divided by a river slowly flowing through the canyon before it disappeared around a bend opposite from them. A rickety-looking bridge linked the riverbanks together. Large groups of men, women, and children mulled around the valley floor, weaving between scraggly brush and slender trees as they entered and exited from the various openings or paused at rough merchant stalls. A couple of makeshift pens held small herds of goats, pigs, and hens pressed close together. Beyond everything, the shoreline of Long Lake hemmed in the ravine. A smattering of tiny vessels rested along its banks.

This must be the refugee camp, Micah realized.

"This way," the lead man ordered.

As he guided them down the weaving trail, Micah glanced behind, noticing the group of men following them, maybe ten or fifteen-strong.

So much for a hundred.

The ledge gradually sloped to the valley floor. Several of the crowds watched with curious expressions as the group descended. All of them looked exhausted, their bodies and clothes in a similar condition to the scouts who had detained them. As Micah and Kelj followed along a path between dense sections of underbrush, the villagers retreated, women pulling their children closer and giving them a wide berth. The leader guided them from the sparsely shaded path to the Winding River, crossing the rickety bridge Micah had spied previously, and then towards a gap in the valley wall Micah hadn't noticed before. Shouting vendors and boisterous men grew quieter as they passed, eyeing them as the group filed away from the heart of the camp. It was clear the dangers these people had faced had sown a deep distrust of the outside world.

The slight passage emptied into another smaller ravine with a set of shallow caves. The openings along one side were fortified with wooden barricades and doorways, creating improvised buildings. More armed men roamed the bare ground, watching them cautiously.

The lead man directed them to the far end, near the shoreline, where an exposed cavern waited. As they entered the dark shelter, the flickering of torches cast a strange pattern of lines along the floor and wall. It took Micah a second to realize the lines were actually the bars of a large, metal cage built into the grotto.

"You will wait here while I inform Aranaias of your arrival," the man directed. "This is only temporary."

Kelj bristled.

"I assure you this isn't necessary," Micah replied. The men behind him shuffled loudly, gripping their rifles tighter.

Micah shook his head, sighing resignedly, and strolled into the cell. Kelj hesitated, and for a moment, Micah panicked, thinking their entire journey was about to end. At last, Kelj relented and stomped in to join him, grumbling all the while.

The man breathed an audible sigh of relief as the metal door creaked shut, and he clasped a small padlock over the bars. He disappeared as the others shuffled out of the cramped cave.

Looking around the desolate space, Micah discovered a scratchy set of beds and a single stool. He collapsed on one of the straw mattresses, resting his back against the cold iron bars as Kelj irritably paced.

"I do not trust these men, Micah," he muttered.

"Nor do I, but I have to believe they'll lead us to Marinaya. Did you notice the state of the camp?"

"Yes. A hard place to live," he observed. "One would have to be truly desperate to flee here."

"This must be the refugee camp, though. We're at the right place. Maybe this Aranaias will be more understanding."

"I am not hopeful," said Kelj sullenly.

Hours seemed to drag by as the faint sunlight beyond the cave waned. Between Kelj's pacing and the absence of their captors, Micah's frustration steadily grew.

As he pondered whether he could summon enough fire to melt the blasted lock, a commotion echoed from beyond the mouth of the cave. A tall, slim man in a billowing robe of black and red stormed through the opening. His bald head sat above a thin, wiry beard while his dark eyes inspected them with fervor. His long face was pulled into a furious glare, accentuating the faint wrinkles in his tanned skin. The lead scout from before silently filed in behind the mage with an embarrassed look on his face. Micah warily approached the bars as they drew closer.

"What is your business here, soldier?" the mage demanded. "How have you found this place?"

"I'm Micah Stormcrown, Warden of the Karthmoor Guard. I'm here on an urgent mission to find a mage who escaped the fall of Hillmarch."

"Warden, my boot," the mage spat. "Anyone can claim such now with the Conclave gone." He waved his arm with agitation, his dark robe billowing with every move. "Who is it you seek?"

"A woman by the name of Marinaya," Micah answered. "I was led to believe she may be one of the mages in charge of this camp."

The man frowned, obviously annoyed by his knowledge.

"That would be a matter of contention, depending on who you ask," he growled. "In any case, what's your business with her?"

"I cannot say. The news is for her ears alone," said Micah flatly, aggravated by the mage's rudeness. His disapproving frown quickly turned into a scowl.

"You are in no position to defy me!" he screamed. "Answer my question, or I will force you to."

Micah quickly erected a barrier in his mind, fearful of another Garrin-like assault. Kelj tensed beside him.

"Aranaias," the other man whimpered, "our orders were not to harm detainees from the canyon. They have complied with all our requests."

"Silence!" Aranaias bellowed at the poor scout. He wheeled back around to Micah. "Well, soldier?"

Micah folded his arms. "I must speak with Marinaya. It's vital to the safety of everyone, including your camp."

A fuming yet gleeful sneer streaked across his face. "Wrong answer, Stormcrown."

Immediately, Micah felt another presence probing the edges of his consciousness. It swiftly collided with Micah's defense, surprised but unbowed. The mage's face contorted with wrath as his mind hammered against the fragile barrier, Micah's thoughts shuddering under the weight of his assault. Micah gripped the bars of the cell, struggling to fend off the barrage of probes peeling away the layers around his mind. Micah felt him withdraw, his energy gathering on the outskirts, and he feebly shored up his battered shield.

Too late.

Aranaias unleashed a colossal blast, splitting Micah's mental barrier and sending his thoughts tumbling in the chaos. His body quaked, vision blurring from the impact as the mage triumphantly marched into his mind, spearing through his thoughts without mercy. Although his assault was significantly weaker than Garrin's, it remained immensely painful as he plowed through Micah's fragile brain.

Just as he reached Micah's memories to begin shredding through them, Kelj shoved his way between them, breaking the connection. As Micah's sight swirled, Aranaias stepped back in surprise before focusing his attack on Kelj. Micah collapsed on the ground, shaking, afraid of witnessing Kelj buckle under the same battering.

But the warrior stood there, silent, his fists clenched at his sides in a calm determination. Micah watched as Aranaias' face transformed from a confident scowl to an annoyed frown and then to hysterical panic.

"Graah!" he shouted in rage, releasing his hold and stumbling back.

Kelj relaxed, defiantly crossing his arms over his armored chest.

"Impossible!" Aranaias shrieked. "You're nothing but a barbarian! An illiterate brute. No one can withstand my power!"

"Your pride will be your downfall," Kelj coolly chided. "You shame yourself."

Aranaias cast a final, venomous glare at Kelj before swerving to Micah.

"You will *rot* in this cell. No one will ever hear of you."

Aranaias stomped out of the cave, the terrified scout giving them one last look of apology before scampering after the mage.

Satisfied they were gone, Kelj turned, extending a hand. Micah grasped it, and the towering warrior easily lifted him from the dirt.

"How did you do that?" Micah gaped.

Kelj gave a satisfied smirk. "While my people outlaw the use of magic, we are not blind to its dangers. All knaerlck learn meditations to resist the wicked snares of mind-whisperers. It is a treacherous magic that only the most villainous warlocks pursue. Were they to dominate our leaders, they would wreak much chaos."

"That's incredible," said Micah, amazed, "and it'll be invaluable against the Firewalkers. Is it something you can teach me?"

"The Way of Resolve is not something to undertake lightly," he warned. "It requires many years to master. That is not time we have."

Micah's excitement melted, thwarted by his words.

"Nevertheless, I will show you what I can. As time permits," Kelj offered.

A small grin broke across Micah's lips. "Thank you, shield-brother."

Kelj nodded, pleased.

Micah glanced at the mouth of the cave, the last light of the day quickly vanishing beyond the canyon walls.

"Well, it doesn't look like we'll be seeing any help today," he remarked.

"Or food," Kelj grumbled.

They returned to the rough cots, their next steps momentarily halted. As the evening faded into obscurity, the soft patter of feet echoed from beyond the cell. Micah looked up to find the scout from before gliding towards them, casting fearful looks over his shoulder. A thick, burlap sack swung from his hand. He shoved it through the bars, a lump of objects rolling around inside.

"I swiped what I could from the barracks," he whispered. "This should keep you 'til morning."

Micah peeked into the bag to find a loaf of bread, apples, and a bit of fresh cheese. A full skin of water poked out from beneath.

"Thank you," said Micah gratefully.

The man nodded.

"Aranaias is mad," he muttered, "but none of us dare defy him. We can't risk our families' lives."

"I understand, but please, get a message to Marinaya. Tell her men from Director Mai are here with a warning."

The man jumped at the sound of laughter from beyond the cave, and they fell silent.

"I can't promise that," he hurriedly answered. "We're not allowed in the mages' hall."

Micah frowned.

"But maybe I can reach someone else," he offered. "There's another mage who'd likely be sympathetic to your cause."

"Please," Micah begged, "whatever you can do. We can't wait much longer."

"Give me tomorrow," the man replied. "I'll try to contact him."

"Very well. Thank you."

The scout retreated, sneaking back towards the exit.

"Wait," Micah softly called. "What's your name?"

"Tarion," he whispered, then vanished into the night.

Chapter 30

The Way and the Wizards

A whine from Edoran somewhere outside the cave startled Micah from his sleep. He rubbed his eyes, squinting to peer out of the darkness into the bright morning beyond. In the stillness of the prison, he faintly heard the chatter of men milling about the gorge outside. The distant clang of metal rang, scouts practicing their swordplay as others laughed and goaded them on. After a while, someone yelled—*Probably Aranaias,* Micah silently groused—and the fight subsided.

He picked at the remains of a chunk of bread as Kelj snored loudly from across the cell. Micah watched the Anderfall, still astounded by his victory over the mage while also wondering how much longer the giant was going to keep snoozing. After an hour or so, with no sign of relenting, Micah's irritableness got the better of him.

"Wake up, you big lout." He lightly tossed a small smooth stone from the floor, hitting Kelj in the chest. Kelj jumped up, growling.

"Whodare chal'nge, m-me?" he groggily slurred.

"No one," said Micah grumpily. "Your snoring woke half the camp."

Kelj shot him an annoyed look before settling back onto the bed.

Kelj scarfed down an apple from the sack, closely eyeing the entrance as Micah leaned back onto his cot. After so long of endlessly moving from task to task, danger after danger, being stuck in a cage with nothing to do only fueled his impatience.

The Mist was out there, growing stronger. So were the Firewalkers. What if they had already reached their prize?

We've got to escape. Today.

Yet, Micah had given Tarion his word they'd try his way first.

"So, what's the Way of Resolve?" Micah asked, hoping to pass the time. Kelj finished his apple, setting the remains neatly on the stool before swinging his legs over the edge of the bed. His rough fingers tugged at the thick beard spilling over his hunched chest as he studied Micah.

"There are several meditations the wise-men of the Anderfalls created to counter the dangers of magic," he began. "The Way of Resolve is the most practiced for disarming mind-whisperers, those warlocks who possess the power to dominate your will. As I said, it is not an easy path. Our greatest warriors spend years secluded from the world alongside a *svensiir,* a Way-Guide, learning how to conquer their own minds and master the meditations."

"And you can teach this?"

"I am no Way-Guide," said Kelj humbly, "but I can pass on the basics of how to quiet your mind and form your thoughts into steel. With practice, you might learn an inkling of what it means to follow the Way of Resolve."

"Well, I don't see us leaving anytime soon." Micah smirked, his excitement growing. "What do you say?"

"As you will." He nodded. "Come."

Kelj slid off the bed and onto the cold floor of the cave. Crossing his legs, he gripped his knees lightly, his serious eyes watching as Micah joined him and imitated the pose. The mysterious warrior was silent, stoic. Shadows of the cave spilled across his grizzled face, making the thin, blue marking running from his temple to his jaw even more imposing.

"Still your mind, Warden," he serenely ordered.

Micah closed his eyes, wrestling with the chaotic tendrils dwelling deep within his conscience. For such a simple request, the effort seemed impossible.

"The greatest wall is born within your strongest memories," Kelj continued. "Think deeply, Stormcrown. Find something powerful, something to bend your mind towards. Let it step into the forefront."

Micah scoured his thoughts, searching.

Images of Fairhollow flashed through his mind. Gerar, Merrick, Rila, and Tala. A multitude of friends and cherished moments. None of them felt quite strong enough.

His mind drifted to adventuring. From the quiet, peaceful reveries amongst lonely nights to exciting discoveries in far-off lands, he found many pleasant memories. Still, none held his attention for long. He turned to where he knew his heart was leading.

Samuel, taking his first, tentative step as his frightened hand left the support of the small table near the sofa. Micah cheering in excitement, startling the poor boy as he tumbled to the ground and cried for his mother.

An evening return from the days before he left his post as warden. Elisa smiled with excitement from the porch as Samuel raced across the swaying grass, crying out for him. Micah reached down, scooping him into his arms as he giggled wildly.

Each was a tender moment he lingered on.

A young Elisa rising from beside the worn, stone well, spying Micah's arrival. Her long, dark hair moved gently in the evening breeze as bright, chestnut eyes bore into him with anticipation. He struggled to maintain a steady pace, longing to race to her. Without a word, they slipped away from her parents' homestead, escaping to their secret grove beyond her father's fields. Free from prying eyes, Elisa relaxed, laughing as he drew her close, feeling the warmth of her skin and the smell of her soft dress. They talked about the life to come and a host of things long since lost to time. She laughed again, thrilling his soul after a passionate kiss.

Micah drank in the moment, intoxicated. His heart ached within his chest, captivated by the tender memory now tinged with bittersweet loss.

"I have one."

"Keep it in focus," Kelj commanded. "Allow everything else to wash gently away, like waves along the lakeshore, until only it remains."

Micah slowly felt his mind relaxing, the tension of a thousand thoughts evaporating as he replayed their sweet embrace within his mind.

"Feel the strength of the memory," Kelj continued. "Form it into a solid wall, allowing the essence of the moment to envelop your heart and mind."

Micah breathed deeply, feeling the emotions and love flow across his soul, blocking out every distraction.

Suddenly, a familiar energy entered the space like a welcome friend. Amidst the pull of his memory, Micah felt the current of magic stirring deep within his consciousness, drawn by the serenity. No barrier remained between him and the immense power. It stood ready, waiting to be called upon as Elisa's warmth surrounded him.

The air around Micah's body began to shimmer. Kelj opened his eyes, watching Micah warily as he tapped into the magic, allowing it to flow freely. The sensation was exhilarating. He felt as if anything was possible.

Micah raised his hand towards the gate, energy softly glowing from his palm. *Deep breath. Exhale.*

CRACK!

A bolt of lightning erupted from his hand, springing wildly towards the metal. The cell sizzled with energy, bolts skipping sporadically between the bars as the lightning connected. Both of them jumped in surprise, and Micah quickly cut the flow.

The solitude and power vanished as muddled thoughts returned. Try as he might to hold on, Elisa's sweet sensation vanished into the void.

"What did you do?" Kelj quietly demanded, stunned.

"I–I don't know," Micah admitted, feeling exhaustion tug at his limbs as the magic claimed his energy. "I felt the barrier form around my mind, and next, I could tap into my magic. There wasn't anything stopping me like before."

"Did you mean to summon lightning?" he asked, incredulous.

"Not exactly. I was imagining fire to melt the door with. There must have been more power behind it than I realized."

"And so fire became lightning," Kelj mused, stroking his beard. "Unforeseen, but curious."

"What do you mean?"

"No svensiir has ever instructed the magic-cursed in the art," he answered. "How the Way will respond to your essence is unknown. Your path will be the first."

Micah marveled at the incredible opportunity before him.

"Again," said Kelj. "Form the shield around your mind. A warning before shocking our cage would be appreciated this time."

"Right, sorry," he awkwardly stammered.

Micah returned to his place on the floor before Kelj, closing his eyes to center himself. He reached out, feeling for Elisa's touch, but a mass of excitement and thoughts crowded his busy mind. Micah struggled to push the tide away, frustration only further hampering his efforts. Try as he might, the tranquility from before remained elusive. He let out an aggravated snort.

"It will take patience. Strong emotions, such as anger, fear, or even anticipation, make it harder to maintain the barrier," Kelj explained. "So it is also with battle."

Micah shook his head. "I can't imagine trying to keep that kind of focus during a fight."

"To still your mind, you must let go of the world. It is one of the greatest challenges in following the Way. You did well for your first attempt. With time, you will gain a deeper understanding of its nature."

Micah nodded, glancing out into the bright day beyond the cave and allowing the full weight of his words to sink in.

"Kelj," Micah asked, his thoughts drifting, "if the Way allows me to tap into magic, how do other mages harness theirs? Protectors are trained to force their way into it, but the mages we've encountered don't appear to struggle like that."

"I cannot say. The Way was not intended to conduct magic, only counter it," Kelj answered. "Perhaps an elder warlock could answer this."

Micah sighed. "Like Marinaya."

He moved to lean against the cage, but Kelj made a noise, nodding at the bars.

"Oh, right." He grinned, tossing a rock from the damp floor at the metal, satisfied after it clattered to the ground, unharmed. Electrocuting himself in a dank cavern cell would have been a pitiful end to their quest.

The morning dragged by as they stared at the unchanging view of the dark hole. Somewhere in the light, Micah heard men and horses, the only evidence as to life beyond. No one appeared, making him even more grateful for Tarion's smuggled meal.

As midday arrived, Micah began toying with the idea of melting through the metal again. Instead, the sound of footsteps suddenly drew his attention. A new mage slowly entered the murky cavern. A timid flame glowed brightly from his open hand, illuminating his startling features. He was strikingly tall, nearly rivaling Kelj. A curious robe with shifting hues of amber and gold covered his burly frame. His skin appeared nearly black in the faint light, contrasted by a fascinating, though terrifying, white design, either painted or tattooed, across his aging face. His dark hair was shaved close to his skull, revealing streaks of white that continued towards the back of his head. Micah stepped back from the bars as the ominous mage calmly approached.

Either this is the mage Tarion mentioned, or we're toast.

"Serah Stormcrown, serah Kelj," he announced in an exotic accent, "we are honored by your arrival in our modest camp. May the moons of fortune shine upon you." The mage bowed with a curious, foreign gesture. Something about him felt familiar.

"You as well." Micah bowed awkwardly in return, thrown off by his greeting. "Your words are very kind."

"I am Narombe," the strange mage continued. "If you would, please follow me to Lady Marinaya."

With a quick wave of his hand, the lock on the cell clicked open. Micah looked at Kelj, astounded. Kelj strode to the door and shoved it open, not about to lose his opportunity. Micah followed close behind. Narombe spun around, striding from the gloomy pit as they chased after him.

Micah's eyes struggled to adjust as he stumbled into the bright sun. After a moment, he noticed the clearing was just as empty as it was the night before. The row of dwellings sat across from him, built into the natural formations of the cliffs. Edoran and Coalfire were tied near a small grove of trees, grazing contentedly in the shade. At the far end of the enclosure, a small group of defenders clumsily fired arrows at a set of straw targets as an instructor shouted irascibly.

Narombe escorted them to a narrow set of stairs carved into the ravine not far from the holding cell. At the top, a wide ledge led to a gap in the rock where the path rose towards the top of the cliffs.

"Were you able to relay our message to Marinaya?" Micah asked, unable to wait as they climbed towards the passage.

"I was not, honorable Warden," Narombe replied. "My duties have kept me busy as the day has grown."

"But you trusted Tarion enough to seek us out?"

"We have many valiant defenders, Tarion numbered among them," he answered. "But where others overlooked your name, the Warden of the West is known to me. It would be a foolish thing to try to impersonate one so highly decorated."

"You'll have to forgive my memory; I don't recall our meeting."

"There was no meeting, serah," Narombe quickly added. "I am merely familiar with your Guard. My position at the Hillmarch Academy frequently included collaboration alongside your companions."

The hilly path squeezed between a rocky opening as the ascent continued.

"I wasn't aware the Guard had any dealings with the Academy," Micah panted, exertion growing in the gentle heat of the sun. "What was your role with the Guard, if I may?"

"In my homeland, I would be known as a Spirit-Hunter," said Narombe solemnly, "but here, it was my duty to assist your peacekeepers in tracking and detaining mages who selfishly abused their powers to the detriment of the innocent."

"A warlock who hunts other warlocks?" Kelj interjected with surprise.

"As you say. It is a difficult duty, but a necessary one. Magic must never be used to harm the blameless."

"A warlock with honor," Kelj softly quipped. "I like this one."

"So, you escaped Hillmarch with Marinaya?" Micah continued.

"Indeed. By her guidance, many lives were saved. I will leave her the pleasure of recounting the tale, should she so desire."

After a moment, the rocky hike leveled, transforming into a wide, stone plateau that overlooked the camp and provided an excellent view of Long Lake as it stretched endlessly to the east. At the back of the cliff, a single, massive cave dominated the dusty formations. The gaping hole loomed above their heads as Narombe led them into its shadowy depths.

Inside, an array of torches and makeshift chandeliers illuminated the grand space, casting warm light along the rocky corridor. A series of smaller chambers and passages riddled the sides of the cavern, many veiled with expensive-looking curtains dyed a rich, sea-blue hue. An intricate symbol of gold and black adorned each of the silken covers; a shimmering circle shifting between the two colors with flowing lines within. At the center, a bright, blue flame glowed against a pale background. The symbol of the Hillmarch Academy. A handful of mages of every age and in an array of colored robes warily marked their progress as Narombe took them deeper into the mighty cavern.

The high roof gradually shrank, leading to a fork in the passages. They turned, taking the right-hand one. Curious glass lamps lined the cavern wall, a magical flame illuminated within by unseen power. After a brief twist, the confining tunnel spilled into a large room lit by more of the odd lamps. A large, glass chandelier hung from the cavern ceiling, surrounded by stalactites. The rough walls were covered with various fabrics and hangings, many bearing the insignia of the Academy. A set of modest rugs provided a cozy feel to the open room. Several bookshelves and tables lay scattered along the edges where mages sat, consumed in study.

Narombe guided them across the room, pupils glancing up in surprise as the group quietly passed. Near the end of the space, Micah saw a small, aging woman in a modest blue robe with silvery hair, intricately braided, bent over a young man. The teen gazed intently at an open tome among a pile of books scattered across the rough table.

"Reread Ibram Tark's *Elemental Considerations*. Chapters one through five," the wizened mage agitatedly directed. "Once you've completed that, review section twenty-seven of Dorian Issachar's *Treatise on Metaphysical Transubstantiations*. I expect a written explanation of their implications regarding your flippant violation of rules concerning the use of magic to gain the attention of certain young girls in the camp, on my desk by evening meal tomorrow."

"Yes, Lady Marinaya," the teen abashedly complied. He stumbled from the chair, grabbing a handful of books before rushing past them. Marinaya cast a final, irritated look at the boy before refocusing her attention.

"Ah, Master Narombe," she said warmly. "I was wondering where you had disappeared to. I see you have brought us guests."

"My discussions with the camp leaders ran longer than expected," he apologized in his strange accent. "It was not until late morning that I was informed we had detained travelers from the canyon."

"Detained?" Marinaya raised a stern eyebrow, her wrinkled face turning serious.

"Aranaias."

Marinaya let out a small, disgruntled sigh. "Naturally." She shook her head and rose from beside the table, her robe ruffling slightly as she joined them in the center of the chamber.

"I apologize for Aranaias' behavior," Marinaya began. "I hope your introduction to our camp was not entirely discourteous."

"We've had worse receptions," Micah remarked, Bowman's Crossing flashing into his mind.

"An unfortunate effect of the dark times we find ourselves," she wistfully replied, "but I digress. I am Lady Marinaya, representative of the Hillmarch Academy for our camp."

"We are honored to meet you, Lady Marinaya." Micah respectfully bowed. "I'm Micah Stormcrown, former Warden of the Guard."

"A warden survives?" she mused, eyebrows raised. "It is a relief to know not all of Karthmoor's leadership was claimed by the Mist. And you, noble warrior." She turned to Kelj. "I recognize the markings of a great champion of the Anderfalls."

"I am Kelj, one of the last of Clan Wulfgrad," Kelj declared as he signaled his customary greeting, "and of my people. I am honored by our meeting, Lady Marinaya."

"As I am honored, Kelj of Clan Wulfgrad." Marinaya repeated the Anderfall welcome. "Aldaria is a darker world without your kin."

He nodded silently, a flicker of pain reflected in his typically stoic face.

"So then. What brings a warden and a warrior of the Anderfalls to a secluded camp in the wilderness?" Marinaya inquisitively asked. "You make for odd refugees."

"We haven't come for shelter, but for knowledge. Information only you may be able to provide, Lady Marinaya," Micah began.

"Information from me?" She stared in surprise. "What led you to think I could be of assistance to you?"

"Not so much what as who. An old friend of yours sent us. Director Mai."

Marinaya's face darkened. "Perhaps we ought to move this conversation outside. I feel I could use the fresh air after spending all morning in this stuffy library."

They followed Marinaya and Narombe back through the twisting cavern. Emerging into the afternoon sun, Micah's stomach churned as he spotted Aranaias stomping towards them from the valley below. The second he spied Micah, his features flared in anger. Marinaya patiently waited as he stormed towards her, his dark robe billowing.

"What is the meaning of this?" Aranaias shouted. "The protection of the camp is my responsibility! Who released these dangerous captives?" His head swerved furiously between Marinaya, Narombe, and Micah—he barely acknowledged Kelj's existence. Narombe moved to speak, but Marinaya interrupted.

"Leader of our defenders you may be," she began sweetly, "but as long as I am here, *I* hold final authority on matters concerning the safety of these people. It was brought to my attention that our guests have information that may prove important to keeping our refuge secure. A goal I expect you share." She looked sternly at Aranaias as he fumed under her gaze, vacillating between anger and shame.

"My interrogation of the outsiders revealed nothing of interest to our security," he bluntly retorted.

"Even so. I will make my own decision regarding this," Marinaya confidently finished.

Aranaias opened his mouth, but she cut him off. "You are dismissed, Aranaias."

His expression turned into a scowl as he jerkily bowed, glaring at Narombe and Micah before stalking towards the cavern.

"Undoubtedly our most delightful resident," Marinaya lightly remarked before leading them farther from the cave.

As they reached the edge of the plateau overlooking the canyon, she turned to face them, her wrinkled features serious.

"Now then, on what business has Mai sent you here? She knows I am not to have dealings with the Collective. Not even the Mist will cause me to throw all caution to the wind and ignore the terms of my banishment."

"No, nothing like that," Micah hastily replied, "though it does involve your work on the time pods." Marinaya's brow furrowed with concern.

"An unfortunate discovery," she grumbled. "It would've been better if the device had never been found. What is your involvement?"

"It's a long story, but the point is we're after a very danger-ous group of individuals who have some connection to the time pods," he explained. "These mages, the Firewalkers as they call themselves, are searching for something related to the pods. We can only guess at what. The director is concerned it's a weapon or some other danger tied to the original time pod. Something they could use to wipe out the Collective and all of the Mist-marked."

"Hmm." Marinaya's aging eyes narrowed. She looked out over the lake, thinking. "Knowing Mai, she undoubtedly revealed she knows next to nothing about the source of the pods. I promise she did not lie."

"Which is why she pointed us to you. Mai believed you could help us unravel this mystery."

She smirked. "Perhaps my apprentice holds too high a regard for me. Unfortunately, I can tell you nothing more as to the discovery of the original pod."

"I see," Micah sighed, his hopes of beating Garrin unraveling.

"Now, not so fast," she continued. "I may not know how or where it was discovered, but perhaps something of its history will assist you."

His face brightened, though he was still somewhat confused.

"The time pods, or at least the original one, are old. Far older than the Collective realizes," Marinaya began. "It wasn't until I began my work at the Hillmarch Academy that I discovered the truth."

"What do you mean?"

She took a deep breath. "When I was forced out of the Heraldan Collective, I was furious—and terrified. The only place I knew I would be fully accepted was the Academy. They had previously offered me an honorary position while I was still serving Archon Valerius.

"I decided to take the offer, using my experience as Valerius' historical advisor to serve as the Academy's Dean of History. My contacts and knowledge of Elvish excavations underway across Edros provided the school with invaluable resources in furthering our students' education. Many were even selected to join expeditions to recover artifacts alongside professional researchers in the field. It was an exciting time.

"It was also during these few years that some of my students abroad brought back odd tales of new ruins being discovered along the forested coast of Westrock. Remnants of a human civilization previously unknown to our community of historians. When such a discovery appeared here in Karthmoor, I couldn't pass up the chance to see for myself.

"I accompanied a set of my brightest students who were selected to join archaeologists on a dig site deep within the Frozen Wastes. After weeks of being surrounded by vicious beasts, pummeled by frigid air, and nearly losing our way in the treacherous, icy swamps, the voyage proved worth the effort." Marinaya cleared her throat as she stared beyond the cliff's edge, lost in recollection.

"Little remained of the derelict ruin along the northern coast of the Wastes, battered by centuries of waves and salty air. Even so, the scale suggested an immense structure whose craftsmanship and stonework were unlike anything I had ever seen.

"In a section where the main level had collapsed into a subterranean passage, we made our most shocking discovery. An underground vault. After untold centuries of decay, a wealth of fascinating carvings and crumbled statues had somehow survived, sheltered from the harsh climate. Intriguing and starkly foreign symbols wove delicately around the ancient murals. We inferred the symbols described the exquisite scenes, though we had no way of deciphering them at the time." She paused, glancing towards the Lonely Isle in the center of the lake, its land shrouded by deep, mysterious woods.

"Regardless, all the evidence made it clear this ruin was strikingly older than other fragments of settlements on Karthmoor, older than even our earliest records of pre-Hamidian society in Edros. The whole area seemed to whisper of a people very different from our own ancestors. A precursor civilization, if you will. Full of wondrous power and magic, existing long before our forefathers rose to take their place."

"Magic?" Micah repeated as Kelj stiffened.

"Indeed." She smiled. "From several of the murals, it was quite apparent that arcane gifts were common, if not intrinsic, amongst these people. A fascinating contrast to our world today, but I digress.

"Of all the depictions covering the stone walls, one in particular stood out to me: a carving portraying persons in regal attire entering a handful of oddly familiar obelisks, though I could not place them at the time. It was not until later that evening, after we had returned to camp, that I grasped the connection. The ruin, those ancient people... The time pods were *their* invention.

"After that, I began to see the evidence around me whispering the truth of my realization. The carvings, the design of the structure, even the stone itself, all of it reflected the same minds who left us the technology of the time pods. It was an exhilarating realization, but also a chilling one."

"Chilling?"

Marinaya turned to him, troubled. "The Archmage was obsessed with the power of the pods. Their mere existence was a closely guarded secret. If he learned of the pods' connection to the excavation, and that I was involved, there was no guarantee the terms of my exile would prevent him from hunting me down to protect his precious secret." Marinaya shuddered. "I could not reveal my knowledge to the archaeologists. Thus, I remained silent."

"The pods are immensely powerful artifacts," Micah mused. "Anything their creators designed likely harnessed iluvan with a similar power. If the Firewalkers weren't concerned with the time pods themselves, what else could they be searching for?"

"I cannot say," she admitted. "We found no remnants of technology at the dig site, only the markings within the vault."

"This is interesting," Kelj interrupted, "but how does it help us defeat our enemies?"

"I was getting to that," Marinaya replied. "While I couldn't reveal the link between the ruins and the time pods, my desire to uncover the origin of these mysterious people led me to continue my research discreetly.

"My students returned to Hillmarch with a cartload of rubbings taken from the walls of the vault. It became their prized project during their time at the Academy. Newer students joined the effort, bringing back additional etchings from locations in Edros whenever possible.

"Over time, and with my subtle assistance, our brightest minds began to decipher a handful of the symbols. We were on the verge of unlocking the key to them when the Mist appeared."

"What happened?"

"Besides the panic as people lay dying in the streets and nameless beasts tore apart innocent victims?" she asked dryly. "The garrison at Hillmarch was not prepared for the attack, and the monsters spread like wildfire through the streets. The chaos hit the Academy quickly. As young pupils and wizened instructors alike were claimed by the Mist, I knew we had to evacuate. Little else mattered beyond survival.

"We grabbed what possessions we could as instructors herded students into a protective barrier and set out for the gate. A group of citizens managed to reach our convoy and escape with us.

"As Hillmarch fell, we fled along the southern road, hoping to reach Harrowmont, but were forced to retreat as more nightmarish terrors marched to join the sacking of the city. At that point, we were trapped. Ocean to the east, a burning city at our backs, and an army of demons closing in from the south. Our only option was to flee towards Long Lake and hope the northern villages remained.

"Dorn survived and initially welcomed our weary group, though their distrust of the Academy proved overwhelming. Thus, we found our way here, settling into a rough existence beside the shelter of the lake."

"And your research from Hillmarch?" asked Micah.

"In the turmoil, I fear nearly all of our efforts were left abandoned at the Academy," Marinaya sadly answered. "Years of passionate study lost to murderous monsters, fire, and destruction. I cannot say whether any of it still survives."

"But there is a chance it remains?" Kelj pressed.

"A chance, yes," she said curtly. "Though it would be a thing of miracles." She gazed once more across the lake, undoubtedly recalling the harrowing journey. She turned to them with a determined look.

"Research on the precursor civilization was confined to the third floor of the Academy. A modest room on the northern side, near my office. If anything remains, it will be there."

Micah glanced at Kelj. "Is there anything specific that we should look for?"

Marinaya thought for a moment.

"Leyana was most involved in translating the runes. Her last paper theorized one of the other carvings from the ruin was actually a map, pointing to a second location on Karthmoor. She was close to deciphering its symbols in the hopes of identifying the site's location. Leyana's notes would likely be scribbled in the small leather-bound journal she diligently kept."

"Maybe her journal could lead to more answers," said Micah eagerly. He turned to Kelj. "Looks like we have a new destination."

Kelj nodded in agreement.

"I will not stop you, but heed my warning," Marinaya continued. "Use all the caution you can muster. Hillmarch is now the domain of the Mist. An army of beasts devastated the city—an army that likely remains. If the survival of our research proves a miracle, your safe passage through the city would be an even greater one."

"We understand," Micah somberly replied, "but the stakes are too great to abandon everything now. We'll be careful."

"I see your determination and wish you safe journeys," she said gently. "We will do what we can to speed you on your way."

Micah politely bowed. "We're grateful for the assistance. It'll be a long road around the lake and across the eastern plains."

Marinaya hesitated, her eyes brightening.

"Perhaps we can shorten the trek, though your faithful horses may not appreciate it." She grinned faintly as a puzzled look crossed Micah's face. "We have a handful of sailing vessels moored along the shore. A trip across Long Lake would save many days' time."

"It would remedy our delay," Kelj concurred. "If we act swiftly."

"Agreed."

Marinaya gave a satisfied nod. "I will have some of the men ready our sturdiest ship and situate the horses. They should remain calm as long as they are properly restrained and blindfolded. In the meantime, Narombe will assist you in gathering supplies for the days ahead."

"It would be my honor." Narombe bowed.

Marinaya cast a final look at the camp below before moving back towards the cave.

"Unfortunately, I have other duties I must attend to before the day is over," she concluded. "I will leave you here, unless there are other matters to discuss?"

Micah glanced once more at Kelj, who shrugged. "I had hoped there'd be time to learn more about the Academy," he admitted, "and about my magic."

Marinaya's eyes widened. "Forgive me. I did not perceive your abilities." She thought for a moment. "As you said, the stakes are dire. I understand the urgency of your quest. Still, should you find your answers, return to us. The Academy and I would be delighted to share our knowledge."

"Thank you, Lady Marinaya," Micah gratefully replied, nodding.

She turned to leave. After a few steps, she paused, looking back. "I am relieved to hear Mai and the others have survived, though I do not envy her position. Thank you."

"You should also know," Micah warned, "the Archmage is alive. Somewhere. Mai and the Greenwatch Collective are refusing his orders."

"I see. The Archmage will find it difficult to banish an entire branch of the Collective." She smiled. "I am glad they renounced that wicked work. Perhaps, as exiles together, we will reunite one day."

With that, Marinaya disappeared as Narombe gestured to the trail towards camp.

CHAPTER 31
BETRAYED

As they returned to the main canyon, crowds of refugees came into view, hustling through their daily chores. A few cast sour looks at Narombe as they passed. He didn't acknowledge them. However, several of the stall vendors and herdsmen called out warmly to Narombe, a heartening sign that not everyone was opposed to the mages' presence.

"It looks like many of the people appreciate your help," Micah remarked as they passed a bustling stall covered in an assortment of meats. Hungry customers noisily bartered for the few fresh cuts that remained.

"There are many kind souls who would see us as friends," Narombe answered in his strange voice. "Though those who distrust the spirit-called are well-numbered."

"Spirit-called?" Micah asked, sidestepping a man rushing past with a cartload of pungent rubbish.

"The magic-born," he clarified. "In my homeland, many view those with arcane affinity as touched by Alakanthu, the Sun

Spirit. Whether it is a blessing or a curse depends upon the one you ask."

It suddenly dawned on Micah why the mysterious wizard felt so familiar.

"Narombe, would your homeland happen to be Neboa?"

He stopped, turning to face Micah with an astonished yet pleased look on his face.

"I am surprised by your knowledge, serah Stormcrown," he eagerly confirmed. "It is indeed. Few of your countrymen have asked this of me. Fewer still who recognize the mere existence of my native land. You must be well-traveled."

Micah chuckled. "Never as far south as that. A merchant from Neboa came to my village before my journey began. Asher was his name. A good man."

"Hmm." Narombe pulled at his beard. "I do not recall an acquaintance by this name. Even so, I am encouraged to hear a brother of my home has survived."

They continued on, collecting an assortment of equipment from several of the vendors, all of whom gifted them supplies at Narombe's direction. They stopped near the center of the wooded valley, where a wide, dusty clearing stood next to the mouth of the Winding River. The center of the camp was awash in a cacophony of men herding multitudes of animals and the loud hammering of metalworkers. A small group of refugees huddled around another food cart where a woman busily prepared a hash of vegetables in a massive cast-iron skillet. With midday well past, the sound of its sizzling grease and fragrant, savory smell immediately made Micah's stomach growl. They joined the boisterous crowd.

With new water skins and freshly patched bags stuffed with supplies hanging from their shoulders, Micah and Kelj returned to the ravine reserved for the camp guards as the sun grew longer in the late afternoon sky.

"I have a final task I must see to before the day is done," Narombe explained as they settled near the horses. "I will return as soon as it is finished." He quickly vanished from the gorge.

Micah and Kelj returned to preparing Edoran and Coalfire for the trip. After a moment, the sound of approaching footsteps echoed off the crunching gravel. Micah turned around to find Tarion and the men who had apprehended them. A relieved expression crossed Tarion's face.

"He found you!" Tarion breathed. "I knew he would, but still. You never know what a mage will do."

"He did, and we appreciate the risk you took," Micah graciously replied, shaking Tarion's hand. "It couldn't have been easy."

"No, but it was the right thing to do." He grinned. "Plus, it's about time someone stood up to that nasty wizard."

Micah smiled at the plucky man's spite.

"Anyways, Lady Marinaya requested we load your horses onto the ship. Are you leaving so soon?"

"Yes, unfortunately. Time isn't our ally."

"Of course." Tarion nodded. "I don't envy you a trip across the lake, but we'll get them situated as quickly—and calmly—as can be."

Micah and Kelj accompanied the scouts as they guided the horses to the shore. A single wide-bottomed sailing boat sat anchored in the sand. A solitary, sturdy-looking mast was situated in the center. Micah noticed the benches around it had been removed to make space for their steeds.

Luckily, the silly beasts didn't even recognize where they were taking them, at least until Edoran's hoof hit the wood. As the object shifted under his weight, Edoran recoiled in surprise, immediately nervous. As he resisted climbing farther into the vessel, Tarion and Micah called sweetly, slowly calming his nerves. Inch by inch, Edoran reluctantly hobbled into the ship where Tarion and another man coaxed him to his knees, gently lashing the horse down.

As they repeated the process with Coalfire, Micah raised a hand over his eyes to block out the rays of the descending sun and spotted Narombe striding quickly towards them from the gorge. His striking face was painted with concern.

"Lady Marinaya has asked for you before you leave," he called as he reached the shore.

"What's wrong?"

"I am not sure," he said nervously.

Kelj looked up from assisting the scouts. "I will finish here. Go."

Micah nodded, turning back to Narombe. "Lead the way."

"We'll have the boat ready to go before your return," Tarion shouted after him.

Narombe and Micah set out for the main canyon, the towering mage striding ahead. Micah nearly had to jog to keep up. As they headed down the trail leading to the camp itself, Narombe swerved left, shoving through a row of prickly saplings. Micah chased after him onto a hidden trail leading up the side of the valley.

"Lady Marinaya and the others are above," Narombe explained. "This way."

They climbed the rocky ledge, obscured from the camp below by a thick canopy of foliage. As they clambered onto a wide bluff, Micah spotted Marinaya along with a handful of other mages and scouts huddled near a cluster of young pines. The crowd was immersed in debate, several clamoring for Marinaya's attention as her head swerved between them.

"Enough!" she called as Micah approached. "When did we last hear from them?"

"Noonday," one scout answered.

"But we sent Bolri's group after them over an hour ago! No one's reported in," another chimed.

"Garland would've sent word. It's not like him," a third added with a note of worry.

"Maybe someone got hurt. Or a wolf pack cornered them."

"Please!" Marinaya commanded as she wheeled back to the first scout. "Has anyone returned from the passage?"

"No, ma'am."

"And where is Aranaias?" she snapped. "This is precisely what he is supposed to assist with."

"I haven't seen him since this morning," a nervous mage piped up. "He stormed out of the cave, grumbling."

Marinaya frowned. "Very well. Organize a watch on the cavern passage. We will begin closing the market for the day. Fenwick, I need you to... Ah, Master Narombe," she said as she spied their arrival, "and Warden Micah. Thank you for coming."

Micah nodded as the handful of scouts rushed to their duties. "What's going on?" he asked, looking around. "Trouble?"

"Hopefully not." She shook her head, gesturing across the wooded ravine. Micah followed her finger to the shrouded entrance to the camp on the far wall. "Two teams of scouts from the canyon have failed to report in," she explained. "It is concerning. I hoped you might remember something before you leave us. Do you recall anything odd as you approached our sanctuary? Any other travelers? Maybe a strange sight or sound that seemed out of place?"

Micah paused, trying to remember their path towards the wild canyon through the rocky labyrinth.

"I can't say that I do," he admitted. "It was an odd route but nothing that would seem out of place. We haven't seen another person since we left Hazelcourt."

"I see," she quietly relented. "Then I thank you for your time and apologize for delaying your departure."

"Not at all," said Micah earnestly. "Is there anything I can do to help?"

"No, no," she quickly finished. "We will sort this out. I think—"

Suddenly, a gush of flame erupted from the mouth of the cavern passage, drowning her words. A man screamed. The scouts who had reached the far ledge cried in fear, retreating.

"Lord above," Marinaya breathed.

As the fire evaporated, a lone figure in dark clothing emerged from the depths. Micah squinted across the trees, trying to identify the shadowy figure. Four additional shapes joined the person as the scouts struggled to regroup. They raised their bows, yelling in confusion. Another bolt of flame exploded from the first figure, blasting the rear man backwards as the first was swallowed in the inferno. Below, men and women shrieked in terror.

"Quickly!" Narombe yelled.

The remaining mages and scouts raced down from the ledge towards the canyon floor, hoping to close off the camp before the invaders pressed any closer. Micah chased after them, drawing his pistol. As they sprinted towards the bridge, scattered packs of refugees fled in every direction, crying in panic and confusion.

At the river, the remaining scouts from the cavern had congregated around the bridge, the shadowy group of attackers crashing through the undergrowth as more bolts of fire roasted the trees around them. The men raised their bows and rifles as mages readied spells, watching the burning brush with fearful anticipation.

Through the trees, Micah heard the cracking of branches. The attackers were drawing closer. The roar of the flames grew louder.

"Steady!" Narombe hollered. Micah strained to catch a glimpse of movement beyond the fiery tree line. Amidst the chaos, everything fell ominously quiet.

"Well, well."

Micah's stomach dropped.

"Your persistent involvement in affairs beyond you is becoming quite an annoyance, Oathsworn."

A sinister smirk rose from Garrin's wicked face as he strode from the scorching brush. The shrouded shapes of his companions emerged as the terrified scouts shrank back.

"These are innocent people!" Marinaya angrily shouted. "Explain yourself!"

Garrin glanced at the small, elderly mage with an irritated glare.

"I assume you are the woman in charge." His frown transformed into a menacing smile. "How... convenient."

As Arksul, Hadrian, and Armeia materialized, a fourth person clambered through the blaze.

"Aranaias!" Marinaya gasped.

"Your disgruntled friend here has been most helpful," Hadrian purred, twirling his wicked blade beside him.

"Your weak guidance has led us to ruin," Aranaias spat at Marinaya, scowling. "It's time the Academy had a new leader. A strong leader."

"Traitor!" Narombe bellowed.

"Enough," Garrin furiously growled, a small flame forming around his fist. "Give us the information we seek, mage, and we'll leave you to your disgraceful existence."

"What are you talking about? What information?" Marinaya retorted, baffled.

"The same that meddling Micah undoubtedly came here for. Where is the source of your research?" Garrin forcefully demanded. "Where is the *iluvashtin*?"

Marinaya scoffed, "I don't know what you're talking about."

Garrin's visible anger evaporated as he clasped his hands behind his back. He leaned forward with a twisted grin, teeth gleaming.

"I don't believe you."

Armeia and Hadrian unleashed a blast of energy, tossing the scouts on the opposing bank into the murky river. The others were flung clear across to the rough dirt. Marinaya flicked her arm and the wooden bridge exploded, splinters pelting Garrin's arcane shield.

The battlefield erupted in chaos as scouts and mages unleashed a barrage of arrows and spells. The water flashed as bolts of lightning and fire danced in the clearing. Aranaias and Hadrian deflected the missiles, casting barriers around the Firewalkers as Arksul began forming an icy bridge across the river.

"Call the men!" Narombe bellowed above the havoc. "Get Marinaya out of here!"

Micah fired his pistol at Garrin before one of the other mages grabbed Marinaya, shielding them as they retreated towards the far gorge. As they sprinted up the stony gap in the cliff sides, Garrin shouted from behind, "You can't run forever, Oathsworn!"

As they tumbled into the wide clearing, a group of scouts jerked around, startled by the commotion.

"We're under attack!" Marinaya cried. "Defenders, protect the camp!"

Additional scouts poured out of the barracks, grabbing whatever weapons they could as they dashed into the fray. Marinaya turned to the other mage. "Summon the others. Get the students into the safe room and lock down the Academy. We need every spell-weaver we have in this fight." The frantic man dashed up the slope to the mages' cavern as Marinaya turned to Micah.

"You fight these men?" she breathed heavily.

"Yes, they're Firewalkers," he answered. "I have to stop them from reaching their goal."

"Then go. Go!" she commanded, pointing to the boat.

"What about the camp?" Micah cried.

"We'll be fine," she replied, exasperated. "We'll hold them off and buy you time. They can't defeat the entire Academy."

"You don't know their power. They'll annihilate you!"

"Then make sure our sacrifice isn't in vain," she furiously demanded. "Go!"

Micah took one last look at the canyon gap, the blasts of fire and horrible screams of men echoing through the rocky walls. Groaning in anger, he jerked around, pounding towards the ship as Kelj shoved the load into the lake. They jumped in, pushing the oars hard against the muddy bottom as the boat drifted into the water. The flashes of spells and rifles diminished as Kelj unwrapped the sail and they glided quietly away. Micah glanced back to where Marinaya's solitary figure stood on the shore. She watched them a moment longer before spinning around, heading back into the fight.

Micah punched the side of the ship. "This is a mistake," he fumed.

"Yes," Kelj grumbled, "but their effort may give us the time to win this race."

Micah stomped past the horses, collapsing in the ship's bow as Kelj steered the vessel into the open waters.

"How did they even find us?" Micah sulkily mused, "and how did Aranaias know?"

Kelj thought quietly as he guided the ship in the growing breeze.

"We do not know the extent of these warlocks' allies yet," he said. "It is possible the camp was already known to them, as was the betrayer, Aranaias. I expect he revealed the elder mage's existence to gain their help in removing her."

Micah gripped the edge of the boat, his knuckles turning white as frustration burned inside him.

How can we just leave them?

"They will turn to chase us once they learn of our escape," Kelj finished. "The battle you crave will surely find its way back."

"It's still one I'm vastly unprepared for."

"Practice," Kelj directed. "We have time before reaching the far shore." Micah cast a final, wistful glare towards the smoking refugee camp before turning to the emptiness of Long Lake.

In the stillness, he closed his eyes, attempting to recall the Anderfall's instructions. Water lapped softly against the wooden sides as the fabric of the sail rustled gently beneath Kelj's steady hands. Micah felt himself drawn to the edge of balance, sweet Elisa sharpening his focus, before ultimately losing his inner clarity. The turmoil of the camp was still too close at hand.

He took a break, discouraged, watching as they drifted silently past the Lonely Isle in the gathering dusk. Strange sightings, along with a string of disappearances, deterred most of the curious from ever setting foot upon its eerie shores. The closer they drew to the mysterious island, the more apprehensive Micah became until it faded behind them in the growing dark.

As the sun disappeared, Micah returned to his meditations, the boat continuing its peaceful drift towards the eastern shore in the faint evening wind. Tiredness soon overtook his concentration, sleep beckoning tenderly as his head began to bob.

Must. Focus.

The crunch of gravel against the boat jerked him from his trance.

"What happened?" Micah exclaimed.

"We are here," Kelj rumbled, tossing a pack onto the pebbly shore. The moon glowed brightly from far above.

"We were just passing the Lonely Isle," he whined.

"Yes, right before you began snoring." Kelj smirked.

Grumbling, Micah rose to free Edoran from his restraints. Sensing solid ground ahead, the foolish horse leapt up, nearly tipping the entire ship over.

"Whoa now!" Micah yelled. He tugged him roughly out of the swaying vessel, hoping to avoid further incident.

Once the boat was unloaded, they retreated towards a line of thick, leafy trees and claimed a grassy clearing for the camp. A choir of crickets chirped loudly around the empty space, answered by the lapping of waves on the shore. Moonlight permeated the boughs as shadows filtered through the leaves onto fallen trunks.

"We will continue at first light," Kelj declared. "It will do no good to go any farther on exhaustion."

They didn't even bother with a fire as they dug out their sleeping sacks, ready to catch what little sleep they could with dawn rapidly approaching.

First light, Micah thought grimly. *Garrin won't win this time.*

Chapter 32
The Eastern Jewel

Topping the grassy knoll, an endless sea of golden fronds billowed softly before them. Beyond the wooded shoreline of the night before, the empty plains of the eastern grasslands stretched infinitely into the distance.

Micah and Kelj rode hard, setting a hurried pace through the swaying fields. At that point, even the horses seemed conscious of the danger pursuing them.

"The plains are just as bleak as the ones near Hazelcourt," Micah called out as Kelj and Coalfire sidled up to Edoran. "Maybe two days' journey to Hillmarch."

"We will make it in less if we push," said Kelj, his jaw tightening.

"Aye."

"How far behind are they?" Kelj asked ominously.

"Two, maybe three, days to ride around the lake," Micah guessed. Kelj nodded.

They pressed on, their eyes ceaselessly scanning the land for signs of change. Only an occasional break for rest or to feed the horses halted their progress. The day passed quickly as the sun drifted across the warm, cloudy sky. At least the weather cooperated.

The hills of the eastern shore gradually faded the farther they traveled from Long Lake. By the time the sun touched the horizon, the bare prairie was monotonously flat. Micah and Kelj continued as the daylight disappeared, a nearly full moon bathing the grass in its soft light.

By then, it was clear Edoran and Coalfire were exhausted. They found a patchy space where rocky soil disrupted the thick stalks and made camp. The horses drank greedily, if awkwardly, from an extra waterskin before Kelj and Micah squared off in a brief spar. The match remained even for most of the fight until Kelj landed a solid blow against Micah's side, his mind distracted by thoughts of pursuers and anxiety over what lay ahead. Defeated, Micah collapsed into bed. Just thinking about another day of hard riding already had him aching before he quickly fell asleep.

Kelj shook Micah awake as a faint dawn spread over the plains. They groggily guided their reluctant steeds back onto the trail. The wispy clouds from the previous day had grown into an overcast sky, though impending rain remained absent.

The bleak, featureless landscape continued through the morning as they kept to their brisk pace. Occasionally, a stray hawk soared above, searching the void for unsuspecting prey. Both of them were silent, lost in their own thoughts as they passed the time.

Near midday, the unceasing grass showed new signs of life as sparse rocky hills and slender trees appeared. Micah pushed Edoran a little harder, encouraged by the change. The eastern coast couldn't be far now. A handful of minutes later, they trekked around a thick copse of leafy trees and discovered a wide, dusty road stretching from the north to the south. Few traces of travelers remained in the weathered dirt, though it was clear the road was once a busy highway.

"Any clues to our location?" Kelj inquired.

Micah studied the road, recalling his previous trips to the great Eastern Jewel. He ran a tired hand through his unkempt hair. "It's hard to say," he admitted, "but I think this is the road between Harrowmont and Hillmarch. It's too large to belong to one of the outlying settlements."

"Indeed."

"Shall we?" said Micah lightly, angling Edoran northwards.

They prodded the horses into a trot, a cloud of dust rising behind them as their powerful hooves thumped loudly against the dry ground. They followed the road as it climbed over gentle hills and around wooded groves, a winding route guiding them through the lifeless landscape. Oddly, no signs of the Mist rose from their surroundings, as if the specter looming over creation was holding its breath.

Eventually, the trees along a stretch of the path lessened, the golden fields returning as they topped a range of wide hills. The plains rolled back, revealing a breathtaking view of a vast ocean shimmering in the east.

"There." Kelj pointed to a great bay carved into the sloping shore in the distance. A rocky ring of hills stretched before it, while a span of short mountains enclosed the far edge. The faint gleam of stone and metal covered the western shore of the bay, surrounded by grassy fields that spread far to the west.

"That's Hillmarch," Micah concurred. "The richest port in Karthmoor."

From their vantage point, Micah discerned a smattering of dark shapes floating in the wide, sheltered bay, though they were too far away to tell what kind of shape they were in.

Kelj spurred Coalfire down the hill towards the city. The captivating view of the ocean disappeared as the riders delved back into the plains.

By the time they neared the city, the land around them had darkened. Imposing cliffs to the east blocked any view of the coast as the late afternoon sun disappeared behind a thick bank of clouds. Micah and Kelj slowed the horses, waiting to spot a glimpse of Hillmarch in the rocky terrain.

At a sudden dip in the road, the cliffs abruptly broke away, and the city slid into view. Micah gasped in horror.

The high stone walls, impeccably built by master masons to display the wealth and might of the gigantic city, lay crumbled and ruined. Entire sections had given way where unknown assailants had smashed the imposing blocks to rubble. Large gouges and cracks covered much of the rest while the high gate of thick, rich wood, adorned with the imposing symbol of Hillmarch, sat in tatters. Above the walls, the tiled rooftops of proud towers and lofty estates whispered of decay and devastation. No sounds of the city's once-bustling streets rose from its deserted ruins.

They stopped the horses, gripping their weapons tightly and searching for hidden foes.

"We should leave the road," Kelj urgently whispered.

Micah nodded. "This way."

He steered Edoran into a grove of small birches nestled a stone's throw from the road. They slipped into the trees and down the hill behind them towards empty fields to the west. An assortment of farms and outbuildings dotted the landscape, all of them abandoned and deteriorating.

Keeping the hill firmly between them and the city, Micah and Kelj moved north, bypassing Hillmarch and crossing back over the road once it was well behind them. Beyond the city's northern edge, they stumbled across a narrow gap in the cliff sides and ventured up the winding trail to a wooded overlook at the foot of the mountains with an excellent view of the festering city below. They tied the horses off, hiding them inside the thicket, before moving for a closer look. Crawling carefully on their stomachs, they inched towards the dusty cliff's edge.

As Micah peeked over the rough rocks, a clearer sight of Hillmarch came into view. Like the walls, many of the buildings lay in rubble across the expansive city. Not a building left standing was free of scars. Most sat with large stone chunks blasted out or wicked burn marks upon their exteriors. Worst of all, thick pockets of sickly blue Mist infested the city, shrouding entire sections from sight.

A thinner layer of low-hanging Mist sprawled over everything, though from their angle, Micah could make out other features of the city. Its cobblestone streets were littered with plaster, stone, and wood from the siege. The once-carefully manicured trees lining several of the thoroughfares were destroyed or burned beyond saving by sporadic fires during the monsters' rampage. Past the twisted wreckage of Hillmarch's extensive docks, he finally got a better glimpse of the ships. A fleet of vessels, ranging from small fishing boats to princely frigates, drifted aimlessly inside the bay. Broken masts and gaping holes dotted the decrepit remnants. The city's famed legion of golden vessels and proud galleons, bringing wealth and splendor to the city of merchants, consigned to a graveyard of husks and bones. Micah's heart broke at the devastation.

"A ruined nightmare," Kelj solemnly proclaimed.

"This was a city of thousands…" Micah gazed painfully at the ruins. "A capital of trade where ships from all over Edros came. Hundreds of merchants and wealthy families with a plethora of resources. Reduced to this."

"Another unspeakable wound from this curse," Kelj spat. "It must be stopped."

"The Firewalkers too," Micah added. "Hopefully, our answers lie in these streets. Somewhere."

"Can we see the Hillmarch Academy from this place?" Kelj quietly asked.

Leaving the destroyed center of Hillmarch, his eyes traveled over a wide stretch of fading gardens and crumbling palatial manors. "Yes, there." Micah pointed to their left.

From their hiding spot, it was clear the structure had suffered just as Hillmarch itself had. Sparse gravel paths crisscrossed the once beautiful grounds, leading to a barren hill surrounded by high wrought-iron fencing. Twisted gaps of broken metal dotted the perimeter before the slope crested onto the spacious grounds of the Academy itself. The ancient sanctuary of wizards and the magically gifted towered over the harbor and city, segregated, though still subjected to the same destruction as its neighbors. Its impressive stonework stood firm even as an array of shattered windows gleamed from the face of the castle.

"We need a path to the Academy," Kelj observed. Micah scanned the layout of the city, mentally drawing a route through the carnage.

"I'm not seeing any Mist Wolves or creatures down there," he slowly noted. "Maybe the beasts have—"

"There!" Kelj softly exclaimed.

Micah followed his finger to a cluster of shingled buildings not far from the main gate. For a moment, he couldn't make out anything through the billowing Mist. Then, a sudden shift in the haze revealed a solitary shape hunched near a crumbling doorway. The lanky creature stood, raising its wolfish head as it sniffed the air. Micah's muscles tightened at the sight of the fearsome enemy. He swept the adjacent area, locating a second Wolf prowling through the remains of a blown-out house. He looked farther into the city, searching for more Mist Wolves, only to find something worse.

"We have a bigger problem," Micah grumbled. They watched as a massive gray shoulder swung a bulky arm out of a thick bank of Mist, before vanishing back into the haze.

"Mist Trolls," Kelj growled excitedly. "Finally, a challenge."

"We'll have to avoid the core of the city. The monsters are clearly more concentrated the closer you get to those thick pockets of Mist."

"We cannot simply follow the wall," Kelj argued. "There is no cover near the edges."

"The middle ground then," said Micah. "We follow the houses along the city perimeter to the Academy."

"Yes," Kelj agreed. "We need a way in as well."

"Well, the gate is the only way into Hillmarch over land." Micah nodded towards the busted gatehouse. "Though, maybe... Yes, right there. That spot in the wall looks like an opening." He gestured towards a depression in the blocks where a massive chunk had crumbled near the ground.

"Very well. If we enter at that point, where does our path take us?"

For the next hour, they lay on the cliff, tracing and retracing the steps to take through the treacherous depths of Hillmarch. They noted every cover break and weakness, trying to guess at alternate routes along the way, should something happen. Ultimately, only speed and a genuine miracle, as Marinaya predicted, would see them through.

As the sun drifted behind the trees, they quietly scrambled back from the edge and returned to where the horses patiently waited. Micah rolled a moss-covered log over near Edoran as Kelj pulled a sack of small apples and dried meat from Coalfire's saddlebag.

Micah shook his head at the dwindling rations. "If this is my last meal, I could use a little less stringy rabbit and a little more roasted pig,"

"Anderfall warriors do not eat before battle," Kelj replied gruffly. "Hunger sharpens our resolve."

"No, thank you." Micah swiped the stiff meat from his massive fist. "So then. Once the sun is down, I say we head for the wall. The horses should be safe enough here." Kelj grunted in agreement.

Micah finished his meager dinner, watching the evening rays fade into obscurity. As the moon began its rise, a tide of insects awakened, drowning the leafy enclosure in their droning chirps. They nodded and stood with grave resolve, grabbing their weapons before heading towards the road.

CHAPTER 33
AMONG THE SHADOWS

BACK OUT IN THE open, Micah immediately felt exposed, the safety of the hidden grove fading with every step as they silently moved through the sparse trees along the cliffs towards Hillmarch. As the rocky ledges ended, he peered out from the brush. An open field was all that stood between them and the crumbling stone walls, tendrils of Mist rising in the cool, moonlit air. They paused, scanning for any Wolves prowling outside the fortifications. Nothing.

Elowë, protect us, Micah silently prayed.

"Go," Kelj urged.

They dashed towards the wall, keeping low and holding their weapons tight to stifle any noise. The towering ramparts loomed above as they raced into their shadows, angling for the breach. Micah scanned rapidly from side to side, alert for any sign of discovery. The haunting world remained quiet as a tomb.

Thankfully, Micah's guess was right, and a narrow hole appeared in the crumbled wall, just wide enough for Kelj to duck through. The Anderfall grunted, shoving his broad shoulders through the crack as Micah nervously glanced behind them. Kelj tumbled through, and Micah squeezed in after him. Inside the walls, a row of modest brick and timber homes shrouded the alleyway in gloom. They stepped carefully through a mess of shattered glass and strewn rubble between the structures, heading for a back door creaking softly against its broken frame.

Kelj guided them into a small, dusty kitchen space. A wooden counter sat smashed into the floor, cooking utensils and pots sprinkled around the splintered frame. A massive fissure in the house's front let in a stream of moonlight where wisps of bluish Mist twisted menacingly over a flattened fabric sofa and a multitude of oddly-shaped sticks scattered across the floor. Micah paused, edging closer. He inhaled sharply. Not sticks.

Bones.

He forced himself to look away from the gleaming fragments as his stomach churned. They cautiously skirted the sitting area, angling for the blown-out corner of the wall facing the next house.

Micah held his breath, staring into the dark street.

"Clear."

Kelj stepped through the opening, striding for the door of the next house. Micah chased after him. The battered door was wedged at an angle beneath a collapsed second floor, forcing them to crawl under it. The inside of the house was in even worse shape. Its upper floor had almost completely fallen through, covering whatever stood before in a layer of wood and dust. A broken child's bed rested atop the mess, the straw mattress impaled on a wooden beam. Micah shuddered, grateful there were no signs of this home's former inhabitants.

They climbed over the mess, searching for the door leading to a garden between the houses they had spotted from the ridge. Kelj shoved a dresser resting on its side, revealing their exit as it tumbled noisily. They halted, listening for anything beyond the house.

Silence.

Kelj reached down through the pile of rubble, searching for the doorknob. After a moment, he huffed in triumph, and the warped door swung open. Mist spilled into the ruined house through the narrow opening as he crouched down, sliding through the gap and into a tangle of vines. Micah bent down, following him into the void.

Squat, stone walls lined the small plot, where an unkempt mass of plants and prickly vines sprawled in every direction. Any vegetables and plants once tenderly kept by its owners had long since died off. A pale door, still firmly in its frame, waited on the far end of the garden, leading to another row of homes and shops. Kelj deftly picked a route through the growth towards it. As he reached the beaten frame, a metal bang echoed from the street.

They froze.

Micah peered over the low, cobbled wall towards a crumbling bakery across the road. Through the bank of cracked windows lining the front, he caught a glimpse of a dark shape rummaging in its depths. Kelj turned back to the doorknob and twisted.

Nothing.

Micah crawled over to him, staying crouched below the garden wall. Kelj growled softly, tugging harder at the knob as it refused to budge.

Something wooden clattered inside the bakery, and a Wolf snarled.

Kelj released the knob and wiggled his hand underneath the peeling, white paint of the door. With a forceful jerk, he ripped the door from its lock, the rusted knob cracking as the splintered wood creaked open.

The noises from the bakery ceased.

"Quick!" Micah whispered.

They slipped inside, gently pulling the door shut behind them. Across a dusty living room of overturned furniture and broken glass, a large gash in the paneled wall opened into a storefront on the other side. They stayed low, staring at the windows at the front. No sign of the Wolf.

The gap in the wall allowed easy access as Micah and Kelj stepped through into a garment shop. Overturned racks of leather coats and soft cloaks covered the floor.

"That way." Micah pointed to a door ajar behind the counter. Swinging the weathered boards open, they found a small set of stairs leading to a second floor.

A low growl emanated from the entrance to the shop, and he jumped. Not missing a beat, Kelj hurriedly mounted the stairs as Micah shut the door.

The stairwell went black.

Micah grasped for a railing in the dark, only to find it dangling dangerously from the wall. Step by step, he clambered after Kelj, who finally found the door at the top and wrenched it open. Moonlight spilled into the small space, and Micah raced to join him.

The next doorway exited into a massive sitting room. A broken wall of windows lined the side facing the street, allowing a steady stream of Mist to filter in. The fog glowed ominously as moonlight danced across the faded crimson fabric of the chairs. A small hall led over the adjacent building, with an array of doors hanging at various angles.

They headed for the sealed door at the end, passing a series of rooms that Micah peeked into, curious. An elegant bathroom, still pristine in condition save for a gaping hole displaying the porcelain tub to the city below. A small bedroom, the roof caved in on a wide bed while a pile of ceramic roof tile crumbled atop an expensive mahogany wardrobe. Across from them, a guest room sat in silence, cracked ceiling plaster covering the ripped bed and painted nightstand.

Kelj pulled open the door at the end of the hall, nearly walking into an abyss before Micah tugged him back.

"Whoa."

The front half of the next house was completely demolished. Both stories had collapsed into an immense pile of brick and wood, leaving the space exposed to the street. It was a high drop from there to the mess below.

Something cracked in the shop, and a Wolf yelped. Micah glanced behind, his fear rising.

"No going back," muttered Kelj.

Kelj leapt from the hall, reaching for a broken wall stud stretching from the ground to the shattered ceiling above. As his gloved hands found the stud, he landed on a slender, broken beam protruding from the pole, and it snapped under his weight. He gasped, gripping the wood tighter and swinging around to slide down the wobbling post onto the rubble. In a graceful motion, he sprang from the stud, landing safely at the bottom.

Micah pulled Hamill's pair of leathered gloves from his pocket, one of his final keepsakes from Fairhollow.

A snarl reverberated from the stairwell.

Micah crouched, breathing hard, and leapt towards the pole. He smashed into the rigid wood, wrapping his arms around it as he held on for dear life. After finding a grip, he slowly lowered himself onto the debris. Just as he reached the ground, another growl echoed through the hall above.

"Quickly," Kelj whispered.

They clambered through the chaos, heading for a broken doorway into the next house.

As Micah slipped through the opening, he was greeted again by shadows. A ruined kitchen was covered in dust, and splintered beams from above sprinkled the room. The only light penetrating the Mist-filled space came from the open doorway at their backs. Micah stared into the darkness shrouding the front room, unable to make out any stairs or even the door.

"This should be the end of the row," he recalled.

Kelj motioned. "The door at the back."

They turned, heading for the kitchen access that led outside. As Kelj turned the rusted knob, a faint glimmer of moonlight gleamed through the crack. Beyond it, an alleyway of shadows awaited between the rows of houses, offering a brief respite in the dark. They paused, listening.

"Clear," Kelj declared.

The heavy wooden door swung open with a creak, and they stepped into the narrow debris-strewn backstreet. Micah gripped his sword hilt tightly as he followed Kelj, dashing from house to house to avoid the moonlight. Micah looked up, realizing they were running out of time as the moon traversed the starry void. His anxiety grew.

The space between houses widened as the city receded. Before long, Micah spotted the edge of the gardens, their overgrown trees swaying gloomily in the Mist. As they reached the final house, he passed Kelj, ready to dash across to the cover of a row of evergreens.

"Wait," Kelj murmured, pulling Micah back. He jerked his head, and Micah followed, spying a set of Mist Wolves near the ruin of a small shop beside the grove. One Wolf was busily clawing through a pile of rubble, searching for something as the second approached. The first turned, a throaty growl rising through the Mist as it detected the newcomer's presence. The other responded with a threatening snarl, challenging the first's claim on the ruined structure. The two paced in a circle, growling and snarling like animals fighting over a kill.

With blinding speed, the challenger leapt, dagger-like claws outstretched for the other's gut. Their talons met, a terrible scraping sound ringing across the square as the Wolves devolved into a whirl of mottled fur. As quickly as it began, the pair sprang apart, the challenger retreating with a whine as it licked at a long gash along its shoulder. The victor howled in triumph, sporting a fresh cut across its forearm.

As the second one scampered back towards the city, Kelj drew a long knife from his fur cloak. The remaining Mist Wolf returned to sifting through its mess, contentedly unaware. Kelj snuck forward, stepping lightly as the beast tore feverishly at the debris, scattering a spray of wood and, to Micah's disgust, more bones. Not a tree length away, it paused, sensing something was wrong.

"Psst."

The monster swerved around, startled. It spotted Kelj and rose indignantly to its hind legs. With lightning speed, Kelj flung the shimmering knife, and it sank into the Wolf's skull. An anguished breath escaped the brute as it collapsed.

Silence.

Kelj slunk forward, tugging the blade free and wiping it clean on the Wolf's fur before returning it to its place. He gestured towards the trees.

Together, they plunged into the dark gardens, leaving the hub of the city. Through breaks in the foliage, Micah spied the Academy atop its hill, the dark castle looming above the murky growth like an ominous ghost in the fog.

Before long, the faint Mist at the edge of the grounds gave way to a thick blanket, obscuring the path through the swaying branches. They stumbled through several groves, searching for a graveled trail to guide them.

With his eyes focused on the ground, Micah nearly collided with a slender iron fence, barely catching himself.

"Kelj," he whispered.

They peered through the fence as the Mist swirled, revealing a large, stately manor in the foreboding darkness.

"I do not recall this one," Kelj glumly replied.

Micah stared at the ornate stone, trying to picture all the buildings they had scouted earlier. "I think it's this way."

They followed the fence line, shoving through a shower of lifeless willow branches as they passed beside its sad trunk. A stony path appeared just beyond the fenced enclosure.

The trail swung away from the barren estate, weaving between rows of once-uniform juniper trees. They passed two more manors along the way. The iron gates of one sat in a twisted heap as the shattered wood and glass entry door swayed ominously in the gloom. Far beyond the solitary jungle, howls of Mist Wolves rose from the city.

As the path steepened along the slope, a sudden break in the heavy Mist finally granted them a brief view of their surroundings. Kelj swore.

Micah looked ahead to find the gravel cutting a wide, arcing route across the lower portion of the hill, heading back towards the harbor end of the gardens.

"We're on the wrong path," Kelj fumed.

Micah stretched to see over a row of shrubs on his left, searching for another route through the Mist that would lead up the hill, towards the lonely castle.

"There!" he cried in a low voice. Beyond several rows of sprawling bushes, a small walk snaked between the trees towards the Academy.

"Quickly! Before we lose it in the Mist," Kelj hissed.

They barreled through the thick, scratchy growth, leaving the trail and dashing for the other path. Branches whipped against Micah's face as he tumbled through a second line of wild bushes covered with pungent, wilted flowers. As they pounded across the grass, he nearly ran feetfirst into a sunken pond between rows of small fir trees.

The Mist thickened again, swallowing the land ahead in a hazy void as they neared the path's last known location. As Micah shoved through a prickly wall of green, his foot caught on the undergrowth, sending him sailing through the brush. He smashed into a rocky surface, pain erupting along his shoulder. Micah groaned, rolling off his injured arm to find he had landed on the path.

"Here," he wheezed as Kelj plowed his way through.

Kelj reached down, pulling Micah to his feet. As Kelj surveyed the trail, a soft growl sprang from a tangle of evergreens. Micah reached for his sword.

Too late.

A dark blur exploded through the brush and plowed into his side, knocking Micah off his feet again. Fabric tore as he hit the ground, a smothering weight sitting atop his middle and pressing him into rock and dirt. His hand fumbled for his hunting knife. The Wolf's teeth gleamed just inches from his face as it howled in delight. Its midnight fur shone ominously in the Misty light of the moon.

Micah yanked his knife from his belt, slashing wildly at the beast's legs pinning him to the ground. The howl transformed into a yelp as the blade sank into its soft flesh. The Wolf lurched back, swiping a deadly fist at his hand. Micah rolled, narrowly dodging the blow, and the claws scraped against the loose stones. As the Wolf turned to pounce, it abruptly recoiled. It thrust its arms wide as a howl of pain escaped its fearsome mouth. Kelj tore a gleaming axe from the beast's back as it stumbled. Micah leapt, lunging without a second thought and planting the knife deep in its furry chest. A pitiful cry sputtered behind its fangs, and it crumpled to the ground, the monster's life extinguished.

"Thanks," Micah breathed. Kelj nodded.

Micah took a step, sending a stinging fire shooting through his leg. He barely caught himself, hobbling and muttering. Looking down, he noticed a tattered patch on the outside of his pant leg. Warm blood dripped down his thigh from a row of three ugly gashes.

"Bad?" Kelj squinted.

"It's not deep." Micah grimaced. "I'll live."

A chorus of howls filled the sky, and they froze.

"Run."

The angry cries closed in as Micah and Kelj sprinted up the gravel, the path becoming steeper as they neared the Academy. They shoved through long tendrils of branches and knotted vines, each step sending a jolt of excruciating pain through Micah's leg. His body refused to submit as the terrible sound of Wolves neared, adrenaline briefly blotting out the pain.

The slope lessened as they passed a barrier of iron bars in the gloom. Micah and Kelj charged out of the thick Mist, greeted by the long stretch of the Academy's lawn. Under the Mist's occupation, the manicured grass had transformed into a waving field of prickly weeds lining the crumbling stone path. It was all that stood between them and safety.

"Go!" Micah yelled, the yelps and howls increasing in tempo.

They raced towards the towering oaken doors, the desolate castle shrouded in shadow. Micah could feel his leg weakening, his stride becoming more uneven, as they neared the entrance. A gleeful howl rose from the path behind as a Mist Wolf spied its quarry.

Kelj crashed into the Academy doors as Micah limped after him. Kelj pulled at the large iron ring, but the massive bulwark refused to budge. Micah's terror surged. Kelj roared, yanking on the handle a second time. A piercing, metallic creak shrieked from the hinges. With muscles straining, He hauled the thick wood open just wide enough for them to pass, the rusted door resisting every inch.

Micah stumbled past him into the dark of the Academy's entrance, the snapping jaws of Mist Wolves right on their heels. Kelj swung around the door, wrenching the barrier closed. The swarm of Wolves lunged ravenously across the lawn, howling furiously. Kelj bellowed, throwing all his might into sealing the gap as the colossal door inched shut. With only a handsbreadth left, a giant Wolf smashed into the timber, slamming it closed with a quaking shudder. A barrage of scratching echoed against the wood as the pack collided with it. Kelj took a step back. An odd metallic clatter rose from the other side.

The ring.

In a moment of sheer horror, the gigantic door began to crack open.

"No!" Kelj dived for the handle, fighting against the beast's incredible strength as it tugged at the ring.

"Find the bar!" Kelj bellowed, nodding at the metal brackets hammered across the backside.

Micah frantically searched the room, tossing broken chairs and clutter aside in the shadows. Suddenly, his boot struck a thick, metallic object under a torn banner. He reached down, pulling a heavy iron rod from beneath. He dragged the massive bar to the entry, a sea of snarls and howls reverberating through the chamber with every step.

Panting, Micah lugged the heavy brace over his shoulders, pushing it towards the brackets as Kelj struggled to keep the doors even. The bar crashed noisily into the slot, echoing through the high stone lobby. While the Wolf still fought against the wood, the exterior ring clanging madly, the sturdy bar refused to budge.

Kelj leaned over, gasping for air.

"That was close," he coughed, wiping sweat from his brow.

"Too close."

CHAPTER 34
THE ACADEMY

MOMENTARILY SAFE, THEY SURVEYED the foreboding castle. Micah walked to the center of the musty entrance hall, marveling at the lofty ceiling with its huge iron chandeliers suspended above the wreckage. Moonlight spilled in from the high, narrow windows, casting dim beams on either side of the castle gates. As his eyes adjusted, he started to make out objects in the chaos.

Where packs of students had once reclined, waiting for class and studying for exams, plush sofas and comfy leather chairs lay in an overturned mess. Tufts of padding were sprinkled across the tiled floor like mounds of snow. Cozy rugs, colorful banners, and artwork littered the room in ripped tatters. Decorative suits of armor and sturdy wooden tables were strewn in pieces across the dusky stone. A bony limb protruded from under the heap of a fractured sofa. Beyond the streams of moonlight, a wide, main corridor beckoned sinisterly in utter darkness.

In the menacing silence, everything about the Academy felt... wrong.

Micah hobbled back to a long, narrow banner still hanging near the doors and cut a band of cloth from its faded length. Wrapping the soft fabric around his leg, the trickle of blood stopped, providing a small measure of relief.

Kelj walked over to a pile of wreckage, inspecting an intricately carved chair. Satisfied, he gripped the end of a leg and jerked back, stomping on the other end and snapping it off. He repeated the attack on the other three, grabbing the load along with the ragged remains of a tapestry.

Micah watched, curious, as Kelj dumped the heap at his feet before ripping the cloth into strips. As Kelj neatly wrapped one length of dyed material around the wooden stick, Micah grabbed the flint from his bag. A moment later, Kelj handed him a makeshift torch, and the room brightened in the warm light. A multitude of jagged shadows danced behind the carnage, animated by the fiery glow.

"Your turn to lead," Kelj said gruffly.

Micah rolled his eyes. "Thanks."

As Kelj wrapped the other splintered legs, Micah slowly paced towards the grand corridor, his faint torchlight revealing a steady stream of rubbish littering the hall. Kelj joined him as Micah took a deep breath, staring into the unknown. They cautiously entered the passage, the sound of the Wolves fading as they delved deeper into the tomb-like Academy.

The castle was eerily quiet. There was scant evidence the beasts of the city had remained within its ancient halls. Very little Mist drifted through the stuffy air. As the wide corridor continued, they passed a multitude of openings, studying every room. Each sat in silent gloom, shattered wooden chairs and damaged desks covered in a layer of dust. Tattered books and writing utensils were strewn carelessly, covering the floors.

"This place is a grave," Kelj muttered.

Eventually, the main hall ended, forcing them to choose between left and right, both veiled in the consuming blackness. Micah turned right, following an expensive-looking rug of delicate golden lines dancing on a maroon backdrop.

The hallway emptied into another wide chamber, where towering stone pillars marched into the unseen void. Long rows of rich, wooden tables accompanied by sturdy benches followed suit.

"This looks like a grand dining hall," Kelj remarked.

"I'd say you're right," Micah concurred, pointing to a smattering of tin plates and silverware littering the polished floors. He spotted a narrow doorway beyond the tables.

"Through there, maybe?"

The modest frame creaked open, its dirty hinges unaccustomed to use. As the light of the torch brightened the shadowy space, Micah could identify various objects in the small room. Massive stone counters were piled high with plates, metal pots, and various utensils. A few blocks of completely molded cheese lay stacked on a wooden carving table near an impressive bank of clay ovens along the back wall. A foul odor wafted from the darkness.

"Just the kitchen," he whispered.

They turned back, scouring the hall for additional doorways, but came up empty-handed.

"Let's try the other passage," said Micah.

They retraced their steps, returning to the fork in the corridor and taking the left route this time. After a series of turns and more classrooms, the hall ended at a wide, stone stairwell spiraling up into darkness.

Micah's boots clicked loudly against the smooth stairs, amplified in the noiseless tower. Even the crackling of the torch seemed to cry out, threatening to reveal his intruding presence. He ran a hand along the thick, rocky banister, its icy surface chilling his skin. As the next floor appeared, he hugged the rail, expecting to continue to the third floor, only to face a blank wall of stone.

"There must be another stairwell," Kelj suggested.

Paintings and portraits hung haphazardly from the walls of the corridor, their startling faces springing from the dark as Micah's flickering light passed. Several displays, along with an assortment of study materials, lay scattered across the carpeted floor. The ceiling above seemed to close in on Micah after the massive corridors of the floor below. Oddly, the Mist was heavier here.

Micah peered into several of the rooms as they passed, spying collections of beds, dressers, and shelves. All of them were in various states of disorder.

"A dormitory floor," said Micah softly. "I wonder how many students lived at the Academy?"

"Given its size, dozens, if not a hundred," Kelj reckoned.

"And not all survived." Micah sighed sadly, thinking back to the smattering of students at the refugee camp. He wondered how many never left the castle, its darkened chambers forever hiding their fate.

At another juncture, they ignored the other halls and continued straight, following the dusty corridor as the torn carpet treaded on into the shadows. After another series of dark rooms, the corridor abruptly ended at a solid wooden door. Micah glanced at Kelj, and he shrugged. Gripping the metal latch, Micah pressed it gingerly, then with force after the lever refused to budge. The bolt unlocked with an echoing click, and the hatch squeaked open. A smaller spiral staircase wound upwards behind it, and Micah breathed in relief. Before they mounted the stairs, he lit the second torch from Kelj and set the remains of the first on the cold stone. Micah gripped the iron rail to ascend.

A blood-curdling screech pierced the hall.

Kelj whipped out his axe as Micah drew his pistol. They stared into the blackness, frozen in fear as they watched the hallway for any hint of movement. The source of the inhuman noise did not appear. Micah could almost hear his heart pounding. Nothing else sounded from the void.

"Go," Kelj murmured as he softly closed the door.

Micah turned around, his hand sweating as he gripped the torch. He quickly climbed the stairs, straining to see beyond the torch's light. Kelj's hard stare never left the bottom.

At the top, Micah found another door and carefully teased it open, scanning the silent corridor before exiting the tower. As they edged farther into the narrow hall, a faint light glowed through a cracked door ahead. They crept to the doorway, discovering a messy study with a row of windows along the far wall. Moonlight cast spooky shadows across the disordered room, strange glass devices and spokes of wooden furniture twisting the beams in every direction. An array of dingy beakers covered a set of long stone tables, reflecting muted shades of light through their dry centers, whatever liquids they had once contained having long since evaporated. Micah stepped into the chamber, eyeing the world outside the castle.

"Is this the room Marinaya described?" Kelj asked.

"No, she said it was on the northern end of the building. Judging by the view, we need to follow the corridor to the far end."

They snuck back into the cold hall, dodging a mess of over-turned bookcases and scattered papers as they trekked on. While this floor of the Academy appeared to be in decent shape, the chaotic flight from the castle had still left behind a muddled mess as instructors and students fled the invading terrors.

At the end of the corridor, another door appeared before Micah, tightly closed. The worn handle initially stuck, but a moment later, the latch jiggled free. Soft moonlight filtered in as the door widened, revealing a bank of windows overlooking the cliffs and fields beyond Hillmarch. Towering bookcases lined the walls of the room, filled with an amazing array of weathered tomes and mysterious arcane objects. A large, ornate desk and an expensive-looking leather chair faced the doorway.

"Marinaya's study," Micah murmured, casting a final look around before turning to a second door on their left.

The creaking door swung open to a gloomy classroom. Several tables piled with books and sketches were dispersed across the tight space. Huge sheets of delicate paper covered in faded charcoal markings hung from nails pounded into thin beams along the walls. A bizarre collection of fascinating symbols and pictures adorned the sheets. The flowing scripts and artistic images were unlike anything Micah had ever seen.

"This has to be it," he declared, stepping into the room. Micah stared at the entrancing rubbings, something about them stirring a deep, unspeakable excitement. Runes in an unknown language, whispering powerful secrets, kindled a spark of long-ing in his soul.

"Do you see the journal?" Kelj impatiently whispered, shak-ing him from his trance.

Micah focused on the scattered notes and research of Mari-naya's students. "Not yet."

Time dragged by as they dug through the clutter, the key to their questions refusing to reveal itself. Micah was beginning to lose hope the journal still remained when Kelj gave a victorious huff. He raised a small, worn book, its leathered bindings battered and scratched. He tossed it to Micah as he wove his way over.

"Precursor Translations," Micah read, opening the soft cover. "Leyana Faircloth."

"That is it," Kelj exclaimed. "What does it say? Where is the Firewalkers' prize?"

"Slow down, give me a moment," he grumbled.

Micah paced to the window, using the torch and moonlight to illuminate Leyana's delicate scribbles. Page after page was filled with curious notes and tangents. Hopeful theories and inspired notes danced between the ends, displaying the brilliant mind of its owner. In several sections, it was clear the mage had attempted to connect the markings in the room with other civilizations, but continued to come up short.

Micah sifted through the fragile sheets, flipping quickly towards the back. After a moment, his eyes caught a glimpse of something, and he stopped, slowly turning back to find it. He raised a brow as he studied the image.

A curious symbol adorned the top half of the paper. Its outline resembled a regal kite shield, the edges curving to a point at the top. Inside the shape, coiling lines flowed through each other in an intricate pattern. A series of mysterious symbols were interspersed between the cardinal ends with a dragon-like creature at the center. At the bottom of the page, a single word was written in large letters.

Oathsworn.

Micah's breath stuck in his throat as he flashed back to Garrin.

You carry a name older than you realize.

"That's ridiculous," he quietly scoffed.

"What?" Kelj looked up as he combed through a stack of papers across the room.

"Nothing," Micah muttered.

He glanced up, spotting the same symbol on one of the mural rubbings depicting a line of powerful looking warriors, each with an arm raised as a nameless spell burned in their palms. A foreboding feeling crept over him.

He focused back on the notebook.

As Micah neared the final pages, the meandering notes began to converge on a single theme.

"Here," he announced. "I think I've got something."

Kelj stopped digging through the clutter and joined him.

Recurring thoughts concerning a map gradually appeared, along with strings of unknown symbols.

"Nineteen," Micah mused, alighting on a number circled on a page dedicated to 'the map.'

He glanced at the classroom walls, realizing each of the massive papers was marked with a number in the lower right-hand corner. He circled the room, his heartbeat rising as the numbers slowly counted up.

"That one." Micah pointed to the drawing marked with number nineteen.

If the charcoal rubbing was a map, it was unlike any map he'd ever seen. The sporadic lines were incomprehensible, with few connections to suggest a landmass. A jagged peak rested in the upper corner, resembling a mountain, but that was where the similarity stopped. A collection of sharp lines and a multitude of curious symbols lay scattered across the face of the drawing. Odd shapes, not quite like the other symbols, were spaced randomly throughout the sheet.

"That is not a map," Kelj astutely confirmed.

Micah looked back at the journal. Leyana had tried to link symbols to places around Karthmoor, drawing odd sketches across the smudged pages before crossing them out with heavy marks. The only one that continued to appear was the mountain which the mage attempted to situate using great peaks throughout Edros, including Tar'auth Eld. Still, her efforts to place the precursor markings remained elusive.

"She was getting close, it seems, but I'm running out of pages," Micah remarked, flipping quickly through an assortment of marked out drawings.

The pages turned blank. He flipped back to the last drawing, a section of Karthmoor overlaid with another furiously scribbled denial.

Nothing. Micah turned to the back of the final page.

Think. *Bigger*.

Below that, a final note, hastily scribbled.

Professor's map.

"Be right back," said Micah, heading for the door.

He ducked into the hall, its shadowy depths eerily silent, and slipped into Marinaya's office. Micah scanned the room, looking for anything like a map. Over a wide shelf in the bookcases, a large frame sat empty, as if something was missing. He moved to Marinaya's desk. Behind a stack of massive tomes, a delicate parchment waited, rolled and neatly bound by a slender thread. A piece of paper rested on top, tucked into the string. Micah pulled out the note, lost to time and forgotten in another age.

Leyana, this rendering was made by one of Archon Valerius' top cartographers. It is more precious than all the wealth of Hillmarch. <u>Be careful</u>. Please return it when you are finished.

Professor Marinaya

A jubilant sigh escaped his lips as Micah hurried back to the research room. Kelj jumped as he rushed in and hastily swept papers off a table before delicately unrolling the ancient map. The aging parchment crinkled as it opened, revealing an ornate depiction of the known world. Delicate lines painted by the hands of a master scribe flowed across the colored page. Inlays of golden ink marked important cities and geography across the Edros, every country given its proper borders. The unknown expanse of the seas hemmed the land in, their mysterious ends left unanswered. It was a beautiful work of art.

"What is this?" Kelj gawked in awe.

"The key, I hope."

Micah walked over to the wall, pulling off the precursor drawing and pinning it over the windows.

He gently lifted the map from the table, making his way to the moonlit glass where number nineteen hung, the light glowing through the thin, white parchment. Kelj watched eagerly as Micah pulled a chair over with his leg. Micah stepped up, searching for the right angle at which to lay the map behind the rubbing. Holding his breath, he slowly raised the map to meet the drawing.

The dark charcoal markings of the rubbing contrasted starkly with the sheet in the moonlight, the image of the mountain appearing exactly where Tar'auth Eld stood on Marinaya's map.

"Incredible," Kelj murmured.

Micah grinned. "Creator, you made a brilliant mage."

The array of lines and symbols painted perfectly across the expanse of Edros as if Elowë himself decreed it; symbols lining up with unknown locations throughout the continent.

"Look there." Micah nodded at a scattering of odd glyphs along Edros' western coast. "That's Westrock. Probably where they found the first ruins."

"There are different symbols throughout the land," Kelj observed. "Dozens of places remain."

"What are the lines?" he wondered aloud. "They don't match up with anything."

"They do follow the land, however," Kelj continued. "Perhaps they marked provinces of this lost nation."

"Amazing."

"What of Karthmoor? I cannot see it well from here," Kelj asked.

Micah looked at the mountain, a tiny speck compared to the breadth of the world below.

"Two symbols besides the mountain," he noted, studying their odd triangular shapes. "That one looks like it's in the Frozen Wastes. Probably Marinaya's ruin."

"Indeed. And the other?"

"Here." Micah gestured to the symbol nestled against the mountain. "The map would put it on the western slopes of Tar'auth Eld, but that can't be right."

"How so?"

Micah cautiously descended from the chair, laying the map back on the table.

"That would put it in the Forest of Midland, not far from my old farm in Aringoth," he explained. "I know the area. The only structure that still exists in Midland is the old cathedral, Angol'daur."

"An unsettling name," said Kelj.

"An unsettling ruin, but definitely not precursor. It was the first temple on Karthmoor, built by our ancestors. As the forest grew, the place was abandoned and fell into disrepair. Now it's only known for stories of hauntings."

Kelj glanced back at the moonlit rubbing. "Are you certain?"

"Yes, this is my home," said Micah, mildly defensive.

"Perhaps history has forgotten," he countered. "Your people may not have been the first."

"So, do you think that's where whatever the Firewalkers are after is hidden?"

"The map is clear, surprisingly so. I see no reason to doubt the sorceress' apprentice," Kelj confidently asserted.

Micah stared at the towering warrior, considering the options. After a moment, he released a conceding sigh.

"You're right. It's too accurate to be a coincidence," Micah admitted. "Something has to be there, or close by, at least."

"It is settled then."

The faint howl of a Mist Wolf from the city below whistled through the brittle windows.

"We can figure it out later," said Micah. "Right now, let's get out of here."

"We should take the research," Kelj added. "There may be more riddles to solve."

"With Garrin, I can only imagine," he muttered.

Micah plucked the precursor rubbing from the window and laid it with the Hamidian map. They grabbed a handful of other interesting looking etchings from around the room, rolling them all together and stowing them in Kelj's small pack along with Leyana's notebook.

Kelj lit the third torch, and together they crept back into the silent hall, passing darkened studies and remnants of classrooms as they headed for the stairwell.

Chapter 35
Escape

At the bottom of the stairs, Micah and Kelj paused again, peeking out into the castle hall and searching for the source of the terrible shriek from before. They stepped onto the plush carpet, heading as carefully as they could for the first floor. Nothing appeared. They staggered down the tower towards the main corridor, the pain in Micah's leg returning as the excitement of their discovery faded behind the danger of the moment.

"What about the Wolves?" he whispered as they strode through the juncture leading to the castle entrance.

"With luck, they will have moved on," Kelj replied, an edge of uncertainty in his voice.

They slowed as they neared the lobby, noticing the uncomfortable silence hanging in the air. No sound came from the front gates shrouded in the encompassing dark.

At least the Wolves aren't still pounding on the door.

The gloom brightened slightly as moonlight from the entry spilled into view.

Without warning, Kelj's muscular arm slammed into Micah's chest, yanking him back.

"What?" Micah gasped.

Then he saw it.

A terrifying monster stood before the Academy doors, turned away from them. Its long, slender limbs were a blackish gray, almost as if charred, with faint streaks of glowing blue light running along them like veins. Instead of fingers, elongated black claws extended from its hands while twisted, wicked-looking spikes protruded from its head. In shape, the horror resembled a Mist Wolf, but at the same time was also more human-like. Micah stepped back, fumbling for his pistol.

The monster sensed their torchlight, its joints contorting at unnatural angles as it haltingly turned to face them. A horrible, warped face, a cross between man and wolf, peered at them with glowing blue eyes. Its mouth opened in a frightening grin, revealing rows of fangs, gleaming with blue streaks.

"Back," Kelj quietly ordered.

The hideous monster let out an ear-splitting scream, and they scrambled to cover their ears, Kelj dropping the torch. Micah raised his pistol.

BOOM!

The blinding flash illuminated the hall. With lightning-fast reflexes, the monster twitched a blackened hand, and the bullet swerved, smashing into a pillar.

It has magic!

They stumbled back as the terror raised another hand, a glowing blue orb expanding around its fist.

"Duck!"

Micah dragged Kelj into the open doorway of a darkened classroom just as a massive wave of energy exploded, sending debris and stone flying down the shuddering corridor. Micah peeked around the doorframe, watching in sheer horror as the monster lurched towards them with a long, slow gait.

"We have to move—now!" he shouted. They rushed out of the room, Kelj flinging a polished knife at the glowing demon as they ran. It deflected the blade with another spell, but the move bought enough time to sprint out of range. The creature unleashed another chilling screech as it vanished in the dark.

"Micah!" Kelj shouted as Micah raced ahead.

Without thinking, Micah turned right, heading towards the dining hall. As Kelj rounded the corner after him, a cone of lightning crashed into the stone wall, and the massive banner with the Academy insignia burst into flames.

They stumbled into the dining space, scouring for an exit.

"There is no escape here!" Kelj bellowed. "We must go back!"

Another earsplitting shriek echoed from the corridor.

"There's no time!" Micah yelled. "Check the kitchen!"

He slid across a row of tables, rushing for the small side door. They filed in, immediately engulfed in darkness. Then he remembered the torch lying at the entrance.

Great.

"I cannot see anything," Kelj urgently muttered.

Running out of options, Micah stopped. Closing his eyes, he tried to calm his racing heart as the wails drew closer.

Elisa. Elisa. Creator, quiet my mind.

The world around him gradually stilled as he recalled her tender memory. Micah slowed his breath, emptying his mind of everything but her.

Then he felt it.

The spark came gently, welcomed by the calm. It drew close, the strange energy filling Micah's body, dulling the pain in his leg. He spread out his hand.

A calm, pulsing light burst from his palm, rising into a steady orb. As it grew, the room sprang alive as if filled with sunlight. Kelj gawked at him, surprise painted across his face. A screech reverberated from somewhere in the dining hall.

"There must be something," Micah said shakily, feeling the slight drain of magic against his vitality.

They looked around the room, objects sharpening in the light of the orb.

"There." Kelj pointed to a small door cut into the back corner of the kitchen. They hurried over, opening the rickety door to reveal a spacious larder.

"Not exactly what I was hoping for," Micah dryly observed.

"Do you feel that?" Kelj quietly asked. Micah looked at him quizzically.

Kelj stepped into the storeroom as a wave of aromas hit Micah's nose. Dozens of ingredients and goods, all rotting. Then he felt it. A faint breeze. Kelj ran his hand along the stone wall at the back.

Something scrabbled against the kitchen door.

"There is something here," Kelj continued.

Suddenly, the door to the kitchen exploded, wooden splinters pelting the walls and ovens as flames licked at the doorway. Micah flinched, nearly losing his concentration, but managed to sustain the flow of energy to his light.

"Quickly!" Micah shouted, spinning around.

"No, Micah!"

Micah stepped back into the kitchen, facing the blue glow of the monster as it searched for its prey. It immediately spotted his light, screaming in delight. Micah heard Kelj frantically pounding against the larder wall behind him.

The creature raised a vicious, clawed arm, its glowing streaks pulsing with power as electricity crackled on its fingertips. Still maintaining the light, Micah raised his other arm, reaching for a spell.

Breathe.

A trembling wall of flickering white sputtered from his hand, growing into a translucent barrier. The monster screeched in fury.

CRACK!

A stream of lightning burst from the demon's claws, crossing the room in a blinding blur. Micah staggered as the blast collided with his barrier, sending the deadly bolts into the walls. The ancient mortar split as energy hammered the blocks, blowing a gaping hole into the dining hall.

Kelj roared, and Micah heard stone scraping in the storeroom.

A renewed energy pressed against Micah's consciousness. He released the shield, drawing his arm back and letting the magic flow as his muscles tensed. A faint glow sprouted from his hand as he clenched his fist, feeling its might.

Almost.

The monster shrieked, furious at his rebellion, as it raised its claws again.

There.

The energy was coursing, pounding through his very veins. Micah flung out his arm, opening his hand and unleashing a flash of light as an invisible wave shook the air. The creature cried out in surprise, raising a barrier to stop the barrage and barely catching it in time.

Energy poured from Micah. The entire room trembled as the air rippled with vibrations, chips of stone splintering from the ceiling as the monster resisted the blast.

"Now, Micah!" Kelj shouted.

Micah yelled, unleashing a final, massive wave.

The monster stumbled back, still maintaining its swirling barrier, but the castle wasn't as fortunate. The kitchen quaked, pillars cracking. Micah cut the flow, backing towards the larder as chunks of ceiling began to rain down. The monster rose, protesting Micah's escape, but it was too late.

With a deafening roar, the ceiling crumbled, an avalanche of stone hammering the kitchen as the floor above collapsed. Micah stumbled as the monster vanished within the chaos, and then sprinted towards Kelj, who beckoned from a narrow opening in the larder wall. The ceiling of the tiny room began to fracture, and Micah leapt into the opening, cutting off his flow of magic, as Kelj shoved the stone door closed. Everything around them went black. Tremors and rumbling shook the earth, drowning Micah's ears, but thankfully, the hidden room stood firm.

In a single, terrifying moment, everything fell silent.

Kelj was breathing hard. Nearly as hard as Micah was as his muscles quivered from exertion.

"Light, Micah," Kelj wheezed.

Micah reached for his magic, but everything, including sweet Elisa, had vanished.

"I can't," he feebly choked. His whole body started to convulse, weakening. Micah lay there, unable to move as the magic drained the life from his body, claiming its due.

Kelj grunted, rustling for something in the dark. After a moment, Micah heard him striking his flint, the spark flashing in the void. A flicker of flame began to glow. Kelj stood, gripping the final torch in his hand as he shoved rubble off of Micah's trapped legs. As he clawed at the rock, Micah's sight dimmed, and he panicked. He was trapped within his own mind, helpless as an enormous energy evaporated from his body to compensate for the taxing spells.

I'm going to die.

"Micah?" Kelj whispered with concern.

Unable to respond, Micah waited in fear, drawing closer to death. Just as he reached the edge, certain he was about to leave the world, the leeching force mercifully subsided.

For several minutes, there was nothing, only his ragged breaths in the dark.

Gradually, Micah's eyesight returned. He feebly curled his fingers, feeling a tingle of life returning to his cold skin. Kelj hovered with worry as Micah shifted a leg, slowly returning to the world. Kelj pulled a waterskin from his pouch, raising it for Micah to drink.

The cold sensation sent a shiver through Micah's core, sharpening his mind. With Kelj's help, he sluggishly rose, sitting shakily on the rocky ground.

"What happened?" Kelj asked in a serious tone.

"The magic," he gasped weakly. "My body wasn't ready to handle it."

"There is a price for using your power," Kelj quietly realized.

"Yes, I was foolish," he admitted, reprimanding himself for forgetting the most basic lessons from the Guard. "Even if I can access the power, my body and mind have a long way to go before I'm conditioned enough to wield it."

Kelj's brow furrowed.

"Where are we?" Micah coughed, studying the sharp, rocky walls. A narrow passage faded into the black void.

"I am not sure," Kelj answered. "Likely a passage under the mountains. Air is entering from somewhere beyond."

"Looks like our only option."

Micah took another drink before Kelj's rough hand pulled him to his feet. Micah wobbled, vision flickering, steadying himself against the chilly earthen wall.

"Are you ready?" Kelj hesitantly asked.

"I'll be fine."

They climbed through the rubble, reaching an uneven, but clear path as the dank tunnel led farther from the Academy. Wherever it was heading, it was certainly not towards Hillmarch.

Time stretched on as they followed the gentle dirt trail, their progress slowed by Micah's injured leg and exhaustion.

"What was that thing?" Micah asked after several minutes of silence.

"Another demon of the Mist," Kelj growled.

"It almost looked like a Mist Wolf," Micah nervously continued, "only more... human."

"With the strength of a powerful warlock," Kelj ominously added.

"You don't think..."

"I do."

"That could have been me, were I not so fortunate." Micah shuddered. "I think I see why you view magic as a curse now."

"Never like that," he replied sadly. "No Anderfall would wish that existence on a magic-cursed."

"A Mist Wraith," Micah declared after a moment of silence.

"Indeed."

At a sudden bend in the path, a stronger breeze of air slipped across Micah's face, smelling faintly of pine.

"There." Kelj gestured as he paced ahead. A sharp rise in the dirt ended at a short ladder stretching towards the low ceiling. The faint glow of fading moonlight peeked between the boards of a battered hatch.

Kelj shoved the trapdoor open, climbing out into the darkened world above. Micah tightly gripped the rickety ladder as he followed. Heaving himself out of the hole, Micah rolled onto the hard, dusty ground, staring at the twinkling sky. Kelj kicked the hatch closed as Micah stood, scanning their surroundings for threats.

The concealed door sat behind a rocky pile, nestled beneath a range of high cliffs at the edge of the mountains. A line of birch trees and tall evergreens enclosed the clearing.

"We must be outside the city walls. Maybe near the grove where we hid the horses?"

"Were we so blessed," Kelj replied.

They made for the woods, weaving their way through the undergrowth in the murky shadows. A howl in the distance called out, and they froze.

"Coyote," Micah confirmed, and they continued.

After an hour of hacking their way through, the forest finally relented, emptying onto an open plain. At first, all Micah saw was the dim waving of grass and swirling Mist. As his eyes adjusted, he spotted a gap in the stalks stretching in both directions. They passed through the field, finally reaching a wide dirt road after what seemed like an unending journey.

Gauging by the waning moon, they turned left, trekking down the dry trail as it followed the mountains to the east. After a lengthy hike, they finally found the shrouded gap leading to their secret grove as sunlight grew stronger on the horizon.

Micah staggered into camp, startling the horses before collapsing near the bags under the trees. He yanked a wedge of bread from the supplies along with his sleep sack, choosing a shady spot beneath a low-hanging branch.

Exhausted, Micah burrowed into the warm fur, hoping to escape the nightmarish events dominating his thoughts. The glowing eyes of the mage-turned-Wraith haunted his mind, and he shivered, grateful once again for his unmerited immunity.

It could have been me.

Chapter 36
An Ancient Hall

THE ROAD VANISHED IN the eerie blue fog, concealing the approach to Aringoth as Micah spurred his horse past the Jacobsens' farm. The poor beast protested loudly as he kicked again. Panicking, he could only watch helplessly as the world was swallowed by the void.

After losing contact with Greenwatch, refugees from western Karthmoor had begun pouring into Starkhaven, spreading word of a terrible curse rising over the land, killing everyone who breathed the air. News of "the Mist" spread faster than the curse itself. The Conclave descended further into chaos, struggling to comprehend this new darkness conquering their lands.

There had been no word from Aringoth.

Micah had bade Berien farewell, leaving the capital. Not knowing the risk, he plunged into the invading fog, losing himself in its depths as he headed for home. Desperate farmers and terrified villagers warned him at every step, calling for him to stop. He could not.

The dusty center of Aringoth was disturbingly quiet as Micah reached town. The door to the general store stood open, no one in sight.

"Hello?"

Silence.

He pressed on, riding out of the village and heading for Jonas' farm. Micah stood in the moving stirrups as hooves pounded noisily in the forsaken dirt, hoping to catch a glimpse of Tar'auth Eld in the distance. Even the great mountain was hidden by the unnatural cloud.

Thankfully, the faint light of day helped him find the edge of Jonas' fence, signaling the beginning of his property. Micah slowed to a trot, not wanting to miss the path to their homestead.

Elisa. Samuel.

Their names rang inside his frightened soul.

The fence abruptly ended, revealing the dusty road to the old farmhouse. The bleat of a terrified goat nearly tossed him off his horse as it scampered across the path, disappearing into the fog. Micah reached the faded house, wisps of haze swirling around its edges, and headed for the door.

Everything was ominously silent as he stepped onto the porch and knocked firmly against the slender frame.

No response.

"Jonas? Elisa?"

Still nothing. The door was unbolted. He opened it and stepped into the gloomy house.

Inside, everything appeared normal. Work boots from the field were lined neatly beneath the coat rack. A partially finished blanket lay draped across a rocking chair alongside a pair of knitting needles. The kitchen was orderly, an assortment of dry goods sit-

*ting on the counter, waiting to be used. The house was unnervingly
still.*

*Micah climbed the stairs, heading for the bedrooms. The second
floor was just as tranquil as below, not a creature stirring. He
softly opened the door to the farmer's room.*

His stomach dropped in horror.

*Jonas and his wife lay completely still on the bed, not a breath
rising from their bodies. Micah felt for a pulse, finding none
beneath Jonas' cold flesh.*

*He sprinted out of the house, shuddering as he climbed back
onto the horse and raced towards home.*

*A pair of chickens clucked happily as Micah galloped into
the yard, oblivious to the dangers around them. The door to his
house was closed, the windows dark. He clambered down, lurching
across the grass for the door.*

"Elisa!"

Micah jolted awake, shouting her name as tears streamed
down his face. Kelj stirred, startled.

Don't. Don't go back.

*He barged through the door, scanning the room wildly. The
long sofa was empty, faint light filtering in through the wide
window. The kitchen he'd entered countless times to find Elisa
cooking in her graceful blur was barren. Micah's boots stomped
loudly against the wooden floor as he hurried towards the back
rooms.*

"Samuel!"

Micah rocked back and forth, hunching feebly in his sleeping
sack while tearing at his hair.

Please, no.

*He paused at the door to their bedroom that overlooked the
gentle northern hills. It was closed. No light came from under the*

wood as if something was blocking it. He pushed, and it resisted. Micah shoved harder, a wrinkle of fabric rubbing beneath the door as he thrust it wider. The quilted comforter and sheets of their large bed were ripped off the mattress, trailing towards the doorframe. He realized the fabric underneath his feet were the sheets.

A beautiful, petite foot stuck out from the far side of the bed. Its delicate form was so familiar as he recalled the warmth of its flesh tangled with his own.

Micah sobbed, memories flashing through his mind as he tried vainly to stifle the horror.

"No, no, no," he cried, trembling and burying his face in his hands.

Kelj shifted closer. "Micah! Speak to me, shield-brother. What is it you see?"

Micah could not answer, struggling to control the whirlwind of pain, grief, and shame rampaging through his soul before he finally choked, "Death."

They sat there in the quiet breeze, the Forest of Midland swaying in the dark. Kelj watched him, patient.

After several minutes, Micah whispered, "I saw the day the Mist came. The day it took my family."

Kelj nodded, a gleam of sympathy in his eyes.

"I left my wife and child alone, halfway across Karthmoor. I wasn't there to protect them," Micah's voice trembled. "They died because of my failure."

"No one foresaw the Mist," Kelj gently contended. "That is a weight you cannot carry."

"It was my responsibility to lead them."

Kelj shook his head. "Do not allow the Tempter to hang such guilt on you. The Mist-curse could not be stopped. Turn the pain it has caused into your weapon. Seek vengeance for them and glory to the Allfather in its destruction."

"And how am I going to stop the Mist?" Micah scoffed, rubbing the moisture from his face. "I can't even face the Firewalkers!"

"In time, your magic will rival theirs," he predicted. "We have set a powerful string of fate in motion. The Allfather will reveal the way."

Micah sulkily looked away, his uneven breath slowly steadying.

"Take heart. Know our efforts will honor your family's legacy," said Kelj softly.

They sat silent in the gloomy campsite, watching the swaying trees ahead as stars twinkled far above. After what felt like an eternity, the horizon behind them began to brighten.

"Come," Kelj murmured, breaking the quiet. "The forest awaits."

They rolled up their bags, loading Edoran and Coalfire as they groggily adjusted in the early morning light. The sea of grass rustled gently as Micah and Kelj delved back into its expanse, the barren cliff where they had stopped disappearing as the hills swallowed it.

It had been three days since leaving Hillmarch, trudging back across the eastern plains towards the center of Karthmoor. The quickest route led them along the northern tip of Long Lake, though it also risked an encounter with the Firewalkers. Pressed for time, they followed the path, thankfully evading Garrin and his allies. After a brief stop in Dorn to purchase more supplies, and while avoiding any mention of magic, they had crossed back into the central grasslands, the empty fields transforming into hills and short cliffs as the riders approached the Forest of Midland. Beyond an occasional blanket of Mist, the journey had remained surprisingly calm. All that stood now was navigating the dense maze of the ancient woods.

They halted at the edge of the towering trees, the faint dawn gathering strength at their backs. The mossy branches of Midland creaked like old bones in the morning air, dissuading any that would enter their haunting depths.

"Ready?" Micah asked, shaking off the last vestiges of his nightmares to focus on the dangers lurking ahead.

"What can I expect within its halls?" Kelj questioned, studying the foliage.

"Midland is the oldest forest on Karthmoor, though no one can really say how old," he answered. "It was here well before Angol'daur. Very little wildlife thrives in its trees. We should pass through relatively unnoticed, though, barring any surprises."

"And this temple lies on the far side?"

"Yes, a couple days' trek."

"There is no time to waste then," Kelj finished with a determined look on his grizzly face.

"Just be ready," Micah warned, Edoran shifting beneath him. "You never know what will happen in Midland."

As the sun peeked over the hills, they guided the horses into the woods, vanishing into the gloom.

The soft sounds of the billowing fields immediately ceased as the trees sealed them in. A deathly stillness hung in the musty air, a silence penetrating the very soul. There was a dark presence to the wood, almost as if the forest was alive, watching their every step with antipathy. Coalfire snorted nervously as Micah steadied Edoran and led on.

As the sun rose beyond the trees, the deep shadows relented, gradually returning to a heavy shade beneath the thick canopy of leaves. The dense undergrowth of the forest's edge lessened the deeper they wound into Midland, the lush bushes and tall weeds fading into gnarled stalks and a short turf of bluish-green grass. Large folds of moss covered the colossal branches creaking over the narrow trail, their hanging tendrils occasionally swaying curiously in the still, stuffy air.

"This is an unnatural place," Kelj muttered, swerving his head around to scan the spaces between the massive trunks.

They followed a slender gap in the trees, carving a weaving path through the ancient growth as they headed westward. Giant roots spilled out of the soil, slowing their progress as the horses stepped carefully through the tangled mess. The rough terrain gently rose and fell as an endless sea of green and brown stretched into the distance.

They stopped around midday, giving the horses a break and taking a quick meal. Without any heavy undergrowth, a small knoll afforded a reasonable view of the forest around them. Beyond the tall trees, coiling roots, and jagged rocks, the land was strangely desolate. Kelj tossed Micah a sack of dried meat, and he picked through the dwindling pouch while Kelj rummaged through the supplies. All of a sudden, a piercing cry echoed through the trees, and the horses whined in fear. Kelj jumped, reaching for his axe as Micah dropped the bag. They whirled around, scouring for the source.

No more sounds rose from the woods.

"Let us be off," Kelj grumbled after several moments.

Back in the saddles, they cautiously watched the trees as they passed, both of them on edge. A few other calls and yelps whispered through the groaning trees as the afternoon drifted slowly by, though they never caught sight of any animal. The ancient forest remained just as unchanging and barren as the day grew longer.

With evening's arrival, the light quickly faded, obscured by the dense ceiling of the wooded hall. They hurried to find an adequate site to stop for the night, unwilling to lose their way in the dark. A small clearing nestled between a cluster of enormous, wizened oaks provided just enough space for them to spread out as darkness overtook the forest. They unpacked their sleeping gear, claiming the least-prickly spots to rest and eyeing the foreboding shadows. Kelj grabbed a dead limb at the foot of the trees, studying it before tossing it into the dark.

He shrugged. "Something about a campfire feels... unwise."

"Can't say I disagree." Micah swept his spot clear and stretched out his sack, laying his trusty pistol and sword at his side, just in case.

As night descended upon Midland, another string of unknown yowls echoed in the distance, unnerving in the gathering gloom.

"Let's just get this over with," Micah muttered, hunkering down into the warm fur. Inside his little shelter, he quickly faded into dreams. The uneasy slumber of Midland settled upon the world.

The sky was still black when Kelj shook him awake. Micah grumbled, pulling the warm cover down from his head.

"What?" he irritably muttered.

"The trees," Kelj urgently whispered. "They are alive."

"What are you talking about?" Micah sat up, his blurry eyes refocusing. He looked around the camp. Everything was quiet. At the far end, the horses were tethered to their branches, resting.

"There." Kelj pointed to a large mossy trunk, a good stone's throw from the clearing. "That one *moved*."

"That's ridiculous," Micah groused, shaking his sleepy head. "It was a dream, Kelj."

"Upon my honor, I swear the cursed tree moved, roots and all."

"Go back to bed," he retorted, collapsing into his sack.

"I do not trust these woods," Kelj growled. "I take back what I said. It is not like the Anderfalls at all."

"Well, leave it alone, and it'll leave you alone, no?"

"Hmph."

Micah was out in seconds.

———◆———

A faint light caught his eye, teasing him from his sleep. Far above, the roof of leaves glowed in the warm, morning sun. Micah sat, stretching as he glanced around the camp. Everything looked to be in place. Except Kelj. The giant warrior sat propped on a tree root, angled towards the spot he had pointed to in the night. His tangled mane hung over his head, resting against his chest. A low snore rose with each of his deep breaths. Micah made his way over, nudging Kelj's boot with his foot. Kelj drowsily lifted his head.

"Didn't get snatched by the trees, I see," said Micah, smirking as Kelj raised his tired face. "Did you stay up all night?"

"I kept watch," he mumbled, rubbing the dark circles under his eyes.

Micah shook his head as he started packing his gear.

The endless trees continued to shroud the path as the day wore on. An occasional rise in the ground lifted them partially above the shorter trees, granting brief glimpses of Tar'auth Eld looming majestically in the distance. The closer they drew to the mountain, the more unsettling Midland seemed to become.

By midafternoon, they spotted its western foothills, a sign they were nearing the ruined cathedral.

"It can't be far now," Micah shouted back to Kelj as Coalfire weaved between two massive roots. "Maybe less than an hour if—"

A fearsome howl reverberated off the trees somewhere from Micah's right.

He reached for his pistol, his eyes flashing as he hunted for the source.

Kelj hefted his battle axe. "That sounded like…"

"Mist Wolf." Micah finished Kelj's thought just as the beast's lumbering figure dashed from behind a gnarled tree.

The Mist Wolf howled again, charging along a wide trail between the overgrown trunks towards them. Kelj roared in challenge as Micah raised his pistol, aiming for the monster as it sprinted into range. The world faded as Micah's focus sharpened on the Wolf's matted fur.

Inhale.

Micah's breathing slowed as he steadied his arm. The beast howled in fury, its terrible, scarred face contorted in rage as slavering jaws bore down on the frightened horses.

Exhale.

Micah rested a finger against the thin trigger, the cool metal warming as he gripped the pistol tighter. The Mist Wolf bounded over a tangle of roots.

In an instant, the forest erupted, the trees around them quaking violently as ancient wood shrieked in protest. Startled, Micah glanced up as leaves swirled through the branches. He turned back to the Wolf just in time to see a huge, mossy branch come crashing down from the heights of a rocking oak.

BOOM!

The ground shook as the enormous limb collided with the earth, the Wolf vanishing as a mass of leaves, twigs, and soil exploded into the air. Another peal of creaking wood reverberated as the massive tree recoiled, pulling its knotted growth back into its boughs.

"No way..."

The rumbling grew as the surrounding trees increased in tempo. Without warning, another gush of dirt erupted along the trail, a twisted tendril of root breaking free of the soil. To Micah's utter shock, more roots ripped apart the ground, unshackling the tree from its hole as he gaped at the sight. *The stories... They're true.*

The weathered trunk flexed in agitation, a whirlwind of leaves filling the air. The twisting roots snaked forward, reaching for the path and dragging the oak's colossal form behind.

"Move!" Kelj shouted, shaking off his paralysis.

Micah whipped Edoran around, spurring him towards the mountain as the woods came alive. Geysers of dirt and rock showered them as Micah frantically chased after Kelj, ducking underneath swiping branches and bushels of roots as more trees awakened. An oak behind Kelj moved, cutting off the trail as he swerved around a hill of quaking trunks and vanished from sight. Micah dug his heels into a terrified Edoran, sprinting towards the gap.

This isn't happening!

He wove through a grove of slender saplings quivering in agitation, spotting a rocky outcropping in the distance. A branch whipped across Micah's face, stinging his cheek, as he steered

Edoran towards the clearing. The shuddering trees pressed in as he raced along the narrow path, barely dodging another swipe from a mossy cluster of enraged twigs. The ground beneath Edoran roiled as a twisting sea of roots pushed towards the surface. Their trunks constricted, forming a massive seal overhead as the daylight disappeared in the solid hedge. Micah's heart pounded inside his chest, his eyes locked on the faint glimmer of the rocky space through the closing branches. He could feel the grip of the forest hemming him in as he spurred Edoran on, escape rapidly fading. Bitter leaves tugged at his clothes as Edoran charged through the foliage. The light of the clearing shrank, angry, leafy limbs groping at his flesh.

"No, no, no!"

Edoran leapt through the leaves like a streak of chestnut lightning, sailing into the meadow as the trees snapped shut like monstrous jaws. The horse stumbled in the dirt, sliding narrowly to a stop before a jagged cleft of rock. Micah slumped in the saddle, gasping for air.

Turning around, he watched the forest begin to calm, its thundering growls fitfully subsiding as the trees returned to their slumber, though they remained a solid wall enclosing the clearing. Micah let out a shaky sigh of relief. Edoran wheezed as his powerful legs trembled.

"You're a lifesaver, friend," Micah gushed, patting the horse's tense neck. "Remind me to find sugar at our next stop."

He sat back up, looking beyond the pile of boulders, and realized he had come to the very base of the mountain. Tar'auth Eld towered high above, its lofty peak lost in a small bank of clouds. For a moment, Micah stared in wonder.

Turning Edoran around, he scanned for Kelj and Coalfire, but the space was empty.

"Kelj!"

No response.

With the trees sated, the forest returned to its eerie solitude. Micah's eyes passed along the barrier of trunks, searching for an escape beyond scaling the high cliffs of the mountain. On the west end of the basin, he spotted a small point of carved black stone peeking above the ancient wood. A lone, grassy trail back through the trees disappeared into the gloom in its direction. The trees on that end appeared to sleep peacefully.

"Angol'daur," he muttered. "Figures."

Micah guided Edoran to the path, the poor beast shrinking back from the ominous boughs as Micah prodded him on. As the shady growth swallowed them, the trunks beyond the clearing returned to their normal spacing. Micah looked around, hoping to spot a glimpse of Kelj.

"Kelj!" he cried again.

For a moment, nothing.

"Micah!" Kelj hollered from somewhere ahead.

He hurried along the path, the gentle earth curving towards the place he had spotted the dark spire. After several moments, the thick canopy gradually relented, the ruined tower peeking through the gap above a mound ringed with trees.

"Kelj!"

"I am here!" he shouted.

The grassy route turned sharply at the base of the hill, revealing a massive clearing. Kelj shifted anxiously atop Coalfire at the end of the trail, hovering beneath the eaves of the thick branches at the forest's edge.

Micah sighed in relief. "You made it."

"Well met, shield-brother." Kelj smiled. "I feared you were lost to this accursed forest."

"Almost, but not quite," he replied, rubbing a line of blood off his cheek. "What happened?"

"In the shifting trees, I chose a narrow gap and followed it," Kelj answered. "Eventually, the forest stilled its wrath, and I found myself on this very path."

"At least we're at the cathedral."

Micah peered into the empty space beyond the trees. The weedy clearing was dotted with piles of weathered rock. Though none of the village's structures remained beyond the temple, several spots across the clearing retained a semblance of places where homes once stood, though nature had reclaimed the land. The eastern side, however, was completely dominated by the towering spire. Its smoky black stone, expertly chiseled, rose high above the green trees. The weathered bricks were old, much of it crumbling after centuries of abandonment. Tall, slender windows sat devoid of their glass, and several sections of the walls were missing entirely. However, much of the structure's patchy slate roof remained, the steeply sloped ceiling sheltering the interior of the building. Above it all, a thin bell tower stretched towards the sky, its cupola damaged and bare. Beyond the impressive temple, the mountain loomed higher still.

"Death whispers in this place," Kelj murmured, gripping his axe close.

The cathedral was forebodingly silent, just like the mysterious woods surrounding it. Micah guided Edoran into the clearing, clopping slowly towards the decaying ruin. The lofty entrance was fully exposed, any hint of its once-majestic doors rotted long ago. As he neared the dark walls, he spotted intricate carvings that reminded him of branches and stars weaving along the sides of the entrance, their beautiful design worn down by rain and wind. Though reduced to bones lost to the annals of time, Angol'daur must have been a sight in its prime.

Near the far wall of the exterior, Micah discovered a short stone pillar with a metal band fixed at the top. They dismounted and tied the horses to the ring before heading towards the temple. Micah paused at the doorway, peering into the silent gloom broken only by shafts of light piercing the cracked ceiling. He glanced back at the warm clearing, then warily stepped into the darkened hall.

Inside, the air hung heavy with dust and decay. Micah looked around for signs of life, finding none. Their boots clicked loudly against the cold, stone floor, any trains of carpet having long since disintegrated.

Along the center aisle, rows of weathered pews hewn from the same smoky rock as the building lined the corridor. Two series of massive columns supported the ceiling looming high above, though a couple had collapsed, one having smashed through a section of seating. The perimeter of the cathedral housed still more rows of pews, intermittently broken by small spaces partitioned by shorter blackened walls. At the far end of the cathedral, the aisle ended at a wide set of shallow stairs rising to a platform. A large, solitary altar of gray stone sat at the center, though the right side had broken away, resting sadly on the grimy floor.

No banners or decorations lined the desolate space as Micah and Kelj headed towards the front of the sanctuary. The ruin felt empty, soulless. They paused at the base of the dais where a rail, long since decomposed, had once partitioned the space. Kelj looked at him and nodded towards the altar. Cautiously, Micah climbed the steps and ascended to the platform as Kelj paced its boundary.

Upon reaching the ancient table, Micah rested a hand against the worn rock. Its hard, dusty surface was cold as ice. Delicately carved animals and majestic-looking figures lined the sides of the altar table, while straight, simple lines ran across its top and border.

He searched the platform, eyeing the walls and recesses around the front of the sanctuary as Kelj explored. A narrow doorway sat hidden from view within an alcove at the back of the space. A faint light glowed from within.

Kelj vanished through the opening, and Micah heard him moving around the room. After a moment, he returned.

"Nothing," he grumbled. "Likely where the priests prepared. What about the altar?"

Micah glanced behind and underneath the stone table, searching for any clues as to the precursor map, but came up empty.

"I don't see anything that stands out."

Kelj moved away from the front of the sanctuary, following the walls of the temple and peering into the recesses. Micah stepped back, watching a band of sunlight streaming through a hole in the dark ceiling above. He looked again towards the altar, eyeing a broken set of windows behind the platform. On the table itself, he mused over the trail of creatures dancing along the edge.

Fantastical depictions of bizarre chimeras and cherubim interspersed between lions, sheep, wolves, and cows flowed along the thick sides, their train interrupted where the one side had collapsed. As Micah moved to the broken piece, he studied the right edge of the border. The repeating pattern of animals continued until he reached the final quarter. A blank spot appeared, as if some poor animal had failed to appear for the dance, before an angled rendering of a dragon. The powerful monster slithered along the bottom of the side, its wings outstretched. Its long neck extended towards the end of the altar's edge, a barbed tongue projected from its mouth. Its thick, stubby leg was raised, a single claw pointing straight ahead. Even with the rest of its curious companions, the beast felt conspicuously out of place.

Micah lingered on the angular claw, tracing its direction to the back wall of the sanctuary. A series of stone columns jutted out of its towering bricks, the rightmost one in particular lining up with the side of the altar. He climbed down the back of the dais to inspect the dark stone. The column itself at first appeared unremarkable. The curving bricks flowed effortlessly out of the flat surface of the wall, speaking to their excellent craftsmanship. He ran a finger along the cracked mortar between two bricks, following it across the column. Suddenly, Micah spied a small symbol. An intricate shield, small as a coin, cut into the side of the rock and hidden in the shadows.

"Kelj," he called, his excitement reverberating through the desolate ruin. Kelj appeared from behind an alcove near the entrance and made his way over. Micah looked back at the symbol, his mind racing with an inkling of suspicion he had seen this marking before.

Kelj strode around the platform, his steps clattering in the empty chamber. Micah motioned towards the shield, giving him room to inspect the shape.

"What do you make of this?"

Kelj paused for a moment, running his hand over the lines woven through the shield.

"The carvings," he murmured, leaning back. "I recall a similar shield on the she-mage's drawings."

"That's right!" Micah exclaimed, remembering the journal.

"Do you see anything else?" Kelj asked as he scanned the wall around the column.

"Not yet, but I wonder…"

Micah rested his palm against the cold symbol, feeling its rough shape against his bare skin. He pressed lightly on the surface.

The stone shifted.

Kelj swerved around as Micah gasped in triumph. He pressed harder, the symbol sliding into the column as the stones grated against each other. As it came to a stop, the wall to Micah's right rumbled, dust spewing from a line of cracks. A panel of stone as wide as his outstretched arms receded from its neighbors. Kelj moved to the disturbance, pushing against the rock. Heavy metal hinges shrieked as the panel swung wider, revealing a set of stairs leading down into shadows.

"Secrets whispered from the past," Kelj mumbled, grasping for a torch in his pack. With the torch lit, Kelj slowly descended the black stairs, and Micah followed, casting a final look across the cathedral's empty hall before the pit swallowed them up.

Chapter 37

The Vault

The rough stairs continued their descent, curving gently as they delved into the earth.

"We must be somewhere under the cathedral," Micah observed, the darkness growing with each passing step.

After a moment, they finally reached the end, the ancient passage spilling onto a smooth floor of the same black rock. A wide hall with short, blocky columns faded into the void, with additional hallways diverging along the sides.

Micah took a step, and the pillars ahead of him blossomed with light. He recoiled as additional rows sprang to life, pulsing with a soft, golden glow. The shadows disappeared as strange lamps erupted along the walls, revealing a lengthy corridor ending at a set of grand wooden doors. The chamber was unlike anything he had seen. Its pitch-black stone and curious design were exquisite, but wholly foreign. Judging by the sea of cobwebs and grime, it was also clear the structure was ancient.

With the room awakened, they slowly crept through the hall, their eyes flicking from side to side as they passed the still-darkened side passages.

"These lamps look similar to the mages' at the lake," Micah softly remarked, studying one of the delicate orbs. Each shining sphere rested in a small ring of golden metal anchored in the dark stone. Their insides were unnaturally absent of any fuel or wicks. Simple golden lights flickered at the very center of the orbs.

As they passed the center of the corridor, another large hallway crossed theirs, its lamps dead. They hurried past, arriving at the sealed doors. Kelj pushed on the ornate iron handle, and the door ominously creaked open. Inside was a large circular room with a wide stone table in the center. Scores of musty, decomposing chairs were strewn about it. A raised, stone panel on the back wall displayed the same shield and dragon crest they had found in Hillmarch.

"Not much left," Micah commented as Kelj wandered the room.

"I feel as if I am in one of our war rooms," Kelj softly replied. "Many battles were planned here."

"How do you know?"

"It leaves its mark. War," he said simply, "war never changes."

They lingered a moment longer, breathing in the stale air and imagining a host of powerful warriors with serious faces debating around the circle.

"Maybe one of the other passages holds more clues?" Micah said at last.

He returned to the main hall, Kelj following more hesitantly. At the central exchange, they weighed the shrouded halls, settling on the one to their left. More magical lamps sprang alive, revealing a turn at the end. Halfway down the corridor, Micah came across a tidy stack of odd, metal canisters resting along the side of the hall. A smaller passage faded into the gloom across from them. The aged iron vessels were void of any markings beyond a faint rust. Kelj halted at one, prying the dusty top off with a knife and revealing a pool of thick, filthy liquid. He bent down, sniffing the contents, and recoiled in disgust.

"Oil," he growled.

"Lamps?" Micah wondered, confused.

He shook his head. "It is unlike any oil from the Anderfalls. To gather it in this quantity can only mean one thing: explosives."

After passing a set of small storerooms devoid of contents beyond a few crumbling shelves, Micah reached a turn, only to find another hall. They walked past more mysterious tunnels bathed in foreboding darkness. They avoided them, closely following the wider hall as it continued to twist into the depths. The cold corridors were devoid of any decoration beyond the lanterns. For such regal stonework, the structure was remarkably stale.

"This place is a labyrinth," Micah grumbled.

Kelj grunted.

After what felt like an eternity in the maze of uniform stone, they rounded another corner, nearly colliding with a set of iron gates. Beyond them, the hall widened into a darkened chamber.

Micah inspected the ancient metal. The gates had no lock. One of its rusted frames sat slightly ajar. He pushed it wider, the gate screeching in a protest that echoed off the walls. As he walked into the room, lamps along the edges awakened. The floor shimmered in the light like black obsidian, thin streaks of silver and white flowing across its smooth surface. Above the center, a massive chandelier of golden glass stirred, spokes of slender, twisting metal flickering in the rousing glow. A huge orb in the center lit with a brilliant flash, bathing the room with light. Rows of high columns curved along the sides of the room before ending at a large set of steel doors covered in dazzling shapes and mysterious runes. A small, jagged pillar of swirling gray and black obsidian carved in the shape of a slender dragon ominously rose from the center of the room.

"Impressive," said Kelj as he joined him.

With the room fully revealed, Micah's mind struggled to comprehend its shape. From the entrance, the outer walls curved outwards towards the far end, only to double back and curve to meet the opposing steel doors, almost like an inverted triangle. The stone columns were equal distances from the walls, placed at peculiar points along the way.

"What is this place?"

"Power and ritual," Kelj growled. "Magic."

Micah slowly paced across the room, the swirling floor glistening in the lamplight and giving the space an intimidating presence. He swiftly passed the dragon statue, avoiding contact with the rough image, and approached the pair of doors. Beyond the fascinating designs, the steel was featureless. He shoved his shoulder against the icy metal, but they refused to budge. *Something must be here.*

"Sealed."

"The room may hold more clues," Kelj suggested.

They split up, roaming the outer walls and searching for any markings or symbols they might have missed. When Micah reached the first column, he glimpsed a short metal rod jutting from the back of it.

"There's a lever here," he called out.

"Here as well," Kelj added, passing another column.

Micah walked along the line of columns. All of them concealed an identical lever.

"Perhaps they are the key?" Kelj mused.

From the entrance, Micah chose the second column, cautiously pulling the worn lever down. The cold rod noiselessly fell, stopping with a soft click. Suddenly, a stream of blue light gushed under the black floor with a whoosh of sound, racing from the column to meet the dragon pillar. A thin streak of blue light wound up its tail, curling around its body and ending at its snout.

"That did... something," said Micah excitedly.

"It shines like iluvan," Kelj observed.

"That must be what's underneath us."

"A dangerous thought," he growled.

"But maybe we're on the right track."

Micah returned to the first pillar from the entrance and quickly pulled its lever. Another streak of blue light dashed under the obsidian. As it reached the dragon, the light fizzled, and both streaks changed into a reddish blur before vanishing. The levers reset their positions. Something near the steel doors rumbled, and an ominous red line appeared above them as the iron gates at the entrance swung shut with a frightening bang.

They were trapped.

"You have chosen poorly." Kelj frowned, crossing his arms.

Micah stepped back, examining the room before shaking his head. *How did I miss that?*

"It's a puzzle."

"Yes," Kelj agreed. "With only so many guesses."

Micah glanced at the warning light, noticing two additional lines of mute crystal.

"Three attempts. Then what, I wonder?"

"This magic can only end in misery," Kelj warned.

"Then let's make sure we do it right."

Micah strolled around the room, looking for clues in the shrouded floor. After a moment, Kelj broke the silence.

"There must be a pattern," he irritably concluded. "A system or something that mirrors this odd room."

Micah looked up from the floor, studying the curious walls. Eventually, his mind wandered to the altar in the cathedral and the hidden symbols that had led them here.

Wait a moment.

He hurried back to the chamber entrance, observing the entirety of the space. Then he marched to the opposite end, carefully following the walls as they passed through the set of odd, pointed corners.

"It's the shield," Micah sputtered.

Kelj shot him a quizzical look.

"The room. Give me the journal."

The towering warrior removed the small travel bag from his back and tossed it to Micah. He opened the sack, pulling the worn leather notebook from underneath the paper rubbings from Hillmarch. He excitedly flipped through the crinkled pages, searching for the symbol he had seen before. After several passes, he finally found it.

"Here." Micah pointed to the curious shield with flowing lines. "Look at its shape. It's the shield from the pillar in the cathedral. The room is the same shape." He gestured to the walls. Kelj's head swerved between the room and the journal, weighing his words.

"I see the resemblance," he finally admitted.

"Right, and here." Micah pointed to Leyana's hastily drawn dragon. "There's a dragon at the center, just like this room. Which means the iluvan markings…"

"Align with those of the drawing," Kelj finished. "Fate is with us, shield-brother."

Thank you, Elowë, Micah silently prayed with relief.

"Now we just have to figure out which columns line up," he declared.

"Hopefully, the she-mage was precise."

Micah walked back to the entrance, counting the pillars and eyeing the shield in the journal.

Eight pillars along each side.

"We know the second column was correct," he slowly started, pulling its lever again. The line of iluvan sprang back to life. Following the symbol on the page, Kelj pulled the opposite lever, and another line of energy raced towards the dragon. The streak of blue light twisted along the pillar, adding to the statue.

"Where is the next?" Kelj asked.

Micah walked past the next column, pausing at the fourth.

"Maybe… here?" He pulled the iron rod, releasing another gush of light. The iluvan awakened, lighting a third streak across the dragon. Kelj repeated the process, and the dragon's light grew stronger.

Micah moved to the sixth column, hoping they'd cracked the pattern, and pulled the lever. As its light hit the pillar, the blue glow vanished, along with his excitement. A second warning light appeared above the steel doors. He looked back at the journal, tracing the lines along the shield and comparing it to where the iluvan ran on the floor.

"Too far," Micah concluded. They repeated the steps, pulling the fifth levers. The third line erupted from Micah's post, racing across the floor and passing through the previous line before curving to meet the dragon. The stone figure brightened as the additional light rose across the shimmering stone.

"There's one last set of lines," Micah called out. With three columns left, he moved in front of the doors, weighing his options against the mage's notes.

"I think it's the final ones."

"Are you sure?" Kelj cautioned.

"Not entirely," he nervously admitted, "but it feels right. We've come too far to just give up."

"Allfather guide us," Kelj murmured.

They slowly moved to the final columns.

"Ready?" Micah asked.

"At your word."

He held his breath, grasping the slender rod behind the rocky column. The icy metal leeched the warmth from his hand as he hesitated.

What if I'm wrong?

With a grunt, Micah slammed the lever. A rush of silvery blue light exploded from the base of the pillar, streaking across the smooth floor. His heart stopped as it reached the carved figure. For a second, it seemed to pause, and Micah's gut filled with terror. Then the light rose into the dragon's tail, filling a dark strip around the rising beast. As it reached the end, the statue glowed brighter. Only a thin line of cold, dull rock remained.

"Do it."

Kelj thrust his lever down, releasing another wave of iluvan. As it reached the center pedestal, the tail of the dragon filled with light, the last stripe of dark stone fading as the glow consumed it. The light reached the top, and the whole dragon glowed brighter. The room started to rumble as if massive machines were moving beneath the obsidian floor. The dragon erupted in a blinding flash of light, forcing Micah to cover his eyes.

BANG!

A deafening noise reverberated through the chamber, and the steel doors shuddered. As the dragon subsided to an excited glow, a loud clicking emanated from the doors, their hidden lock released. The steel barrier unsealed, grinding loudly as it swung open.

The metal slammed against the walls, ringing madly before everything fell silent. Beyond the warm glow of the puzzle room's lamps, a black abyss beckoned.

Micah squinted into the darkened room, still adjusting after the dragon's flash. Slowly, his eyes focused on a pale, muted light, glowing in the dark. He glanced at Kelj, cautiously gripping his sword hilt.

"Lead on, shield-brother," Kelj said solemnly.

Micah halted at the edge of the shadows. After a tentative step into the void, a lone lamp stirred atop a small stone table just inside the chamber. The reaction awakened another set of golden orbs set into gray stone walls deeper in the room. A couple of decrepit wooden chairs along another slender table came into view, a thick layer of debris and filth collecting on the surfaces. A bank of steel racks sat neatly lined against the opposite wall, whatever objects they had once held lost to the unknown. As the light illuminated the far end, the odd glow from before took shape, revealing a small podium of dark stone. A jagged crystal adorned the stand, no larger than a dinner plate. A muted, silvery blue glow emanated from it. Behind the shard, a detailed rendering of the mysterious shield and dragon was carved into the smooth stone wall. The mural was flanked by two expertly crafted statues of white stone—warriors in elaborate, flowing armor. A wisp of stony flame rose from each of their outstretched palms.

"A treasury perhaps?" Kelj wondered as they treaded through the small space. "There is not much left."

"Except that," Micah replied, pointing to the crystal. As they neared the pedestal, he noticed the face of the object was completely smooth. A swirling cloud of the same silvery blue hue floated behind the surface.

"What is this?" Kelj asked.

"If I didn't know better, I'd say it's an iluvan mirror. I've never seen one so small, though."

"Iluvan mirror?"

"Magical devices for communicating across distances," Micah explained. "They're extremely rare. The only two I knew of belonged to the Governor of Greenwatch and the Conclave. They were imported from the Hamid Empire for an incredible sum."

"Constructs from heathen mages of the South," Kelj spat. "How did one come to rest in this forgotten tomb?"

Micah paused for a moment, baffled at the iluvan's bizarre presence.

"I'm not sure. The Empire was the source of the Conclave's mirrors, though that doesn't necessarily mean they created them. Maybe the iluvan mirrors are another relic of the precursor nation, like the time pods?"

"Perhaps," Kelj allowed, still unconvinced.

Without warning, the cloud within the mirror began to swirl, coiling around itself. Kelj jumped back in surprise. Like the Conclave's mirror, Micah expected the murky surface to transform into an image, but instead the color simply drained away, leaving a peculiar black void.

"What trickery is this?" Kelj bristled.

They fell silent, staring into the nothingness.

"It awakens." A calm, masculine voice emanated from the crystal. "Curious."

"Who's there?" Micah demanded.

"One you need not fear—" A presence, gentle as a falling feather, brushed his consciousness, "—Micah Stormcrown."

Kelj gripped his weapon as his eyes widened. "Vile sorcery!"

Micah quickly erected a barrier around his mind, terrified by the Voice's incredible ability. It sensed his defense and immediately vanished.

"I mean no harm, brave warrior," the Voice apologized, "but I had to know your intentions."

"How did you do that?" Micah asked in fear-inspired awe. "The mirrors only allow sound and images through."

The Voice gave a wizened chuckle.

"Your people may use the *iluvimír*, but they remain ignorant of its true potential. An understandable oversight."

"Who are you?" he pressed defensively.

"One who holds the answers you seek, Eldvenir."

Micah's gut twisted as he recalled Garrin's proclamation.

"What did you call me?"

"Your heritage is clear," the Voice solemnly replied. "To end the curse ravaging your home, you will need its power."

"Explain yourself!" Micah shouted at the rock.

The Voice was silent for a moment as he scowled at the formless image.

"All will be revealed at the proper time, but it is not now," it finally declared. "You are no longer safe within these walls."

"What do you mean?"

"There are intruders within the vault," it said hurriedly. "Seek me out in the city of Starkhaven." An image of a mighty tower enclosed in a column of light flashed across Micah's mind. "All will be made clear."

The dark pit of the mirror lightened as a cloud of blue gushed to the surface. In a moment, the Voice was gone, the crystal returning to its serene, swirling glow.

"Grab the mirror, and let's get out of here," Micah said to Kelj, turning back towards the doors.

"Well, well, an Oathsworn in his vault. How quaint."

Too late.

Micah froze, staring in dismay as Garrin and the other Firewalkers crossed the puzzle chamber towards them.

Garrin grinned menacingly. "While I appreciate you opening the doors, your little quest ends here."

"How, how did you find this place?" Micah stuttered, stepping back towards the podium, gripping the end of his pistol.

"One of the old crone's underlings had memories of their research," Garrin casually replied, scanning the safe room. "Images taken from the other vault were clear before his feeble mind collapsed. From there, it was a simple matter of narrowing down which location. The Oathsworn of old were nothing if not predictable."

"And so you murdered another group of innocents just to find this place," he angrily retorted.

"I will not debate the supposed innocence of these corrupt people," Garrin hissed. "If it is any consolation, Oathsworn, we did not linger once we obtained our information. Our mission takes priority over purging the rest of this ridiculous island."

"You killed them for this?" he scoffed, gesturing to the little mirror in Kelj's massive fist.

Garrin rolled his eyes. "Hardly. Their pathetic existence is not even worth such a trinket. But the iluvimír are never made alone. If the old woman's research led to this, its twin will lead to our prize."

"What has it shown you, Stormcrown?" Armeia furiously demanded, her green eyes flashing in the lamplight. "Give us the truth or face annihilation."

"It showed me nothing."

"Tsk, tsk, these games you play," Garrin chided.

"What did it speak then, Micah?" Arksul sternly commanded. "Do not avoid the question."

"Nothing."

Hadrian gave a short laugh. "He's lying, Garrin. Playing us for fools."

"Of course he is," Garrin replied, turning to Micah with a wicked smile, "but even amongst the tombs of your forefathers, you cannot hide from us."

He stepped forward, resting a hand on the dragon pillar. The blue light of the dragon's snout began to change, an evil, purplish hue creeping down from the palm gripping the stone. "Final chance. Give us the mirror, and I promise a quick death."

Micah looked at Kelj, the warrior's face furrowed with an angry scowl as he shook his head. Then a small glint on the back of the mirror's pedestal caught Micah's eye.

A lever.

He cast a defiant glare back into Garrin's wicked eyes.

"No."

Garrin's frustrated face twisted into a wrathful sneer as he unsheathed his dark, menacing sword. Out of the corner of his eye, Micah saw Kelj raise the iluvan mirror. Garrin's fury shifted to him, exchanged for a look of horror.

"Stop!" he yelled, raising a hand.

The Anderfall hurled the crystal onto the solid ground as a spear of flame sprang from Garrin towards him. A shower of blue splinters exploded, the mirror detonating with a blast of smoke and light that sent everyone sprawling. In the blinding chaos, Micah lunged for the tiny lever, his flailing hand slapping it down. The floor rumbled loudly as the Firewalkers clambered to their feet, scanning the chamber for traps. Just as Garrin took a step, the massive steel doors slammed shut with a deafening bang.

Garrin screamed in rage beyond the thick metal.

Micah's vision blurred as he turned to Kelj, the warrior in a heap against the wall. As his mind made sense of the scene, he gasped. "Kelj..."

Smoke drifted from the singed furs around Kelj's waist, dangling above a gaping wound of seared, red flesh shining across his thigh. The Anderfall groaned, grasping at the slender table as he struggled to his feet. A horrid, burning smell filled Micah's nose.

"Kelj, stop," said Micah, scrambling towards him. "We've got to—"

"There is no time," Kelj growled through clenched teeth. Sweat beaded on his forehead. "We must move."

The sound of flames erupted from the doors.

Micah's eyes widened. "They're melting their way in."

"There!" Kelj pointed. Micah spotted a narrow opening in the dark corner near one of the statues, the passage quietly appearing in all the commotion.

He raced towards the tunnel, grabbing one of the lamp orbs from the wall. To his surprise, the glass was cool. He glanced back at the struggling warrior who waved him on, then he ducked into the opening.

Kelj limped after him as Micah wove through the tight shaft. He sprinted around several turns, slamming against the cold bricks at each curve, wildly praying for an escape. After a series of sharp corners, Micah stumbled into a tiny room.

Dead end.

"Lever," Kelj panted as he staggered into the room, motioning to a rod on their left.

Micah flung the rod down with a loud click. Another round of gentle rumbling released the wall with a cloud of dust. The doorway swung inward, and they stepped into a wide hall. Micah's gaze skimmed the space, trying to get a bearing.

"Looks like the hall leading to the puzzle chamber," he wheezed.

"That way," said Kelj, pointing to their right.

They tore down the lamplit hall as fast as Kelj's lurching gait could carry him, their boots pounding on the bare floor. A couple of turns later, a small blast echoed from somewhere behind. Micah's pulse raced, his mind urging him to move faster. Kelj groaned, tripping against the wall before Micah caught him by the arm, dragging the warrior forward as the charred stench slammed into him again.

The hall twisted several more times before Micah finally sensed the central corridor nearing.

"We're close," he said.

Hadrian yelled. The Firewalkers were gaining.

"Not close enough," Kelj exhaustedly puffed.

As they passed the mound of canisters, Kelj abruptly stopped, resting a shaky hand on one of them as his other grasped at his oozing thigh. Micah stumbled to a halt, whirling around in a frenzy.

"What are you doing? Let's go!"

"There is no time," Kelj roared. "Even if we reach the horses, they will overtake us before we clear the trees."

"So we fight!" Micah cried.

Kelj hobbled over, his somber face looming over him.

"No."

Kelj slipped his sturdy bag across Micah's chest. Then he raised a firm but gentle hand to Micah's shoulder, Kelj's deep eyes staring into his with sorrow. Micah stared back, confused and exasperated. He felt Kelj's other hand pulling his pistol from its holster.

"You have shown me the honor and courage a warlock is capable of," Kelj said softly.

"What are you doing?!" Micah demanded.

"Through your actions, I see the magic of our world may one day be worthy of glory. I thank you for this, Micah Storm-crown."

"Kelj—"

The warrior stepped back, holding Micah's pistol firmly in his large hand. The faint sound of footsteps echoed through the hall behind him.

"By the strength of my axe, the honor of my ancestors, and the blood of our enemies, I vowed and joined my honor with yours," Kelj affirmed with a look of pain and tender pride. "We sought greater glory and higher honor, achieving it all to the shame of our enemies."

The footsteps drew closer, Garrin yelling in rage.

"May it be so in death. Let my deeds be done for this purpose, to the glory of the Allfather."

"No, Kelj!" Fear welled inside Micah's chest. "Come on!"

Kelj's serene expression held his frantic gaze.

"See our journey through, shield-brother. Seek justice for my people. Become the Eldvenir our world needs."

Kelj turned away and moved beside the doorway across from the canisters, his axe outstretched in one hand, Micah's pistol in the other. The sound of the Firewalkers reverberated from just beyond the corner. Kelj jerked back with a final, serious look.

"*Run!*"

Micah spun around, sprinting towards the central hall. As he reached the turn, he glanced behind just as Hadrian rounded the far corner. The Firewalker let out a triumphant yell as he spied Kelj.

At the same moment, Kelj raised the pistol towards the stack of canisters.

Oh no.

Its barrel erupted in a blast of light.

BOOM!

The canisters exploded in a wave of fire, rocking the hallway and sending Micah halfway across the corridor. The hall where the canisters stood collapsed in a torrent of rock and debris. Kelj was nowhere to be seen. Stone columns along the edges cracked and crumbled, the entire structure trembling in an earsplitting roar as the ground shook. Micah staggered to his feet, spinning with vertigo. He could barely hear past the ringing in his head.

The whole complex is falling!

The roar grew into a scream as the war room at the far end trembled. A second later, it was swallowed in a landslide of stone and rocks. Micah whipped around, sprinting for the stairwell to the surface. The floor split and threatened to suck him into the abyss as he leapt for the stairs, the arch around the doorframe shuddering as the thick stone bricks faltered. A thunderous roll shook the air as the massive hall cracked, pummeled by the imploding ground.

Micah mounted the stairs, three at a time, racing towards the surface. At the first curve, he looked back in terror as the earth consumed the grand hall where he had stood seconds before.

He didn't look again.

The short ceiling of the stairwell crumbled as Micah raced upwards. Shards of rock pelted his head, forcing him to squint as the light around him vanished, save for the orb still somehow in his hand.

In an agonizing flash, Micah clambered out of the passage and into the cathedral. He gasped for air as dust filled his lungs, spewing from the shuddering tunnel. He glanced around, noticing the shaking, ruined walls.

Great.

Chips of stone and plaster rained from the looming ceiling as giant cracks raced up the ancient structure. As he bounded over the altar platform, the roar of the earth split the cathedral in every direction. Micah raced towards the open doorway, swerving as chunks of the roof slammed into the pews. A massive shard cratered into the path ahead as the walls around the altar exploded. He slid over the ceiling chunk, hurtling towards the faint light of the entrance. The colossal pillars holding the ceiling snapped with an earsplitting boom, the fragile stone overwhelmed by the quake as they smashed into the sanctuary floor.

Almost...

A piece of debris slammed into Micah's shoulder, tearing his shirt and sending a bolt of pain through his arm. He stumbled forward, recovering as the roof caved in behind his feet, nearly crushing him. With a last, desperate push, he flung himself through the trembling entrance, sailing onto the cool grass beyond the ruin's edge as the last of the ceiling gave way. Micah glanced up, watching the front exterior and bell tower shudder precariously. It swayed back and forth, threatening to squash him into the dirt. By the grace of Elowë, it teetered back, cracking under its own weight, and fell into the rubble of the ruin in a cascade of blackened stone. A deafening blast reverberated across the clearing as the tower toppled onto the cathedral's remains.

Silence.

With ears pounding, Micah could still feel the earth beneath rumbling. Shaking in exhaustion, he attempted to stand.

"Kelj," he choked, before stumbling to his knees.

He scanned the warped earth and jutting stones, plumes of dust filling the clearing. Nothing moved.

Creator, no, Micah silently pleaded. The cost of the proud warrior's sacrifice shattered his soul. Tears welled behind his eyes, that final moment replaying time and again in his mind. In the fading daylight, he stared at the mystical orb in his hand, its light fading as the centuries-old magic failed.

How am I supposed to do this alone?

He glanced over to where they'd tied the horses. Gone. The Firewalkers' horses were nowhere to be found, either.

Micah finally stood, his legs feebly recovering as fresh air rejuvenated his weary lungs. Instinctively, he gripped the leather satchel around his shoulders. Kelj's bag.

"I will avenge your people," he whispered, tears streaming. "Rest in peace and honor, shield-brother."

He turned around, facing the southern edge of the clearing. With heavy feet and a heavier heart, Micah walked across the soft grass, stepping over splinters of debris that had escaped the cathedral's demise. In the empty clearing, all alone, the weight of the broken world threatened to bury him in pain.

Micah barely noticed as he reached the forest's edge, his watering eyes focused on the ground, almost running straight into a thick, mossy trunk. He jolted back, looking for a path around the tree.

What the...?

Looking closer, he realized the entire edge of the forest had shifted into another uniform barrier.

"They've moved again," Micah whispered, frustrated. He scanned the ring around the clearing to find nothing—he was completely sealed in. He wiped the wet grime from his face.

"This can't be happening."

Finally, Micah spotted a gap in the trees on the far side. He hurried over, peering into the darkened trees. A final scan confirmed the trail as his only escape.

With a tentative step, he delved into their branches, the musty air of Midland roiling his nose as the odor washed over him.

The solid ring of trees relented beyond Angol'daur, though the current path remained the only traversable one through the forest's tangled depths. With the sun sinking on the horizon, the forest soon became a shrouded maze.

Micah walked on, lost in thoughts and grief, not caring where the trail led him.

"Why?" he rasped, rolling a rock under his boot.

After several minutes of trekking, a snort shook Micah from his mourning. His eyes darted up to find Edoran, happily grazing in a small, grassy clearing.

"Edoran!" he exclaimed, rushing over to the faithful horse. He hardly acknowledged Micah's arrival, chomping contentedly at the bluish grass as the stars twinkled faintly through the break in the trees. Micah rubbed his hand along Edoran's neck, feeling the powerful muscles beneath his glossy coat.

"Where's Coalfire, boy?" Micah asked, looking around for his companion. Edoran refused to answer, and the poor warhorse was nowhere to be found.

Micah sighed, his pain returning. "Hopefully, Midland is kind to him."

He stood there, watching Edoran finish his meal, weighing what to do. After the chaos of Angol'daur, his body was exhausted, his heart and soul pierced, but his mind burned with anxiety. There wouldn't be any restful sleep that night.

"Think you can go a little farther?" Micah pleaded with the sturdy beast. Edoran snorted patiently.

"I'll take that as a yes."

Micah checked his saddle, confirming the bags were still in place, and swung into the hard seat as the horse finished his meal. Beyond the clearing, the easy trail continued south, disappearing into the trees.

"Starkhaven it is."

CHAPTER 38
ROAD'S END

Two days after losing Kelj to the Firewalkers and narrowly escaping the fall of Angol'daur, Micah finally reached the end of the Forest of Midland. The sunny fields and cries of birds sent a jolt of relief through his aching heart after long, painful hours under the dreary boughs of the old forest. Around midmorning, he reached the banks of the Winding River, heading south-southeast towards the capital city of Karthmoor. At a shallow ford in the river, he paused, looking longingly to the west.

"Fairhollow's that way," Micah wistfully commented to Edoran, who lapped ignorantly at the river. "I hope Gerar and everyone are safe."

As much as he wanted to retreat to the cozy village where his friends waited, he knew he could not. The Mist remained a deadly threat, including to those he loved in Fairhollow.

At least the Firewalkers are gone.

"We have to see this through," Micah murmured.

He guided Edoran across the babbling stream, entering the tall pines of Binthir Forest. Under its towering trees, the woods were as ominous as ever. Edoran's hooves stomped softly on the bed of dead needles covering the forest floor as eerie birds called out from the depths. Several pockets of Mist drifted through the barren pines, and he longed for his pistol and his shield-brother at his side. Thankfully, Mist Wolf sightings were absent. Only an occasional timber wolf howled in the distance, searching for companions already claimed by the killing fog. As the afternoon wore on, a young doe pounced from behind a tree, startling Micah as he reached for a weapon. In a flash, the poor creature dashed off into the gloom, swallowed by shadows. After many days in Midland, Binthir Forest seemed positively teeming with life.

As the sun sank beyond the trees, Micah urged Edoran over a modest hill, revealing the forest's southern edge.

At least I won't have to spend a night here.

Beyond the dark pines, fields of golden fronds broken by sparse, leafy trees swayed in the evening breeze. He spotted several large banks of Mist rising from the flat grasslands, causing him to tense.

Leaving the cover of foreboding Binthir Forest, Micah reached a pairing of young birch trees near a small hollow. By that point, the sun had disappeared behind the range of small mountains to the west, where the Winding River flowed towards Stark Bay. He tied Edoran off on one of the low-hanging branches, retrieving his sleep sack from the saddlebags and clearing a small space for the night.

As he sat there, staring into the embers of the campfire, Micah's mind wandered to the words of the Voice.

Eldvenir.

A thrill mixed with apprehension filled him. What sort of power had the Voice alluded to? Was it his magic, or was his magic a result of something deeper? Why did Garrin seem to despise him, even as he claimed to fight the Mist? And the Mist... *Was the curse somehow tied to it all?*

Questions exploded in Micah's thoughts as he frowned at the flames, all of them frustratingly unanswered. He wanted nothing more than to stop all of it. To return to a simpler world, free of the horrid Mist that plagued all he knew before it consumed all that remained.

There's no going back.

But maybe there was a way forward. It was the only prayer he had to hold. And the Voice was his key.

Please, Elowë, he silently prayed, gazing at the twinkling stars, *let it be a way to end this. Whatever this path is, please show me how to end this curse. To protect those I love, to avenge my family, to avenge Kelj...*

His breath stopped. Their journey was now his. He would see it through, as Kelj had wanted.

Even though Micah's heart was slowly mending from the events of the ancient vault, the silence of the campsite was a painful reminder of his friend's absence. A dull ache tugged at Micah's chest as the loss hammered into him anew. Hoping to escape the sorrow, he retreated into the warm fur of his sleep sack. Instead, he tossed restlessly, his mind fighting sleep.

The next morning, the sweet melody of a songbird awakened him, a faint dawn gathering beneath a sky of patchy clouds. Micah retrieved a handful of dried meat from the saddlebags, realizing he was dangerously low on supplies.

Hopefully, there'll be something near Starkhaven.

He quickly packed up the camp, waiting as Edoran took a drink from a small pool near the edge of the hollow. By midmorning, he was back in the thick of the plains, marching south through the yellow sea. The land was just as bleak as the plains around Fairhollow, devoid of any life beyond preying hawks or an occasional rustle of the weeds where a small critter fled at his approach. Beyond it all, thick clouds of Mist sprang up. All of them seemed to hound Micah's progress across the prairie.

Eventually, the flat grassland gave way to rough, stony hills—a sign he was nearing the massive expanse of cultivated farms and ranches that surrounded Starkhaven, which lay just beyond the hills.

As the sun reached its zenith, he caught a glimpse of something past the sloping mounds. Micah spurred Edoran forward, climbing an embankment for a better look. Starkhaven finally came into view as they reached the top, the colossal city spreading to the edge of sight in both directions. Yet, what Micah saw quickly turned his anticipation into dismay.

Ahead, tangled fields of withered crops lay in ruin before the feet of the capital. Except for jumbled dwellings along the capital's edge, the entire city was shrouded in a vast blanket of Mist. Its sheer scale defied all attempts to measure it, suggesting Starkhaven had become the central focus of the consuming curse's grip on Micah's homeland. The gleaming tips of magnificent towers were all he could see of the once-proud capital. His gut sank with fear and sorrow.

How am I supposed to navigate that?

The strange image from the Voice flashed in his thoughts.

That tower could be any one of those poking through. It could still be covered, for all I know, he somberly mused, eyeing the cloud of Mist looming monstrously above the desolate fields and squalid shacks.

Micah led Edoran down from their vantage, angling towards the wide cobblestone road between the town of Stonecroft and the capital. As he neared the city's edge, the immensity of the Mist filled him with dread. An army of monsters assuredly stalked the streets of Starkhaven.

He took shelter in a deserted barn just off the main road, finding several bundles of hay left by its previous inhabitants. The meager stores would provide a welcome distraction for poor Edoran while Micah infiltrated the city.

"You've been a faithful friend," Micah gently told the tall warhorse, feeling the coarse mane behind his sturdy face, "but this is where your path ends. I'll come back for you if I make it, but if I don't..."

He choked, unable to say another goodbye so soon.

"Take care of yourself, Edoran," he murmured, kissing his powerful neck.

Creeping back onto the road, Micah gaped at the city and the wall of bluish haze enveloping its buildings. Even in the daylight, a dark aura gripped the capital.

He trudged forward, grasping his sword with white knuckles as he approached Starkhaven's perimeter. The world around him was deathly still, save for an eerie breeze whistling through the disheveled farms and broken cottages. A thin bank of Mist swirled around the outskirts before giving way to the impenetrable fog beyond. Micah slipped off the cobblestone, sneaking along a row of dead hedges towards the first house. As he approached, tendrils of Mist reached out from the lazy swirl, groping hungrily for his flesh, but unable to harm him. As he slid up to the house's clay exterior, the entire atmosphere shifted; the peaceful world outside the Mist replaced by a haunting presence whispering evil threats at the edge of consciousness.

Micah peered around the corner for a better look at the main road. From his time in Starkhaven, he knew the highway from Stonecroft ran straight into the heart of Starkhaven, joining a frenzy of roads converging on the Circle of the Conclave and Tar'auth Ben. Unfortunately, the wide thoroughfare remained ensconced in an impermeable wall of writhing Mist. He waited a moment longer, hoping the fog would shift and provide some hint as to what was in store for him. Instead, a chorus of howls cried out from deeper in the city, only to be answered by another pack somewhere far to his right.

Mist Wolves.

After a moment, a lumbering roar joined the choir from straight ahead, followed by a faint boom, suggesting a massive Mist Troll somewhere in the depths of the fog.

There would be no coming back.

Micah took a deep breath, steadying himself against the cold house as he sized up the busted doorway of a small, timbered shack just inside the cloud of Mist. From there, everything would be up to chance.

Protect me, Elowë, he pleaded. *Lead me safely through this hell.*

Micah flexed his legs, ready to dash across the open road.

"You don't want to do that."

The voice nearly sent Micah to his knees as he stumbled in surprise. He whipped out his sword, the blade gleaming in the daylight as he spun around. Behind him, a young woman sat atop a crumbling stone wall enclosing the remains of a small garden. Her dark, wavy hair was tied back in a loose ponytail, revealing a beautiful, light-brown face. Bright brown eyes with a golden tinge studied him, while a teasing smile played along her small lips.

"What are you doing?" Micah whispered fiercely. "Get down!"

"They don't come this close to the outside. At least, not usually," she lightly answered, waving her delicate hand. "There's far more of interest to them deeper in the city."

He cast a final glance at the road, checking for any sign of Wolves before creeping over to the captivating woman.

"What are you doing out here?" he hissed.

"I could ask the same of you," she challenged, dropping from the wall and brushing dust off her hands. Her slender body was covered by a dark, woven shirt and pants with pieces of matching leather armor for protection. A large cloth pack rested on her shoulders, stuffed with unknown objects. A quiver of expensive-looking arrows rested beside her pack, while an unusual sword hung from her hip. For a moment, the object drew Micah's attention. The sheath looked like thin, smoky glass inlaid with silver, enclosing a gently curving sword of white metal with a hilt of wood and silver, unlike anything he had ever seen. An ornate bow of rich, dark wood rested against the wall behind her.

"What are you doing on the road? Everyone knows it's not safe." She scolded him as a mother does her child.

"What do you mean?"

"You're clearly not from around here," she chided with a smirk. "Some simple advice? One: stay out of Starkhaven unless you have a death wish. Two: stay off the main roads. Even though the monsters *tend* to stay in the city, they can get adventurous. The main roads into the capital are their favorite haunt when they get antsy. They catch a whiff of you and poof!" She flicked her fingers at his face. "You're Wolf food."

"I get that," Micah grumbled, salvaging his pride, "but I have to get into the city. It's important to the survival of Karthmoor."

She laughed. "Wow, we're jumping to that already? Not even a 'my wife left a precious family heirloom, and I simply must recover it to restore our family's honor' blah, blah, blah?"

"I lost my wife to the Mist years ago," he flatly retorted. "I'm serious about this."

The woman's face soured with regret. "I'm sorry, that was callous. The Mist's taken plenty of loved ones."

"I appreciate it," Micah relented. "You couldn't have known, anyway. I take it you've lost someone?"

"Pretty much everyone close," she said matter-of-factly. "I think I may have a relative or two who escaped somewhere south, but I'm not really sure."

They paused for a moment, awkwardly surveying the swirling Mist.

"Micah Stormcrown," he said, breaking the silence and extending a rough hand. "Formerly of Aringoth, formerly of Fairhollow."

She flashed a relieved smile.

"Navaeya Endalië," she replied, her gentle hand shaking his. "A pleasure."

"A curious name."

"It has a curious story too, if you stick around long enough," she coyly added. "Just not while prancing along the edge of a death zone."

"Right." Micah chuckled grimly.

She glanced over his shoulder as the howl of a Mist Wolf rose from the street.

"Look, I won't stop you if you're set on gambling your life away," she said, turning serious, "but I'd take some time to scout out the place before blundering in."

"Meaning?"

"Meaning I'm not the only one interested in the capital. The Guard in Stonecroft has the last official reports on the city, and there's always an odd fellow around the pub with a juicy bit of information."

"The Stonecroft garrison survived?" he gaped in astonishment.

Navaeya shrugged. "Not all of them, but enough. The survivors have kept Stonecroft relatively secure, so they've done alright in my book. At least for soldiers."

"What does that mean?" he asked indignantly.

She shook her head, dark hair fluttering around her face. "Another story for another time."

Another Wolf sounded in the distance, closer than the last.

"And that's my cue. So, what'll it be?" she finished, crossing her arms.

Micah turned around, weighing the dangers lurking beyond the wall of Mist. He sighed.

"Stonecroft it is."

"Cheer up, Micah," Navaeya happily replied. "Starkhaven's a big place. There's always a way in."

He cast a final, defeated look at the forsaken city.

"Come on." She gestured behind them.

Navaeya grabbed her bow from the ground, striding along the wall away from Starkhaven. Micah reluctantly followed, mulling over what to do next.

After stepping through several tangled fields and darting around crumbling houses, she glanced back, satisfied with their distance from the capital, and led them onto the highway towards Stonecroft. Ahead, Micah spotted the barn where he'd left Edoran.

"Hold up," he called as she strode away.

He dashed inside to Edoran and coaxed him back outdoors, after clearly interrupting his meal. Navaeya raised a thin eyebrow as he guided him over.

She smiled. "Quite a handsome stallion. What's his name?"

"Edoran." Micah beamed. "He's been with me since my journey began."

"If you're set on entering Starkhaven, I'm sure someone will offer to care for him, for a price."

He nodded, holding Edoran's reins as Navaeya led on.

"The garrison is only a few leagues from the capital," Navaeya announced in her pure, lighthearted voice. "We'll be there before you know it."

"About three leagues," he added, moving to her side.

"Oh, you've been there?" she said with surprise.

"In... another lifetime."

Micah could feel her energetic eyes burning with curiosity, but she remained silent.

"How has the garrison survived this long when they're this close to the Mist?" he asked as they passed the time.

"It's odd, you know," Navaeya mused after a moment. "Everywhere else the Mist and its goons show up, they kill anything that moves, but here... I don't know. There's the occasional party of Wolves that hounds the walls, sure, but for the most part, it leaves Stonecroft alone. Something about the capital holds its attention."

"Odd," Micah softly agreed, pondering the implications.

"But at least it means we all get a decent night's sleep, right?" Her gentle face brightened.

"Very true."

The patchy clouds above slowly transformed into a billowing blanket as the afternoon arrived. In the west, a dark bank appeared, hinting at a coming storm. They trekked silently along the cracked cobblestone, the desolate fields of Starkhaven giving way to golden plains before the terrain shifted into rocky cliffs. Edoran's hoofs echoed loudly against the stone as the road dipped through a small ravine.

"Almost there," Navaeya murmured.

A handful of minutes later, they rounded a rough cliff, bringing Stonecroft into view. An easy slope in the highway ran into a wide, shallow canyon. At the center stood a large fort of high stone walls separating the road. Dusty plains around the fort provided clear sightlines in every direction.

"A sight for sore eyes," she mumbled with relief.

Micah watched the small shapes of men pass between the parapets towering above as the road headed towards the settlement. Its high gate of iron and wood was sealed, preventing the Mist's creatures from entering the town.

When they were within a bowshot of the gate, the gleam of a Guardsman's helm appeared by the gatehouse.

"Navaeya!" a grizzled man called. "Good hunting today?"

Beyond the gate, a loud rumbling began, and the thick doors slowly inched open.

"Not bad," she shouted back, hoisting the pack on her shoulders. "Even brought home a stray!"

"So I see. Make sure to inform the captain of his arrival," the man directed.

"I will!" she happily replied, then under her breath. "It's not like it's my first time, Gerrald."

The grand gates came to a shuddering stop as Micah followed Navaeya through the opening, Edoran obediently tagging behind. Inside the fort, a vast yard opened up where a handful of muddy streets separated rows of rough cabin-style homes and buildings along one side. A wall of iron bars ran across the opposite end, dividing the Guards' training grounds and barracks from the town. Above the squat shacks and olive-colored tents, the clash of metal echoed in the air.

Dozens of citizens roamed the streets as Navaeya led him farther into Stonecroft, many casting a curious eye in his direction. A large well marked the center of the fort, drawing crowds of soldiers, citizens, and a variety of others with small carts of goods, all yelling above the fray, hoping to draw the attention of onlookers. On the left of the square, a high iron gate stood open, a pair of heavily armored Guardsmen keeping watch.

"You'll want to head in there." Navaeya pointed through it to the towering keep at the far end. "That's the garrison's headquarters. Captain Hawthorne's the one in charge. He's a serious fellow, but decent enough. His priority will be gaining whatever insight you can give him into the rest of Karthmoor."

"You're not coming?" Micah asked, surprised.

"I prefer to avoid mingling with the Guard if I can." She grinned. "Don't worry, you'll be safe without me."

Her teasing face succeeded in drawing a smirk out of him.

"Then I guess this is farewell," said Micah, strangely disappointed. "Good luck, and thanks for talking me off the ledge."

She stopped, tilting her head slightly as a tangle of hair fell over her shoulder.

"Something tells me I haven't seen the last of you, Micah Stormcrown," she declared playfully. "There's simply too much mystery left."

She spun around, gracefully weaving through the crowd and vanishing from view. Micah stood there, baffled.

Always something new.

CHAPTER 39
THE LAST BASTION

MICAH TURNED TO FACE the gates to the keep as the Guards watched cautiously.

"We heard, newcomer," one lazily replied as he stepped forward. "You can tie your horse there—" He pointed to a modest stable to Micah's right, where a group of warhorses waited in a line of stalls. "—then head across the field to the keep."

Micah guided Edoran over to the enclosure, where a young apprentice rushed up to take his reins. Returning to the bumpy trail through the camp, he passed several Guardsmen, exhaustion clear on their faces. After crossing a training yard full of fresh recruits, wildly sparring with dulled or wooden blades, he reached a wide set of stairs leading to the keep. The enormous structure was set into the northern wall of Stonecroft, a series of stout pillars supporting a covered porch beneath the unbroken tower of dark gray stone. The only variation beyond the sparse windows was a small balcony several floors above.

At the set of heavy oaken doors leading to the atrium, another set of Guards stood watch.

"What's your business here, civilian?" one challenged with a gruff voice. A stubbly beard jutted out from his iron helm.

"I'm a traveler to Stonecroft. I was told to see the captain of the garrison."

"Right. Head in and take the stairwell straight ahead. Fourth floor, the door at the end," he grumbled.

"Thank you."

The thick door creaked open as Micah entered the keep. A sea of candles and torches flickered off the dim stone, giving the space a cave-like feel. After a short hall, the entrance opened into the lofty atrium. A narrow stairwell with an iron railing rose along the walls, the cavernous room open all the way to the top floor above. An array of doors and halls branched off the main floor, as did additional passages at regular balconies along the angled stairwell.

A troop of Guards in jingling armor shuffled through a door at the far end, and Micah jumped out of the way before heading for the stairs. He jogged up the rough steps, his clunking boots echoing up the tower as he climbed. On the fourth floor, a short hallway offered three closed doors. He headed for the last one at the end. Through the ancient wood, muffled voices reached Micah's ears as he knocked.

"Yes, yes, come in," called a man's deep voice. Micah pulled the latch, pushing the door open on its dreary hinges.

An older man in heavy, polished armor stood peering down at a large desk, his brilliant gauntlets resting on the wood. A wild tangle of fiery red hair sprouted from his head and face, the thick beard spilling onto his breastplate. His wicked looking mace peeked over the back of his armor, a powerful weapon Kelj certainly would have appreciated. A younger man with short, dark hair, also in heavy armor, faced him from the other side of the desk. The men looked up as Micah entered.

"I haven't seen your face before, stranger," the fiery warrior said, straightening to face him.

"Just arrived," Micah answered, crossing to shake his armored hand.

"Well met then, and welcome to Stonecroft," he boomed in his gritty voice. "The last bastion of hope at the end of the world."

The younger man smirked as he stepped to the side of the desk, nodding a silent greeting.

"I'm Captain Hawthorne," the large Guardsmen continued, "commander of this fort and likely one of the last officers of the Karthmoor Guard. A sobering thought."

"I wouldn't jump to conclusions too quickly, Captain," Micah replied, smiling. "Micah Stormcrown, honored to make your acquaintance."

The man's proud smile immediately exchanged for shock, as did the other man's.

"Stormcrown?" he sputtered. "As in Warden Micah Stormcrown? The Warden of the West?"

"As you say."

The captain fumbled backwards, jerking his arm into an awkward salute.

"Warden Stormcrown, sir. I, I had no idea you survived. That anyone survived!" he exclaimed.

Micah chuckled and returned the soldier's hasty gesture. "At ease, Captain. Karthmoor is full of surprises these days."

The man lowered his arm, relaxing slightly, though clearly bursting with questions.

"Warden, sir, we haven't had any contact with other settlements in years, other than Karthport," Hawthorne began. "How have you survived? Are there other garrisons still functioning?"

"I spent several years in the small logging village of Fairhollow, though I've made quite a trek across Karthmoor these past few weeks. The Guard still operates in some areas, though none of the old garrisons truly remain," he gravely reported. "There are remnants of the Guard protecting Fairhollow and Greenwatch. Beyond that, I cannot say."

"So Greenwatch lives," he breathed in relief. "What of Hillmarch?"

"Gone. Fell to the Mist not long after it arrived."

"I see." His bright eyes saddened.

"Take heart, Captain," added Micah. "There are many places that still resist the curse. Our people are resilient. Karthmoor hasn't given up yet."

"That's good to hear," he said solemnly, a small confidence growing.

"You've done well here," Micah commended, observing the captain's office. "I'm impressed Stonecroft has stood this long with the Mist in Starkhaven so close."

"It's been a challenge, but Stonecroft is a hardy place. As are its people," he crowed.

"Lieutenant Maran, sir," the second man introduced himself with a salute. "Welcome to Stonecroft. If I may, many of the civilians were eager to enlist once the Mist attacked. We have them to thank for outlasting this curse."

"Indeed," Captain Hawthorne concurred. "Although, come to think of it... I suppose Stonecroft falls to your command,

Warden Stormcrown. You're likely the highest-ranking officer in the entire nation now."

"Don't go proclaiming me Warden-Commander yet," Micah warned with a chuckle. "I left the service long ago."

"Even so," the captain countered.

"A worthy gesture, Captain, but I'm not here to relieve you of command. My journey is leading me elsewhere."

"At your command, sir." Hawthorne nodded. "But I must admit, Stonecroft could desperately use you."

"I'm flattered, Captain, but you're clearly doing an excellent job of defending these people. I trust your hands are capable."

"Yes, sir," he said sadly. "Very well then. How can the Guard assist you, Warden?"

Micah glanced at the maps and letters strewn across Hawthorne's desk.

"I need information on Starkhaven. Scouting reports, enemy movements, safe house locations. Whatever you have."

"Of course, sir. The lieutenant here will gather everything we have on the capital."

Lieutenant Maran saluted, rushing from the room.

"I must warn you, Warden, we have very little information on Starkhaven's current situation. We haven't had the manpower to spare for regular scouting runs in months, and the blasted Mist shrouds the entire city, preventing us from monitoring the monsters' movements. As far as we're concerned, nowhere is safe within the city."

"I understand," said Micah with a frown, "but it's of the highest importance I gain access to the capital. I'll take anything that might help."

"If I may, sir, what could be so important in a dead city? Even if it is our crowning jewel?" Hawthorne asked.

"I wish I had a good answer for you," he admitted. "All I can say is there may be answers there to help put an end to the Mist, once and for all."

"I wouldn't have believed it from anyone else, sir, but that'd certainly be a cause for action. Anything to throw off this murderous fog. I'll spare any men I can to get you to your goal," Hawthorne loudly declared.

"Unfortunately, it isn't that simple," Micah replied. "I don't have an exact location, and I won't risk your men on a suicide mission. Their place is with Stonecroft."

"As you say."

Lieutenant Maran stumbled back through Hawthorne's door with a mound of crusty papers and leathery books piled in his arms. Captain Hawthorne cleared his desk, spreading out a map of Starkhaven and selecting a handful of dusty reports. The three of them huddled around the worn parchments in the torchlight.

"Our last detailed reports on Starkhaven are nearly as old as the Mist," Captain Hawthorne explained. "The weeks following the invasion of the capital and its subsequent evacuation were filled with vain attempts to retake sections of the city. Nearly all of the Starkhaven Guard and many soldiers of Stonecroft were lost in the skirmishes. Without the Conclave and Warden-Commander Berien, the colonels were at a loss."

"Much of the city will be a ruin by this point," Micah observed. "Traversing the rubble will be difficult, perhaps impossible, in certain places."

"Yes, and we have no updated information on where the Mist is concentrating," the captain continued. "The deadliest locations could be anywhere."

"Your best bet would be to use the side streets and alleys," Lieutenant Maran offered. "The larger beasts have trouble entering the tight spaces between the buildings."

"Only catch is that's also an easy way to get pinned between roaming packs of Wolves, or worse, those screaming demons," Hawthorne countered.

"Mist Wraiths." Micah shuddered.

"Aye, Wraiths," the captain agreed. "Do you have a general idea of where you're heading?"

"Not exactly," he slowly answered, replaying the image of the mysterious tower in his mind. "I'm looking for a tower, seated on a wide city square and expertly built. The exterior is quite lavish."

"Hmm." Hawthorne pulled at his bushy beard. "If it's a property of Starkhaven's elite, I would place my bets on either the Government or Upper Districts." He pointed an armored finger to the center and southeastern corner of the map.

"Those will be the most difficult places to reach," Maran warned. "You have to pass through half the city just to reach the Circle of the Conclave. Even more to reach the Upper District's waterfront properties."

"Is it accessible by sea?" Micah wondered aloud.

"Ignoring the Mist hanging over Stark Bay, we haven't found any seaworthy vessels to even try with," the captain flatly stated. "The bay is likely not an option."

Micah stared at the dusty parchment, wracking his brain.

"Has anyone else tried to map the city recently?" he asked with a hint of frustration.

"Not to my knowledge," Hawthorne glumly replied. The room fell silent with despair.

"There might be someone in town who could help," Lieutenant Maran hesitantly piped. Hawthorne and Micah jerked their heads in his direction.

"What do you mean, Maran?" the captain pressed.

"A couple of our more… adventurous citizens have spent some time around Starkhaven," he explained. "One of them might know something we don't."

"Hmph," Hawthorne grumbled with a frown. "You're talking about that Endalië girl."

"Navaeya?" Micah asked, astonished.

"Yes, that's her name." Hawthorne raised a brow. "Pretty girl, but I wouldn't show her any trust, sir. She's a foreigner, supposedly from Istwyneir. Mark my words, she's hiding something. Likely an Imperial spy."

"Even if she is, sir," Maran argued, "she's spent more time around the capital recently than most anyone else. She may know a way through that we're not aware of."

Captain Hawthorne pulled back from his desk, crossing his arms with disapproval.

"As much as I hate pointing you in her direction, the lieutenant has a point," he grouchily admitted. "The girl may have information we don't. Frankly, Starkhaven has been less of a concern to us than fortifying Stonecroft."

"I completely understand, Captain," said Micah approvingly. "Navaeya was the one who persuaded me to come here in the first place. I'll take any help I can get."

"Right," Hawthorne replied. "Lieutenant?"

"Sir." Lieutenant Maran nodded. "Word around town is Miss Endalië keeps an odd schedule, though you can usually find her at her stall in the market square. I've passed her wares. An odd assortment of trinkets, likely gathered from Starkhaven.

I also hear from the men who patronize Stonecroft's tavern that she's a regular presence there in the evenings."

Micah glanced through the open glass door to the captain's balcony. The descending sun had completely disappeared behind the thick clouds. A soft rumble of thunder echoed from the doorway. Rain was coming. Soon.

"Right, check the market, then the tavern," he repeated. "Anything else?"

"I took the liberty of ordering a ration of supplies from the quartermaster for you, sir. I'll have them delivered to Laring, the tavern keeper," Maran continued. "And one of the apprentices informed me of your horse. Rest assured, it will be well kept until your return, should you decide to leave it here."

"Excellent work, Lieutenant," Captain Hawthorne bellowed. "What ever would I do without you?"

"It's my pleasure, sir." He smiled proudly.

"Thank you, Maran." Micah nodded. "Sounds like I'm set."

"We wish you were staying longer, Warden Stormcrown, but I understand the importance of your mission," Hawthorne finished, he and Maran moving to salute. "Remember that the Guard of Stonecroft stands with you, should you need us."

"Thank you, Captain." Micah returned the gesture. "Elowë watch over your people."

"You as well, sir."

He firmly shut the heavy door to Hawthorne's office, descending the slick stairwell at a brisk pace.

There was no time to lose.

Chapter 40

Pathfinder... for a Price

As Micah exited the keep and returned to the covered entrance, a scattering of rain began to fall across the training field.

He rushed past groups of soldiers, the men hurriedly packing up gear and moving it out of the weather. No one took a second glance at him as he slipped out of the garrison's camp and into the market. As the mist turned into a steady sprinkle, the villagers began hurrying towards the houses along the narrow streets, covering their heads. The remaining vendors busily swung awnings and doors shut on their wares, moving them out of the rain. Micah scanned the crowd, looking for a glimpse of the mysterious woman.

Nothing.

Maybe the tavern then.

He spotted an elderly street merchant fumbling to gather a pile of apples that refused to stay in their basket. Micah hurried over, deftly snatching one as it rolled past his wrinkled hand and off the cart.

"Thank you, sir," the man rasped with a toothy smile.

"Of course. If I may, where is the tavern?" Micah asked.

"Ah, take this street to the second turn. Go left," he directed, raising a shaky arm. "The second building on the right, young sir. You can't miss it."

"Thank you."

Micah set off, along with a mob of others, hoping to get out of the weather before the sky really broke loose. The world grew darker, evening gathering its strength as he turned onto the busy street. Ahead of him, the tavern was a sea of activity. Dozens of patrons were noisily shuffling their way in, ready to pass the rainy night with a drink or two. Micah joined the throng, jostling his way through the narrow door and into the smoky room.

Much like Fairhollow's boisterous tavern, the modest structure was awash in a din of laughter and noise. A multitude of men and women, farmers and soldiers, all celebrating the end of another day. A couple of men slid around behind a wide, well-worn bar, passing thick glasses of golden liquid across to thirsty patrons.

Weaving his way to an empty corner, Micah gripped the back of a worn wooden chair, searching for Navaeya. Nothing yet.

A cheery, older woman tapped him on the shoulder. "Can I get you something?"

"Just an ale, please." Micah passed her a coin, and she hurried off toward the bar. He angled the seat to where he could see most of the room and vanished into the sea of patrons. The woman returned in a flash, placing a tall glass of rich ale in front of him before scurrying to another table.

For the next hour, Micah jumped every time someone entered the bustling tavern. Outside, the sprinkling gradually rose to a roaring pour, rain pounding the roof of the floor above. Even so, the racket of the gloomy bar nearly drowned out the storm. Halfway through his second glass, a mischievous voice from behind cut through the clamor, startling him.

"If I didn't know any better, I'd say I have a stalker." Navaeya's graceful figure slipped into a rickety seat, eyeing Micah with a spirited grin. Her hair was undone, a cascade of wavy strands flowing around her shoulders above her dark clothing. Micah scooted over, making room in an attempt to cover up his awkward lack of response. She laughed lightly, tossing her hair and drawing the attention of several men around them.

"About time you showed up," Micah grumbled over the cacophony of the bar.

"Micah Stormcrown," she replied with feigned hurt, "when did I give the impression that a dingy pub was the place to find me?"

"Apparently, you frequent it enough to draw attention," he teased back.

"Ignoring the fact I'm associated with this grimy shack, it sounds like I need to switch up my routine."

The old woman appeared again. "Usual, Navi?"

"Yes, please. Thank you, Arla," Navaeya answered. The woman disappeared again.

"Navi?" Micah asked, grinning.

"I hate it. Makes me sound like a fairy," she muttered. "*But* when it's one of your best customers, you find out just how much you're willing to put up with."

"What do you sell?" he casually continued.

"All sorts of fascinating things from my many, many travels," she said elusively.

"Like ones to Starkhaven?"

Navaeya shrugged with a subtle grin. "Perhaps."

Arla returned with a delicate cup of steaming tea, setting it before her. Next to Micah's towering pint, the dainty drink seemed laughably small.

"So then, Navaeya, what were you doing out there, anyway?" Micah questioned with narrowed eyes.

"Scavenging," she answered curtly.

"Scavenging?"

"Yes. And don't look at me like that!" she scolded as Micah frowned. "There's plenty of treasures hidden in Starkhaven, their owners long since dead or gone. You just have to know where to look... And where to hide."

"There's a lot of danger delving into the Mist," he observed. "You're lucky to at least be immune to it."

"I decided long ago I'd rather find something out on my own terms than wait for it to sneak up on me," she asserted. His respect for the enigmatic woman was growing.

"Fair enough. So, who would pay for old trinkets when the Mist is breathing down their necks?" he scoffed.

"You'd be surprised. With so much loss, plenty of people are looking for anything to recall happier days," she explained. "Anything can become important to a soul who's lost it all. An old locket, a fine dress, a fur cloak. Some even pay a premium for rarer items."

"Rarer items?"

Navaeya looked around anxiously, eyeing the gruff men around their table, before leaning closer.

"Besides artifacts from the Conclave, a few of my... clients are very interested in iluvan remnants, if you've ever even heard of that this far north. Your nation is quite removed from the world. No offense."

"We know iluvan," said Micah defensively. "Karthmoorans aren't as backward as you think. Conclave property, though, is another matter. That's a high crime."

"Please," she huffed. "The only people left who care are the Stonecroft Guard. The rule of law died when the Mist took over. Unless..."

Navaeya leaned back, studying Micah with her dark, piercing eyes.

"Stormcrown," she mumbled. "Come to think of it, your name seems familiar..."

"I was a Warden in the Guard. Before the Mist," he awkwardly revealed.

"Yes! That's it," she exclaimed. "That's where! You were quite persistent in rooting out the Thieves' Guild forming in Farshore when you were a city captain."

"Wait, how do you remember that?" he asked with a quizzical look. "That was ages ago, well before anyone knew me."

"I may have dabbled with the Guild along the Strait," she answered slyly. "For all the damage you did, your name was legend among them. After the Farshore branch fell apart, I always wondered where you'd end up without that ragtag crew to hunt."

"I see."

"Honestly, they were a rough bunch," she continued breezily. "Pirates and all. I wouldn't have stuck around, anyway. Always preferred the Guild inside the Empire. Still, your battle with Captain Skrilas' ship always made for a thrilling tale."

"I'd almost forgotten about that one." Micah smiled, recalling a desperate chase along the Fallow Strait, along with a near collision in the southern coves. "So, you're a thief then."

"Not anymore, least not professionally," she admitted. "But when you're young and on your own, with your only options being to sell your body in some slum or slog around a grubby tavern filled with filthy men, I opted for something different."

"I'm sorry, I didn't realize… You didn't have parents or family to—"

"Forget it," she cut him off, her voice unexpectedly strained. "It's none of your business."

"Of course. I apologize."

She turned away for a moment, her face hidden behind her wavy hair.

"So, what's your aim, Micah Stormcrown? Why'd you seek me out?" she finally asked, turning back.

"I need a way into Starkhaven."

"Still holding onto that death wish," Navaeya jokingly grumbled. "No one returns from the capital unscathed. Why? What's so important?"

"I'm looking for a building, either near the Circle or somewhere in the Upper District. A tower ringed in light."

Navaeya nearly fell out of her rickety chair, laughing wildly.

"You're joking, right? You'd go roaming through a dead zone, looking for some mystical, glowy tower? Even if it's real, no one's ever gone that far into Starkhaven and lived to tell about it."

"I'm serious. I wasn't jesting when I said it was important to Karthmoor's survival," Micah argued.

"What makes you think I can give you a way through?" she demanded, her skepticism clear.

"Word is you know Starkhaven better than anyone. Surely, you have a way in if you've scavenged in the city," he replied. "I need you to lead me through."

Navaeya shook her head furiously, her deep eyes flashing as she frowned. "I dig up stuff along the outskirts, sure, but actually *entering* the capital is entirely different. I don't do that for the fun of it and certainly not for cheap. Someone wants something special from deeper in? They'll pay for it. Up front and with a lot of coin."

He ran a frustrated hand through his hair, his narrowed eyes locking with hers in the flickering candlelight.

"What if I pay?"

"How much are you offering?" she brusquely retorted.

Micah felt the dwindling coin pouch from his delivery to Greenwatch at his side, and his heart sank. There was no way he could afford what she was asking.

Unless...

He reached behind his neck, untying the simple cord holding Elisa's pendant. Micah raised the dim crystal above the worn table, gleaming in the candlelight.

"What about this?" he somberly asked. Navaeya stretched out a curious hand, and he dropped the shard into her smooth palm. She rolled the crystal around, shielding it from prying eyes and studying it from various angles. After a moment, she glanced up, her eyes boring into him with a fearful look.

"Do you even realize what this *is*?" she hissed through the noise of the bar.

"Not exactly, but I have a guess."

Navaeya glanced around the table, making sure no one was watching before discreetly stowing the crystal in a pouch at her hip.

"I'll consider it down payment. We'll cover the rest with any treasure we find along the way," she offered.

"Deal."

She smiled. "Looks like you've got yourself a pathfinder, Stormcrown."

"Just like that?" Micah asked, incredulous.

"Yep!" she happily replied.

He shot her a suspicious look, his mouth turned in a slight frown.

Navaeya continued smiling. "If you want a better answer, you'll simply have to follow me."

Suddenly, she jumped up from the table, elegantly twirling her hair back through the band Micah had seen holding it along the road. She strode deftly through the crowd, weaving towards the door as he carved a jostled path after her. Not two tables later, a large, burly man stumbled up from his drink, blocking her exit.

"Leaving so soon, beautiful?" he slurred. "Why don't you sit your pretty self down? I'll get you a drink."

"I'd rather kiss a pig," said Navaeya, bristling. "Out of my way, please."

"W–what did you say?" the man stuttered angrily.

"You heard me," she growled. "Move your stinking, drunken self out of my way!"

The man's shock turned to wrath, and he lunged for her arm. In a flash, Navaeya twisted, slapping his hand away and lashing out with a piercing jab at his neck. The man's lumbering mass recoiled, but not before she delivered a swift kick to his knee and another to his other foot. Something cracked, and he howled in pain, collapsing into his chair only for it to explode under his considerable weight. Two of his companions leapt up, yelling in surprise as the entire room fell silent, swerving in their seats to watch the scene.

"I said *please*." Navaeya stepped around the man and resuming her stride towards the door without a second look. The crowd melted out of her way as Micah scampered after her.

"She broke my foot!" the drunken man yelled as Micah slipped out of the tavern.

Outside, a deluge poured as the storm flashed across the blackened sky. Rain obscured everything on the muddy road beyond a smattering of sheltered torches flickering faintly in the vicious wind.

Navaeya pulled a long, thin cloak from her small bag, throwing it over her shoulders and head as she hurried down the street. Covering himself with his arm, Micah chased after her. She turned onto a side street, vanishing into the shadows. Micah was drenched in seconds, fighting to keep the rain out of his eyes as he tried to keep up with her.

After a series of twists and turns in Stonecroft's darkened lanes, Navaeya stopped at a small door along a row of tired-looking houses. The two-story buildings loomed ominously above them in the dark, lightning flashing over their creaky roofs. Navaeya pulled a key from her side, unlocking the door and slipping through the opening. Micah leapt after her into the black, but dry, interior. Instantly, he stumbled into an unseen object. Metal clanged loudly against the wood floor.

"Just a moment," said Navaeya, her soft feet moving away in the formless space. Micah shook his soaked head, spraying the ground, before squeezing a tub's-worth of water from his clothes. A gentle light sprang from a darkened doorway to his left, slowly revealing the area as she returned holding a small lamp. Looking around, Micah noticed piles of trinkets and worn cases lining the room. Everything from chipped tea sets to walking canes to pieces of Guard armor poked out of wooden boxes or were heaped on top of each other. Stranger still, towers of dusty books and tomes sat in tidy stacks along the walls, organized into unknown groups. A wide, patched sofa along with two crusty, wooden seats surrounded a small oak table before a low fireplace. A few tattered rugs were spaced across the creaky floorboards.

Navaeya threw her soaked cloak into a basket and moved over to the fireplace, lighting a long match from her lamp to kindle a pile of dry straw and sticks. After a few moments, the fire caught, slowly bringing the old stone enclosure to life. Micah joined her, leaving a dripping trail across the floor. She glanced up as he approached, his wet skin eager to dry out in the flame's blossoming heat.

"Sorry," she mumbled, vanishing back into the side room before returning with a heap of thick woolen blankets. Micah kicked off his sopping boots, undoing his gear on the floor before throwing one around his shoulders. Between the blanket and the fire, he immediately felt the cold moisture evaporating from his tired bones. Navaeya removed her belt and gear, kicking off her small, dark boots before removing Elisa's crystal pendant from her pouch and grabbing another blanket. Micah plopped into one of the chairs as she curled her legs onto the couch, glancing at him from across the table. For a moment, they were silent, watching the growing flames cast dancing shadows around the dreary room as the storm raged outside.

"It isn't much, but it's home. For now," Navaeya said quietly, breaking the still air.

"It's... nice."

She snorted. "Please, this is Stonecroft."

Micah's face burned awkwardly.

"But I appreciate it." Navaeya smiled, her gentle face glowing in the firelight. "If you hadn't guessed, I'm terrible at hospitality. It isn't often I let someone into my home."

"I'll consider myself lucky."

She laughed. "You should. But anyway. I promised you an explanation." Her carefree expression turned slightly more serious.

"So," Micah started, "what about my crystal changed your mind?"

Navaeya pulled the pendant from under her blanket, dangling it in the air. The small shape shimmered faintly in the firelight, its silvery, white interior swirling in curious patterns.

"Where to begin... You said you've heard of iluvan, the magical blue rocks people use for power?"

Micah nodded.

"Regular iluvan is rare enough these days. Most of the time, the Mist swarms wherever you find it in large quantities. Still, plenty of mages, tinkerers, and collectors pay well for me to retrieve shards of the stuff from Starkhaven. It's becoming harder to find on the outskirts though, forcing me to raise the price and risk going deeper into the city," she continued. "Occasionally, you get the half-mad wizard asking for black iluvan too, but I refuse those. Too many risks, especially the Mist. You might be able to avoid the Mist with just a small bit of iluvan, but hold even a fingernail's worth of black iluvan, and the Mist will chase you to the end of the earth."

"Right, I've seen all this in my travels," Micah replied slowly. "Where are you going?"

"I'm getting there," she said irritably. "So, loads of people chase after those two, but you see, they aren't the only forms of iluvan. Twice, and only twice, during my time scavenging, I've had individuals request I find a third form of iluvan: white iluvan. Like your pendant." Navaeya glanced at the stone, eyeing it with a look of fascination, but also a tinge of fear.

"I've only heard a rumor of it from a mage," Micah added. "I had a suspicion then that my pendant might be iluvan but had no way to confirm one way or the other."

"I'd always assumed it was just a myth. Until now," she responded. "It's rumored white iluvan can absorb and store a nearly unlimited amount of magic, though it has to be fed in some way. The only ways I could see that happening is if someone figured out how to transfer power from another iluvan or a mage transferred her power into it. You'd have to find a mage who knows how to do that, though."

Micah shook his head. "That makes sense."

I wonder if I could do that...

"Still, the rarity makes it almost priceless. Where did you find this, anyway?" Navaeya asked, her eyes flashing with excitement.

"Far away, exploring a forgotten shrine in the Anderfalls. I brought it home as a gift for my wife."

A shadow of guilt crossed Navaeya's face. "Oh."

"Don't worry about it." He shrugged, masking his disappointment.

"You're asking me to risk a whole lot, going into the heart of Starkhaven," she reasoned. "If you have anything else of value, I'd consider it in trade."

"I don't."

Navaeya nodded, slipping the pendant back underneath her blanket. They fell into awkward silence again, the sound of the rain echoing in the room.

"It's late," Navaeya said at last, shedding the woolen cover before standing. "Assuming the rain lets up, we'll head out at first light, if that works for you."

"Sounds good."

"You can use the couch." She gestured to its warped frame. "Sorry, I don't have much here."

Micah nodded.

"Well, it's been a lovely evening," she proclaimed, stretching her slender form. "You've turned out to be quite the surprise, Micah. Or should I call you Warden Stormcrown?"

She shot him a teasing grin, and he returned a smirk. "Micah is fine, thief Navaeya." She gave a small laugh before turning towards the open doorway.

"Goodnight," Micah called after her.

At the doorframe, she stopped, spinning to face him as he moved to the couch. A small but threatening smile played at her lips.

"Don't get any ideas about creeping into my room, Warden," she cheerfully warned. "There are simply so many places to hide a knife. Goodnight!"

Micah stared after her in shock and confusion as she whisked around, quickly throwing her bedroom door shut. The bolt locked with a loud click.

Shaking his head, he stretched his damp legs out on the wide couch, the fireplace still crackling across the table. Micah's entire body flooded with exhaustion as he pulled up the warm covers. Even on the rickety lump, he was immensely grateful for the peaceful safety of what could be his last night.

Please Elowë, he silently prayed, *lead us safely through* Starkhaven. *Show me how to end this curse.*

CHAPTER 41
POINT OF NO RETURN

A soft thump jolted Micah awake. The dingy living room was dark and quiet, the faint sounds of Stonecroft stirring outside the tired house as gentle morning light crept in through the cracks.

Another thump.

He rose from the couch, his joints aching from a night on its rough frame. He looked over and noticed Navaeya's door was still shut.

Micah grabbed his gear from the floor, strapping it back over his mostly dried clothes before roaming into the kitchen on the opposite side of the house. A few shaky cabinets with barely attached doors supported a cracked wooden counter. In the corner of the counter, a wide, clay bowl filled with water rested below an odd spout cut into the ceiling. A small cabinet beside it held a few remnants of edible food.

"Grab whatever you want."

He turned to find Navaeya entering the room. Her hair was tied back in the same style as before, still perfectly shaped. Her dark clothes were covered with the same piecework leather armor. She tugged down a corner of her shirt while clasping the exotic sword to her belt, her bow and quiver slung across her back.

Micah grabbed an only partly molded chunk of bread and an apple, watching as she retrieved her own meal. After scarfing down the stale food, he returned to the couch, throwing on his boots while Navaeya paced anxiously.

"Ready?"

He nodded.

Together, they slipped out of the house, and she locked the door. Navaeya rested a hand on its worn shape, lost in thought, before shaking her head and whisking around.

They reached the gate long before most of Stonecroft had woken. A tired sentry above watched as they approached. The young soldier rested a mailed arm on her battered spear, dusty hair poking from beneath a light helm gleaming in the stirring light.

"Heading out early today, eh, Navaeya?" she called.

"You never know, might catch the Mist napping!"

The woman laughed as two other Guardsmen pulled the gates open.

Micah and Navaeya hurried down the cobblestone road, the weak morning sun rising in a cold sky. The stormy clouds from the night before had scattered in its rays, though the smell of damp earth hung in the air. Near midmorning, they caught a glimpse of Starkhaven across the golden plains, its white stone spires glistening above the immense cloud of Mist blanketing the capital.

Instead of following the road, Navaeya darted to the left, cutting through a grove of young evergreens and eventually stumbling into the remains of an old crop field. Ahead of them, a large, pale farmhouse stood crumbling near a section of the city jutting out from the towering, sickly blue Mist.

"Where are we going?" Micah whispered. She didn't answer.

At the edge of the creaking house, Navaeya peered out, looking for any of the Mist's fearsome monsters. Satisfied the area was clear, they snuck around the weathered boards, slipping towards a modest wood and brick storefront closer to the city's edge. A faint haze of Mist rolled around the corners of the abandoned building.

Inside lay an array of farming tools scattered across the room. Shovels, rakes, and hoes sat in forgotten, dusty rows along the store's shelves while piles of rough sacks, heavy ropes, and horse tack rested on long tables and atop low beams above the shelving. An oversized doorway on the side of the shop emptied onto a wide cobblestone street where a couple of small houses marked the city's end. An embankment dipped behind them where a large stone drainage channel ran off to the east and south, heading towards its eventual end in Stark Bay.

Navaeya prowled towards the opening, eyeing the silent buildings where the Mist curled threateningly. The deadly cloud scattered the sun's bright rays over a graveyard of broken wagons and splintered merchant carts strewn along the desolate street.

She turned, her brilliant, serious eyes boring into Micah.

"Last chance," she whispered. "You sure you want to do this?"

Micah stared at the wall of Mist waiting beyond the decaying structures. Images of Elisa and Samuel flashed through his mind, their smiling faces a tender reminder of an aching loss. He shifted to friends from Fairhollow—Gerar, Delvin, Rila, and Tala. The dangerous yet comforting time he had spent amongst them. Last, he thought of Kelj. The pain of that final moment laced with bittersweet respect and friendship born where it was once unlooked for. He couldn't turn back, not for their sakes.

"Yes."

Navaeya nodded, breathing deeply.

"Stay low, stay quiet," she commanded. "Right behind me. Not a word until I say so."

He nodded obediently.

She whirled back, eyeing the Mist one last time.

"This way."

Navaeya leapt from the shadowed doorway, sprinting for the opposite side of the road and taking cover alongside a cracked wagon. Micah dashed after her as she rounded its back end, watching the road before slipping beside an overturned cart. From there, she angled towards the last house on the row before the road trekked into the empty fields and farmhouses to the east.

Where are you going? thought Micah. *The city's the other way.*

In a blink, Navaeya disappeared beside the collapsing porch along a narrow timber home, riddled with cracks and holes in its dark wooden exterior. She leapt down the rocky slope towards the muddy drainage channel. He followed, slipping into the gorge shadowed by silent, looming houses.

As they reached the damp, dirty floor of the channel, Navaeya straightened, relaxing slightly. A high wall of massive stone bricks, too high to scale, supported an outer road of the capital bordering the channel's far side. A few howls from prowling Mist Wolves echoed faintly within the enclosure, the sources hidden deep in the city proper. She cast a hesitant look at the wall as they crept along the old waterway, twisting beneath the lofty ruins above.

Several paces into the canal, the faint Mist of the capital's border gave way to a thick pocket of the suffocating smog. Except for the buildings along the channel, the city vanished from view. Navaeya skirted a large mound of dirt and debris from a crumbling building above. Micah followed, only to stifle a gasp and flinch back as a pair of dark, empty sockets stared at him from a human skull, half-buried in the muck. Navaeya shot him a scowl as he hurried after her.

After a sharp curve, the walled channel ended, an intersecting street above cutting a route farther into Starkhaven. A huge, circular opening loomed in the stone blocks supporting the street, a faint trickle of water dripping through its warped iron bars. Navaeya looked at Micah with a teasing grin.

"Hope you're not afraid of getting wet," she whispered before slinking towards the grate.

An old access hatch along one side sat ajar, its metal bars fused in place by years of rust. Navaeya curved around the door, and Micah followed, climbing the stone incline along the sewer's rounded wall. The foul stench of rank water and decaying refuse slammed into Micah's senses, hanging in the breezeless air. A short trench ran through the muddy center of the tunnel where a soggy channel trickled its way out into the Misty air. Past the entrance, the shaft disappeared into the shadows.

Navaeya reached into a pile of wooden rubble, her small hand finding a hidden torch. Micah grabbed his flint and handed it over. After a few strikes, the end caught, a tender flame awakening the dank sewer walls with a glistening sheen as the light danced across the moist bricks.

"We're clear for the moment, if we're quiet," Navaeya softly explained. "These sewers stretch all across Starkhaven. I've found a few exits to the Market District, and one that *might* lead to the Government District. Everything beyond that will be uncharted territory."

"So, this is how you get around the capital safely," he realized, admiring the woman's cleverness.

"For the most part. But you'd be a fool to think these are safe," Navaeya warned, her warm eyes unusually stern. "Mist Wolves also blunder into the tunnels, searching for who knows what. From here on out, we have to be extremely careful. We'll run out of room fast in a fight."

Micah nodded. "Lead on then."

Torch in hand, Navaeya stepped along the narrow ledge, moving into the passage before vanishing around a corner in the tunnel. Micah glanced back, watching the last light of the outside world disappear as the murky sewers swallowed them.

◆

The Mist slowly lessened the deeper they traveled into the gloomy tunnel, following its twisting course beneath the city streets. Beyond the soft crackle of the torch and interminable dripping of water, the sewers were conspicuously still. They passed several junctions where additional passages trailed away into the void, their mouths briefly illuminated by passing flame as Navaeya bounded across the gaps. After rounding a gentle turn, a dim light filtered through a grate in the road above, revealing a massive exchange ahead. As their tunnel joined the fray, Navaeya slowed, her back brushing against Micah's chest as she leaned towards him.

"We're below Merchant's Row," she whispered. "Lots of Trolls over us."

He glanced up nervously.

Merchant's Row was the largest and most popular marketplace in Starkhaven. A colossal span of open squares covered in a sea of street vendors and shops for both the working and upper classes. It was one of the rare places people from all walks of society came together, enjoying the wondrous goods of the vast world beyond their island home.

A wide pool shimmered below the faint light passing through the grate. Mist swirled through the opening, groping lazily as it lurched down into the sewer before curling back towards the ceiling. Navaeya scanned the circular room, her gaze lingering on the veiled opening of each tunnel branching off along the walls. A series of narrow stone bridges formed a connected ring around the rim of the sewer basin. She turned right, crossing the bridges and glancing at each opening they passed. At the fourth passage, she stopped, rubbing her dark glove against a damp stone near her waist. Squinting through the gloom, Micah spotted a thin, white arrow scratched on the surface of the brownish gray brick. She motioned him over and leaned into his ear again.

"This is the one with the exit to the Government District. I think," she whispered.

"You *think*?"

"Well, it's not like I come traipsing through here every day," she muttered indignantly. "I haven't had a job pay well enough for me to risk finding out what's up there. But given the other points I've discovered, this one should line up with the district's northern edge."

"What if we need to go farther?" he quietly asked.

"Then we either follow the tunnels deeper or find a way across the Circle of the Conclave. But I'd only recommend that if you're willing to take on a horde of shrieking Mist demons," she cautioned.

"The ones with magic?" Micah asked, Hillmarch briefly crossing his mind.

She nodded grimly.

"I hate Mist Wraiths."

"Sewers it is," she declared with a smile. "Someone owes me a nice, warm bath after this."

Navaeya took off, creeping along the ledge of the new tunnel, much like their previous one. A steady stream of foul water trickled through the passage's canal, muffling their footsteps and filling the shaft with its rank smell. As the tunnel intersected with additional waterways, Navaeya made a series of turns, following a winding route through the darkened sewers. Micah quickly found himself lost in the capital's sunken labyrinth, completely reliant on the mysterious woman guiding him.

After a while of following a single tunnel, she slowed, falling beside him.

"Should only be a few more turns," she whispered. "There'll be a ladder on our right that—"

A grunting growl reverberated off the tunnel ahead, and they froze. Micah reached for his holster, only to find his trusty pistol absent.

Oh, right.

He grasped the leathered hilt of his sword instead.

Another growl echoed in the dark, followed by an angry snarl.

Mist Wolves!

Navaeya carefully stepped back, tugging at Micah's shirt before reaching for her own sword. He retreated, still staring into the void in front of them as the two Wolves continued quarreling. Suddenly, his foot struck an object, nearly sending him into the dank water. His gut twisted in fear as the rocky surface shifted beside his ankle.

Splash.

The growling stopped. Micah glanced down, watching a ring of waves spread across the surface of the water. Navaeya bent down, extinguishing her torch in it.

The tunnel instantly went black.

A low growl emanated from somewhere as the clicking of Wolf claws entered the passage. Navaeya's hand groped for his, pulling him away from the water and into a narrow recess in the slick wall. Micah could feel the warmth of her trembling body pressed against his as the cold, clammy stone seeped into his back.

The growl continued, followed by another snuffling Wolf, the sounds growing as the pair moved closer. Micah moved his hand back to his hunting knife, sliding it from the sheath at his thigh. Navaeya's breath stopped, the beasts' threatening sounds closing in. His fingers twitched as he gripped the knife tighter, his cheek pressed against the cold stone as he stared vainly into the dark.

The snarling stopped.

The sewer fell deathly silent, Micah's ears straining to catch any hint of sound.

Nothing.

He felt trapped, smothered by the menacing gloom.

I have to do something.

He closed his eyes, attempting to still his mind in the tense darkness. Micah thought back to Kelj's lessons, calming his breath and his frenzied emotions. As Micah's world slowed, he summoned Elisa's memory to steady his mind. Her loving face and touch filled his thoughts, allowing the barrier to form around his mind as it recalled Kelj's words. Instinctively, he felt the spark of magic bloom at the edge of his consciousness. It drew closer, the fibers of his being entwining with its limitless power. Micah immediately felt his body relax, the power pulsing just beneath his skin. Navaeya lightly nudged him, worried.

With his energy focused, Micah took a step out of the nook, extending a hand into the void like he had in Hillmarch. An orb of white light sprang into existence, exploding across the tunnel. His eyes recoiled at the sight, but not before spotting two Mist Wolves prowling on either side of the watery trench, one only a few steps away.

"What are you doing?" Navaeya gasped in horror.

The Wolves shrank back, whimpering and shielding the horrid pits of their burning eyes. The one beside Micah recovered, locking its beady pupils on him. It raised an arm of patchy, gray fur, its gleaming claws extended as it howled in rage. Micah lunged, lashing out with his knife before the Wolf could strike. The tempered blade sliced across its forearm, and the beast stumbled, yelping in agony. Its companion snarled, doubling back towards a narrow bridge leading over the canal to their side.

"Run!" Micah yelled.

Navaeya's hair whipped around her face as she spun, sprinting down the tunnel. Micah raced after her, his bright orb casting a frenzy of shadows on the dull stone.

"*You have magic?*" Navaeya shouted furiously. "Why didn't you tell me you had magic?"

"Later!"

A chorus of howls erupted as the Wolves stumbled in confusion. To Micah's dismay, another mass of howls burst from the passage where the Wolves had appeared.

There's more of them!

The sewer exploded with a deafening horde of howls, snarls, and yelps as the pack gave chase, breathing at Micah's heels as he and Navaeya dashed through the maze of tunnels. Navaeya led him on a twisting route along the dangerous paths, leaping over crumbling bridges and taking sudden turns to try to lose the Wolves, to no avail. After sprinting through several passages, they found themselves back in a large sewer exchange. A set of small openings in the ceiling dumped gushing water into the central basin, the waterfalls only adding to the thunderous noise as the Wolves neared the chamber.

"This way!" Navaeya yelled, heading for a tunnel on the far side.

"Where are we going?" Micah shouted.

"No idea!"

Just as he slipped into the shadowed opening, the pack reached the exchange, furiously searching for their scent. He took off after Navaeya as she bounded through another passage, deftly avoiding spots where the ancient stone had collapsed into the murky water. After several more turns, angry howls rang off the cold stone of the shaft, the Wolves closing in.

Another tunnel appeared, and Navaeya slipped around the corner. Micah dashed around the turn, narrowly avoiding a collision with her back. Ahead of them, a wide, stone platform spanned a deep drainage trench. Four Wolves, pawing at debris littering the moldy floor, leapt up in surprise. The leader, a massive Wolf with a healthy-looking coat of brown, let out a gleeful howl.

"Back, back!" Micah hollered, pushing himself between the Wolves and Navaeya. They turned, sprinting back down the sewer passage. As they leapt across the intersecting trenches, the first pack of Wolves barreled around the corner, nearly colliding with the newcomers. The din of howls grew to an ear-splitting level as they ran through the dark corridor, searching wildly for an escape.

Just ahead, the dank passage made an abrupt turn, Micah's feet sliding on the slick stone and nearly sending him into the muddy channel. As he struggled to regain his footing, Navaeya scrambled up a rusty ladder set into the curving stone wall. A shrouded gap in the ceiling revealed a hatch to the surface. He raced over, flinging himself at the rough bars and clambering after her. A faint light appeared above as Navaeya shoved the heavy metal grate out of the way, and Micah extinguished his orb.

As he reached for the last rung, the Wolves tore around the corner below, spotting his flailing boots. The leader let out a wrathful howl, launching its massive shape into the air and aiming its piercing claws at his legs. Micah scurried up, narrowly escaping the sharp claws that clattered against the metal. The monster wailed in rage as Navaeya dragged Micah out of the hole and into a swirling haze of Mist. Looking down, his blood ran cold as the Wolf recovered, then began clambering up the ladder.

"Cover it!" Navaeya cried.

Micah lunged for the metal grate, grunting as he pulled the heavy disc over the gap. Another fist of jagged claws shot upward as he struggled to seal the drain, but the Wolf was too late. The grate dropped into the opening with a shuddering clang. Micah collapsed, watching as Navaeya shoved a heavy-looking wooden cart towards the drain. The metal cover rumbled ominously. She groaned, pushing the cart over it, and it tumbled onto the hatch with a loud crash. Beneath the mass of cracked wood and metal, a dull clanging continued, but the rubble refused to budge.

They looked at each other with wild eyes before Micah fell back onto the cold pavement, gasping for air.

"Too close."

Chapter 42
Starkhaven

Micah stood, shaking with adrenaline and from his use of magic, as Navaeya steadied her hands on her knees, breathing hard. As strength slowly returned, he surveyed the area, trying to make sense of it. Beyond the bright stone pavement and smothering cloud of Mist, the faint outlines of timbered and pale plastered buildings surrounded the small enclosure. Narrow gaps between them beckoned with darkened paths as the alleys disappeared into the unknown. A few twisted trees, their dead branches jutting through the thick Mist, lined the edges of the courtyard.

"Where are we?" Micah panted.

Navaeya straightened, collecting herself and analyzing the abandoned lane.

"Not a clue," she answered tiredly. "An alleyway?"

He crept through the groping Mist towards one of the shrouded buildings. Its smooth, pale brick towered several stories above him, casting a long shadow in the dim daylight. Peering into the passageway between the silent structures, he faintly discerned the alley's end, emptying onto a street beyond. Hugging the cold blocks, Micah hesitantly edged his way towards the open space.

"Where are you going?" Navaeya furiously hissed.

At the corner of the street, he stopped, carefully peering around the stone wall into the gloomy Mist. A row of desolate storefronts lined the narrow street, many of the glistening windows and doorways shattered and broken. Signs for a bakery, butcher, and alchemist creaked ominously in the swirling fog. Several other obscured signs dangled from broken hooks in the gloom before Micah's line of sight faded into the sickly blue void. He snuck back to where Navaeya waited with a disapproving stare.

"Well?" she grumbled, folding her arms over her dark shirt.

"Storefronts. We must still be somewhere in the Market District."

Navaeya cursed under her breath.

"I knew I shouldn't have taken that turn."

The roar of a Mist Troll broke the alley's tomblike silence, making them both jump.

"We need to get our bearings, fast," said Micah. Navaeya scanned the shadowy circle, another roar echoing through the passageways as the beast lumbered closer.

"There." She pointed to a small door on one of the far buildings Micah hadn't noticed in the heavy Mist.

They hurried over to the weathered entry, its rusted latch stubbornly giving way with a loud groan. Slipping inside, they were immediately greeted by a darkened storeroom. Shelves of dusty boxes and spider webs lined the walls of the tiny space before a doorway opened to a small, quiet shop. Inside, a handful of delicate glass shelves and wooden tables were stacked with assortments of glassware, utensils, and tea boxes atop a thinly carpeted floor. A short oak counter separated the back room and a small kitchen from the wares on display, the various hues of colored glass sparkling faintly in the light filtering through the grimy front window. Directly across from the store's entry, a small stairway led to a second floor.

Micah and Navaeya carefully wove through the precarious mounds of glass, heading for the stairs in hopes of gaining a vantage over the shroud covering Starkhaven. After ascending the creaky boards, they found themselves in a quaint tearoom overlooking the street. Small sets of parlor tables and chairs dotted the cozy space. Dusty teacups and saucers covered the tables, as if their owners had left for a brief stretch and never returned. The only object out of place was a single overturned table near the stairwell. A half-opened door jutted out from the papered wall on the far side. As Navaeya wandered the room, Micah moved to the door, coaxing the gnarled wood open with a gentle groan to reveal another set of darkened stairs. He shot her an impatient look.

She shrugged. "Nothing of value here, anyway."

Micah placed a tentative foot on the first stair, spying a hint of light below the thin door at the top. His boots creaked loudly in the cramped space as he climbed, fostering fears that he'd assuredly drawn monsters lurking in the streets below. After jostling the loose doorknob at the top, the door opened to a small living space with a set of closed rooms off a short hall. Mist obscured the buildings beyond the room's windows, though not as thickly as below.

"Look." Navaeya nodded, moving to a narrow door in the corner. Yet another set of rickety stairs. At the top, Navaeya thrust open the heavy door and foggy daylight burst onto the stairs. They found themselves on the roof of the teashop, the flat surface providing a mostly clear view of the other storefronts and of the alley behind. It was then that Micah finally got a better sense of the state of the capital.

The wide street below the shop was littered with rubble and abandoned carts. Micah spotted the pale, sickening form of bony remains mixed into the debris, scattered victims of the Mist's assault. Charred and withered trees dotted the edges of the road—any signs of growth destroyed long ago. Buildings lining the thoroughfare sat in various states of disorder. While some were relatively intact, sporting only moderately damaged windows or doors, most had sustained heavier injury. Many had lost entire banks of windows that once displayed their goods or had wide, gaping holes in the wood and stone exteriors. Some had been reduced to ruined heaps, their upper floors collapsed in a mountain of rubble. A small blacksmith's shop at the far end barely stood amongst its cracked columns supporting another floor above. A watchmaker's storefront, where incredible devices powered by exotic iluvan from the Hamid Empire were once sold in their growing popularity, was completely gutted, the remains of display cases strewn across the street. Another mound of rubble sat silently, one section down. The only distinguishing feature left was a freestanding sign emblazoned with the words *Hadri's Magical Wares*, over a curling flame.

"Even the lamp makers got a share," Navaeya sadly observed, nodding towards a store where items from simple lanterns to iluvan-powered candelabras were sold. "You see it, though, right?"

"See what?"

"The pattern," Navaeya explained impatiently. "Where the Mist hit the hardest. Look." She pointed to the various ruins.

"The stores where iluvan was present got the worst of it. Like the monsters are drawn to the stuff."

"You're right. Even the streetlights are gone."

In the early days, when iluvan was growing more commonplace, the capital had spent a lavish sum to import the simple, yet miraculous lights to brighten its dim streets. The power of the iluvan virtually guaranteed they would remain lit forever. Except now the only remains were an occasional base of iron jutting from the cracked cobblestone, the tips of the modest lamps twisted off and scattered to Elowë only knows where.

"I wonder if that's why the Mist is so heavy here. Not just all the people, but also all the iluvan," Micah mused with a growing realization. "Starkhaven housed the majority of the nation's crystal. There's a reason people saw the capital as a technological wonder. Maybe there's some arcane connection between the Mist and the crystals."

"Of all the harebrained theories I've heard since coming here, yours might be the sanest." Navaeya grinned. "Except that bit about a glowing tower."

"Well, I guess we'll find out," he lightly retorted. "Now then... Where are we?"

Micah looked above the desolate buildings, watching the Mist writhing high above the street. Occasionally, a gust of wind or another unseen force separated the thick blanket, offering a glimpse of the sky. After several minutes of waiting, he finally spotted something.

"There!" Micah shouted triumphantly.

To the right, a cloud of Mist shifted ever so slightly, revealing a gleaming spire in the haze. A bright glimmer of glass sparkled in the daylight at the top, ringed by shining white stone. As quickly as it had appeared, the tower vanished as the Mist curled back on itself.

"What was it?" Navaeya asked.

"Tar'auth Ben. The Circle of the Conclave at the center of the Government District. I'd know that spire from anywhere."

"Based on what I know of the city, and guessing at the distance, I'd say we're right at the edge of the three districts," she replied. "Which means you have a choice."

Micah leaned back from the brick wall at the roof's edge, looking at Navaeya as she pushed a curling strand of hair out of her face.

"Which way to your enchanted tower, oh mighty wizard?" She smirked. "Right or left?"

He looked back at the street, eyeing each end as it dissolved into the rolling Mist. The Voice's vision whispered in the corners of his mind, the curious tower shifting behind its shroud of light. Instinctively, Micah knew his choice.

"Left," he declared.

"The Upper District?"

"It has to be."

"If you say so," Navaeya slowly complied. "Well then. If we're at the edge of the Market District, we can't be far from the river."

"Correct," said Micah, recalling the canal separating the majestic estates of the Upper District from the rest of the city. "I say we head down to the other end of the street. Maybe find an alley that'll get us close—"

A howl emanated from below.

Navaeya whipped out her bow, both of them creeping to the edge for a better look. With his eyes barely above the short stone wall, Micah caught a glimpse of a Mist Wolf prowling near the shop's corner. Seconds after the first howl, an answering call rose from somewhere down the street.

"Reinforcements," he muttered.

"We need to get out of here, fast," Navaeya furiously whispered.

They snuck back to the stairs, moving towards the ground floor as quietly as they could. Back in the tearoom above the shop, a wicked crack resounded from the floor below, like the front door snapping under the massive weight of a Mist Wolf.

"Up, up," Micah urged, pressing gently into the back of Navaeya's leather armor as they retreated up the stairs. At the top, he gingerly pulled the door shut before a cascade of breaking glass erupted in the shop, the barks of three Mist Wolves echoing in surprise as one overturned a table.

Micah and Navaeya hurriedly crept to the closed doors in the living quarters, hoping for access to the adjacent building, only to find a set of bedrooms and a small bathroom. A faint scratching rose from the door to the lower stairs.

"The roof," Navaeya softly snapped.

After twisting up the narrow stairs to the roof again, Micah pulled the heavy door closed, sliding an old rain barrel in front of it.

"What now?" he said, exasperated.

Navaeya climbed onto the short brick partition neighboring the adjacent structure.

"How are you at jumping?" she asked forebodingly.

"Um, what do you mean?"

Something from the floor below them cracked, followed by a yelp reverberating behind the closed door.

"Guess we'll find out!"

Before he could respond, she leapt off the ledge.

"Navaeya!" Micah cried, rushing to the wall.

He collided with the rough stone, afraid of what might lie beyond. Thankfully, he quickly spotted the nimble thief standing safely on the roof of the next building. He gripped the cold rock, staring nervously at the narrow alley separating the teashop from the next roof a half-story below.

"It's not far!" Navaeya called quietly. "Just jump!"

"I'm... not great with heights." Micah jerked around as the heavy door at the other end of the roof began to shudder. "Okay, okay."

He shakily climbed onto the ledge, struggling to balance in the faint gust blowing through the tendrils of Mist. Navaeya watched with a nervous look. He took a deep breath, bending his knees while still eyeing the precarious drop threatening to render him a lifeless puddle nearly four stories down. Micah's legs tensed, preparing every ounce of force he could to launch himself across the chasm.

Crack!

The ancient barrel behind him careened across the roof as a huge, mottled Wolf shoved open the beaten door. Micah twisted around to lock with beady, dark-ringed eyes, scowling in hatred. It let out a piercing howl, splitting the silent street.

"Jump!" Navaeya yelled.

Micah hurtled from the ledge as the Wolf raced across the roof. His stomach dropped as his body flew across the gap, unbound from the anchor of solid ground. A horrible fear swelled inside him.

I'm not going to make it.

A moment later, his feet stumbled as they smashed into the hard surface of the other roof, his wobbly legs unable to compensate. With an agile swipe, Navaeya grabbed his chest, catching him before he gracelessly planted his face into the ground. They turned around, watching as the Wolf peered down at them from the teashop. It let out an enraged howl, unwilling to risk a similar leap. The head of another furious Wolf joined the first, their horrid eyes boring into Micah and Navaeya before vanishing from the ledge. Across the Mist-shrouded rooftops, the roar of a Mist Troll answered the Wolves' indignant calls.

"They'll find a way," Navaeya panted. "We have to move, now!"

Micah scanned the area, looking for access to the building below. Unlike the teashop, the slate roof was devoid of any distinguishing features.

They raced across the worn structure towards the next house, relieved to find the series of buildings ahead were all evenly connected. Near the end of the rooftops, a small stone spire jutted from the corner of the last house, containing a slender doorway on its rear.

Side by side, they hurdled over the first ledge dividing the roofs, sprinting through the Mist coiling over the desolate stone. A multitude of howls erupted from the street below, Wolves racing alongside in pursuit.

As Micah leapt over to the next store, his feet nearly slid through a crumbling hole into a room beneath. He rolled to the side, tumbling onto the cracked roof beside the pit, breathing hard. Navaeya pulled him up, and they swerved across the decaying roof, weaving along the patchwork surface between more gaps exposing the shadowy ruins.

Ahead of them, the Mist Troll roared again, closer.

"This won't be good," Micah gasped, vaulting over another wall. Navaeya grunted in agreement as he focused on the doorway, only a building away.

They sprinted across the solid ground, scaling onto the final roof. Navaeya raced ahead, heading for the weathered wooden hatch. Mere paces from the door, a terrifying crack split the roof. Micah's feet stumbled as the battered stone broke, fissures rushing in all directions as tiny chunks began to fall. Navaeya thrust the door open as the roof gave way, a large splinter crashing through the top floor. Nowhere to go, he jumped, barely clearing the gap as the last of the roof collapsed. They dove into the rickety stairwell, tumbling down the worn stairs as the sound of raining rock drowned out the world. They burst into a musty living space just as a massive square of the ceiling plowed into a stained fabric sofa in the center. Huge cracks ripped across the walls, small glass windows cracking as the entire structure started to fail.

"Down!" Navaeya shouted above the noise.

They swung around the stairwell to the bottom floor, bounding down the creaking boards as a threatening roar consumed the building. A shower of dust and debris rained from the ceiling as they spilled into a ruined shop. Through the chaos, Micah barely registered the racks of fine clothing and cloaks as they sprinted towards the battered entrance, daylight streaming through a spray of filth spewing out of the shop. Halfway across the busted floor, an ear-splitting boom shook the central pillar, the thick stone buckling under the weight of the imploding floors. He raced onto the street after Navaeya just as the windows along the storefront exploded, sending a shower of gleaming shards onto the street. With a deafening shriek, the entire structure caved, rock and boards flying as a cloud of debris raced towards the earth. A building away, the pack of Wolves halted in fear, the thunderous calamity splitting the ground and sending a plume of smoke into the air. Mist whipped past as the dirty cloud displaced the deathly fog, briefly obscuring the Wolves. Micah and Navaeya quickly fled, dashing towards a wide intersection.

As they reached the crossroads, a looming warehouse of dark, damaged brick appeared on their right, across from an open-air market of covered patios and ruined merchant stands. A short row of tiny shops ran along the northern side, the street littered with twisted rubble and shattered glass, enclosing the graveyard-like square.

Micah rushed around the corner of the warehouse, squinting to see through the thick Mist. A booming roar immediately rattled the road, stopping him in his tracks. The Mist ahead of him swirled violently.

Thud, thud, thud.

The cobblestones beneath Micah's feet vibrated, and his terror rose with each pounding blast.

"Uh oh," Navaeya muttered.

Through the dense fog, a towering shape began to take form.

"Back!" Micah yelled, spinning around. The quaking intensified as the thuds quickened, closing in.

The Mist Troll let out another hair-raising roar, its smooth, gray hide lumbering out of the Mist. Burning eyes fixed on them as they swerved around the warehouse. Micah halted once he rounded the structure, spotting the Mist Wolves heading straight for the market as the shop's destruction subsided.

"This way!" he shouted, grabbing Navaeya's arm and pulling her towards the ruined warehouse. They slipped through a narrow gap in the large iron loading doors, entering the gloomy building. The Troll and Wolves cried in dismay as their prey disappeared.

Faint beams of light drifted into the cavernous room through its fractured ceiling. Pockets of hazy Mist wrapped around endless rows of crates and shelves of boxes, giving the warehouse a similarly eerie feeling to the one he and Kelj had traversed in Greenwatch. Except for the immense, creaking beams high above, the building was silent.

BOOM!

The giant door behind them shuddered on its track as the Troll's fist hammered the metal. A Mist Wolf stopped to sniff at the gap between the door and the brick, slowly squeezing its way in. Micah and Navaeya dashed into the sea of cargo without a second look.

Immediately, they were surrounded by spires of crates, following narrow aisles weaving uneven paths through the abandoned goods. Each time they passed a short stack of boxes, Micah peered over, hoping to spot an exit from the warehouse, only to find more rows of dusty shelves blocking his view.

A loud howl, followed by another, filled the air, echoing over the mounds.

The Wolves were in.

The warehouse door rattled again as the Troll pounded away. Micah looked up, judging them to be a little over halfway through the structure.

"It won't last much longer," he whispered to Navaeya as they crept around a collapsed row of shelving.

"Then we'd better find another door before that Troll rips the building to shreds," she hissed.

Rushing down a line of worn crates, he paused at a narrow gap between two boxes draped in tattered cloth. An iron stairwell led to a catwalk just beyond a couple of rows of identical containers.

"Navaeya, here," Micah softly called out.

They squeezed through the opening, dashing across the exposed floor. The ancient metal grated loudly under their boots as they mounted the stairs, surely drawing the relentless Wolves. As they climbed, Micah noticed the iron catwalk wrapped around the majority of the warehouse, providing a view of the sea of crates below. A wide band of light streamed into the building through a massive hole in the far end, the catwalk along that wall reduced to twisted poles poking through a mountain of brick. If there had been a door on that end, it was lost under the ruin.

An ear-splitting shriek jolted the warehouse. Micah watched in horror as a massive iron door flew off its track, smashing into the first rows of boxes and sending a torrent of crates crashing. The Mist Troll roared, its hulking form crouching to enter the warehouse in search of them. A frenzy of howls erupted from the labyrinth below.

Micah and Navaeya tore down the catwalk, the metal floor ringing out and drawing the gaze of the Troll. A horrible cracking sound exploded behind them, the Troll swatting towers of weighty crates like pesky flies as it charged towards them. The Wolves flitted in and out of sight as they wove through the warehouse, marking their escape.

"There's no door!" he called out as Navaeya sprinted towards the far end.

"Good thing someone already made an exit for us!"

As they reached the end of the building, Micah realized the gaping hole in the wall was higher than he thought, the mound of rubble still far below the opening. Luckily, the fissure was just level with the catwalk where a twisted remnant of the iron floor ended at the edge of the opening. Navaeya breezed around the turn, heading straight for the gap. At the last moment, she leapt out, swinging over the damaged bricks and slipping through the hole. A Wolf cried out in fury as its quarry vanished from view.

Behind Micah, the Troll roared in anger; the catwalk swaying dangerously as the beast barreled towards him. Following Navaeya's example, he ran to the edge of the rickety metal, jumping out and grabbing the crumbling remains of the brick. With a heavy grunt, he hoisted himself over the wall, swinging his legs into the air. Then he noticed the drop. As Micah released his hold on the brick, he twisted around, landing hard on the packed earth and collapsing in an awkward roll to absorb the impact. Navaeya waited a few steps away, helping him to his feet after he tumbled to a stop.

"I should charge extra for catching you every time." She grinned, a wild look flashing in her dark eyes.

"You'll be lucky to make it out of here with anything at—"

A chorus of howls echoed through the gap in the wall, the furious pack searching for a way through.

"Let's get out of here," she finished.

They raced down a wide alley between the warehouses, heading back towards the desolate square. At the street, Micah discovered the market stretched farther than he thought, the closest buildings still several blocks away. Their left led back to the warehouse and row of shops from before, filled with the sound of more Wolves closing in from that direction. He looked to the right, and for a moment, the Mist painted a confusing picture. Then he grasped what lay ahead.

The canal!

A wide, stone bridge with ornate walls of ruined steel rose out of the Mist, the haze shrouding the far end from view but leaving enough to recognize the gap dividing the Market and Upper Districts.

Suddenly, the hole in the warehouse behind Micah exploded, a shower of brick and dust erupting as the Troll's massive fist pulverized the weathered stone. A lone Wolf sprinted out of the cloud, its ruddy body heading straight for them.

The Troll stumbled out of the rubble behind it.

"What I wouldn't give for my pistol," he muttered angrily.

"Over the bridge!" Navaeya shouted, and they raced down the street beside the decrepit buildings.

Glancing back, Micah noticed the furious Wolf quickly gaining in the open air. Farther in the Mist, the pounding Troll struggled to keep up. As they reached the bridge, panting hard, he looked at Navaeya.

"The Wolf!" Micah gasped.

The creature howled in delight, nearly upon them.

He gripped his sword, a single, clear note ringing out as he unsheathed its deadly edge. Navaeya retreated onto the bridge, reaching for an arrow. Micah raised his blade, digging in his feet as the Wolf bore down on him.

Mere paces away, the matted beast snarled violently, launching into the air with gleaming claws, its snout of razor-sharp teeth exposed in a wicked grin. Micah ducked, rolling to the side as the Wolf sailed past, fruitlessly swiping the air. At the same moment, a soft twang echoed from Navaeya's bow, a gleaming arrow splitting the heavy fog.

The Wolf landed hard, yelping in anguish as the arrow buried into its shoulder. Its gaze immediately flicked to Navaeya as she rummaged for another bolt. The Wolf rose, preparing to chase after her as she backed farther onto the bridge. With a furious yell, Micah rushed the beast, recapturing its attention.

A row of razor-like claws clashed against his gleaming blade, the unnatural peal ringing through the Mist. The Wolf growled, swiping with its other hand. He leapt back, its puncturing tips mere inches from his gut. A second arrow buried itself in the creature's back, its patchy jaw releasing another pained cry. The Troll roared in response, drawing closer.

With the Wolf weakened, Micah struck again, landing a bloody cut across the beast's arm. It howled in agony, stumbling back. With a final, desperate lunge, he thrust his blade into the Wolf's shaggy chest; the howl ending in a squeaky whoosh as its final breath escaped. The Wolf's massive corpse crumpled to the ground, lifeless.

Micah glanced at Navaeya, her face smiling in triumph.

Suddenly, the Troll roared in Micah's ear, its hulking shape blasting out of the Mist as it charged the bridge. Micah sprinted after Navaeya as she fled over the shaking road, the raging behemoth looming behind him. He quickly realized there was no escaping this one.

Halfway across, he turned, facing the maddened beast as it bellowed again. It slowed as he paused, its bare skin gleaming strangely in the enveloping Mist. Micah's heart pounded in his chest. Every fiber of his being screamed for him to run. The Troll took a wrathful step forward, a snarl of broken teeth thundering at Micah's defiance as he raised his sword. The bridge shifted beneath him, a large crack splitting the cobblestone under the Troll's massive, rounded foot.

"Come on!" Micah yelled.

Enraged, the Troll stomped closer, the bridge cracking under its enormous weight. The beast raised its colossal hands, preparing to splatter his puny body into the ground. With a terrible roar, its fists came crashing down. Micah leapt to the side, the whistling blast slamming into the rock and sending the chunk of bridge sailing into the swirling water below.

Scores of cracks rushed from the gaping hole. The entire bridge began to shudder and rumble with an ominous sound. The Troll raised its hands, confused once it realized he was no longer there. Then it spotted him, its surprise exchanged for a scowl of pure hatred across its ugly, wrinkled face. It growled, taking another step towards Micah. The bridge cracked again, the Troll's foot shifting as more cobblestone gave way. The low rumble grew to a fever pitch, stopping the Troll in its tracks. Gaping fissures raced along the bridge around them, sending more pavement into the canal. The Troll gave a final bellow, raising another raging fist above him. In a horrible flash, the bridge split under the beast's vast weight, the cobblestone disintegrating with an appalling shriek. Micah watched in awe as the Troll's towering form was sucked into the chasm. With a terrified cry, the beast tumbled into the roiling water. A knobbly, flailing hand rose from the surface, groping for solid ground, only for more debris to smother it before vanishing forever.

Micah's shoulders slumped, his body quivering with adrenaline.

"Run!" Navaeya screamed, shaking him from his stupor.

The entire bridge shuddered dangerously, more chunks giving way as the structure crumbled. Micah sprinted towards the end, leaping over holes as more of the ground plummeted into the abyss. The road beneath him wavered, thousands of unstoppable seams splintering towards the bridge's edge only seconds away. With a great metallic groan, the center of the bridge collapsed, dragging the remaining structure into the canal. The ground disappeared, greedily pulling Micah into the watery grave. He lunged with all of his might at the far wall, groping wildly for the edge. Navaeya's firm hands grasped his own as he slammed into the side of the canal, dangling from her outstretched arms as his weight dragged her down onto the road. She cried in pain, attempting to pull him onto the jagged precipice as Micah flailed helplessly. A shower of rock and debris rained from the gaunt skeleton of the bridge beside them. Slowly, she shuffled back, bringing his hands to the ledge where he could find a hold. With her gripping his arms, Micah dragged himself up, wheezing in agony. Inch by inch, he rose above the edge, Navaeya still tugging him towards her. In an instant, he was free of the canal's clutch. The force sent him flying into Navaeya as they collapsed on the rough street, gasping for air.

"Too. Close," she wheezed, her body trembling from exertion.

"Thanks," Micah gasped, shaking.

"Anytime. Now get off!" He feebly rolled onto the stony surface beside her, staring up at the swirling Mist. Feeling gradually returned to his aching hands, and his breathing slowed, allowing him to sit. Micah reached over, pulling Navaeya up with a wobbly hand.

An abrupt howl echoed from across the canal, jolting them back to reality. Through the hazy Mist, a band of restless Wolves prowled the far bank, sniffing the remains of the bridge.

"There are other bridges," said Micah, steadying himself. "We'd better get to cover."

With a final glance at the indignant Wolves, they slipped away in the endless gloom.

Chapter 43
The Tower

As they crossed the quiet cobblestone street bordering the canal, the mass of buildings abruptly stopped. An empty void of Mist swirled ominously in front of them.

"Where are we?" Navaeya asked, slinging her bow over the rough leather protecting her shoulder.

"If I didn't know any better, I'd say this is Geirand Park," Micah replied, eyeing the desolate field. Prickly weeds covered the once-fertile ground, along with rows of brown shrubs. A plethora of dry, gnarled trees dotted the land before the Mist thickened into a solid wall.

"So, you know where we are," said Navaeya excitedly. "Finally!"

"Maybe, let's find out."

They jogged through the scraggy growth, the outlines of buildings bordering the gardens vanishing in the eerie fog as the green widened. A gigantic stone basin drifted into view as they approached the center of the grounds. They stopped at its edge, marveling at the empty channel stretching infinitely into the Mist.

"What is it?" Navaeya softly wondered.

"It used to be a pool running through the middle of the park," he explained. "Ornate fountains lined the center, and arcane lights illuminated the water through little iluvan devices. We're definitely in Geirand Park."

"The Upper District..." She grinned. "We're either the bravest, or craziest, explorers Starkhaven's ever seen."

Micah glanced over his shoulder. The Misty sky was darker than before.

"Let's find that tower," he said. "We're losing daylight."

"There'd better be treasure," Navaeya mumbled.

They continued through the ruined grounds, a faint breeze rustling the dead branches and withered grass. The world around them was completely silent, save for an occasional howl or roar in the distance. Thankfully, none of the beasts sounded close.

They stopped at the end of the park, peeking across a wide road through a row of lifeless hedges. A set of towering manors loomed across the street. The windows of the ground floors were completely shattered, though ones cut into the exquisite stone higher up were in better shape. Through the Mist, Micah noticed the door of the rightmost estate was battered in.

"So... stick to the street?" Navaeya whispered. "I doubt all these palaces are connected."

"Let's follow that one south," he replied, pointing to the road beside the manor on the right. "Hopefully, any Wolves are busy elsewhere."

Satisfied the coast was clear, they crept across the empty cobblestone. Halfway there, a dark shape in the Mist caused Micah to jump, only to reveal an abandoned carriage. As they passed the shadowed door of the crumbling manor, Navaeya paused.

"What?" he whispered, looking back.

"Just a second. I want to look inside."

"Are you mad?" he hissed.

Ignoring him, she slipped through the darkened entry. Micah followed with a frustrated growl, carefully stepping over the embellished oak door shattered on the tiled floor.

The foyer of the manor was impressive. The gilded walls above the polished tiles were covered in an array of fine paintings. A marble staircase wrapped along one side, opposite a bank of high windows overlooking the street. Through an open set of double doors, the faint outline of a massive formal room loomed in eerie darkness.

He spotted Navaeya, slowly creeping up the rich staircase towards a shrouded hall above. Micah scrambled after her, finding himself at the start of a long hall at the top. Cracked windows and tattered curtains let a wealth of light into the corridor where a faint sheen of Mist drifted across the parquet floor. He passed several doors leading to grand libraries, sitting rooms, and bedrooms before finally locating Navaeya in a large study.

Inside, rows of expensive-looking books lined one wall, a small sliding ladder providing access to higher shelves. Beyond a cozy sitting area with embroidered couches, tall, thin windows overlooked the city to the south. An immense mahogany desk surrounded by glass cases of fascinating objects and trophies marked the far end of the study.

As Micah snuck into the room, Navaeya carefully opened a grimy case filled with an assortment of valuable gems and odd instruments scattered on its velvet surface.

"Now here's a catch," she breathed, gently scooping the loot into her open bag.

"What are those?" he asked, forgetting his annoyance as he peered at an odd set of dusty, golden orbs. Each one was about the size of an apple.

"Easy coin," Navaeya cheerfully answered, plucking them up by the maroon cloth beneath them. As she lifted the pile out of the case, the cloth began to shake. The metallic shells clanged loudly against each other, vibrating with unnatural energy. Navaeya dropped the cloth with a startled gasp, and the orbs sprang into the air. Suddenly, the largest one started to glow, transforming into a muted orange ball as the others drifted lazily around it, flickering with sparks of multi-colored light across their metallic surfaces.

"Magic," she whispered in awe.

"They're orbiting the central one," Micah observed. "You know, I think it's an arcane version of an orrery."

"Incredible," Navaeya responded with a hint of delight. "I wonder how it works?"

As the smallest orb passed in front of Micah, he lightly tapped its edge. Its gentle lights immediately vanished, and the ball crashed to the ground, its golden case cracking against the hard floor.

"You broke my planet!" cried Navaeya furiously.

He bent down, discovering at a faint, bluish light emanating from the center of the husk.

"There's your answer. Iluvan."

"Really now?" Navaeya crouched beside him. "Maybe I should crack open the rest of them then."

"Later," Micah growled with a frown. "Let's go."

They swiped the orbs out of the air, returning them to Navaeya's satchel. After browsing several of the other cases, they turned to leave, only for her to stop again at a display of musty tomes.

"It can't be!" she gasped, pressing against the glass.

Micah rolled his eyes. "What now?"

She scanned the corners of the case, looking for a latch. Unsuccessful, she swiped an ivory cane from beside the desk, and in a quick motion, rapped the glass before he could even react. The thin sheet shattered with a deafening crash.

"What are you doing?" he fumed.

"We're not leaving without this," she said indignantly, delicately extracting an ancient-looking book from the case. She lifted the heavy volume into the air, inspecting its edge before displaying the cover. The thick leather bindings were engraved with an array of exotic, golden symbols. The image of a flying dragon inside an inverted triangle rested at the center.

"What is it?" Micah asked.

"Forbidden knowledge," she replied mysteriously. "I thought all of these had been destroyed."

"What do you mean? What is it?"

"The *Imperium Fallum*, the writings of a mage who defied Imperial cult worship of the Archon when the Hamid Empire ruled the known world centuries ago. The Empire attributed their power to their god-like ruler, but this mage argued if the world actually owed their allegiance to anyone, it was to a single god and long extinct civilization who'd left artifacts of power for the first Hamidians to find. Needless to say, the Archon didn't appreciate his theory."

As Navaeya's excitement grew, an ominous feeling crept over Micah, recalling the catacombs of Angol'daur he'd seen with Kelj.

Micah snorted. "That sounds ridiculous. Why would the Empire bother with a crazy mage?"

"Believe it or not, he actually inspired a following," Navaeya continued. "Normally, I'd figure an Archon wouldn't care, but the fact they questioned his power made them a target. You have to remember, the Empire ruled Edros with an iron fist. Ask the wrong questions, you're dead."

"Did the mage have any proof?"

"It's hard to know. Everything I've heard about this book says he doesn't offer anything concrete. Apparently, he had a penchant for absurd riddles. A lot of his so-called proof was never deciphered. But still, the Archon wouldn't have had the man executed and wiped from history if there wasn't *something* to what he was writing."

Micah smirked. "Whatever you say."

"If anything, I'd wager the mage was closer to the truth than we think," said Navaeya, ignoring him. "We'd just started to find new ruins across Edros before the Mist arrived. They could be theirs for all we know."

The smile instantly dropped from his face. "Wait, what do you know about the ruins?"

"I spent most of my life in Edros," she answered, eyeing him shiftily. "I've seen a few."

Micah slowly rolled his fingers into a fist, resisting the urge to place a hand on Kelj's pack. "So why the book? Who cares now?"

"Like I said, the Hamid Empire had nearly all the copies destroyed. Scholars outside the Empire pay a great deal for scraps of the *Imperium*. Imagine what a complete edition will fetch!"

A piercing scream ripped through the manor, and they both froze, glancing at the open door.

"Wraith," Micah whispered.

Another scream from the street below answered the call.

"Make that two," Navaeya added.

He growled bitterly under his breath. "We need to leave, now."

"Right behind you."

Micah glanced towards the high windows, the afternoon sun slowly fading into evening light somewhere beyond the wall of Mist. At the same moment, the deathly fog outside shifted, revealing a penetrating column of golden light shining brightly through the haze.

"It's there," he breathed. "It's real."

"What?" Navaeya whipped around just as the Mist coiled back, obscuring the sight.

"That way." Micah pointed out the window.

She smirked at him. "You're jumping first."

"Come on," he said, shaking his head.

Back in the hall, they snuck along the billowing curtains, heading for the stairs. Another scream split the air, cracking a window ahead of them. At the balcony's edge, Micah peered down, scanning the foyer for the demon.

"Clear," he whispered.

They slowly descended the marbled stairs, the thin, gilded rails exposing them to the empty room. The street beyond the broken entrance swirled with thickened Mist, tendrils of the curse rolling through the desolate entry. Micah cautiously stepped over the warped door, exiting the manor, and Navaeya followed. Just as she cleared the doorway, an angry screech blasted from the forsaken mansion. He jerked around, spotting the terrifying glow of the Wraith inside the gloomy sitting room. Its ashen face contorted in a wicked smile, those pulsing blue eyes fixed on them as they stumbled away in fear.

Another shriek reverberated from the street to their right. Micah's eyes snapped back to the manor where the first Wraith slowly sauntered across the pale tile. It raised an elongated arm, veins pulsing rapidly with the unnatural light leading to its black claws, groping for them. A red aura blossomed in the monster's palm.

"Move!" he yelled, grabbing Navaeya's arm as he leapt away, and they tumbled to the ground.

A beam of blood-red energy erupted from the Wraith, blasting apart the stone doorway and slicing through the Mist. The bolt whizzed just feet from Micah, the hair on his arms standing on end. It collided with a patch of earth in the park, sending a geyser of dirt into the air and leaving a gaping crater in the dead soil.

He clambered to his feet, watching as the horror crept closer to the door. Just as they turned to run, the Wraith's form shimmered, its solid, charred body fading to an ethereal image before vanishing with a whoosh. Suddenly, the monster materialized several paces outside the manor's entry with a loud crack.

How did it do that?

At the same moment, the dark shape of a second Wraith shuffled around the mansion's corner, its bright glow pulsing through the stirring Mist.

They sprinted away from the Wraiths, dashing past the second manor and heading for the far street. A spear of lightning flashed over Micah's head, instinctively causing him to duck. The monsters wailed again, infuriated.

Rounding the weathered blocks of the building, they stumbled onto a narrow road bordered by small but elaborate houses, all pressed together. The remnants of withered trees dotted the walks along the ruined cobblestone as it gently sloped downward into the Mist. While most of the stone buildings were only moderately damaged, a handful of costly houses were missing entire sections of their polished exteriors. Others sat as decomposing rubble. With the Wraiths shrieking behind them, Micah and Navaeya rushed down the street, passing the shattered doorways and windows.

At the bottom, the path evened out at a large, circular intersection. A looming fountain, long-since dried up, rested in the center, surrounded by more twisted stumps and weathered benches. Colossal manors and princely tower estates ringed the plaza, their crumbling exteriors languishing under dead vines and faded glory.

They followed the circle around to the next road, and a new sound rose from the Mist.

The long, drawn-out howl of a Mist Wolf pierced the sky, answered by a scream from the Wraiths. A cluster of howls joined the choir, heading straight for the plaza. Dread filled Micah as blood pounded in his ears.

"Wherever we're headed, you'd better get us there fast," Navaeya panted, shoving her hair back.

They raced away from the cries, taking the westward route and leaving the plaza in the consuming fog. An assortment of gated mansions and lofty towers interspersed with the shattered storefronts of cafes and clothiers whizzed past as the shrieks and howls grew fainter. As another street materialized in the Mist,

Micah angled towards it, preparing to swing around a row of dead shrubs enclosing a small, desolate manor.

Without warning, a Mist Wraith stepped from the shadows of a structure on the far side, vanishing in an instant only to reappear in the middle of the road with a jolting crack. A gleeful scream erupted from its glowing fangs, its charred limbs flexing with delight. Micah staggered to a halt, searching for an escape.

"This way!" Navaeya shouted, dragging him around the lifeless shrubbery. A fount of lightning sprang from the Wraith's claws as it shrieked again, and the dead brush burst into flames. They leapt over a short row of hedges, tumbling into a narrow alley between the manor grounds and a walled tower. In the enclosed space, the yelps of the Wolves sounded like they were right on top of them.

Micah chased Navaeya down the backstreet, his boots sloshing through muddy puddles in the warped stone as the Wraith's cries bounced off the walls. Ahead of him, the alley ended at the Mist-shrouded wall of another building. Sheer terror overtook his limbs. A moment later, he thankfully realized another alley cut through the gloom. A way out. As Micah rounded the sharp turn, the hazy shape of the Wolf pack entered the alley, running hard.

Micah and Navaeya spilled onto the main street, where another series of smaller houses enclosed the road in both directions. The shriek of the Mist Wraith blasted across the ruined boulevard. There was nowhere to go but forward. He quickly felt his legs weakening after a day of racing through the city.

Please Elowë, let the tower be close, Micah desperately prayed.

After passing several more crumbling houses, breathing hard and with the howls rapidly gaining, an unusual glow appeared in the fog. With menacing shadows growing in the failing sun, the light gradually turned from the whitish, blue hue of the Mist to a soft yellow.

"It's just ahead!" he gasped as Navaeya sprinted madly through the angry haze in front of them.

In an instant, the Mist vanished, the abrupt change startling Micah as the air cleared. They ground to a halt, mouths gaping in shock.

At the center of a swirling storm of Mist, a massive column of sharp, golden energy radiated into the sky, displacing the consuming fog as it spilled into the cobblestone streets of the intersection. A monumental tower sat at the center of the translucent barrier, an extravagant rounded structure of pale, weathered stone with sparkling windows rising high above the stately manors around it. The roof of the spire was rounded, a curious sheen of bronze metal glistening in the evening light. While the tower showed signs of damage, pieces of its exterior chipped and sections of the fence sitting in twisted gaps, it was in far better condition than its neighbors.

"So, you weren't crazy," Navaeya breathed, astonishment clear on her exhausted face.

A terrifying shriek shook them from their awe.

"Quick!" Micah shouted. "Into the tower!"

"Are you insane?" she cried. "That barrier will vaporize us!"

The baying of the Wolf pack filled the air, seconds away in the swirling Mist.

"Either we risk it or get eaten alive!"

He took off towards the shimmering column. Navaeya let out a furious growl before chasing after him.

The soaring column loomed over Micah's head as he approached its shifting surface, the golden light lazily swirling in a uniform ring. With the Wolves howling at their heels, he plowed forward. There was no stopping now.

Deep breath.

Micah plunged into the energy, a curious, tingling sensation coursing through his limbs as he sailed through, unharmed. Navaeya breezed in just as the Wolves burst out of the Mist. He caught her as she stumbled, breathing wildly. Micah glanced out, watching as the Mist Wolves cautiously padded towards the barrier, sniffing angrily. He unsheathed his sword, placing himself between Navaeya and the ring of energy. The world stopped, everything still as he and the Wolves stared at one another. Hostility burned within their soulless eyes.

But the pack refused to move closer. The leader, a massive Wolf with a thick coat of peppery fur, rose to its hind legs. Summoning its courage, the Wolf paced forward with its unnatural gait. For a moment, it studied him, a light snarl playing at its lips. Then, with a terrible howl, the beast spread its gaunt arms, flexing rows of razor-sharp claws in the dying light. At the same instant, a Mist Wraith lurched out of the fog, its ear-splitting shriek entwining with the howl. The Wolf shot him a final scowl, returning to the pack prowling at the border of the Mist. Micah stepped back, lowering his blade as he moved closer to where Navaeya was still bent over, breathing hard.

The Wraith screamed again, and he jumped. It raised a dark palm, a blue pulse increasing along its body. A blast of lightning erupted towards them, and Micah impulsively flinched. The blinding energy crashed into the barrier, the golden shield brightening with a sudden flash. The blast sizzled against the curtain, sending a ripple of pulses along the surface. In seconds, the magical barrier returned to its lazy swirl, completely unchanged. An indignant cry escaped the Wraith's jagged teeth. It stared at them, willing a way to claim their lives but unable to broach the arcane column.

"Come on," he gasped to Navaeya, turning towards the tower. With legs shaking from exhaustion, they staggered into the tower's courtyard, vanishing behind iron and stone.

Inside the enclosure, a smooth walk of polished tiles led to a small, bronze statue of a mage. The hooded figure held two flaming metal orbs, staring into the distance. Beyond it, the path ended at a tall pair of wooden doors set into the base of the tower. As they approached the sealed entrance, a soft clatter rose from the doors, and they gently swung open. They paused, looking at each other.

"This is your show now," Navaeya breathed, drawing back. "You first."

Micah shrugged, walking towards the faint light spilling from the opening. He rested a tentative hand against the sturdy wood, the door quivering at his touch as he scanned the marbled floor of the entry. Then he stepped inside.

CHAPTER 44
ANSWERS IN THE MIST

WITHIN THE TOWER, A massive chamber greeted Micah. Dozens of metal-encased glass orbs lined the sides, bathing the entrance in warm light. Their glow flickered off cultured stone floors and walls. At the center of the hall, a gentle waterfall gurgled down a wall of natural, jutting stones, filtering into a fountain pool lined with lush plants and woody foliage. Above it hung a lavish chandelier of silver and glass. Benches of smooth, marbled stone surrounded the woodland feature, giving the space a calm, meditative feel. A wide staircase curled around the room's circular wall, vanishing behind the curious waterfall.

As Micah examined one of the orbs, he recognized them as the expensive, though common, iluvan lamps, once found all over Starkhaven in its prime. Similar lamps had once adorned the walls of the Conclave chambers.

"This is... beautiful," Navaeya murmured, admiring the woodland scene.

"Karthmoor's wealthiest citizens lived in this district," he explained. "This was clearly one of the richest."

He looked around, studying an array of dim passages branching off from the foyer, and pondered where to go. He headed for the marble stairs leading to the tower proper.

With a hand on the smooth, stone balustrade, Micah warily began the ascent. Beyond the sound of his boots and the soft flow of the falling water, the tower was unnervingly silent. Above them, the curving stairwell disappeared, hiding the next floor behind the pale rock ceiling.

At the top, a wide sitting area appeared. Plush couches and mahogany end tables were arranged in a tidy square before a massive fireplace on the far wall. A series of smaller doors concealed the rest of the floor before the marble staircase continued its curving climb.

"I don't think I've ever seen a tower quite like this," Navaeya mused.

"I wonder what else we'll find," Micah murmured, thinking back to the mysterious Voice. They slowly made their way to the next set of stairs.

On the next floor, they found themselves in a gallery. Intricate paintings and masterfully sculpted statues lined the circular chamber, hinting at the owner's refined interests and immense wealth. Navaeya paused for a moment, twirling the end of her hair as she studied a beautiful painting of a lush, forested coastline.

Another floor revealed a row of open doors along the edges of a space lined with bookshelves. They peered into one, discovering a modest room filled with cases of alchemical agents behind frosted glass. An assortment of vials, gadgets, and utensils were spread across its rich wooden tables. Moving to the next door, they found a large study with a wall of windows overlooking the city. Arcane instruments of golden metal and shimmering crystals dotted the corners of the office, shelves of thick texts and unknown devices scattered near the shadowed walls.

"Now we're talking." Navaeya grinned, stepping towards the darkened room.

Suddenly, the thick wood slammed shut, the lock clicking in its slot. Navaeya jumped back, startled.

"There will be time for trinkets later," the secretive Voice boomed across the room. A hint of disapproval played at the edge of its wizened tone. "The stairs, if you will."

Everything fell silent.

"Who was that?" Navaeya hissed, gripping her elegant bow.

"The tower's owner, I guess," Micah replied, trying to make sense of it all. "He's the one who led me here."

Navaeya frowned, her wary eyes narrowing. "You never mentioned that."

"It didn't seem important. Regardless, if anyone knows how to end the Mist, it's got to be him."

She stared at him with her eyebrows raised. "You brought us on a hairbrained trek through a monster-filled city *to destroy the Mist?* I take back what I said. You're still crazy."

Micah shrugged, heading for the next staircase.

They followed the circling stairs up a couple more floors, each lavishly decorated like the others. They resisted opening any more of the doors, however.

As they approached the final set of stairs, Micah noticed the floor above was completely dark.

"This feels like a trap," Navaeya whispered as Micah tentatively climbed, ignoring her. As the stairs neared the opening, his eyes tried to adjust. The first thing he spotted was an array of tiny lights gleaming across the ceiling, casting a faint glow in the darkened room. He took a deep breath, stepping into the chamber. The lightless void grew, shrouding the tower's spire as he struggled to see. Beyond the twinkling dots, everything was black.

"Where are we?" Navaeya murmured, her hand groping for his shoulder in the consuming shadows.

"Hawkmoon Observatory," the Voice called from the dark, making them both jump. "Once the property of a particularly gifted, and wealthy, clan of mages."

Faint glass orbs awakened along the edges of the room, the sleepy lamps spreading their light. As the darkness receded, Micah could finally make sense of the tower. A wide floor of marble spanned the room, lined with walls of glass. Curious bronze shutters enclosed the panes from the world beyond. Elegant tables piled high with books and writing materials were scattered around the circular space, along with occasional bookcases of still more tomes and bizarre objects. A massive cylinder of bronze metal, set at an angle and reaching to the ceiling, rested on a chiseled pedestal at the far end. An odd track cut into the stone floor traveled along the perimeter of the room, hinting at the intricate device's ability to move.

Then Micah saw him.

A wiry old man in a simple robe of fitted gray material sat on a plush mat near the center of the spire. His face was bowed, his eyes closed, as if deep in thought. His palms rested patiently on his knees. White hair reaching almost to his shoulders hung from his wrinkly head, and a short, matching beard covered his sharp jaw.

The man opened his eyes, revealing piercing blue irises that immediately locked with Micah's. He froze, unsure of how to react. The man raised his weathered head, his pointed nose wrinkling as he studied Micah with a slight frown. Whether in amusement or disapproval, he could not tell. Beyond that, the man's expression was completely unreadable.

"Who are you?" Micah cautiously asked, resting a hand on his blade.

The man's wizened face watched him, expressionless. Then he straightened, his hands releasing their hold.

Suddenly, he rose. His entire body floated into the air, hoisted by an unseen power. Micah gaped in shock as the man settled gently onto his feet and extended a hand towards the ground. A slender rod of obsidian rock effortlessly glided to his open palm. Whoever he was, his magic seemed effortless, beyond anything Micah had ever known.

"I would ask the same of you, Micah Stormcrown," the man rasped, leisurely stepping forward. "Though you may not know yourself."

His robe swirled around his legs as he approached, the cane clicking softly against the hard stone.

"The Warden of the West, Guard of my people," Micah carefully answered, then more solemnly. "Husband to a slain wife, father to a slain child. One who seeks justice against their killer."

"You speak of titles, names that have defined you," he said gently. "And of vengeance. Important, yes, but something rests deeper than all these. Something waiting to be awakened."

"Eldvenir," Micah murmured.

"Indeed." The aged man nodded. "But what of your inheritance, Eldvenir? Do you truly grasp its nature?"

"A dead house has no inheritance," he said, recalling Garrin's proclamation. "But whatever remains I will embrace, if it helps me defeat this curse."

"You may find more than you presume," the man replied, his eyes twinkling. "If you are willing to learn."

"What do you mean? Who are you?"

The elderly man stopped several paces from them, still watching Micah intently. He could feel Navaeya tensing.

"I had assumed the worst. In an ironic twist of fate, I believed myself to be the last voice of a once-great people," the mage softly began, gazing at the floor. "I see now that Elowë had other plans." He snapped back to Micah.

"I am Silvanus Aerulion, Grandmaster of the Oathsworn Order. Its final leader, imprisoned in disgrace. The last Andaayan, awakened to mourn the passing of my people."

Micah's mind reeled at his declaration, the words failing to register.

"That's... impossible," he stuttered, struggling to comprehend the frail elder before him.

"Only a closed mind sees something as impossible," Silvanus chided. "I ask no blind faith for your trust."

"How?" Micah gawked, unable to reconcile his existence with everything he had learned. "The precursors lived centuries ago—maybe longer!"

Silvanus nodded.

"In the last days of my people, I was betrayed, thrown before a false tribunal and imprisoned for crimes conceived in slander. Placed within the iluvashtin and sealed deep beneath the earth, it was my punishment to slumber for eternity, unknowing, as my homeland withered away," Silvanus explained, sorrow lacing his weathered voice. "By unforeseen design, fate saw my prison uncovered and brought to the world of men as I slept. The invasion of the Mist brought awakening, a new world greeting with fire and ruin. This tower became my new cage, shrouding my ancient soul from the Young World beyond the clouds."

Navaeya stared at them, dumbfounded, as questions raced through Micah's mind.

"Wait, that word you used, iluvashtin," he recalled. "Garrin used that. You were imprisoned in a time pod?"

"Time pod, yes." Silvanus gave a short chuckle. "A fitting name. My long years were stretched even further. Further than any alive today has endured. Until men of the Young World found me."

"Young World? Do you mean us?"

"Yes. You *see*, but you fail to *comprehend*," he slowly continued. "When my people walked your lands, your ancestors were just emerging. To them, we were as gods. Now, the time of the Andaayans has passed, just as it did for the Elves. True Man, in all his glory and ruin, rises to claim the Mantle."

"I've never heard of Andaaya."

"Ah, a legacy of my people," he explained. "The maps of the Young World are incomplete. As we designed it to be."

"What do you mean? And what Mantle?"

"Much pain has befallen your world because of the trespass," Silvanus sadly replied. "Have patience. In time, this will be revealed to you."

"Very well," Micah hesitantly conceded.

"Um. I'm lost here," Navaeya interjected with a baffled look. "Something about the Mist and the end of the world and you being our great, great, great, great grandfather. Or thereabout." She glanced at the old mage with a smirk.

"Strange." Silvanus frowned, eyeing the sprightly woman. "Your energy differs from the one whom I felt beside Micah through the iluvimír."

"You felt Kelj," said Micah, pain crossing his heart.

Suddenly, Navaeya froze, her eyes furiously locked on Silvanus.

"Get out of my mind," she growled through her teeth. After a moment, she relaxed, slightly.

"I apologize, Navaeya." Silvanus nodded. "But I had to know your intentions, as I did the other. Your heart is wounded and confused, and I lament the pain you have endured. Though, in time, you may heal once again. Your blood calls deeply. It will lead you to the truth."

"Her blood?" Micah asked, confused.

"Forget it," she snapped. "It's not your concern."

"As you wish," Silvanus said, before turning back to Micah. "Does the fog of your thoughts begin to clear?"

"Sort of... But why didn't you warn anyone about the Mist when you were freed?"

"There was little time as I adjusted from my slumber," said Silvanus wistfully. "When I awoke, my iluvashtin was cracked, a support underneath this tower fracturing the chamber. Much of the building was in flames. The mages were fleeing as I awoke, oblivious to my existence. Ultimately, I was in a foreign world. I did not know where to go and so remained inside Hawkmoon Observatory, constructing the shield beyond from the remnant of my pod and instruments the mages left behind. From their writings, I slowly came to understand the Young World around me."

"Mages?"

"The only symbol of their order was this." Silvanus gestured to a crumpled banner strewn over a table to Micah's right. He knew the white hand instantly.

The Heraldan Collective.

"It's an organization of mages from Edros," he explained. "They've reverse engineered the time pods, making new replicas of it."

Silvanus frowned. "A dangerous path. They do not comprehend the implications of their folly."

"They aren't the only ones," Micah ominously replied. "Another group was searching for your time pod. The Firewalkers."

Silvanus' brow furrowed even more. "Hmm. Then my suspicion from our previous encounter is confirmed. I did not believe any of their order had survived. It is not the iluvashtin they are concerned with, but me."

"What do you mean?"

"You have faced the Firewalkers, tasted their power. Did it not feel... wrong, in your mind?" he asked with a knowing look.

"Everything about them was wrong. Garrin's magic was beyond anything I'd ever seen." Micah shivered, reliving the crippling grip on his brain.

"No doubt. Their abilities are not of the Young World. The Firewalkers, regrettably, are of mine." His gaze saddened. "They are Andaayan, though their hearts and minds are twisted by the dark teachings of one cast from the Oathsworn Order."

"They're Oathsworn too?" Micah choked, nearly falling where he stood.

Silvanus shook his head. "No. The Firewalkers you encountered are far removed from the first initiates who were exiled from the Order. I can only assume their cruelty and malice has grown over the centuries," he answered with a hint of pain.

"So, maybe more of your people survived?"

"I had no reason before now to believe so, but it may be. Clearly an enclave of Firewalkers managed to survive the curse, only to follow as it spread to the Young World," he surmised.

"Even so, it is clear they still retain the power of Andaayan blood. Along with an apparent knowledge of my imprisonment. If they discovered the iluvashtin held by this mage community, their logical conclusion would be my escape."

"So, they were hunting *you*," Micah grasped with growing worry. "That's why they left Greenwatch."

"I expect as much. Had they discovered me, it would have ended in my execution."

"That shouldn't be an issue anymore," he said grimly. "Kelj, my companion you felt in Angol'daur, sacrificed himself to stop them. The vault was destroyed, along with everyone in it."

"A noble, mournful deed," Silvanus murmured. "The warrior's honor cannot be praised higher. Still, we must be cautious. The Firewalkers are relentless. If any of them survived, or if there are others yet to be revealed, they will continue their quest to see us exterminated. Even with my abilities, age and imprisonment has taken its toll. I would be no match should they attack in force."

"You don't look that old," said Navaeya.

"I was five hundred and sixteen when I was sentenced to eternal slumber, a respectable age for my people. By the movements of the heavens tracked by these mages, I project my age has grown roughly by another five hundred years."

"You're bluffing," she said flatly, struggling to close her gaping mouth.

"No way," Micah muttered.

"It is an improbable age, even for an Andaayan whose blood blesses him with long life," Silvanus confessed. "Such is the power of the iluvashtin."

"So, you're a thousand-year-old Oathsworn who knows the origins of the Mist," Navaeya replied, rubbing her head. "Why stay here once you'd understood more? Why Starkhaven?"

"My home is lost. I am an orphaned voice, belonging neither to this world nor the world that has passed. But the Mist... The Mist is a curse the Young World should never have suffered. I fear its awakening and arrival on your shores has some connection to my own. I believed myself to be the last voice of my people, the last Eldvenir. As such, it is my duty to see it ended," Silvanus humbly asserted. "It would seem I now share this duty with Micah."

Micah shook his head. "I want to destroy the Mist more than anything, but I'm not an Oathsworn. I'm just a retired soldier."

"Even so. You possess the gift passed down by your ancestors." Silvanus tapped his staff against the stone. "The call of Andaaya has merely grown faint in the centuries since your forefathers left, rendering you little different from the men you see as brothers. The magic intrinsic to your lineage need only be restored."

"How?"

"*Iluvasil*, our rarest treasure. One must be found and taken to a Well of Souls. When mixed with the gift of my own power, Andaaya will waken within you once again," he sagaciously explained.

"Iluvasil?"

"Iluvan in its scarcest form, the few shards found throughout our world brought from the Elvish homeland beyond the eastern sun, which no mortal has ever seen, where the Creator's Song began," he continued. "You will know it by its silver or white appearance, in contrast to the calm blue of its siblings."

"You mean this?" Navaeya pulled Elisa's pendant from her belt.

Silvanus' eyes brightened in surprise, and he smiled. "Indeed. You have resourceful friends, young Micah."

"You could say that."

"Events are set into motion, the winds of change, rustling," Silvanus announced in his wise manner. "You have the keys to unlock your potential, Eldvenir, if you would see your world freed from this curse."

"What would you have me do?" asked Micah humbly, watching as Silvanus slowly walked to the center of the room.

With a flick of his wrist, a low clang vibrated the floor, followed by the deep rumble of moving gears. Around them, the bronze shudders retracted, revealing the fading dusk of Starkhaven beyond. Micah walked over to the edge of the room, staring through the golden barrier outside and across the blanket of Mist engulfing the capital. In the swirling mass, occasional towers of ruined stone jutted from the unseen earth like grasping fingers. To the west, Micah spied Tar'auth Ben, the lone spire feebly gasping for clean air. Starkhaven, as he knew it, shrouded beneath the deadly cloud. Past it all, the faint glimmer of Stark Bay sparkled in the dying sun.

"Become my final apprentice, the last initiate in the ways of the Order," Silvanus offered. "Reclaim your power, vanquish this curse, and restore the honor of the Oathsworn."

Micah glanced at Navaeya, her bright eyes watching him expectantly. She raised an eyebrow, but remained silent.

He had crossed the breadth of his homeland and risked everything to protect those he cared for. He had witnessed horrors, desperation, courageous resolve, and heroic sacrifice. All of it guiding him to this moment. All of it driven by a fate so clearly beyond his hands.

Micah retreated from the glass, moving to meet the ancient mage. He knew his answer.

"For Karthmoor, for those I love, and for those I've lost, I will follow your teaching." Micah sank to his knees, offering his sword in outstretched arms.

Silvanus walked forward, his shimmering staff clicking softly. He placed a wrinkled palm above Micah's forehead, releasing a brief flash of golden light that sent a shiver across his scalp. His body quaked with excitement as the air hummed with anticipation.

"I take you, Micah Stormcrown, as my apprentice. By my vow before our sovereign Creator, I shall teach you all that I know, bestowing on you the blessings and responsibilities of the Oathsworn Order," Silvanus nobly recited. "This power is entrusted to you for the good of all people. May faith in our Creator guide you to righteousness, holding your guardianship of the weak, the poor, and the afflicted, in honor of the highest virtue. So let it be."

The elderly wizard withdrew and Micah stood, a bold determination growing in Micah's heart.

"Thank you, Grandmaster." He solemnly bowed.

"My dim years within this tower provided only a growing despair," Silvanus mused, a warm smile growing on his weathered face. "I place my hopes in you, young Micah. Complete the quest I could not."

"I will," Micah solemnly promised, "though, I do not know where to begin."

"I shall guide your way. First, to your powers, then, to the heart of the Mist."

"And maybe then I will better understand your—my—history," he added.

"Indeed." Silvanus gave a small smile. "As such, your time upon Karthmoor is drawing to its end. If you seek to reclaim your inheritance, the Great Continent awaits." Silvanus set his staff against the colossal telescope and raised an arm towards the open window, his fingers extended towards the bay.

"Edros?" Micah exclaimed. "I thought the source of my power was Andaaya?"

"Andaaya is its birthplace, but the way is closed to you, for now," Silvanus shrewdly answered. "No, to reclaim your inheritance, to truly become Eldvenir, your path lies within the Great Continent. The wisdom of your allies shall guide you."

The mysterious mage cast a knowing look at Navaeya. Completely lost, Micah followed his gaze to where the intriguing woman shifted uneasily.

"I knew I should've charged more," she muttered.

After a moment, she let out a conceding sigh. "Look, I still think you're crazy," she admitted, gazing at Micah with her serious, brown eyes, "but there's too much for all this to be a coincidence. Stuff is happening around you, Micah Stormcrown. I don't know what or why, but I do know one thing: there's no way I'm missing this adventure."

Micah grinned.

"Just think of the stories! And treasure!" she added gleefully.

Wait, does this sound like a good idea?

"Besides." She eyed him mischievously. "You need someone who knows the land *and* how to save your tail when the trouble starts." She tossed Elisa's pendant to him, the cool crystal swirling faintly as it hit his palm.

He looked at her, surprised.

Navaeya shrugged. "Consider it a gift. There'll be greater finds in Edros."

"Thanks."

Silvanus cleared his throat, and they turned to where he patiently waited, the last rays of the sun vanishing in the Mist behind him.

"The path is set," he declared. "Are you ready, apprentice?"

Micah glanced at Navaeya.

"I am."

Silvanus nodded, folding his hands behind his back.

"Then let us begin."

THANK YOU

Thank you for reading *Awakening*! If you enjoyed the story, would you help me out?

Ratings and reviews are one of the biggest ways you can help indie authors connect with more book lovers. The minute or two you take to add your thoughts on the story (or even just a couple seconds for a rating!) can make all the difference in how the algorithm shares it out

Leave a review!

with more curious readers. It also means the world to me! Pick your favorite place to review (Amazon, Goodreads, etc.), and thanks!

Join my newsletter!

Ready for the next book?
Book Two of *The Oathsworn Chronicles* launches on Kickstarter in 2026. Join the vanguard of its supporters by going to www.zrmccorm ick.com to learn more, or by joining my newsletter using the QR code to the left. My amazing subscribers are

always the first to hear the news about Kickstarter, new releases, and freebies.

Still want more?

Don't you hate when a story ends and there are still a dozen more places or things you wish you could explore? Me too. That's why I created a whole page of awesome bonuses for you to dive into while you wait for the next book! From high-resolution maps to

Explore the extras!

short stories to other exclusive content, go to www.zrmccorm ick.com/extras, or scan the QR code to the right to learn more about the world of *The Oathsworn Chronicles*!

Kickstarter Acknowledgments

It's a scary thing releasing your book into the world, especially your first one, not knowing how things will go. Everyone listed below gave generously to support this story's creation, and it simply wouldn't be what it is without them. To those of you who joined together to make *Awakening's* campaign successful, I can only say thank you. Your faith in bringing this story to life is humbling, and I hope it lived up to your expectations.

A. CHAN
AARON DEWAARD
ANGELA MILES
ANNAROSE WILLHITE
ASAKUNOTOMOHIRO
AUSTIN HOFFEY
BEN PETITT
CAMY TANG
CHASE MCGLINCHEY
CHESSCOMMANDS
CHRISTY S
CL "ZENNY8" GONZALEZ
D.V. COLE
DAKOTA PAWLAK
DAN DAETZ
DAVID MUSSELMAN
DEREK BARRIOS

E. A. HENDRYX
E.R. PAIS
EILEE
ENALIA T
ERICA MCCORMICK
ETHAN ESHLEMAN
GERALD P. MCDANIEL
GHOSTCAT
GIANNA CHRISTOPHER
GISELLE
GORDON STURGEON
HANNAH GAUDETTE
HUGO ESSINK
IAN BROWN
IN LOVING MEMORY OF
BASIL MARTIN
J. THOMAS

JACK BAER
JACOB SMITH
JAN B
JARED ORR
JASON BOWDEN
JAVIER VEGA
JEREMY LOCKE
JOHN IDLOR
JOSIAH DEGRAAF
KANDI J WYATT
KATHY BRASBY
KENNETH LUCARELLI
KYLE WESTJOHN
LIZ SEMKIU
LOST GIRL WENDY
LATHEM
MADGE WATSON
MAIRA O.
MARK KLEIN
MATTHEW VARLEY
MAX W.
MELISSA B.
MICHAEL BOX

MIKE GALLIGAN
N. GUSTAFSON
NALAMBA
NICHOLAS STEPHENSON
NICK M.
NOLALISSE HAN
PAUL SMITH
PETER "TONOUR" BASAK
QAVEE
R.S. JOHANSEN
ROBERT JONES
RODNEY VAN VALBURG
SAMANTHA LANDSTRÖM
SEAN
SHERRI SHIRRELL
STEPHANIE BRUNNER
TARA GRACE ERICSON
THE BLACKSMITH OF
CODELL
TRENA
WADE KLINGLER
XAVIER SCHWINDT

AUTHOR'S ACKNOWLEDGMENTS

There's a misconception that writing a book is the author sequestered away from the world, emerging only once this pristine, final version of the story has flowed from his or her pen and onto the pages. I almost laughed out loud writing that, because it couldn't be further from the truth. In reality, there are dozens of unseen faces behind every book, and no story would exist without them.

Angela and Meghan, I can't thank you enough for your editing and abilities to help shape this story into a tale worthy of being told. From every misplaced comma to every misused word, your tenacity for details sharpened not only *Awakening*, but my skills as an author. The rest of my writing career owes a lot to what you've shown me. (Angela, hold on to #JusticeForKelj just a *little* longer. I promise.)

Rachel, my goodness, I couldn't have asked for a better designer. I offered some vague concepts of what I thought *might* work, and you crafted something stunning not just once, but *twice*, to showcase both of the editions. I can't thank you enough for sticking with me and delivering such beautiful covers and chapter images for the series.

Stephanie, when I came to you, a nerdy IT guy with this crazy idea to jump into writing fantasy, you didn't hesitate to share your knowledge and experience, even blessing me with training for the world of publishing. Thank you for being the encouragement at the moment I needed it to take the plunge.

Thomas and the Author Media community, stumbling upon you was like finding a port in a storm. It was that first home, amidst the confusion of navigating the waters of publishing, where I finally found clarity through your courses and a wealth of experience and support in its community. That's made all the difference in how I approach storytelling.

Ben, Lathem, and Karley, I can't thank you enough for being my guinea pigs and graciously agreeing to poke holes in my manuscripts. Having you along as beta readers challenged me to think deeply about my craft, and each story I write gets a little better because of your feedback.

My boys. Every question you ask, each moment of excitement and pride you show in "daddy the author," is precious to me. It's such a joy knowing you're cheering me on, even when you run off with my notebook just to look over my maps and doodles. Maybe someday I'll even pen wild stories of the Rawr Patrol and other ideas brewing in your imaginations.

Erica, I owe so much of this to you. The countless hours you've granted me to transform this inkling of a hobby into something bigger. You saw its potential almost a decade before I did, and quite literally, this story wouldn't exist without you. You've been there for every misplaced detail, every incoherent subplot, and every brainstorming session to solve them. Most of all, you've been an unfailing support whose worth can't be measured. God blessed me with such an incredible partner to walk this journey with. Thank you for being there, encouraging me every step of the way.

For it all, thank you, Jesus, for the daily grace you give me, and the blessings of all those above and more not mentioned. Let my stories be pointers to you. Let them whisper of your love for us, and that restless hearts would respond to you, our true Creator.

THE ALDARIAN COMPENDIUM

If, like the many others before, you've flipped or scrolled to the back of this story because you have no idea what that person just said or where in Aldaria they're at, welcome! Several of the Heraldan Collective's brightest minds have curated this appendix to help you keep everything straight. Within the Compendium, you will find terms listed alphabetically for ease of use. Bear in mind, several scribes continue to work on this ever-expanding tome. Be sure to check back as each new story is discovered!

Administrator Arland - an official of the city of Greenwatch

Alakanthu (ah-lah-KAHN-thoo) - the Neboan spirit of the sun

Aldaria (ahl-DARE-ee-ah) - the planet and known mortal world

Allfather - the Anderfall name for the Creator (see *Elowë*)

Alvin - the former blacksmith of Fairhollow who vanished in the Mist

Andaaya (an-DIE-ah) - the lost continent of the Elves and birthplace of the Oathsworn and Firewalker Orders; home to the first humans awakened by Elowë

Aranaias (air-ah-NIE-uhs) - a mage from the Hillmarch Academy who escaped its fall

Araphon (AIR-ah-fahn) - a large province of the Hamid Empire in northern Edros well known for its vast, uninhabitable desert; most of its cities lie in its grasslands north of the Dragontail Mountains or near oases on the desert's edge

Archon Valerius (vah-LAIR-ee-us) - the ruler of the Hamid Empire

Aringoth (AIR-in-goth) - a small farming village in central Karthmoor near the Forest of Midland

Arksul (ARK-sool) - a middle-aged Firewalker warrior accompanying Garrin on his quest

Arla - a barmaid at Stonecroft's tavern

Armeia (ar-MAY-ah) - a powerful Firewalker woman accompanying Garrin on his quest

Asher - a merchant from Neboa who arrives in Fairhollow with a mysterious delivery for Greenwatch

Battlemaster Carlin - a weapons specialist of the Karthmoor Guard; resides in Greenwatch

Beirand (BEER-and) - an elder of Fairhollow, known for his laziness and affection for strong drinks

Benrick - a farmer of Hazelcourt

Bergi (buhr-GEE) - Lisra's young son

Bolli - a farmer of Fairhollow and husband of Emina

Bowman's Crossing - a small fishing village in northern Karthmoor known for its annual glowfrog competitions

Captain Hawthorne - the leader of the Karthmoor Guard in Stonecroft

Captain Logan - the current leader of the Karthmoor Guard in Greenwatch

Caspin - a young defender of Hazelcourt

Coalfire - a warhorse gifted to Kelj for his service to Greenwatch

Cole - a farmer of Fairhollow and widower of Kara; father of Sadi and Mark

Colonel Clovis - the former leader of the Karthmoor Guard in Greenwatch; slain in a skirmish with the Mist

Coraline - a chicken farmer of Fairhollow

Darian - a young orphan boy of Greenwatch; taken in by Winslow as an apprentice baker

Delvin - Fairhollow's tavern keeper and husband of Maven

Director Mai - the leader of the Heraldan Collective branch in Greenwatch

Dorn - a small fishing village in northwestern Karthmoor

Edoran - a warhorse gifted to Micah by Asher

Edros (EH-droas) - also known as the Great Continent; the largest known landmass in Aldaria and birthplace of modern mankind

Eldvenir (EHLD-vin-eer) - Oathsworn, in Elvish (see *Oathsworn Order*)

Elisa - the wife of Micah Stormcrown

Elowë (EHL-oh-way) - the Creator, in Elvish; also referred to as the Creator in the modern era; the sole deity and maker of all things known and unknown

Emina (eh-MEE-nah) - a resident of Fairhollow and wife of Bolli

Endwaith (ind-WAYTH) - the westernmost island of the Anderfalls

Fairhollow - a small farming and logging village in central Karthmoor

Farshore - a coastal city in southwestern Karthmoor

Ferrald - a mage of the Heraldan Collective branch in Greenwatch

Firewalker Order - founded by Lornan and other Oathsworn cast from the Order for their use of blood magic and violent pursuit of power, Firewalkers are native humans of Andaaya who combine the intrinsic abilities of Andaayan mortals with blood magic; they primarily view the world though survival of the strongest and pride themselves on being the antithesis of the Oathsworn Order

Forest of Midland - an ancient forest in the center of Karthmoor

Francis - an elder of Fairhollow known for his blunt, cynical personality

Frederic - a young blacksmith of Fairhollow; formerly Alvin's apprentice

Frostharbor - a remote fishing village in northwestern Karthmoor

Garrin - a dangerous mage and leader of the Firewalker remnants; devoted to destroying the Mist, but the means by which he intends to end the curse are potentially catastrophic to the world

Gerar (guhr-RAHR) - a captain of the Karthmoor Guard and resident of Fairhollow; leads its defenders in Micah's absence

Gerrald - a soldier of the Karthmoor Guard in Stonecroft

Glorious Rule (GR) - the naming convention for chronology in the Hamid Empire; events are recorded based on the founding of the Empire and unification of the Hamidian tribes, which began in 0 GR

Glowfrog - an amphibious, frog-like creature native to the Lake Hemeth region of Karthmoor

Governor Beckett - a former leader of Greenwatch and husband of Lady Mira; killed when the Mist arrived in Karthmoor

Governor Larius - a former governor of Greenwatch

Greenwatch - a large city on Karthmoor's western coast; boasts the largest fishing exports for the island

Grimloth - one of the smaller Anderfall clans; primarily found on Endwaith

Hadrian - a young, sarcastic Firewalker mage accompanying Garrin on his quest

Halvid - a young farmer of Fairhollow and an initiate to its defenders

Hamidia (hah-MID-ee-ah) - the central most nation in Edros; birthplace of the Hamid Empire

Hamill - Fairhollow's resident tanner

Harrowmont - a village in southeastern Karthmoor; primary stop for travel between Starkhaven and Hillmarch

Hazelcourt - a small farming village in northern Karthmoor

Heraldan Collective - a secretive sect of mages founded centuries ago in Hamidia; while technically independent, their connections to the Hamid Empire give it much influence over the Collective's activities

Hillmarch - the second largest city on Karthmoor and its eastern provincial capital; also known as the Eastern Jewel; central in Karthmoor's trade with Edros since it was an Imperial territory, owing to generous subsidies for merchants and mineral-rich mountains north of the city

Hogrom (HOE-grohm) - one of the last surviving members of Clan Wulfgrad of the Anderfalls; bodyguard of the Governess of Greenwatch

Iluvan (ih-LEW-vihn) - silver stone, in Elvish; blue-gray crystals found deep underground containing stores of magical energy

Iluvashtin (ih-lew-VASH-tin) - silver dream, in Elvish; a rectangular chamber of polished stone, glass, and metal powered by iluvan; known more recently as a "time pod" for its ability to provide suspended animation; knowledge of its construction, including its interior instruments and relationship to iluvan, was lost with the passing of the Elves

Iluvasil (ih-LEW-vah-sil) - silver star, in Elvish; also known as white iluvan; rare shards of pure white crystal were brought by the Elves from the Ageless Realm; only form of iluvan capable of absorbing and storing nearly limitless quantities of magical energy

Iluvimír (ih-LEW-vih-meer) - silver mirror, in Elvish; large formations of iluvan that are shaped and tuned to respond to another through the lost arts of the Elves; allow instantaneous communication of sound and images

Istwyneir (IST-win-eer) - a small province of the Hamid Empire on the eastern coast of Edros; known for its incredibly dense forests; once home to the largest Elvish population in Edros until the last of their ships sailed east in 175 GR and the Empire conquered the nation

Jarl Angvarn (YAHR-uhl AING-vahrn) - the last leader of the Anderfalls; slain when the Anderfalls besieged Farshore and the Mist invaded

Jonas - a farmer of Aringoth and Micah's former neighbor

Kara - the wife of Cole and a resident of Fairhollow; mysteriously vanished in the Mist

Karthmoor - a large island nation off the northern coast of Edros

Karthport - a coastal city in southern Karthmoor; stopping point for trade vessels from Edros sailing on to Starkhaven and Hillmarch

Kelj - one of the last surviving members of Clan Wulfgrad of the Anderfalls; bodyguard of the Governess of Greenwatch; accompanies Micah on his quest to thwart the Fire-walkers

Kelso - the husband of Lisra and a resident of Fairhollow; slain by the Mist

Knaerlck (NAIR-lick) - a battle master or war leader, in the Anderfall language

Lady Mira - the current governess of Greenwatch; widow of Governor Beckett

Laring - a tavern keeper of Stonecroft

Leyana - a student at the Hillmarch Academy; assisted Marinaya in her precursor research

Lieutenant Maran - an officer of the Karthmoor Guard in Stonecroft

Lisra - a chicken farmer of Fairhollow; widow of Kelso and mother of Bergi

Lurker - a scaled, amphibious monster created by the Mist; resembles a glowfrog but is also more humanlike in its composition and movement

Marian - an elder and healer in Fairhollow; a retired priestess for the Karthmoor Temple

Marinaya (mair-in-NIE-ah) - the former director of the Heraldan Collective in Greenwatch; former advisor to Archon Valerius; exiled by the Archon before accepting a position at the Hillmarch Academy

Mark - the son of Cole and a resident of Fairhollow

Matthias - a former Karthmoor Guard sharpshooter and defender of Fairhollow

Maven - a tavern keeper of Fairhollow and wife of Delvin

Mayor Stern - the resident official of Hazelcourt

Merrick - a former Karthmoor Guard instructor and current defender of Fairhollow

Micah Stormcrown - a Karthmoor native and retired Warden of its Karthmoor Guard; led the defense of Fairhollow after losing his family to the Mist; undertook the quest to rid the village of dangerous iluvan that unearthed his connection to an extinct order of magic-wielders

Mist Troll - a naturally occurring Troll warped and dominated by the Mist; has paler and more deformed features

Mist Wolf - wolf-like, semi-intelligent monsters created by the Mist; capable of movement on two or four legs; extremely hostile and dangerous

Mist Wraith - aggressive, magic-adept monsters created by the Mist; capable of short-distance teleportation; identifiable by their charred, ashen skin and blue veining; body structures similar to Mist Wolves though solely bipedal

Narombe (nah-ROHM-bay) - a member of the Hillmarch Academy who helps lead the Refugee Camp

Navaeya Endalië (nah-VAY-ah in-DAH-lee-ay) - a mysterious woman residing in Stonecroft and scavenging the ruins of Starkhaven; agrees to lead Micah through the capital for a price

Neboa (neh-BOH-ah) - a small nation on the southeastern coast of Edros; unfamiliar to most in the Hamid Empire; known for its tropical climate and unique wildlife

Niala (NEE-ah-lah) - the wife of Merrick; slain by the Mist

Oathsworn Order - an order founded by the first men of Andaaya who embraced faith in Elowë and the Elves' teaching on the Mantle of Stewardship; members of the Order undergo a secretive ceremony bestowing enhanced magical abilities and lifespans

Percy - a tavern keeper of Greenwatch; assistant to Teig

Perentius - a young soldier and messenger of the Karthmoor Guard

Protector - a mage trained as a scout and investigator for the Karthmoor Guard; most serve in secrecy, assisting in high-risk situations or when magic is involved

Rawls - a young defender of Greenwatch

Refugee Camp - a makeshift settlement of Hillmarch survivors near the Winding River on the west bank of Long Lake

Reigmar (REEG-mahr) - the largest island of the Anderfalls; houses the Anderfalls' capital and bulk of its population

Rila (REE-lah) - an apprentice healer to Marian and twin sister to Tala; resides in the village of Fairhollow

Sadi (SAY-dee) - a young girl of Fairhollow; daughter of Cole; assists Marian and Rila

Samuel - the first son of Micah Stormcrown; perished in the Mist's invasion of Karthmoor

Serah (sir-AH) - sir, in Neboan

Shield-brother - A familial title for another warrior to whom an Anderfall warrior has vowed to join with in pursuit of honor; Warriors often band together with multiple shield-brothers; (see *Shield-pact*)

Shield-pact - A group of Anderfall warriors who have vowed to fight as a single, unified group; all warriors are shield-brothers to one another within a pact; Anderfall armies are thus made up of numerous shield-pacts; (see *Shield-brother*)

Silvanus Aerulion (sil-VAHN-us air-ROOL-ee-in) - Grandmaster of the Oathsworn Order and native of Andaaya; seeks to end the Firewalkers' power by any means necessary

Speaker Olan - a leader of Karthmoor's government; slain when the Mist invaded the island

Starkhaven - the capital city of Karthmoor; its original settlers are unknown, though it has been the centerpiece of Karthmoor civilization since before the arrival of the Hamid Empire in 250 GR

Stonecroft - a small fortress city in southern Karthmoor; home to one of the island's larger Guard garrisons

Svensiir (SVEN-seer) - way-guide, in the Anderfall language; similar to a sage or guiding elder

Sylmach (sill-MAHK) - the council of chieftains who advises the Anderfall Jarl

Tala - a young, adventurous girl native to Karthmoor and twin sister to Rila; resides in the village of Fairhollow

Tar'auth Ben (TAHR-oth ben) - Tower of Minds, in Elvish; a large, ancient structure on the island of Karthmoor; restored in 310 GR by the Hamid Empire to house its governing body for the island

Tar'auth Eld (TAHR-oth eld) - Tower of Oaths, in Elvish; a solitary mountain at the center of the island of Karthmoor; the tallest of its peaks

Tarion (TAR-ee-in) - a scout in the Refugee Camp

Teigan (Teig) - a tavern keeper of Greenwatch known for his connections and access to information

The Anderfalls - a collection of small islands northwest of Edros, west of Karthmoor; its remote location and warrior-centric culture left the Anderfalls cut off from much of the world, even as they retained their independence

The Archmage - the enigmatic leader of the Heraldan Collective

The Conclave - the primary governing body of Karthmoor; tasked with legislating its laws and overseeing its military

Thieves' Guild - a network of thieves and criminals across Edros

Tolsten - a former Karthmoor Guard soldier and defender of Fairhollow

Tomas - a mage of the Heraldan Collective branch in Greenwatch

Torvin - a lumberjack and resident of Fairhollow

Troll - an extremely large, vicious creature found throughout northern Edros; tend to inhabit mountainous or densely forested regions where their thick gray or brown hides easily camouflage with the terrain; semi-intelligent but have no known speech

Warden-Commander Berien (BEAR-ee-in) - the highest leader of Karthmoor's Guard; slain when the Mist invaded the island

Westrock - a province of the Hamid Empire on the western edge of Edros; primarily composed of dense forests and mountain ranges; a hub of merchants and commerce throughout the continent for centuries

Winslow - a baker of Greenwatch, who took Darian as his apprentice

Wulfgrad (wolf-GRAD) - one of the larger Anderfall clans and Kelj's birth clan; controlled a large portion of eastern Reigmar

Also By
Z.R. McCormick

The Oathsworn Chronicles

Novels

Book One: Awakening

Novellas

The Cataclysm
A Legacy of Ashes

About the Author

Have you ever imagined exploring another universe?

When Z.R. McCormick outgrew his childhood of cloaks, wooden bows, and plastic swords (which were likely burned to the joy of his neighbors and their landscaping), that wonder inspired by stories of the fantastical was never quite left behind.

He began voyages into the world of Aldaria in between a career in IT, enjoying time with his beautiful wife, and chasing his own rambunctious younglings, culminating in his debut novel, *The Oathsworn Chronicles: Awakening*, released in late 2025. But until that darkness in Aldaria is vanquished, Z.R. is content to read about someone else's adventures with a cold brew and a cozy chair, which, as you might agree, is rather sensible.

Find out more about Z.R. and the world of Aldaria by visiting him at www.zrmccormick.com.